This special signed edition
is limited to 500 numbered copies
and 26 lettered copies.

This is copy 34.

At the Foot of the Story Tree

An Inquiry into the Fiction of Peter Straub

by

Bill Sheehan

Subterranean Press • 2000

At the Foot of the Story Tree

FIRST EDITION
June 2000

ISBN
1-892284-77-4

Subterranean Press
P.O. Box 190106
Burton, MI 48519

email:
publisher@subterraneanpress.com

website:
www.subterraneanpress.com

Contents

Introduction p. 11

Section I: Mainstream Experiments, Gothic Beginnings p. 17

- Chapter One: Marriages p. 19
- Chapter Two: Under Venus p. 31
- Chapter Three: Julia p. 45
- Chapter Four: If You Could See Me Now p. 61

Section II: Lighting Out for the Territory p. 77

- Chapter Five: Ghost Story p. 79
- Chapter Six: Shadowland p. 101
- Chapter Seven: Floating Dragon p. 125
- Chapter Eight: The Talisman p. 145

Section III: Blue Roses and Buffalo Hunters p. 165

- Chapter Nine: Koko p. 167
- Chapter Ten: Mystery p. 189
- Chapter Eleven: Houses Without Doors p. 211
- Chapter Twelve: The Throat p. 237

Section IV: The End of the Century Is in Sight p. 259

- Chapter Thirteen: Uncollected Stories p. 261
- Chapter Fourteen: The Hellfire Club p. 279
- Chapter Fifteen: Mr. X p. 301

Appendices: p. 323

- Appendix A: Ghosts: The HWA Anthology p. 325
- Appendix B: The General's Wife p. 329
- Appendix C: Putney Tyson Ridge p. 333
- Appendix D: Twenty Questions: An Interview with Peter Straub p. 339

Primary Bibliography p. 347

Acknowledgments p. 349

Index p. 351

This book is dedicated to Janice, Eileen and Molly
for the times they let me work on it
and the times they didn't

and to my mother, Anne Theresa Sheehan,
in loving memory

*"Most people will tell you growing up means you stop believing in Halloween things—
I'm telling you the reverse. You start to grow up when you understand that
the stuff that scares you is part of the air you breathe."*

"Pork Pie Hat"

"Sometimes life is like a book."

Mystery

Introduction

Peter Straub first came to prominence with the 1979 publication of *Ghost Story,* a gaudy, expansive novel of supernatural terror that was deeply rooted in the classic tradition of the American Gothic tale. *Ghost Story* was an immediate popular success that quickly established itself as one of the seminal works of late twentieth-century horror fiction. Like the very best examples of its kind—Shirley Jackson's *The Haunting of Hill House* and Stephen King's *The Shining* spring immediately to mind—it offered conclusive evidence that art and entertainment, literature and "popular fiction," need not be regarded as mutually exclusive categories.

Despite his apparent status as an "overnight success," Straub had been a working writer for more than a decade before *Ghost Story* put him on the map, having published two slender volumes of poetry *(Open Air* and *Ishmael),* a modest, rather tentative mainstream novel *(Marriages),* and a pair of striking, increasingly ambitious horror novels *(Julia* and *If You Could See Me Now).* With *Julia,* Straub achieved a modest degree of financial success and began the process of discovering his own true voice. At the same time, he demonstrated an instinctive affinity for the requirements of the Gothic form, a form that proved particularly suited to his own sensibility and narrative gifts. With *If You Could See Me Now,* his grasp of those requirements deepened. With *Ghost Story,* he achieved a new level of mastery, and made the form his own.

In the aftermath of *Ghost Story*'s unanticipated success, Straub began what would become his lifelong habit of confounding conventional expectations. He followed *Ghost Story* with *Shadowland,* a dense and very different sort of novel that combined magic, fairy tales and Gnostic religious philosophy to describe the coming of age of a latter day Magus. His next novel, *Floating Dragon*, was a phantasmagorical horror novel that challenged the limits of the form. After *Floating Dragon*, his fiction evolved in a variety of directions, departing from—and occasionally returning to—the realm of the supernatural, crossing and combining genres to create an ambitious, highly intelligent series of thrillers that function both as colorful, deeply involving narratives, and as intensely personal explorations of a number of recurring themes: the power of past events, the nature and effect of childhood traumas, the existence of the sacred, the primal power of empathy, and the interconnectedness of life and art, to name only a few. To date, this restless aesthetic has resulted in thirteen novels and a substantial number of shorter pieces. Taken together, they represent what is arguably among the most significant—and underrated—bodies of popular fiction published in America in recent years.

Peter Straub was born in Milwaukee, Wisconsin in 1943, the oldest of the three sons born to Gordon Anthony Straub, a salesman, and Elvena (Nilsestuen) Straub, a nurse. As Straub later remarked, "the salesman wanted him to become an athlete, the nurse thought he would do well as either a doctor or a Lutheran minister, but all he wanted to do was learn to read."[1] And so, almost from the beginning, his life was dominated by his obsessive fascination with books. He taught himself to read while still in kindergarten, and by the time he arrived in first grade, he had already developed a taste for fiction of an exotic and adventurous nature. At the same time, his youthful penchant for storytelling began to emerge, and he found himself much "in demand around campfires and in backyards on summer evenings."[2]

All in all, except for his singular regard for narrative and its effects, Straub lived the normal, unexceptional life of a middle-class child in a blue-collar American city. But normality ended abruptly when, at the age of seven, he was struck by an automobile and very nearly killed. He underwent a classic near-death experience, survived, and went on to endure a lengthy, traumatic period of recovery. The accident left Straub with severe internal injuries, multiple broken bones, and the unalterable conviction that the world was a dangerous place. In the extended aftermath of that accident, Straub was subjected to numerous operations, was kept out of school for more than a year, and was confined to a wheelchair for many months. Eventually, he would recreate this experience in two separate novels, *Mystery* and *The Throat*, each of which would present the event from the perspective of a different character.

The accident left Straub with a long-standing speech impediment, which was eventually corrected, and a variety of unspecified "emotional quirks."[3] But the most enduring legacy of the accident took two very different forms. First, it intensified Straub's already obsessive preoccupation with books. In a world in which pain was a constant presence, books provided ready-made, readily available avenues of escape; and the boy who had been simply a voracious reader became an omnivorous one, a condition which would prove immensely valuable to the writer he would eventually become. Second, the accident provided Straub with an indelible sense of the physical, emotional and psychological realities of trauma. It also provided him with a sort of empathic basis for his later recreations of the tortured histories of a wide variety of characters: abused children, tormented Vietnam veterans, violated women, all of whom share the common experience of having—however briefly—lived at "the bottom of the world."[4] "Early experiences of my own," Straub has noted,

> ...permitted me greater access to the traumas of being under fire, of enduring extended periods of fear and panic, of ongoing extremity, than ordinarily would be possible for a lifelong civilian. I realized that all trauma was in a sense the same, and I understood its consequences.[5]

Eventually, Straub's life resumed its interrupted progress and proceeded, "as if scripted," through a series of intellectual stages that continued to shape his essential character. He received a scholarship to Milwaukee's Country Day School (an institution he would cheerfully malign in his 1980 novel, *Shadowland*), where his interests in literature and, additionally, music would continue to evolve. He discovered jazz, which would become a lifelong passion, and which spoke to him "of utterance beyond any constraint: passion and liberation in the form of speech on the far side of the verbal border."[6] Within the verbal borders, he discovered, at just the right moment, the classic interpreters of youthful angst and adolescent restlessness, Thomas Wolfe and Jack Kerouac, and began to develop the vague but powerful impression that a form of "transcendent wholeness"[7] was potentially available through precise, rigorously developed forms of artistic expression.

From Country Day School, Straub moved on to the University of Wisconsin, where he earned an honors degree in English and continued to encounter new and vital aesthetic influences. (Henry James, among others, entered his life at about this time.) Afterward, like the unnamed narrator of his 1994 novella, "Pork Pie Hat," he moved to New York City, acquired a masters degree from Columbia University, and then returned to the Midwest. In 1966, he married the former Susan Bitker and took a position as an English teacher at his old alma mater, Country Day School, now known as the University School of Milwaukee.

Straub's teaching career lasted for three years, and they were largely good ones. He was permitted to design his own courses, and elected to introduce his students to a number of his own favorite novelists: Jane Austen, E. M. Forster, D. H. Lawrence, the Brontes, etc. In the academic year of 1967/68, he encountered what amounted to a personal aesthetic revolution: the poetry of John Ashbery. Ashbery's second volume of poems, *The Tennis Court Oath*, had a revelatory effect on Straub, forcing him to reexamine his most fundamental notions about the nature of literature, and freeing him, eventually, to pursue his own writing. In 1969, in desperate need of change, he left his teaching position and departed, with Susan, for Ireland, where he enrolled in the Ph.D. program at Dublin's University College.

Straub lived in Dublin from 1969 to 1972. During that period, he wrote (and published) a great many poems whose influences included Marianne Moore, Elizabeth Bishop, Mark Strand, Ted Hughes and (of course) John Ashbery. A number of French contemporaries, ambitious experimenters such as Jacques Dupin and Yves Bonnefoy, provided additional inspiration. At the same time, Straub worked on a doctoral dissertation whose center kept shifting, moving away from its original subject, D. H. Lawrence, to a larger, more shapeless subject called The Surface of the Novel, whose first two hundred pages virtually ignored Lawrence, concentrating instead on the works of Charlotte Bronte and Anthony Trollope. Concurrently, and almost in secret, Straub worked steadily away on the manuscript that would eventually become his first novel, *Marriages*. Eventually, with *Marriages* complete and his dissertation still foundering, Straub sent the novel off to the London-based publishing firm of Andre Deutsch, where it was accepted for publication. At this point, Straub yielded to his deepest inclinations, and abandoned academia forever. He felt, in his own words,

> ...as though I had come into my real life, the one I was supposed to have, at last...I felt rescued, restored. I knew that I had only barely begun, but that what I had begun was the process to which I had all along been meant to submit...[8]

In 1972, the Straubs moved to London, where they lived for the next seven years. For two of those years, Straub worked on his problematic second novel, *Under Venus*, while simultaneously absorbing the almost infinite variety of British cultural life, and spending a great deal of time in the company of essential new friends, such as the poet Ann Lauterbach and the poet/novelist Thomas Tessier. In 1974, after numerous rejections, he abandoned *Under Venus* and turned to a new project: *Julia*, which was published successfully in 1975 and later turned into a feature film starring Mia Farrow and Keir Dullea. Suddenly, Straub found himself launched on a viable new career. *Julia* was followed by *If You Could See Me Now*, which was followed in turn by *Ghost Story*. In the wake of *Ghost Story*'s extraordinary success, the Straubs—Peter, Susan, and newborn son Benjamin—returned to America after ten years abroad, settling for a while in Westport, Connecticut, then later finding a more suitable home on Manhattan's Upper West Side, where he continues to live with his wife, son, and second child, Emma Sydney Valli Straub.

In the decades that have passed since his return, Straub has amassed a substantial body of fiction that is notable for its vigor, variousness, and emotional strength, and for its implicit refusal to acknowledge the existence of traditional, genre-related limits. Underlying this entire body of work is the notion that writers, not genres, set both the terms and the limits by which stories of all types are ultimately governed. From *Julia* up through *Mr. X*, Straub has consistently demonstrated his belief in the infinite flexibility of all modes of storytelling, from horror to suspense to that other, slightly more respectable genre known as mainstream fiction. He is one of a number of writers—others include John Le Carré, Ursula Le Guin, John Crowley, and Dan Simmons, to name only a few—whose work has helped reclaim a number of genres too often debased by the shallow, the silly, and the second-rate. In Straub's hands, the entire range of thriller fiction—of which horror, mystery, suspense, etc., are simply subdivisions—has proven itself capable of absorbing and reflecting the deepest, most vital influences from the past, and of creating moving, memorable representations of the real lives led by real people in a violent, equivocal universe. As Straub, commenting on the work of graphic novelist Neil Gaiman, once remarked: "If this isn't literature, nothing is."[9] The same sentiment applies to Straub himself. His novels and stories add up to a large, and largely unrecognized, accomplishment. If they don't represent literature, nothing does.

1. The Peter Straub Website—www.net-site.com/straub—Biography

2. Ibid.

3. Ibid.

4. *Under Venus* (New York: Berkley Books, 1985), p.19

5. "The Quintessential Terrorist: A Chat with Peter Straub"—Online interview conducted by William Mark Simmons, 1998

6. The Peter Straub Website

7. Ibid.

8. "Peter Straub: Connoisseur of Fear"—Interview with Paula Guran for Omni Online (http://www.omnimag.com), June 1997—now available at http://www.darkecho.com/darkecho/archives/straub.html

9. "On Mortality and Change"—Afterward to *Brief Lives* by Neil Gaiman (New York, Vertigo/DC Comics, 1994)

Section I

Mainstream Experiments, Gothic Beginnings

Chapter One:
Marriages

Marriages, the first, tentative fictional creation of a discontented doctoral candidate, was written during the spring and summer of 1970 in the Reading Room of The National Library in Dublin. Its author, then mired in the Ph.D. program at Dublin's University College, yielded, in his own words, "to psychic necessity"[1] and, as a kind of respite from his never-to-be-completed dissertation on the novels of D. H. Lawrence, blindly embarked on the complicated business of writing fiction.

Marriages was written at the steady rate of five hundred words a day, without an outline, without a formal plan, without anything other than the author's nerve, narrative sense, and deep-seated belief that he was, at heart, a novelist. And he was right, although the results of that initial effort were mixed, at best. By August of 1970, the novel was completed, while the dissertation had rambled through some two hundred pages of preliminary material without once engaging the work of its central subject. Discouraged by his dissertation director's negative response to those 200 pages, Straub decided to send his novel out into the world, offering it first to the British publishing firm of Andre Deutsch, where it was immediately accepted. The book was subsequently accepted for American publication by Coward, McCann, and Geoghegen, and, thus encouraged, Straub abandoned his abortive academic career in favor of the deeper, if chancier, satisfactions of full-time fiction writing. At the same time, the publication of *Marriages* signaled a major shift in the direction Straub's creative energies would take from that time forward. Poetry, once the centerpiece of his literary ambitions, faded, like the world of academia, into the background, to be absorbed and replaced by the very different demands of narrative prose.

Still, poetry remains very much at the heart of *Marriage*'s governing aesthetic. Written in a consciously—sometimes self-consciously—poetic style, its sources of inspiration range from the stately gravity of Henry James to the groundbreaking experimentation of John Ashbery, particularly the extended prose poetry of *Three Poems* and the radical rejection of traditional linear expression embodied in Ashbery's 1962 collection, *The Tennis Court Oath*. Straub's encounters with Ashbery's work opened up a window on a world of liberating, previously unsuspected literary possibilities:

> What excited me about *The Tennis Court Oath* and Ashbery's work in general was that it overturned everything I had been taught about literature. It was serious without taking itself seriously. Lots of it was very funny, including the diction levels. Much of it was fragmentary and disjointed, and a lot of the language seemed more to float above rational sense than to represent it. A lot of it was beautiful, and all of it had unmistakable authority. I liked the disjunctions, the playfulness, the bravery. Reading Ashbery's work filled me with a sense of freedom and possibility. The book struck me as a kind of revelation. That I had no idea what it meant was a part of the revelation...[2]

At their most extreme, the Ashbery poems of this period gleefully bypass most commonly accepted standards of poetic discourse, reveling, instead, in a deliberately disconnected, dissociative technique that is startling, striking, and at times almost willfully obscure. Witness this fragment from a poem called "America:"

> Ribbons
> over the Pacific
> Sometimes we
> The deep

additional
and more and more less deep
but hurting
under the fire
brilliant rain
to meet us.
Probably in
moulded fire
we make it
times of the year
the light falls from heaven
love
parting the separate lives.[3]

Galvanized by Ashbery's example, Straub turned to fiction with the intention of creating "a sort of antinarrative, Ashberian novel with a lot of Fitzgerald and Henry James in it."[4] The result of this confluence of radically different elements is an odd, unengaging novel whose eccentric structure flies in the face of its author's most fundamental narrative talents, which are, despite whatever density or convolutions would attend their eventual deployment, basically straightforward and traditional. Thus, *Marriages* is not only the least effective and satisfying of Straub's novels, it is also, with its insistence on the disjointed, nonlinear presentation of an essentially simple story, the least characteristic.

Here, freed from the discontinuities of its chosen structure and recast in more or less chronological order, is the story that *Marriages* labors to tell: Owen, the narrator, is the thirtysomething manufacturer of an unspecified product line. Having weathered "the minor recessions and losses of faith of the sixties,"[5] he leaves his nameless Midwestern city and moves to Europe with two purposes in mind: to tap into the burgeoning European market and "to redirect the growth of [his] personality,"[6] which, he believes, has become more and more staid and colorless over the years. Arriving in Dublin in advance of Morgan, his wife of eight years, he searches for a suitable place to live and begins the process of establishing himself in the Anglo-Irish business community. While awaiting his wife's arrival, Owen has several glancing encounters with a beautiful stranger who, in one of Straub's more pretentious and regrettable decisions, is referred to throughout the novel as, simply, "the woman." Eventually, Owen and the woman meet, fall for each other, and are deeply enmeshed in a clandestine affair by the time of Morgan's arrival. After several furtive encounters in a Dublin hotel, the two are unexpectedly granted an entire month together when Morgan is called away to provide aid and comfort to her emotionally embattled sister, Joanie, who has just been ejected from an Israeli kibbutz on the basis of immoral conduct.

With Morgan gone, the two set out from Dublin to Paris—the woman's home—and from there head out on a journey across France to the messy, embittered resolution of their relationship. Somewhere between Paris and Arles, they pick up a boisterous American hitchhiker named Magruder, who is en route to a self-chosen exile in a monastery in the French Pyrenees. Once in Arles, the three tour the ruins of an ancient outdoor theater, where Owen glimpses a strolling couple who remind him, impossibly, of the participants in a sinister encounter that took place at his wedding, several years before. This encounter leads to the novel's single most effective sequence, a chase through the streets and alleys of Arles in a futile attempt to confront and identify the elusive couple. Later information indicates that the male member of the couple, Charlie La Rochelle, has recently been murdered while serving a term in prison, thus giving *Marriages* the sudden and unexpected aspect of a ghost story.

As the journey continues toward the town of Aix-en-Provence and the relationship between Owen and the woman spirals downward toward its end, she confesses to an abortive act of infidelity, having taken the ultimately impotent Magruder to bed while Owen was chasing his ghosts across the length and breadth of Arles. Owen responds with predictable dismay and, in what might be the novel's single dreariest sequence, spends the bulk of his remaining time with the woman guzzling scotch and brandy and clutching his stomach in an endless bout of psychosomatic pain.

Finally, in a completely unconvincing moment of epiphany, he comes to understand that their relationship has reached its preordained end, that they have learned all that they can from each other, that he loves her still, but in a new and different fashion. Forced to endure his idiotic happiness in the face of this revelation, the woman all but spits in his face before driving recklessly away, with Owen clinging to the passenger seat. She loses control of the car on the rainy streets, and their love affair ends with an auto wreck that sends the woman into the hospital for an extended period while Owen, largely unhurt, returns to his wife, his business, and the old, familiar circumstances of his life.

That is the primary narrative, and Straub supplements it with a scattering of subplots involving Morgan's reckless, promiscuous sister Joanie; Jack and Sylvia Goldsmith, a pair of Dublin-based Americans whose marriage is shattered by Sylvia's repeated acts of infidelity; and Abe Gabriel, a fast-talking ladies' man from Israel who moves in and out of the lives of a number of susceptible women, including both Sylvia and Joanie. There are frequent epistolary interludes, most provided by the woman, who relentlessly anatomizes every aspect of the affair in a breathless, frequently overripe language. A few examples:

> ...for I want us—though this is part of my recklessness—to get down into the center of one another's lives, to be able to converse with the mystery that inhabits the center. There is a violence there, a riskiness. For me this is given. It takes equal place with the other, the kernel of self-interest and passivity, the necessary, unchangeable self.[7]

> ...and now I have to try to write to you, to see what coherence there is in the midst of this ferocious and boisterous tenderness that is boiling in me. You make me afraid to write. What I fear is that I will falsify by touching the wrong word, coming down with a crash on something I don't know how to say correctly.[8]

On a more pedestrian note, Poppa, the beleaguered father of Morgan and Joanie, weighs in with his own flurry of letters, baffled communiqués to the daughters whom he loves but does not understand. His letters end, sadly and invariably, with offers of the only thing he can think to give them: money.

Straub adds a bit of context to all this through a series of crucial flashbacks. In one, we are given an extended, well-executed recreation of Owen's and Morgan's wedding day. The scene is slightly marred by Straub's clumsy rendering of a dope smoking interlude involving Joanie and her hippie husband, Fred. ("You turn on, don't you? Do you want to turn on grass?")[9] On the whole, though, it has energy and a sense of detail, and is mostly notable for the aforementioned sinister encounter between an alcoholic family friend named Sandy Bosch and Charlie La Rochelle, who will later return (possibly) as a ghost. Another flashback concerns the immediate aftermath of Joanie's separation from husband Fred. After returning, temporarily, to her childhood home, Joanie finds a sympathetic listener in Owen, who promptly seduces her, or allows himself to be seduced by her, within shouting distance of Morgan. It is thus with some justification that Owen later refers to himself as "an anthology of betrayals."[10] At the very least, he comes across as something of a sexual opportunist, a judgment which impairs the reader's ability to sympathize with, or even fully believe in, the purity of his subsequent passion for the woman.

Straub dispenses the various elements of the drama in resolutely erratic fashion. Unfortunately, the disregard for chronology and the insistence on a nonlinear presentation of events are really only surface effects. Beneath that surface, the underlying narrative is essentially conventional and frequently pretentious. Straub had not, at this stage of his career, fully absorbed the Ashberian principle of being serious without taking himself seriously. The portentous nature of the entire enterprise is hinted at before the novel proper even begins, through Straub's peculiar rendering of the obligatory Author's Note, which informs the reader, right up front, that the author of this book is a smart, serious guy.

> The characters in this novel do not represent any real people, living or dead. In some cases, there are composites of living people, their voices, anecdotes or gestures; in others, not. Like all fictions, this novel intersects and crosscuts the real world, but is independent of it. "I," like the other people in this book—and the places too—is imaginary.[11]

Marriages isn't by any means a badly written novel. Even starting out, Straub seemed incapable of writing below a certain, consistently literate level. At its lesser moments, though, the prose does become uncomfortably stiff and formal, and cries out for the lighter touch its author was unable to provide. Examples abound. Here, referring to the indelible speech patterns of his Midwest upbringing, Owen tells us:

> ...the flattened and minutely rising inflections at the end of clauses clearly label me. They are like baggage tickets, telling from where it is that I have come.[12]

The descriptions of sexual activity strain mightily for some form of poetic approximation, but end up seeming merely overheated and selfconsciously artistic:

> The gold of her face breaks beneath me: teeth. I am full, full and sliding. Mysterious, she is wrapping, warm, about me, tensing and releasing. Her legs slide up over mine, her back arches. She holds me, riding it out. Fuller and fuller. I ride her wave, teased and urgent; then the signal comes; I burst; I shake like an emptying sack, shaking into her. My heart pounds, pounds. Her hands on my ears.[13]

Taken individually, none of these examples is either fatal or particularly disruptive, but the cumulative effect of these and too many similar moments is an overriding sense of the laboriousness, the essential humorlessness, that infects the novel.

On the other hand, the prose does come periodically to life. Straub was always a shrewd observer and *Marriages* captures, with a nice economy of means, the ambiance of its multitude of settings: the streets, pubs, and clandestine hotel rooms of Dublin; the yacht clubs and upper middle class residences of the American Midwest; and the sights and sounds of an adulterous journey across urban and rural France, from Paris to Albi, from Arles to Aix-en-Provence. In addition to the scene setting, there are a number of nicely stated, brightly observant touches throughout, such as an early description of the character, "peculiarly and revealingly American,"[14] of a young girl's face seen against the backdrop of a seaside bonfire; an account of a dinner party hosted by a Dublin businessman who seems "to have been born with all his clothes on"[15]; a moment of uncomfortable insight in which Owen responds to the plight of his cuckolded friend

Jack Goldsmith with a brief flash of atavistic contempt, thinking: "I have two women. He cannot keep one."[16]

Dialogue, on the other hand, is a fairly consistent problem throughout the novel. Straub's characters simply cannot relax into the rhythms of natural human speech. A stiff, nonidiomatic formality governs far too many of the characters' endless exchanges on life and love. Here, for example, is the woman, sitting in an outdoor cafe in Tours, earnestly addressing Owen:

> "I can't understand," she tells me, "your reluctance to simply accept me—the way you would accept the weather, or a present. At times, you make me feel a dreadful failure, as though there were something terribly wrong with me, or the way I see you. I thought I could make you—*make you*—outgrow your Puritanism. (Of course, I love that in you, too.) Yet, lovely as you are, you stand out of arm's reach."[17]

Here's a brief exchange that occurs just before the two go swimming together in the Rhone River:

> "It's so beautiful," she said. "The water is really white. I never expected it to look so powerful. It actually seems to have a will. It looks as though it would like to come up and take back the land."
>
> "You're a real romantic," I said.[18]

Pillow talk is equally fatuous:

> I love the way you fuck. You're wonderful.
>
> Why?
>
> Oh, you monster, you just want compliments. Because you're bulky—here, across your back, and in your chest. I love your shoulders.

I love yours too.[19]

And so on. People rarely sound like people in this novel, a failing that contributes in large part to the pervasive feeling of artifice that keeps *Marriages* from assuming a genuine, felt life of its own.

Stylistic issues aside, the story itself is fundamentally ordinary and uninvolving, and neither the author's efforts to invest it with a highly charged, poetic language nor his deliberately disjointed presentation of its component parts is able to pump much life into it. The most interesting aspect of the book remains that latent Gothic element suggested by the possible, if unverified, appearance of the recently deceased Charlie LaRochelle. And even this element, intriguing as it is, is tangential to the main thrust of the book, a lively but anomalous offshoot that never really connects with the larger issues of love and passion, infidelity and erotic obsession, that the novel attempts to address. Still, given one's knowledge of the author's subsequent career, it's hard not to see in this offshoot the first tentative stirring of a narrative impulse determined to assert itself among the alien surroundings of a sedate, and extremely literary, first novel.

The key word here is literary. *Marriages* is best and most charitably viewed as the work of an extremely intelligent young man who has read a great many good novels, and whose sensibility has been shaped by those books and by his own emotional and intellectual responses to them. For all its learning, sophistication, and sexual forthrightness, it lacks the quality of actual, deeply considered experience that characterizes Straub's later, better work. Even the underlying notion that drives this book—the notion that a novel about marriages is ipso facto a novel about infidelity—seems like an essentially literary one, a lingering aftereffect of novels such as John Updike's 1967 portrait of adultery in suburbia, *Couples*.

Straub does make a conscious, if perfunctory, attempt to distance the narrative from the dangers of an overly literary viewpoint by making his narrator a businessman rather than a writer or artist. In his role as inheritor of a modestly successful manufacturing concern, Owen makes the occasional token reference to the realities of commerce. There are vague references to business meetings, offstage discussions of import duties, attempts, usually successful, to get Owen's product (whatever it is) into the retail outlets of Dublin. But in all of this, not a single item of concrete information regarding Owen's business ventures ever emerges. Straub isn't even interested enough in the subject to fake it. Similarly, Poppa, Owen's father-in-law, is, on the basis of available evidence, extremely successful at something, but we are never given an inkling of what that something might be. The whole thorny question of how people who aren't teaching, writing, or making their way through graduate school actually earn their livings is one that *Marriages* chooses deliberately to ignore. In the context of the novel, there is a void where this particular dimension of human life should be. And that void is filled with the one subject Straub knows better than anything else: literature.

Everyone in this book reads, and everyone talks about what he or she has read. Within the first few pages, we encounter references to Andre Gide, D. H. Lawrence, Henry James, Pauline Reage (pseudonymous author of *The Story of O*), the poet Yves Bonnefoy, and a controversial figure on the French literary scene in the mid-to-late sixties, Henri Charriere, author of *Papillon*. (Charriere is a curiously persistent figure throughout *Marriages,* cropping up at least half a dozen times in a variety of contexts. Charriere's bestselling account of his adventurous career, which included a spectacular escape from the French prison colony of Devil's Island, was believed by many to be at least partially fraudulent. Whether Straub intended him to serve as an oblique commentary on the more questionable, even fraudulent, aspects of his characters' lives; or whether he is present simply as an iconic emblem of a particular time and place; or whether, in fact, he represents an apotheosis, much desired, of the adventurous life, the life fully and completely lived, is never made clear. But he is an odd and ubiquitous presence nonetheless.)

As the novel progresses, literary references continue to proliferate: Dostoevsky, George Eliot, Virginia Woolf, Shakespeare (naturally), Forster, Proust, Dickens, and others. Owen and the woman spend almost as much time in bookstores as they do in bed. The woman is a particularly voracious reader who, at the time of the affair, is working her way through the complete works of Henry James, both in the original and in French translations. In an almost comically ineffectual attempt to consolidate his position as a soulless, uncultured man of business, Owen claims he is "not much of a reader—in comparison to the woman, not a reader at all."[20] The internal evidence, however, constantly contradicts this assertion. Owen is forever viewing his own life and the life of the world around him in literary terms. He walks into a bedroom and sees the woman silhouetted in a "golden bowl"[21] of light (James). He envisions himself and the woman as passengers on a ship "beating against the current"[22] (Fitzgerald). He recommends *Anna Karenina* to the woman, casually recalls comments made by H. G. Wells on the character of Henry James and, when asked by Magruder why people waste their time reading, he mounts a spirited defense of the reading life:

> "I suppose people read for different reasons," I said. "Escape might be one of them. I don't think it's the only one, though. Some people read to find out about the author's problems or his beliefs. His values, what sort of life he approves. Some people read because they enjoy the way different writers use words—or the way they put scenes together. It's like looking at a painting and responding to its balance, or to the use of color. I don't know what else; in fact, I don't read a whole lot myself. But I know that some people read novels because they are like little worlds, worlds in which everything is organized—a world built on your toenail, say.[23]

That last sounds very much like a reference to William H. Gass' essay on the fiction of Malcolm Lowry, "In Terms of the Toenail." Interestingly, Magruder the nonreader responds to this by discussing some of the books in his own life: "a big huge thing called *The Idiot*," and, unsurprisingly, *Papillon*. ("I liked that too. It was real adventurous."[24]) In the end, *Marriages* is a book both characterized and limited by its author's literary predilections and grad school sensibility. Its roots are in the library and not in real life. Making creative use of one's personal literary pantheon is not necessarily a bad thing, of course, and Straub would, in time, build a distinguished career writing novels that incorporated within their complex and varied structures affectionate and respectful reflections of, and responses to, the novels, stories, poems and essays that have spoken most directly to his creative consciousness.

But at the time in which *Marriages* was written, he had not yet found a way to combine the effects of his wide-ranging reading with the fluency, narrative density, and emotional depth which mark his most memorable work. He would not, in fact, find his way to that level until a few more years had passed, and a few more books had been written. *Marriages*, in spite of its weaknesses, started him on his way. In the aftermath of its publication, his writing began almost immediately to move away from the nonlinear, Ashbery-inspired style of his apprenticeship toward a more orderly, coherent narrative technique much more suited to his particular gifts. Ironically, at least a dozen years would pass before anyone would have the opportunity to view the initial result of that change in direction: his ambitious, problematic, infinitely superior second novel, *Under Venus*.

1. Interview with Paula Guran for Omni Online
2. Ibid.
3. John Ashbery, The Mooring of Starting Out (Hopewell, NJ: Ecco Press, 1997), p. 66
4. Interview with Paula Guran for Omni Online
5. Marriages (New York: Pocket Books, reprint date 1977), p. 3
6. Ibid., p. 3
7. Ibid., p. 105
8. Ibid., p. 71
9. Ibid., p. 124
10. Ibid., p. 101
11. Ibid., Author's Note
12. Ibid., p. 5
13. Ibid., p. 77
14. Ibid., p. 6
15. Ibid., p. 65
16. Ibid., p. 142
17. Ibid., p. 17
18. Ibid., p. 101
19. Ibid., p. 98
20. Ibid., p. 21
21. Ibid., p. 184
22. Ibid., p. 175
23. Ibid., p. 187
24. Ibid., p. 88

Chapter Two: *Under Venus*

Under Venus, Peter Straub's "secret"[1] novel, was begun in Dublin in 1970 and completed, two years later, in London. The bulk of the book was written in the tiny bed-sitting room in Belsize Square to which the Straubs had relocated following the acceptance of *Marriages* by Andre Deutsch, and its author believed that the long and arduous process of composition had resulted in a second novel that was "better, more ambitious and accomplished, more novelistically solid"[2] than his first. And while his judgment in the matter was essentially correct, his ability to anticipate the whims of the publishing world was underdeveloped. His novel, known at that time as *The Scarred Girl*, met with unexpected resistance from both British and American publishers, and would languish in limbo—the proverbial trunk novel—until 1984.

It seemed, at first, that *Under Venus* might meet that kinder fate its ambition and accomplishment had earned for it. Its first reader, Straub's English literary agent, pronounced the book a triumph, informing the author that only the fact of his American citizenship would keep *Under Venus* out of the running for England's top literary prizes. On that heady and confident note, the manuscript went out into the world, where it met with repeated rejection. Two intensive periods of trimming and revision followed, all of which left the novel cleaner and tighter, but still essentially its original self. Eventually, Straub began contemplating more drastic revisions, such as recasting the book as a first-person narrative. In the end, exhausted and aware of the desperation that underlay that notion, he put the book aside and turned his hand to a new and very different project, *Julia*.

Seen from the perspective of Straub's subsequent career—a perspective conspicuously missing in 1972—the nonpublication of *Under Venus* was not altogether a bad thing. In his introduction to *Wild Animals*, the collection in which his lost book was finally resurrected for public consumption, Straub noted that the novel's failure

> shocked me into compressing perhaps a decade's anxiety, growth, and introspection into a fifth of that time. It may be that this was the only time in the history of the often adversarial relationship between writer and publisher that the publisher rejected a book with sufficient merit to be published, did so quite properly, and with wholly beneficial results.[3]

The main beneficial result was the change of direction which immediately followed this debacle, forcing Straub more quickly than might otherwise have been the case to abandon the mainstream and strike out in the direction dictated by his underlying Gothic sensibility. Still, the failure of *Under Venus* to find a publisher on either continent was a bruising and dispiriting experience and, given its manifest superiority to the successfully published *Marriages*, an ironic one as well. Despite its flaws—and it is still very much the work of an inexperienced and overly literary young writer—*Under Venus* is an intelligent and fundamentally vital narrative that captures, with a novelist's eye for character and detail, the inner and outer weather of its particular time and place.

Under Venus, which is set during the waning days of the tumultuous sixties, is a story of exile and return, of a rapidly changing America seen from the perspective of a visiting expatriate composer. The novel opens on the closing moments of a journey from Europe to the unfamiliar homeland of America, and closes with the opening moments of the journey back. In between these bookended images of arrival and departure, the novel takes us into the emotional heartland of its protagonist and allows us to experience, along with him, a variety of dilemmas both personal and political, public and private. Unlike *Marriages,* the language of *Under Venus* is spare and direct, the structure clean and linear. The result is a book which contains within itself an implicit rejection of the earlier novel's more eccentric characteristics, and an equally implicit recognition of the need to bring a greater clarity and directness to the craft of storytelling.

The man at the heart of this particular story is Elliott Denmark, whose surname, given the novel's preoccupation with the viewpoint of European expatriates, is a bit heavy-handed. Elliott is a composer—moderately successful, moderately avant-garde—who has lived and worked in Paris for the past several years. As *Under Venus* opens, Elliot is returning with his wife, Vera, to their mutual hometown of Plechette City, Wisconsin, where Elliot is scheduled to conduct an evening of his own compositions at a local university. But in the three weeks that elapse between their arrival and the night of the concert, the couple find themselves caught up in a multitude of emotional issues. One of these concerns a hotly contested land development scheme which pits each of their families against the other. Another concerns the lingering aftereffects of an old romantic entanglement of Elliot's, one which, despite the intervention of years and distance, has never quite died away.

Many of the novel's central elements are introduced, or at least alluded to, in the effective and densely detailed opening chapters. Beginning with a panoramic, bird's-eye view of the Plechette City skyline, then digressing briefly on the city's history—which is, in part, a history of the Denmark family in America—the narrative follows Elliot and Vera on the scenic drive from the airport to the home of Vera's parents, local alderman Herman Glauber and his wife, Tessa. In the course of the drive, the two are introduced to much of what passes for progress in the America of 1969: ten-acre shopping centers, miniature golf courses, cocktail bars, and an endless array of fast-food franchises. Another, controversial symbol of progress mentioned in the early going concerns Nun's Wood, a large area of wooded land occupied by a soon to be vacated convent. Nun's Wood stands at the center of a proposed development scheme which has divided much of Plechette City into two armed camps. The ramifications of this issue will reverberate throughout the novel.

Alongside these references to commerce and the march of events, two key characters, each of whom has enormous emotional resonance for Elliot, are also introduced. One is Kai Glauber, Herman's older brother, a concentration camp survivor who "had been to the bottom of the world and come back speaking another language."[4] Kai is a man who has reduced his life to the bare essentials. He lives alone, without friends or illusions, working quietly and patiently on the monumental study of Goethe which has become his life's work. His Olympian detachment from the affairs of the world, together with his complete "rejection of customary human ends and solaces,"[5] makes him a powerfully totemic figure to Elliot, whose own life comes to seem more and more disheveled the longer he remains in America. The other key figure—and the major source of Elliot's emotional dishevelment—is Anita Kellerman, a beautiful and charismatic widow with whom Elliot had an adulterous affair shortly before his and Vera's departure to Paris. The affair has long since ended, but the obsessive nature of his feelings for Anita remain undiminished. His return to Plechette City places him in direct contact with the source of his most volatile emotions.

A number of ancillary characters and subplots help fill out the crowded canvas of *Under Venus,* among them the romantic entanglements of two old schoolmates, Joanie Haupt and Lawrence Wooster; the tensions, difficulties, and personal conflicts that attend rehearsals for the climactic concert; the nervous disorder affecting Anita's seven-year-old son, Mark; the rumored presence of a predatory wolf prowling the outskirts of Plechette City. Mostly, though, the central dramatic elements arise either from the depth of Elliot's absorption with Anita Kellerman, or from his unwitting involvement in the Nun's Wood controversy, two essentially separate plot elements that become more and more interconnected as the novel progresses. Characters from one aspect of the novel cross without warning into the other, and the whole complex web of public and private events becomes a mirror of the emotional confusion and cultural disorientation that color so much of Elliot's problematic homecoming.

Anita represents Elliot's most profound connection to the America from which he has voluntarily exiled himself. His affair with her, which began when he was an instructor in the Plechette College music department and lasted for several months, was a life-altering disruption from which he has never fully recovered. Anita is an embodiment of "the disorderly irruptive life of the emotions"[6] and her commanding, powerfully erotic presence very nearly shattered the delicate balance of his marriage to Vera, who intuited the depth of Elliot's feelings for Anita when she stumbled on a mildly indiscreet interlude that occurred between them at a faculty party. Vera's response was to force Elliot to choose between his marriage and his affair. He chose his marriage but remained haunted by the afterimage of the affair, having discovered in his relationship with Anita "a level of feeling that had all his life been given to music."[7] Now, once again in America, he must struggle to maintain the uneasy stability of his life, his work, and his marriage in the resurrected presence of a woman who occupies a larger than life position in his memory and imagination.

The Anita whom Elliot reencounters is a woman with problems and emotional entanglements of her own. The widow of a Plechette College professor who was killed in an automobile accident, she now shares her home, and the care of her disturbed son, with another victim of an auto accident, a scarred but compelling young woman named Andy French. Andy's presence lends another layer of lust, longing, and general emotional confusion to Elliot's already fragile and chaotic mental state. Even more significantly, Anita is embroiled in an enigmatic relationship with a local business tycoon named Ronnie Upp, who is the man most responsible for the plan to develop the virgin acreage of Nun's Wood and who may, as Elliot comes to suspect, be the father of Anita's child.

Ronnie Upp, who is largely an offstage presence for the first two thirds of the novel, is the primary mover and shaker of the Plechette City business community. Before coming into somewhat sharper focus later in the book, he is presented to us through a series of glancing, essentially predatory images: standing in a snowy field, wielding a shotgun; bow hunting in the company of the seven-year-old Mark; striking Anita in a moment of frustration. He also carries what Elliot refers to as "unusual psychic baggage for a tycoon,"[8] having, in his childhood, shot and killed his abusive father after ostensibly mistaking him for a burglar. Ronnie's actions and associations reach into almost every corner of *Under Venus*. He himself is, or has been, Anita's lover. His father, a notorious local character named Harrison Upp, was once the lover of Elliot's uncle, Kai Glauber, and was primarily responsible for Kai's incarceration in Nazi Germany. Additionally, Ronnie's company, The Globe Corporation, has taken over the Chambers-Denmark factory, a local business run by the Denmark family for generations. Most centrally, he is the prime mover behind the plan to develop the Nun's Wood acreage.

In essence, the Nun's Wood controversy is centered around Ronnie's plan to purchase Nun's Wood from the departing order of Catholic nuns and turn the land into an industrial park. His plans include cutting down approximately forty percent of the existing trees, converting the convent into an office building, adding two more office buildings in the cleared areas, and then renting space to companies like IBM and other big, "respectable" corporations. Upp's major political supporter is alderman Herman Glauber, Elliot's father-in-law. His major opposition takes the form of an aristocratic cabal headed by Chase Denmark, Elliot's father. Herman, who is a curious mixture of the cynical and the pragmatic, believes, deep down, that "the past works, not the future,"[9] but still feels compelled to support any reasonable development scheme that will bring new jobs and new opportunities to the area. Chase Denmark, an old-school gentleman newly awakened to the virtues of political activism, is fighting to maintain the existing ecological balance and to preserve the world he knows, and believes in, from the barbarians he hears pounding at the gates. Elliott, caught in the middle of an unresolvable family conflict, must make his own decision on the issue, knowing that whatever stance he takes will alienate someone close to him. At the same time, he must find his way through the surrounding minefields of love, lust, and personal responsibility in which he finds himself and into an elusive, perhaps impossible, state of intellectual and emotional clarity.

The journey toward clarity, toward an end to the discord created by unruly emotions and the uncontrollable forces of the outside world, lies very much at the heart of *Under Venus*' concerns. Confusion is a fundamental element of the novel, the medium through which the characters must make their way. All of them, Elliot in particular, clutch firmly at whatever small or large satisfactions—love, work, values, duty, tradition—are most effective in keeping the encroaching chaos at bay. Elliot's visit to Plechette City is, among other things, an evocation of the many forms—political, cultural, sexual, familial—that chaos takes, and the essential movement of the novel is the movement toward some dimly perceived sense of coherence. Elliot's concert, which concludes the visit, is a case in point. Though the concert itself is never actually described, the implication is that it ultimately comes together, in spite of the cacophony, feuding, and endless plays of ego which precede it. Art is, however temporarily, a form of coherence, often the only one available.

In telling this story, Straub presents us with several early renderings of what will become familiar themes, images, and devices. Foremost among these is the image of a man in thrall to a powerful female and struggling to free himself. Straub created a clumsy prototype of this relationship in *Marriages*, then developed it to much greater effect in his account of Elliot Denmark's obsessive attachment to Anita

Kellerman. In subsequent novels, he would add an interesting and effective supernatural element to his portraits of romantic and/or sexual thralldom, notably through the characters of Allison Greening of *If You Could See Me Now* and Alma Mobley of *Ghost Story*. (It's difficult to ignore the fact that the very literary Straub has given all of these characters—each of whom is in some sense "the other woman"—first names that begin with the proverbial scarlet letter. It's equally hard to ignore the way the name Anita Kellerman seems to echo the name of Anna Karenina, that classic literary adulteress and eponymous heroine of a novel that is of obvious importance to the author, one that receives significant mention in at least two of his other works, *Marriages* and the 1990 novella, *The Buffalo Hunter*.)

In fact, the power that Anita wields over Elliot seems, from the perspective of Elliot's sometimes overheated imagination, almost supernatural, as in this passage, which might have been lifted wholesale from the pages of *If You Could See Me Now:*

> She was a white uncertain lucency in his consciousness, a troubling presence...It was as though she were willing him to think about her. [He] felt as though he were being physically pushed back into the sensations of four years before; as if, over a great distance, he were being manipulated by her. He knew that she expected him to come to her house, and that when he arrived she would confound him once again.[10]

In the end, Elliot is able to free himself from his obsession with Anita by consciously seizing all opportunities—her relationship with Ronnie Upp, her occasional misunderstandings of his personal and artistic intentions, her varied sexual history—to demythologize her, to reduce her to the level of an ordinary mortal with ordinary claims on his energy and attentions:

> In the cold gray darkness of the morning, Elliot felt that his own problems might be moving toward a clarification, a resolution. Anita had always possessed a significance for him that was nearly mythical; he had

> seen her as though she were a giant figure in an epical drama of liberation, and now he could approach her more practically, with a realistic love that honored their situation.[11]

Elliot's attempts to reduce this relationship to the manageable proportions of a "realistic love" involve a certain amount of rationalization on his part, a certain narrowness of focus that brings her flaws and her fundamental human fallibility into greater and greater relief. His revisionist view of Anita is ultimately as skewed as his previous mythologizing had been, but it does allow him to step outside the sphere of her influence and resume his life.

Another characteristic theme, sounded here for the first time, is embodied in the title of the opening section, "The Past in the Present." As Miles Teagarden, narrator of *If You Could See Me Now,* a kind of supernatural sibling to *Under Venus,* tells us: "No story exists without its past, and the past of a story is what enables us to understand it."[12] This belief is fundamental to Straub's fiction, and informs virtually every one of the varied stages of his career.

The past, in *Under Venus,* manifests itself in a variety of forms. First of all, there are the personal pasts of the characters, which are always present to some degree, and which are usually messy and frequently as raw as an open wound. Examples include Elliot's affair with Anita and its defining effect on his life, marriage, and personality; Ronnie Upp's memories of a childhood dominated by an abusive, unpredictable father, and of a single moment of violence that may have been the action of a confused child or may have been a deliberate act of patricide; Andy French's traumatic accident, which left her scarred, distrustful, and separated forever from the fundamental innocence of her previous life; and Kai Glauber's disastrous liaison with Harrison Upp, and his subsequent imprisonment in the concentration camps of Nazi Germany.

Then there is the more distant, impersonal past, the past that has solidified into history. In *Under Venus,* the history of Plechette City and the surrounding region is memorialized in the names of the towns, such as Plechette, Racine, Prairie du Chien, Fon du Lac, lingering reminders of the period of French colonialism that marked the Midwest. Other reminders of a mixed European heritage (French, German, Polish) are present in the forms of murals, architectural monuments, street names, family names, even in the residue of specific cultural influences. (Music in Plechette City is described as "largely an affair of brass bands, accordions, and zithers,"[13] a musical heritage from which Elliot Denmark and his "difficult" compositions have radically retreated.)

Finally, there is that aspect of the past, still very much present, which rises out of a kind of middle distance, and takes the form of stories, legends, and reminiscences that heighten our understanding of the people and places that form the heart of the novel. Out of this arises another characteristic strategy, present here for the first time: the prevalence of independent, internal narratives—stories within the primary story—employed by the characters for a variety of purposes: to illuminate the past; to place the present in some kind of perspective; to define, for themselves and their listeners, the sources of their traditions, values, and beliefs; to augment the sense of a larger, ongoing story of which they are a part; and, most essentially, to amuse, to entertain, to pass the time together in one of the most basic and necessary of all human pursuits. In *Ghost Story,* the propensity for storytelling has become a formalized ritual in which a group of frightened old men—the Chowder Society—meet at each other's houses and tell each other stories that help keep the darkness at bay. In *Under Venus,* the storytelling impulse is considerably less ritualized, but no less important.

One of the basic structural elements of *Under Venus* arises from the domestic circumstances surrounding Elliot and Vera's homecoming. They spend the first half of the visit at the home of Vera's parents, then move to the home of Elliot's parents for the second half. These two very different households, with their very different social, cultural and educational backgrounds give rise to very different kinds of stories. These differences add a sense of variety to the novel, broadening the context against which the present day dramas are played out. In the first half, Tessa Glauber talks about her younger days, and about her surprising romantic aspirations—hidden completely from her husband—regarding the young Kai Glauber, who had been a teacher in her rural Wisconsin school district many years before. Herman recounts his youthful career as the manager of a rough-and-tumble, hot-sheet motel, and of the early exposure to cruelty, violence, and sexual scandals that helped form his understanding of the dark side of human nature. Chase Denmark, on the other hand, tells stories that reflect a different, and much more fastidious, world. His favorite story features a man whose name will be familiar to readers of Straub's 1989 novel, *Mystery:* Lamont von Heilitz. Chase's story concerns the elaborate patriotic gala planned by von Heilitz in 1944, which was largely ruined by a sudden epidemic of measles and was held, in the end, for an audience of one. Von Heilitz's story is variously funny, noble, and pathetic, depending on the listener. But it is always, in Chase's view, about values, the altogether admirable values of another, better, age.

There is one more household in which stories are told: the squalid, claustrophobic apartment in which Kai Glauber secludes himself. Even Kai has a story he feels compelled to tell: a story that encompasses his love/hate relationship with Harrison Upp, his education in the realities of corruption and betrayal, and his experience of life in the death camps of Nazi Germany, "the bottom of the world."[14] This particular segment of Kai's autobiography is told only to Elliot, not to the reader. Straub wisely refuses to cheapen the experience with the inevitable inadequacy of words. Sometimes, silence is best.

The final result of all this is a digressive, deliberately old-fashioned narrative that focuses not simply on the multitude of events, past and present, that drive the plot, but on the wide range of issues, ideas, and moral concerns that arise naturally from those events. *Under Venus* forthrightly engages themes of loyalty and betrayal, as exemplified by Harrison Upp's betrayal of Kai to the Nazis and Elliot's smaller, less dramatic betrayal of his wife; the need for meaningful work, such as Kai's (nearly) endless labor on the life of Goethe and Elliot's bone deep devotion to music; the importance of faith, love, and responsibility in the quest for a coherent life; and the inevitability of painful change at every level of our lives.

Like *Marriages, Under Venus* is often a derivative book, and borrows freely from a variety of sources. Unlike *Marriages,* it reflects a genuine emotional commitment to its freight of characters, issues, and events, and its literary borrowings are placed firmly in the service of a personal vision. In his introduction to *Wild Animals,* Straub openly acknowledges the nature and extent of the novel's underlying influences. Saul Bellow, particularly the Bellow of *Mr. Sammler's Planet,* is a distinct presence here, and certain passages are heavily influenced by the mandarin prose style of John Updike. Alison Lurie's *Love and Friendship* provided the inspiration for a sequence involving Elliot at his father's piano, and two comic walk-ons—"objectionable musicologists"[15] named Wattman and Donadio—were derived from a novella by Richard Stern entitled *1968*.

The most pertinent influences, though, came from two very different novelists: John O'Hara and Iris Murdoch. The O'Hara of the Gibbsville stories or such later novels as *Ten North Frederick* and *From the Terrace* provided a working model for those aspects of *Under Venus* that revolve around social and political issues. The battle over the fate of Nun's Wood, and the wide-ranging vision of democracy at work in Plechette City that arises from that battle, are largely the result of O'Hara's influence. Iris Murdoch, a figure of enduring personal significance to Straub, helps bring a decidedly less naturalistic ambiance to the proceedings. A number of the more dreamlike moments in *Under Venus* bear her peculiar stamp. These include a disorienting, otherworldly walk through Nun's Wood that is marked by the actual (and startling) appearance of a nun's black figure framed against the background of a fresh snowfall; a dream in which the Wisconsin landscape is filled with burning corpses; unexpected sightings of various wild animals, such as a pair of wounded foxes, a hunting owl trapped in the bedroom of a newly constructed, faux English housing development, a wolf which may not be a wolf. Throughout the novel, anomalous images of the natural world intrude on the quotidian reality of Plechette City, as though asserting themselves in the face of the encroaching forces of urban development.

Seen in its entirety, *Under Venus* is ultimately more ambitious than accomplished, the problematic product of a gifted young writer's apprenticeship. Still, problematic or not, it provides clear evidence that the talent struggling to express itself here is a considerable one. It represents, in every major respect, a clear advance over the ponderous gropings of *Marriages*. The structure, as noted, is clearer and less annoyingly experimental. The prose is cleaner, less strained. The dialogue, while not exactly inspired, is much improved, and indicates that Straub was beginning to pay serious attention to the way real people from different backgrounds actually talk. And the professional life of Elliot Denmark, composer, is presented with much more depth and believable detail than Straub was able to bring to his dimly conceived portrait of Owen, the businessman/narrator of *Marriages*.

Under Venus also marks an advance in the effective employment of landscape and setting. The sharply observed backdrop of Plechette City, resonant with memories and filtered through the newly Europeanized viewpoint of its expatriate protagonist, is deeper, richer, more inherently dramatic than *Marriages*' diametrically opposed presentation of a variety of European settings seen from the somewhat shallower perspective of a visiting American.

Finally, Straub's ability to populate his setting with a diverse and reasonably distinctive cast of characters shows a similar improvement. His developing sense of character is particularly evident in the effective and economical deployment of the novel's large supporting cast, among them the pragmatic Herman and Tessa Glauber, the aristocratic Chase and Margaret Denmark, an irredeemably foolish old school mate of Elliot's with the Wodehousian name of Lawrence Wooster, and a pair of slightly dotty old opponents to the Nun's Wood development project, Pierce Laubach and Hilda Usenbrugge.

Set against these undeniable advances are some significant problems that keep *Under Venus* from fully realizing its ambitions, and which probably contributed to its initial failure to find a publisher. First of all, the narrative, for all its inherent conflicts of character and plot, is too sedate, too essentially polite, to generate a sense of genuine dramatic effect. There is a great deal of light here, and not enough heat. The book cries out for the kind of narrative tension that Straub's subsequent movement toward the outré and the horrific would shortly provide. Straub himself once remarked that "*Under Venus* drifts toward the Gothic without quite knowing what to do about it,"[16] and he is absolutely correct. Beneath the naturalistic facade that governs so much of the story, *Under Venus* is a novel of ghosts, guilt, and haunted landscapes whose underlying Gothic impulse remains frustratingly unengaged. A couple of novels later, Straub would revisit some of the central concerns of his still secret book and recast them, to greater effect, in the overtly supernatural thriller, *If You Could See Me Now.*

The second and greater problem is the diffuseness of the narrative. There are simply too many competing story lines clamoring for our attention. Not one of the novel's many subplots ever asserts itself quite enough to provide a thematic or emotional center, to serve as an anchor for the diverse concerns of this very busy book. The result is a rather rambling concatenation of dramatic occurrences, rather than an authoritatively constructed novel. As interesting, even vital, as it often is, *Under Venus* ultimately fails to cohere. By rights, Elliot's obsessive attachment to Anita Kellerman should have provided this primary focus but, as the novel progresses, even this element is shifted off center by the constant press of events. Too much is happening here, and the endless interplay of elements—political cabals, personal confessions, family histories, incidental sexual encounters, musical interludes—leaves the novel searching, furiously and futilely, for a single still point around which to revolve.

The title chosen to christen this crowded enterprise comes from the poem "Evening Star" by Louise Bogan:

> Light from the Planet Venus, soon to set,
> Be with us.[17]

This request for light, for illumination, is entirely appropriate to the circumstances in which Straub's characters find themselves. The title is also relevant in a very literal sense, since much of the action of the novel really does take place "under Venus," whose unblinking presence is repeatedly invoked as it gazes imperiously down on the human comedy playing itself out in Plechette City. Witness Elliot's pratfall as he stumbles clumsily toward a Christmas party at Anita Kellerman's house:

> He staggered, one of his feet slipping sideways, then windmilled his arms...He knew he was going to fall; he fell in that instant. The whiteness broke and dissolved before him into points of light. His back hurt. Elliott opened his eye and was looking straight up toward the black sky. A single enormous star hung above him.[18]

Later, in the melancholy aftermath of Ronnie Upp's victory in the Nun's Wood public referendum, Elliot and his father sit silently in Chase's office, looking through a window to where "a single bright star vibrated in the sky."[19] At moments like these, *Under Venus* feels like Peter Straub's version of Ingmar Bergman's comic meditation on romantic folly, *Smiles of a Summer Night,* in which the moon smiles three times as it bears witness to the shifting tangle of relationships below.

By the time exhaustion, frustration, and a heightened sense of self-doubt caused Straub finally to abandon further revisions and put the novel aside, it had become, in his own words, "a tar baby."[20] In desperate need of a new project, he adopted a suggestion shrewdly put forward by his English agent, changed directions once again, and began to write "a Gothic." His first venture into this new territory, *Julia,* very nearly saved his life, rescuing him from the deepening morass of *Under Venus* and setting him on his proper, and inevitable, path.

1. *Wild Animals* (New York: G. P. Putnam's Sons, 1984), p. 8
2. Ibid., p. 8
3. Ibid., p. 8
4. *Under Venus*, p. 19
5. Ibid., p. 69
6. Ibid., p. 31
7. Ibid., p. 31
8. Ibid., p. 28
9. Ibid., p. 131
10. Ibid., p. 147
11. Ibid., p. 231
12. *If You Could See Me Now* (New York: Coward, McCann & Geohegan, 1977), p. 13
13. *Under Venus*, p. 6
14. Ibid., p. 19
15. *Wild Animals*, p. 10
16. Ibid., p. 10
17. *Under Venus*, epigraph
18. Ibid., p. 208
19. Ibid., p. 242
20. *Wild Animals*, p. 8

Chapter Three: *Julia*

Julia appeared, unhindered by rejections or insurmountable editorial obstacles, in 1975, a year that saw the initial publication of Robert Aickman's *Cold Hand in Mine,* James Herbert's *The Fog,* David Morrell's *Testament,* and Stephen King's groundbreaking and influential vampire epic, *'Salem's Lot.* Despite this flurry of significant titles, and despite the recent popular success of novels like William Peter Blatty's *The Exorcist* and Thomas Tryon's *The Other* and *Harvest Home*, horror fiction was, at the time, commonly perceived as "a tawdry, low-rent subgenre written largely for teenagers,"[1] a situation, in Straub's view, not without its peculiar advantages.

> For some reason, that [horror] was so completely marginalized appealed to me. I saw no reason why it could not include books better than the stereotype, and I liked the notion that I could work away in a disregarded area, learning what I had to learn free of scrutiny and free of critical attention. I also liked the idea of earning a living.[2]

The liberating effects of this change of venue became almost immediately apparent.

> As soon as I started writing *Julia*, by which I mean while writing its first sentence, I

> felt a sudden, reassuring charge of excitement. I knew it was going to work. What I was doing was right for me—I had stumbled into the emotional territory most accommodating to my natural gifts, and I was writing as well as I knew how.[3]

As if to validate the assumption that art and commerce can, in fact, go hand in hand, *Julia* was published immediately and successfully in both England and America, and film rights were sold for a sum large enough to allow Straub to purchase his first house, and to continue his idiosyncratic exploration of this low-rent literary district he had wandered into.

His extensive academic background gave Straub at least a nodding acquaintance with the classical roots of his newly chosen field, as exemplified by such figures as Poe, Hawthorne, and James. His initial exposure to some of the field's more recent—and arcane—practitioners came as a result of his acquaintanceship with fellow expatriate Thomas Tessier. Tessier, a poet, playwright, and managing director of a London-based publishing house, had not yet embarked on his own career as one of the most stylish and eloquent of modern horror novelists, but he was deeply conversant with the field and spent many hours with Straub, discussing the works of older writers like Oliver Onions, Algernon Blackwood, and H. P. Lovecraft, and introducing him to the works of such contemporary figures as Robert Bloch, Richard Matheson, and Fritz Leiber. Tessier himself rather modestly minimizes the importance of these discussions, claiming that

> at the time, I may have thought I was actually telling Peter a thing or two that he didn't know...but I wasn't telling [him] anything. The penny eventually dropped, and I realized that he had been leading me all the way. Peter understood the Gothic instinctively, and he made it his own with astonishing speed. More than any author of our generation, I think, he grasped its huge range and exquisite elasticity, its very special relevance to the times in which we live.[4]

In Tessier's view, true "Gothic" fiction is rooted less in matters of style, genre requirements, or literary techniques than in the sensibility of the individual writer, a sensibility typically informed by "a deeply tragic vision of life and the world."[5] Seen in these terms, *Julia*, despite its occasional reliance on overly familiar elements and its periodic infelicities of character and plot, is a manifestly successful embodiment of the form. A dark, unrelievedly grim account of a life destroyed by the combined forces of guilt, grief, and an external power with an almost limitless capacity for cruelty, *Julia,* in its author's words, "nakedly reflects the psychological condition of the thirty-year-old man who wrote it."[6] In one very general sense, *Julia* represents a kind of spiritual or psychological self-portrait, focusing as it does on one woman's attempt to reconstruct her life in the immediate aftermath of domestic tragedy, a situation which roughly parallels Straub's own attempts to reestablish his writing career in the wake of his demoralizing experience with *Under Venus.*

Julia tells the story of a haunting, but is structured in the manner of such Ross MacDonald mysteries as *The Galton Case* or *The Chill,* stories which explore the connection between traumatic present day events and the events of a violent and unresolved past. The primary victim of this haunting is Julia Lofting, who, as the novel opens, is in the process of moving into a house near London's Holland Park, a house she has impulsively purchased following her questionable recovery from a breakdown brought on by the recent death of her nine-year-old daughter, Kate. Kate's death is one part—the most recent part—of a complex past that threatens to rise up and overwhelm Julia Lofting. The details of that death, revealed only gradually and filtered through the distortions of Julia's tortured psyche, are as follows:

Some months prior to the primary narrative, Kate Lofting, in the presence of both parents, choked on a piece of meat, blocking her air passage. Unable to clear the obstruction, and fearful that Kate would die before emergency medical service arrived, Julia performed a tracheotomy, using a steak knife from the Lofting kitchen. Frightened and unsure of herself, she botched the operation, causing Kate to bleed to death before her parents' eyes. Unable to cope with this memory, Julia collapsed and was confined to a London hospital for several weeks, all spent under heavy sedation. By the time she emerged, she had shifted responsibility for the bungled tracheotomy onto the shoulders of her overbearing husband, Magnus. Desperate to create a new, more endurable life for herself, she leaves Magnus and, yielding to a sudden compulsion, purchases a house, furniture and all, at 25 Ilchester Place in Kensington. It is against this backdrop of tragedy, trauma, and psychological disarray that the narrative begins.

The second, and more remote, remnant of the encroaching past concerns Magnus Lofting, the house on Ilchester Place, and an enigmatic blonde child who enters Julia's life in the very first sentence of chapter one:

> The little blonde girl, about nine or ten—Kate's age—and enough like Kate to make Julia feel dizzy, ran floating up from nowhere along Ilchester Place and, windmilling her arms at the streetcorner, flew into the path to Holland Park. Standing on the steps of the house with the man from Markham and Reeves, Julia's first sensation was the sharp, familiar ache of loss, now so strong as to make her feel that she might shock the man from Markham and Reeves by being sick into the wilting tulips.[7]

Although neither Julia nor the reader are made immediately aware of the fact, the appearance of this nameless blonde girl—who has, quite literally, floated up from nowhere, her moment finally at hand—effectively marks the beginning of the haunting which forms the novel's centerpiece.

After briefly following the girl, only to lose her in the crowds of children in Holland Park, Julia resumes the process of moving into her house, which almost immediately begins to manifest certain inexplicable phenomena: heaters, though set firmly in the off position, continue to generate heat; figures seem to hover just out of sight in the wall-to-wall mirrors that adorn each bathroom. Later, Kate once again catches sight of the girl, follows her into the park, and watches as she holds court before a rapt and ultimately frightened group of children, mesmerizing them with a strange display involving a knife and an indeterminate green object. After the children leave, Julia unearths the object from a sandbox and discovers that it is a turtle, and that the girl has mutilated it in a grotesque parody of the disastrous tracheotomy that cost Kate Lofting her life.

Following this incident, the remaining major characters drift, one by one, into the frame of the story. First, Julia pays a visit to Magnus' sister Lily, whom she views, quite mistakenly, as her friend and ally in her struggle to free herself from Magnus. Lily gives Julia a housewarming gift: a book of photos and stories about Julia's new neighborhood entitled *The Royal Borough of Kensington*. Later, she goes back on her word and reveals Julia's whereabouts both to Magnus and to her handsome, disaffected, adoptive brother, Mark Berkeley. Mark comes to visit Julia the next day, insinuating himself, with clear sexual intent, into her life. Magnus also comes to visit but remains, for a time, an offstage presence, watching clandestinely from the garden, breaking and entering by night. His actions are often deliberately indistinguishable from those of the supernatural forces which inhabit the house, and which manifest themselves more and more directly as the novel progresses.

Those supernatural forces are first identified as such in the climactic seance that concludes section one. This seance comes about when Lily, a dabbler in occult matters, co-opts Julia's house for the weekly meeting of her spiritualist society. Chaos ensues when Rosa Fludd, a genuine sensitive whose usual performance consists of good-natured theatrical fakery, enters the house and finds herself in contact with a genuinely "malefic"[8] power that terrifies and overwhelms her. She manages to warn Julia that she is in danger from "a child and a man"[9] and that she should leave, not just the house, but England itself. Soon, someone else catches sight of some unspecified menace in the bathroom mirror, and the meeting dissolves in panic. Shortly afterward, Rosa Fludd is killed in a suspicious hit-and-run accident, and Julia becomes convinced that Mrs. Fludd's vision was genuine, and that the child and the man whose presence she sensed are Kate and Magnus Lofting. She is wrong on both counts, and will spend much of the remainder of the novel working her way through her various misconceptions toward the final and surprising truth.

The truth first presents itself to Julia in the form of a book: Lily's housewarming present, *The Royal Borough of Kensington*. One of the more scandalous stories recounted in that book concerns a murder that took place some twenty-five years before in the very house that Julia now occupies. The murder victim, nine-year-old Olivia Rudge, had been stabbed to death by her mother, an expatriate American socialite named Heather Rudge. Heather defended her act on the grounds that her daughter was irredeemably evil and, in fact, Olivia—the purported leader of a group of children referred to in the press as

"The Holland Park Child Terror Mob"—had been questioned in connection with the murder of a four-year-old boy named Geoffrey Braden, a crime for which a local vagrant was eventually tried and executed. Struck by the similarity between Kate's death and Olivia's, Julia sets out to investigate the circumstances of Olivia's short life. She visits the asylum to which Heather Rudge was committed years before, then tracks down and interviews the two remaining members of Olivia's "Child Terror Mob," both of whom are murdered after being questioned by Julia about their involvement in the death of Geoffrey Braden.

Shortly after learning the truth about the Braden murder, Julia is herself nearly killed in an unsuccessful attempt to duplicate the hit-and-run death of Rosa Fludd. By this time, she understands that the force behind the haunting at 25 Ilchester Place is not her daughter, but Olivia Rudge.

> Olivia had murdered Geoffrey Braden; she had murdered Paul Winter; she had murdered Mrs. Fludd; and she had tried now to kill Julia. She had been called up from whatever rank, resentful obscurity she had inhabited; Julia's appearance on Ilchester Place had clothed her in flesh, and now she was a bodily presence in the house.[10]

With Julia's subsequent discovery that Magnus had been Heather Rudge's lover and was in all likelihood Olivia's father, and her literally ultimate realization that she, not Magnus, had—"with merciful intent"[11]—performed the fatal tracheotomy, the pattern, the web of connections linking these two widely separated accounts of children stabbed to death by their mothers, is finally complete. The vengeful and unleashed spirit of Olivia Rudge pursues Julia onto the rooftop of Ilchester Place—that high place she has visited repeatedly in dreams—and then watches as Julia, immersed in her memories of Kate's final moments, leaps to her death.

In many respects, *Julia* remains Straub's darkest novel. While a number of the later novels contain scenes and situations as desolating as anything found in these pages, they are, as a rule, more various, more diverse in their presentation of events, interleaving moments of love, pleasure, comradeship, even triumph, throughout even the most nightmarish scenarios. *Julia*, on the other hand, is a stark, consistently grim story, and its eponymous heroine is one of Straub's most beleaguered characters, a woman victimized by friends, family, and external circumstances, then cut off from all meaningful forms of comfort and support. Julia is permitted perhaps two brief interludes of unalloyed pleasure in the entire novel. The first is a solitary dinner at a local French restaurant on the night of her arrival at Ilchester Place, a night when the future, unlike the past, still seems relatively benign. The second is an afternoon spent shopping for household necessities with her brother-in-law, Mark Berkeley, whom, as with Lily, she naively regards as an ally in her struggle for an independent life.

Julia is victimized in a number of ways and from a number of directions. Olivia, of course, has chosen to add her to her ongoing list of victims; her own husband stalks and terrifies her; her friend and sister-in-law, Lily, has joined with Magnus in the attempt to subdue and control her; guilt, grief, and memories of her daughter permeate her life. In the face of all these forces, Julia remains alone and friendless, isolated by the circumstances of a supernatural incursion in which she alone believes and which she can neither mention nor describe without seeming hopelessly deranged. She is equally isolated by the fact that she is a very rich woman, and therefore a target of opportunity to those closest to her.

Julia is the descendent of a fabulously wealthy nineteenth-century railroad baron, a man, in Magnus' words, with "blood on his hands up to the elbows."[12] Reflecting on the source of Julia's fortune, Lily notes that "there was a taint, a historical stain, to [her] money,"[13] but this imagined stain is not sufficient to prevent her from joining in the effort to have Julia declared incompetent, with full control of her money passing into Magnus' hands.

> "She must be put back in the hospital and kept there until she is docile. And I suggest that you take whatever steps are appropriate to ensure that her money is accessible. You must be able to control her money. You must be able to control *her*."
>
> Magnus was leaning forward, his elbows on his knees, staring directly at her. "You are being very frank, Lily."
>
> "It is too late to be anything else," she said

> straight to him. "In truth, Magnus, we all desire to own her. You, I—and Mark. We wish to possess her."[14]

Mark, though a self-proclaimed Maoist and avowed enemy of the monied class, feels much the same way. Here he is, sitting in a pub with Julia, contemplating a round of drinks he can't afford to buy:

> Mark had counted his money a few minutes before in the men's room, and knew that the last round had left him with sixty-three pence. He owed twenty pounds to a colleague, and when he'd paid that, his next check from school would leave him with just enough to pay his rent and buy a month's food and drink. Still, he supposed, he could always put off Samuel for another month...He watched hungrily while Julia withdrew a small purse from her bag and took from it a ten-pound note. With a start of anticipatory pleasure, Mark realized that he already thought of Julia's money as his own. "That's sweet of you, darling," he added. He took the note from her fingers.[15]

Julia's life is a battlefield on which a number of individual actions are being fought. Every aspect of her life—her history, her inner nature, her personal circumstances—has conspired to make her the perfect victim, the perfect receptacle for the various acts of predation, natural and supernatural, that power the plot of this book. Her life is a literal embodiment of that fundamental principle set forth in the Doris Lessing epigraph that opens the novel.

> ...when a war has been going on for a long time, life is all war, every event has the quality of war, nothing of peace remains. Events and the life in which they are embedded have the same quality. But since it is not possible that events are not part of the life they occur in—it is not possible

> that a bomb should explode into a texture
> of life foreign to it...[16]

Straub handles this relentlessly grim scenario with the ease and confidence of a veteran horror writer. It's clear, quite early in the novel, that the author is onto something here, that he has finally found a fictional form in which his intelligence, narrative gifts, and genuinely gothic sensibility are allowed free reign. The result is a novel which, though relatively modest in scope and occasionally awkward in execution, is far and away Straub's surest, most fully realized work to date.

Much of the awkwardness arises from Straub's dogged attempts to place the actions of Olivia Rudge within a rational framework. The detective story structure—in which investigation unearths clues, clues form patterns, and patterns lead to revelation—provides useful and interesting background material but is not enough to explain what is essentially inexplicable: the phenomenon of Olivia Rudge. Straub labors mightily to create a sense of recurring patterns opening outward from a single, central image: two children, each fathered by Magnus Lofting, each killed by a knife wielded, for very different reasons, by their mothers. The idea that patterns, recurrences, coincidences can come together forcefully enough to activate whatever mechanism opens the door between the human world and whatever dank limbo has housed Olivia's malevolent spirit is, in the end, an arbitrary one that fails to illuminate the darkest levels of this book.

Another unresolved problem concerns Mark Berkeley and his ambiguous role in the proceedings. Mark is a lecturer at a local polytechnic, an adoptive brother infinitely resentful of Magnus and all his possessions, a member of various fringe political movements, and a ladies' man handsome enough to cause Julia, on first meeting him, to reflect that "she was not sure she approved of men as beautiful as this."[17] He attends the seance at Julia's house and catches the immediate attention of Rosa Fludd, who tells Julia

> "...there's another cloudy aura," nodding to Mark. "Dirty as an old pond. But that one's open to things. He's receptive. Maybe too receptive...He wants to be filled, like a bottle."[18]

References to Mark's status as a "vessel waiting to be filled" are made repeatedly and the implication is clear that Mark, not Magnus, is the man referred to in the threatening vision of "a child and a man"[19] that comes to Rosa Fludd that night. Just what this means, though, is left deliberately unclear, although specific possibilities abound. For instance, after learning of the death of Paul Winter, a childhood companion/victim of Olivia's, Julia is faced with the realization that

> someone had visited his room and butchered him. Someone under Olivia's control, some man driven by hate so that Olivia could enter him...Maybe he wouldn't even remember committing the murder—maybe Olivia could sweep into a mind and then out again, leaving no real memory of her occupation. This thought weakened Julia's legs.[20]

Internal evidence certainly never suggests that Mark is aware of committing any kind of crime, but the unproved possibility remains. Shortly after stumbling on the dying, just mutilated body of David Swift, another of Olivia's childhood cohorts, Julia rushes, panicked, through the rain to Mark's flat, only to find that he himself has just returned, "his damp coat [hanging] uncomfortably on his shoulders."[21] The timing is suggestive, but no more than that. Deliberate ambiguity is, of course, a legitimate literary device and, elsewhere, Straub has quite properly criticized what he calls "the sentimental desire to wrap everything up with a fatal neatness."[22] Still, Straub's reticence regarding Mark's role in the furtherance of Olivia's plan approaches coyness, and the resultant ambiguity adds nothing of value to the narrative. Add to this the fact that Olivia never really seems to need the kind of help that Mark, or any other human being, might provide, and Mark's presence comes to seem more like an extended irrelevancy than a vital element of the plot.

The virtues of the novel are reflected in an enhanced grasp of those novelistic basics of scene-setting and characterization that first appeared, though somewhat less consistently, in *Under Venus*, together with a newly discovered gift for unsettling, tightly constructed set pieces. *Julia*, as Stephen King has noted, is very much an English ghost story,[23] and the varied ambiance of London is conveyed with an ease and intimacy born of long familiarity, as in the descriptions of children at play in Holland Park; of casual acts of violence carried out against the background of seedy, second-rate pubs; of teenaged gangs patrolling the glass-strewn streets outside of Rosa Fludd's flat on the Mile End Road.

Likewise, Straub's increasing grasp of character provides one of *Julia*'s most consistent sources of pleasure. The major characters—including Julia herself, who is first seen as an almost comically disconnected woman, increasingly adrift, increasingly "less responsible to the world of ordinary truth,"[24] but who deepens under the weight of her experiences into a creature of genuinely tragic dimensions; Magnus Lofting, by nature commanding, even imperious, now visibly eroding under the combined pressures of Kate's death, Julia's departure, and other, less explicable forces emanating from the house on Ilchester Place; and Lily Lofting, whose aristocratic exterior conceals a willingness to do whatever is necessary to protect her privileged lifestyle—are all observed with a real novelist's eye, and come sharply, immediately, into focus.

The secondary characters are equally well drawn, particularly that tiny group of damaged survivors of Olivia Rudge's original rampage, twenty-five years before: Heather Rudge, confined for life to a lunatic asylum and radiating bitterness and rage; David Swift, a widowed and alcoholic loser responsible for the ruin of his family's wine business, a man who is unwisely willing to answer Julia's questions about what really happened to Geoffrey Braden; and Paul Winter, a general's son cashiered from the army for sexual preferences recognized and exploited by Olivia Rudge as far back as his childhood. Straub's portrait of Winter, a prissy and affected wreck of a man, is particularly vivid. Here's Julia taking his measure in the opening moments of their meeting:

> He was preening himself before her, and Julia caught an odd mixture of failure and arrogance in the man...he saw himself as an Oscar Wilde, but the absurd vanity of his toupee made him pathetic. In a minute, she sensed, he'd begin inventing weak epigrams...
>
> Julia said, "I'm sorry to bother you like this,

> [Captain], but for personal reasons I'm interested in something in your past."
>
> "Oh, God," he groaned theatrically. "The past doesn't exist." He considered that a moment, revised it. "No intelligent man believes in the past." Finally he satisfied himself. "Those who believe in the past are condemned to live in it."[25]

Interspersed throughout the novel are a number of sequences that demonstrate Straub's newfound affinity for the dark and the horrific. One, already mentioned, is the seance in which the supernatural character of the events unfolding around Julia Lofting is first clearly identified. Straub takes the overly familiar elements of such scenes and invests them with a sense of mystery and impending violence that gives the scenes force and an unexpected freshness. Then, there is a sequence, strongly reminiscent of Owen's pursuit of Charlie LaRochelle through the streets of Arles in *Marriages*, in which Julia follows Olivia through the twists and turns of Holland Park, only to find herself very nearly lured to her death in the traffic on Holland Park Avenue. This time, though, the scene is not simply an interesting, if anomalous, diversion, but a logical dramatic outgrowth of the novel's central concerns. Late in the book, there is a strikingly composed, hallucinatory vision of London transformed into a vast and teeming necropolis.

> In the high, curved, bald forehead of a man thrusting past, she saw death, the skin tightening on his skull; and she saw in a woman's colored lips death, as they parted over her teeth. And she saw they were all dead, sweeping past her in the noise of raised voices and automobiles. The dark gained on them all...It was the world of her dream life.[26]

Julia's dream life, in all its various and troubled forms, adds a great deal to the overall emotional life of the novel. A primary example is the series of recurring nightmares in which Julia finds herself moving through the streets of London with the corpse of her daughter in her arms, headed toward an unfamiliar rooftop peopled by shabbily dressed men emanating "a despairing, criminal atmosphere of moral failure."[27] These dreams both foreshadow the novel's ending and effectively convey the desolating sense of loss which characterizes Julia's life in the aftermath of Kate's death. Julia is also visited by a series of graphic, intensely perverse sexual dreams which are, in effect, forms of sexual violation precipitated by Olivia Rudge.

> Once again, she was being caressed. She was being touched by lingering, stroking hands beside her own hands. Small hands moved lightly down her body. They paused and began again, stroking. Julia saw Kate beside her: they clasped one another. Kate was with her...
>
> Flickering touches ran insinuatingly over her opening body. Mark and Kate: then, shockingly, only Kate. "No," she said, groaning, and her voice brought her up through sleep. "No." She could still feel the last touch of the hand, stroking between her thighs: she felt sickened and frightened, aroused...[28]

She wakes from such dreams feeling "soiled for life,"[29] her violated body giving off the smell of "loss and failure, of airless exertions."[30] The suffocating sense of moral failure common to both these dreams, referred to elsewhere as "the comprehensive atmosphere of moral loss,"[31] is a notion Straub returns to repeatedly during the course of the narrative, one that goes to the very heart of the novel's beliefs and intentions, its underlying sense of the nature and essential reality of that most amorphous of concepts: genuine evil. Beneath its melodramatic surface and its attendant array of supernatural effects, *Julia* is built on the assumption that evil is, at bottom, a small, mean, comprehensible thing whose most common by-products are, not blood and violence, but squalor and depression, and whose prevailing color is a dominant, uniform gray.

> Julia walked through rooms which seemed alien and dead, utterly apart from her. She

> heard none of the by now familiar noises of the trapped echoes and spirits of the Rudges. Julia thought, as she sat wearily on the McClintock's ugly couch, that Olivia might have withdrawn, leaving Julia in her world forever: that was the strength of evil, she saw, its absence of hope, its stink of moral failure. For a moment she saw the tramp on Cremorne Road savagely stuffing a dog into a bag; from an accumulation of such sordid, hopeless moments evil was condensed.[32]

Straub focuses with such intensity on these "sordid, hopeless moments" that he ends up limiting the emotional range of his novel. At the same time, though, the very narrowness of this approach provides the basis for *Julia*'s considerable, often claustrophobic, power, and successfully connects the book to the larger, if less dramatic, issues of the everyday human world. Most importantly, *Julia* marks an end to a period of false starts and tentative explorations, and the beginning of a more promising apprenticeship in the marginalized world beyond the boundaries of the mainstream.

1. Interview with Paula Guran for Omni Online
2. Ibid.
3. Ibid.
4. Thomas Tessier—Afterword to *Shadowland: The 15th anniversary Edition* (Springfield, PA: Gauntlet Publications, 1995), p. 595
5. Ibid., p. 595
6. *Wild Animals*, p. 8
7. *Julia* (New York: Pocket Books, reprint 1976), p. 2
8. Ibid., p. 70
9. Ibid., p. 81
10. Ibid., p. 227
11. Ibid., p. 285
12. Ibid., p. 129
13. Ibid., p. 129
14. Ibid., pp. 217-218
15. Ibid., pp. 165-166

16. Ibid., epigraph

17. Ibid., p. 19

18. Ibid., pp. 63-64

19. Ibid., p. 81

20. Ibid., pp. 227-228

21. Ibid., p. 250

22. *The General's Wife* (West Kingston, RI: Donald M. Grant, 1982), p. 16

23. Stephen King, *Danse Macabre* (New York: Everest House, 1981), p. 243

24. *Julia*, p. 22

25. Ibid., p. 178

26. Ibid., p. 208

27. Ibid., p. 57

28. Ibid., pp. 91-92

29. Ibid., p. 92

30. Ibid., p. 92

31. Ibid., p. 75

32. Ibid., p. 220

Chapter Four:

If You Could See Me Now

That apprenticeship effectively ended with the publication of *If You Could See Me Now,* an ambitious and evocative ghost story set against the haunted landscape of the Wisconsin farm country. A more expansive exploration of the theme of supernatural revenge introduced in *Julia,* the novel also revisits—and successfully reworks—some of the central concerns of Straub's still secret second novel, *Under Venus.* This characteristic tendency to examine and then re-examine certain key ideas and areas of experience makes its first significant appearance here. As Tim Underhill, "secret hero"[1] of *Koko* and narrator of *The Throat,* will eventually remind us: "...you write what comes back to you, and then afterward it comes back to you all over again."[2]

Even more than in most Straub novels, the true emotional center of *If You Could See Me Now* is located in the past. Before introducing us to any of the story's present day characters and concerns, Straub takes us into the unresolved heart of that past: July 21, 1955, a day whose aftereffects will resonate across twenty years of subsequent history. On that day, which begins on a pastoral, even idyllic, note, Miles Teagarden and Alison Greening, cousins from opposite ends of America, are lying together looking at the stars above their grandmother's farm in rural Wisconsin. Miles is thirteen years old, prone to trouble, too often at the mercy of feelings he cannot control. Alison is fourteen, but powerful and prematurely seductive. Her personality, like her profile, is "fox-sharp, ardent, and if will could lift her off the earth, she would already be sailing away..."[3] Miles, not surprisingly, is totally in thrall to her, and accedes without argument to her suggestion that they escape the confines of farm and family to go swimming in a nearby quarry.

En route to the quarry, with Alison illegally driving and Miles catching sporadic glimpses of distant headlights behind them, she pulls off to the side of the road and impulsively proposes that the two of them vow to meet one another, there in Wisconsin, in twenty years time. They agree that "whether married [or] not married, living in Paris or Africa," they will meet at the farm on July 21, 1975, "if there's still a world."[4] "If you forget," she tells him, "I'll come after you. If you forget, God help you."[5] They seal their vow with an uncousinlike kiss, and Miles finds himself literally overwhelmed by the power of his love for his cousin. ("[He] would have given her anything; he would have died for her on the spot.")[6]

The sexual character of the evening intensifies when they reach the quarry. She invites him to swim the way "we do in California,"[7] which means, of course, skinny-dipping. The ensuing swim is marked by several minutes of erotic roughhouse, which quickly begins to undermine Miles' already tenuous control over his emotions.

> The trouble spread thickly through his mind, canceling all else. He glided up beside her, bruising all that foreign heartland and wilderness of skin...Alison's arm clamped around his neck...her hard cheekbone pressed his jaw. Using all his strength he broke the hold of her arms, and turned her into him. His head went under water...His legs kicked around hers. They were back under, thrashing, and the trouble in his mind forced them to roll deeper into the cold water. His ears boomed as she struck them...Booming was everywhere.[8]

The final image is of Miles and Alison, locked together, "fighting the trouble, fighting the water and fighting for air and fighting for trouble,"[9] while the cold quarry water geysers and booms around them. The prologue then ends, but the outcome of this chaotic encounter remains, for the moment, deliberately undisclosed. At this point, the narrative switches from July of 1955 to June of 1975 and from third person to first as Miles Teagarden, suddenly our narrator, returns to the Midwest, and to the scene of his adolescent vow, for the first time in almost twenty years.

Ostensibly, Miles is returning to complete his doctoral dissertation in a setting of "dull, green peace."[10] In reality, he is returning because he is still, after all these years, helplessly in thrall to his memories of Alison Greening, and is determined to fulfill his half of their vow. It is here, in the image of a man returning, after long exile, to the site of his most enduring passion, that *If You Could See Me Now* most resembles its unpublished predecessor. In his preface to *Wild Animals,* Straub comments that

> The story of Eliot Denmark and his heartsick, frustrated, skeptical love for Anita Kellerman is really very similar to the story of...neurotic Miles Teagarden, widowed and obsessed with the memory of his cousin Alison. Miles is a kind of failed Eliot—if Miles could have written fiction himself instead of having to write a book about other books, he would have been as happy as it would have been possible for him to be...Anita Kellerman is Alison Greening grown up, or a version of her. *If You Could See Me Now* is *Under Venus* from another angle; but this time, the disturbingly intense feeling has a focus.[11]

This is absolutely correct. *If You Could See Me Now* is in every way a stronger, more focused novel, entirely lacking the diffuseness of effect that blunted the impact of the earlier book. That focus is provided almost entirely by the figure of Alison Greening, who takes command of the narrative in a way that *Under Venus*' Anita Kellerman never manages to do. Though primarily an offstage presence, Alison provides a powerful dramatic center around which virtually every major element of the novel ultimately revolves.

In that same preface, Straub noted that a hypothetical rewriting of *Under Venus* would involve the following changes: the use of a first-person narrative voice; the elimination of such extraneous subplots as the Nun's Wood land development issue; and the addition of an element of mystery and melodrama to the lives and histories of its characters.[12] This, in effect, is exactly what *If You Could See Me Now* does. The result is a straightforward, fundamentally simple narrative that is hugely enriched by the complex emotions and lovingly described levels of detail within which the story unfolds. Here, stripped to its essentials, is that story:

Miles returns, as noted, to the "critical landscape"[13] of his youth—Arden, Wisconsin—with the avowed intention of completing his moribund doctoral dissertation on the novels of D. H. Lawrence. His arrival coincides with the first in a series of murders of young Arden girls, murders committed with an inexplicable and escalating savagery that is without precedent in the community's history. Surrounded by the resulting atmosphere of fear and paranoia—which will, as the novel progresses, focus more and more exclusively on him—Miles settles into the farmhouse once owned by his grandmother and now owned and maintained by his widowed cousin Duane (pronounced Dew-ane) Updahl, whose history includes a long-standing antipathy toward Miles as well as a series of hostile, luckless romantic relationships which have left him with a distrustful, overtly misogynist vision of the entire female sex. One of those luckless (and very brief) relationships was with Alison Greening, after whom his own rebellious teenaged daughter, Alison Updahl, was named.

Miles, unable to work, quickly abandons his dissertation and focuses, instead, on two activities: alienating the locals, many of whom have unpleasant memories of his troubled adolescence; and obsessing on his forthcoming rendezvous with Alison Greening. On several occasions, Miles believes he glimpses her on the outskirts of the surrounding forest. Once, he actually searches the forest for her, only to find himself lost and disoriented, and filled with a sense of mounting terror that sends him running blindly for safety. His panicked flight takes him to the temporary haven of his Aunt Rinn's chicken farm. Rinn, Miles' oldest living relative and the only Arden resident who remembers him with sympathy and affection, takes him in, calms him down, and responds to his wild statements concerning his planned reunion by reminding him of a truth that has never been stated explicitly before this point: that Alison died in the quarry twenty years before, and that Miles was thought to have killed her. "I don't believe that,"[14] he tells her, and on that ambiguous, flatly assertive comment, Section One, "To Get to Arden," abruptly ends.

In Section Two, "I Light Out for the Territories," their dialogue resumes immediately.

> "Miles," [Rinn] said, "your cousin died in 1955 while the two of you were swimming in the old Pohlson quarry. She was drowned."
>
> "No. She drowned," I said. "Active verb. I didn't kill her. I couldn't have killed her. She meant more to me than my own life. I would rather have died myself. It was the end of my life anyhow."[15]

This crucial scene between Rinn—herself something of a mystic who speaks quite matter-of-factly about her conversations with dead relatives—and Miles—who believes mostly in the power of the past, and who has returned to Arden to resume his interrupted connection with that past—touches on a number of the novel's central elements. The most important of these is the revelation that Alison is dead, that Miles understands this fact, and that he is determined, nonetheless, to hold to his vow and meet with Alison on the twenty-first of July. At this point in the story, *If You Could See Me Now* crosses over into the realm of the supernatural, and becomes a ghost story. At the same time, we are introduced to the element of mystery surrounding Alison's death, a mystery whose solution will reveal much about the current climate of violence and fear that has lately descended on the community. Finally, we are presented with two wildly divergent visions of the character and essential nature of Alison Greening.

To Rinn, Alison was, even as a child, destructive, calculating, and fundamentally corrupt, a sexual tease who "hated life, [who] hated everything but herself."[16] To Miles, Alison represented the vital center that was removed from his life in 1955, and never replaced. To Rinn, her return means death and destruction. To Miles, it means freedom and life. "I am only an old farm woman," Rinn tells him,

> "but I know you. I love you. You have always been troubled. Your cousin was also a troubled person, but her troubles were not innocent, as yours were. She chose the rocky path, she desired confusion and evil, and you never committed that sin."[17]

To which Miles can only reply:

> "I don't know what you're talking about. She was, I don't know, more complicated than I was, but that was part of her beauty. For me, anyhow. No one else understood her. And I did not kill her, accidentally or any other way."[18]

Much of the rest of the novel turns on the question of whose version of Alison's character is closest to the truth. It is clear from the outset that Miles is in the grip of a genuine obsession, and that any form of objectivity, at least on this subject, is beyond him. Straub does a superb job of articulating the nature and depth of this obsession and gives us, in the process, a painful and complex portrait of a man who has never fully recovered from the traumatic disruption of twenty years before. The essential character of his obsession is perfectly encapsulated by his response to a photograph of himself and Alison holding hands in the summer of 1955, a picture taken just weeks before her death.

> If I had not already been kneeling, it would have brought me to my knees—the force of that face next to mine squeezed all the breath from me. It was like being punched in the stomach with the handle of a rake. For if we were both beautiful, stuck there in ignorance and love in June of 1955, she was incomparably more so. She burned my intelligent young thief's face right off the paper, she canceled me, she was on another plane altogether, where spirit is incandescent in flesh, she was at the height of being, body and soul together. This live trumpet-blast of spirit, this illumination, put me altogether in shadow. I seemed almost to be levitating, carried by the currents of magic and complication of spirit in that face which was her face...[19]

The purity of Miles' feelings for Alison leave no room whatsoever for conflicting viewpoints, and he leaves Rinn's farm with his beliefs intact, still convinced that "all of my life since our last meeting had been the project of finding her again."[20]

The second half of the novel centers on the tension between Miles' attempts to prepare for—and to help evoke—Alison's return, and the escalating atmosphere of xenophobic dread that has taken root in Arden. After formally abandoning his dissertation—destroying all notes and drafts and giving his Lawrence books to Alison Updahl's boyfriend, a Manson-like local renegade named Zack—Miles sets to work creating what he refers to as "the Alison environment,"[21] the physical and psychological environment most likely to facilitate her return. To that end, he restores his grandmother's original furnishings to the positions they occupied in 1955, buys books and jazz records that were important to the fourteen-year-old Alison, even begins drinking her favorite drink: martinis "with a twist."[22] At the same time, he immerses himself in the writing of a memoir centered entirely around his memories of her.

Meanwhile, in Arden, the murders continue, and remain unsolved. Miles, whose drinking, questionable reputation, and eccentric, often insulting, behavior, continue to alienate the Arden residents, emerges, in the general view, as the most likely suspect. The police chief, an acquaintance from childhood named Galen "Polar Bears" Hovre—who was himself once enamored of Alison Greening—warns him, in classic fashion, not to leave town. As the inflammatory atmosphere intensifies, Miles finds himself more and more isolated, more and more suspect. His car is destroyed. He begins receiving hate mail and anonymous phone calls. At one point, he is even stoned in the street by a roving local mob.

Eventually, almost accidentally, Miles stumbles across the identity of Alison's murderers: Galen Hovre, the chief of police, and Duane Updahl, his own misogynist cousin. In the wake of this discovery, aided by dreams and an escalating feeling of dread, he begins to suspect an even more uncomfortable truth: that Alison's spirit is, as Rinn has warned him, essentially malignant, motivated entirely by hatred of the living and the desire for revenge. He comes to believe that Alison, awakened by his arrival and fully capable of taking life, is responsible for the murders of the Arden girls, each of whom bore a distinct physical resemblance to her. He also suspects that he is likely to become her next victim, that his failure to protect her on that long ago night represents "the greatest sin of my life. The crime for which she could not forgive me."[23] When the evening of July twenty-first arrives, he goes to the quarry to meet her, fully expecting to be killed. Much to his amazement, he survives.

While Miles is waiting at the quarry, Alison is elsewhere, murdering her murderers, leaving their mutilated bodies pinned to trees in a clearing within Arden forest. Believing that the other Alison, Duane's daughter, will be murdered next, he races from the forest to the Updahl farm to protect the girl and confront his long-dead cousin. In doing so, he earns the right to live.

> I understood, being looked at by her or what looked like her, that a contract was being made. I understood that she would rather have me dead, but that Duane's daughter, her namesake, was the reason I would live...Yes, there was a contract: I did not wholly comprehend it, I never wholly would, but I was bound to it.[24]

As a result of this enigmatic pact, Miles not only survives, but is reconnected, after twenty years, to the human world of accommodations and manageable illusions. Accompanied by Alison Updahl—and accompanied also by the original Alison, who, he understands, will be with him forever "as a gesture seen on a crowded street, or as a snatch of music heard from an open window"[25]—he leaves Wisconsin, feeling both heavier and lighter, "freighted with responsibilities"[26] that are the new and unalterable conditions of his life.

If You Could See Me Now marked the logical next step in Straub's steady progression along the learning curve of fiction. Propelled by a nuanced, remarkably authoritative narrative voice, and deeply grounded in the story's underlying emotional reality, Straub's fourth novel successfully combines the intensely personal concerns of *Under Venus* with *Julia*'s dramatic embodiment of an external, supernatural source of evil. Written according to stringently maintained literary and aesthetic standards, *If You Could See Me Now* achieves a kind of modest, formal perfection that has prompted several commentators to place it at the top of Straub's considerable body of work. While that judgment seems questionable, and may just reflect a taste for the sort of quiet, relatively restrained fiction that Straub would begin to move away from with his very next book, there is no doubt that the story of Miles Teagarden and Alison Greening represents a major step in Straub's astonishingly rapid assimilation of, and mastery over, the requirements of Gothic fiction.

If You Could See Me Now works as well as it does, not because of any one element, but because of the complex, mutually illuminating interaction of all its elements. Nothing in the novel stands in isolation from the rest. All of its component parts—characters, setting, events—act upon and influence each other, giving the book a unity and dramatic coherence greater than anything found in Straub's previous work. Of all the elements that contribute to this newfound coherence, three stand out: Miles, Alison, and the carefully created backdrop of rural Wisconsin.

The Midwest embodied by Arden and its environs feels worlds away from the urban Midwest of *Under Venus*' Plechette City. It feels, at times, like the resurrected remnant of an earlier era, in much the way that Stephen King's Jerusalem's Lot reflects an aspect of Maine that has passed into history. Commenting on the setting, Straub noted that it represents

> a conscious attempt to get back to a landscape that I knew as a child. It was a wonderful experience to conjure all of that up in my head, to wander those little streets and look at the woods and the streams and the farmhouses in my mind, and then to try to work out their emotional nuances on paper.[27]

Straub's portrait of Arden, which takes in both the town and the surrounding farmland, is a cumulative one, constructed out of overlapping observations of landscape, character, local history, and prevailing attitudes. The range of physical settings, all evoked with the clarity and immediacy of vivid memories, encompasses the haunted precincts of Arden forest, where the spirit of Alison Greening establishes her dominion; the threadbare town, with its feed stores, competing bars, third-rate department store, and rows of "frame Andy Hardy Houses;"[28] local institutions like the general store that sells everything from candy to gas cans, from silage to suitcases; and, of course, the farms themselves, with their crops, cattle, dilapidated barns and toolsheds, their henhouses smelling "like ashes and dung and blood,"[29] with hens nesting together like "books on a bookshelf."[30]

Straub populates this setting with a sizable cast of credible, highly individualized characters, including: cousin Duane, whose life has been indelibly marked by his inability to understand or tolerate the women in his life; Galen "Polar Bears" Hovre, a policeman who views rape as a reasonable response to the provocations of the female sex; Rev. Bertillson, the community's spiritual leader, who sees Miles as the "abomination"[31] at the root of Arden's current troubles; Tuta Sunderson, who keeps house for Miles, and whose duties include reporting all of his suspicious activities to a hostile populace; Zack Hovre, slightly demented son of Arden's police chief, and a social misfit with a penchant for the apocalyptic; Alison Updahl, Duane's daughter and Zack's girlfriend, a girl who deserves more than the circumstances of her life are ever likely to offer; and Paul Kant, a sexually suspect loner forced into seclusion and ultimately destroyed by the weight of his neighbors' ignorance and disapproval.

The Arden that emerges from these pages is characterized by its relentless insularity, a condition exacerbated by the unsolved murders occurring in its midst. As one local resident, referring to the self-evident strangeness of Miles and his "ways of talking" and "ways of being"[32] puts it: "I guess you don't know what will happen to your children if you bring them up in funny places."[33] Funny places, in this case, means anything outside the immediate vicinity of Arden, Wisconsin. Miles falls victim to this attitude even before setting foot in Arden proper. Stopping for lunch at a diner in the nearby town of Plainfield, just after the discovery of the first victim's body, Miles is interrogated, threatened, then ejected from the diner by a gang of roughnecks because, as the waitress tells him, "you're not from around here."[34] This encounter sets the tone for Miles' entire visit. There is not a moment in this book, outside of two brief visits to his Aunt Rinn's poultry farm, when Miles is not made to feel like an unwelcome stranger, an intruder from the alien and incomprehensible outside world.

It is, of course, Miles who shows us all this, Miles whose outsider's perspective is brought to bear on the events unfolding within Arden. The voice that Straub creates for Miles is his most flexible and persuasive to date, notable both for its depth of feeling and for its overall range of effect. Changing in response to the variety of stimuli—internal and external, past and present—which the narrative provides, that voice encompasses moments of pedantry, reportorial exactness, ironic self-assessment, lyrical bursts of feeling—such as the description of the photograph of himself and Alison taken in the summer of 1955—together with precise, sensuously rendered recreations of the emotionally charged landscapes where time past and time present are inextricably linked. Here, for example, is Miles making his way by moonlight to the place he has come to think of as "the bottom of the bottom of the world"[35]: the quarry where Alison Greening was murdered; the place where he himself expects to die.

> In the darkening sky hung the white stone of the moon. I took a step up the drive: I was a magnet's negative pole, the lunar pole. My feet throbbed in their city shoes. A random branch of an oak stood out with supernatural, almost vocal clarity: a huge muscle rolled beneath its crust of bark. I sat on the edge of a pebbly granite shelf and took off my shoes. Then I dropped them beside the rock and, finding what I had to find to move, moved. The air breathed me...Air caught in my throat. Alison Greening seemed profoundly *in* the landscape, a part of all of it. She was printed deeply into every scrabble of rock, every tick of leaf. I went forward, the bravest act of my life, and felt invisibility stir about me.[36]

Miles represents Straub's most complex, most seemingly personal creation thus far, and his story seems to play out against a carefully chosen soundtrack, in which the ironic strains of Les Brown's "Lover Come Back To Me" give way to Dave Brubeck and Gerry Mulligan, the music of the "Alison environment." (*If You Could See Me Now* is, incidentally, the first Straub novel in which modern jazz, a subject of central importance to the author, is integrated into the story. It is also the first time in which this predilection is reflected in the choice of a character's name. "Miles Teagarden" can be read as a purely jazz-related reference—i.e. Miles Davis/Jack Teagarden—or as a combined literary/musical reference connected to the character of young Miles from *The Turn of the Screw*. Either way, this kind of gamesmanship is typical of Straub, and will become a commonplace element of future books.)

Miles is a man whose character has been formed by loss, and whose natural condition is one of turbulence and emotional confusion. His life, marked from the beginning by errors of judgment and a propensity for trouble, has grown more and more unmanageable in the years since Alison's death. At the time of his return to Arden, he is a widower whose marriage fell apart long before his wife's death, a second-rate academic pursuing a Ph.D. in a subject that has no real significance for him, a man fundamentally out of step with the world around him. Miles believes, with some justification, that there are "secrets of competence and knowingness"[37] from which he has always been locked away and—just as he did in an adolescence marked by thefts, auto wrecks, and endless petty indiscretions—he blunders through the Arden of 1975 with an almost comic ineptitude, antagonizing virtually everyone in the already unsettled and xenophobic community.

There is another side to Miles, though, one that is reflected in the nature of his feelings for Alison Greening. However absurd, neurotic, even—given our eventual understanding of Alison's character and intentions—misguided this obsessive attachment might be, there is a kind of quixotic nobility to it. Miles is governed by what he calls "the complications of feeling,"[38] and he has committed the best of himself to fulfilling an adolescent promise that he cannot believe has been obviated by death. Beyond this, he believes in perhaps two things: the power of the past and the existence, however remote or inaccessible it seems, of another world: the world of Spirit.

Reflecting on his cousin Duane's statement, made early in the novel, that "It don't do to hold to the past,"[39] Miles remarks: "I thought he was wrong. I have always held to the past. I thought that it could, would, should be repeated indefinitely, that it was the breathing life in the heart of the present."[40] As to the world of Spirit, Miles believes in it implicitly, and even thinks he glimpsed it once, in the form of a runaway stagecoach careening toward him on a road outside of Boston. He comments repeatedly on the efficacy of "magic substances,"[41] and believes that certain people, like Aunt Rinn, are "inhabited by Spirit"[42] in a way that most of us are not. Most fundamentally, he is convinced that the barrier separating him from Alison is permeable and temporary.

> By telepathy, we had been in communication all our lives—all my life I had been in

> touch with her...She was in another state; she was in another condition. We were apart but (I knew) not finally apart.[43]

In the end, the same purity of purpose that has fueled his lifelong obsession with Alison Greening allows him, in the face of all his manifest limitations, to become a kind of hero. His instinctive urge to protect the living Alison from the murderous designs of her dead namesake ensures his survival, even as it binds him to the enigmatic terms of a new and unspoken vow, a "contract" based on his continued acceptance of the responsibilities he has voluntarily assumed.

The third and last of the novel's critical components is, of course, Alison Greening herself, who bears a certain superficial resemblance to that other monstrous revenant, Olivia Rudge. In much the same way that Olivia is "clothed in flesh"[44] by the replicated patterns of Julia Lofting's life, so Alison is given life (together with the power to take life) by Miles' return to the Midwest. In *If You Could See Me Now,* however, the motive force behind this resurrection is not the arbitrary imposition of complex patterns but the power of the emotional connection that has dominated Miles Teagarden's life for almost twenty years. The result is a novel whose supernatural elements arise more directly from the tragic personal histories of its characters, and are more seamlessly integrated into its overall design.

Alison is also a more original, more vividly imagined creation than Olivia. She is a spirit whose body is buried half a continent away, and who is "forced to put herself together out of available materials. Or be just a wind, the cold breath of spirit."[45] Miles seems to realize this intuitively. In dreams, he sees her as a creature composed of elements borrowed from the forest where her spirit has taken up temporary residence.

> Her mouth was open. I saw that her teeth were water-polished stones. Her face was an intricate pattern of leaves; her hands were rilled wood, tipped with thorns. She was made of bark and leaves. I threw back my hands and felt smooth wood. Air lay in my lungs like water. I realized I was screaming only when I heard it.[46]

Most importantly, Alison gives the novel its center of gravity, just as

Miles gives it its voice, its character, and its emotional range. She is the always silent, mostly invisible presence around which the entire dramatic structure coheres, and everything of importance that happens here, happens because of her. Miles' return; the murders in Arden; the death of suspected deviant Paul Kant; the climactic murders of Duane Updahl and "Polar Bears" Hovre; the undisguised hostility which characterizes Arden's response to Miles' homecoming; an unplanned sexual encounter with Alison Updahl in which the spirit of the original Alison becomes an active, if ghostly, participant—all are either the direct or indirect results of Alison's actions and influence.

The stylish, highly readable, and very cohesive novel that resulted from all of this marked a major advance for Straub, and confirmed him in his belief that horror fiction can be as thoughtful and well-written as the best "literary" fiction without sacrificing any of the genre's traditional pleasures. And, though this was not immediately apparent, *If You Could See Me Now* marked the end of a particular period in the author's development, a period devoted to the creation of modest, tightly-focused, increasingly accomplished fictions that successfully tested the viability of the Gothic subgenre, established Straub's reputation as a literate, intelligent storyteller, and paved the way for the more ambitious, wide-ranging experiments that were to follow. The first of these experiments, *Ghost Story,* appeared two years later, in 1979. From that point forward, nothing in Straub's life or literary career would ever be the same again.

1. *Houses Without Doors* (New York: Dutton, 1990), p. 357
2. *The Throat* (New York: Dutton, 1993), p. 3
3. *If You Could See Me Now*, p. 13
4. Ibid., p. 18
5. Ibid., p. 18
6. Ibid., p. 19
7. Ibid., p. 20
8. Ibid., p. 22
9. Ibid., p. 22
10. Ibid., p. 26
11. *Wild Animals*, p. 9
12. Ibid., p. 10
13. Ibid., p. 9

[14] *If You Could See Me Now*, p. 128
[15] Ibid., p. 131
[16] Ibid., p. 132
[17] Ibid., p. 131
[18] Ibid., p. 131
[19] Ibid., p. 93
[20] Ibid., p. 93
[21] Ibid., p. 173
[22] Ibid., p. 14
[23] Ibid., p. 193
[24] Ibid., p. 284
[25] Ibid., p. 286
[26] Ibid., p. 284
[27] Interview with Douglas E. Winter—*Faces of Fear* (New York: Berkley Books, 1985), p. 225
[28] *If You Could See Me Now*, p. 74
[29] Ibid., p. 68
[30] Ibid., pp. 68-69
[31] Ibid., p. 256
[32] Ibid., p. 72
[33] Ibid., p. 40
[34] Ibid., p. 28
[35] Ibid., p. 267
[36] Ibid., p. 266
[37] Ibid., p. 31
[38] Ibid., p. 269
[39] Ibid., p. 51
[40] Ibid., p. 51
[41] Ibid., p. 49
[42] Ibid., p. 50
[43] Ibid., p. 93
[44] *Julia*, p. 227
[45] *If You Could See Me Now*, p. 271
[46] Ibid., p. 158

Section II

Lighting Out for the Territory

Chapter Five:
Ghost Story

What was the worst thing you've ever done?

I won't tell you that, but I'll tell you the worst thing that ever happened to me...the most dreadful thing...[1]

Shortly after completing the novel that would make him famous, Straub, in a moment of unguarded insecurity, wrote a letter to fellow horror writer Ramsey Campbell in which he described *Ghost Story* as "a big bird which stubbornly refused to fly"[2] and as "a book with maybe one good scare in it."[3] He was, to put the matter simply, wrong. The bird flies, all right, and offers, in the course of its flight, a great number of scares, together with a host of other narrative pleasures, some subtle, some quite spectacular. A more objective assessment of these pleasures can be found in the response of novelist Carlos Fuentes, who, on meeting Straub at a Manhattan literary gathering in 1980, informed him that "he liked *Ghost Story* so much that he had put off reading the last section, for once that was read the book was done."[4] Fuentes was right. *Ghost Story* is that kind of novel.

Ghost Story was, of course, an immediate popular success. In addition to spending some twenty weeks on the New York Times best-seller list, it was acquired by The Book-of-the-Month Club as a main selection, and paperback rights were sold to Pocket Books for a considerable sum. At the same time, film rights were sold to Universal studios (who eventually transformed the book into a big-budget Hollywood extravaganza that remains, to this day, a marvel of missed opportunities.) Remarkably, Straub achieved this breakthrough into the popular consciousness without lowering his literary ambitions or sacrificing his newfound penchant for complex, richly allusive narratives. With the possible exception of Stephen King's *The Shining*—which Straub himself has called "a masterpiece, probably the best supernatural novel in a hundred years"[5]—no Gothic novel in recent memory had attempted or achieved as much as *Ghost Story*. No other novel had succeeded so completely in creating art by "infusing realism with images of mystery and terror."[6]

Ghost Story was the direct result of Straub's deliberate attempt to understand and assimilate the history of the Gothic literary tradition. In his own words,

> The novel refers back to the classic American novels and stories of the genre by Henry James and Nathaniel Hawthorne...I was moved by a desire to look into, examine, and play with the genre—to take these "classic" elements as far as they could go.[7]

After finishing *If You Could See Me Now*, Straub embarked on a virtual crash course in supernatural literature that encompassed not only the form's foremost nineteenth century practitioners—Poe, James and Hawthorne—but broadened to include most of the major American and European figures of the last one hundred years, including Ambrose Bierce, Edith Wharton, M. R. James, and Arthur Machen, as well as H. P. Lovecraft and his circle of disciples, among them Robert Bloch, Frank Belknap Long, Clark Ashton Smith, and Fritz Leiber. His investigation of the form culminated with his discovery of one of the most vital—and certainly the most popular—of twentieth century Gothic voices, Stephen King.

King, Straub has written, "first appeared in my life as a name on a blurb."[8] At the publisher's request, King had supplied a brief paragraph in support of *Julia*, and his comments were "easily the most insightful of the ten or twelve responses"[9] the book received. "...King showed in a few sentences that he understood what I was trying to do—he had a sort of immediate perception of my goals. So I filed the name away..."[10] In 1977, King supplied a second, more extensive comment for *If You Could See Me Now* that "amounted to a mini-essay: two pages of generosity and insight." To Straub,

> ...it was clear that if I had an ideal reader anywhere in the world, it was probably Stephen King; and it was also clear to me that the reason for this was that his aims and ambitions were very close to my own."[11]

The 1975 publication of *'Salem's Lot*—followed, a year later, by *The Shining*—brought King's own fiction to Straub's attention, and the effect was galvanizing, like that of "discovering a long-lost family member—of finding a brother."[12]

> ...he was, very simply, a writer first, and then a writer of horror and fantasy...He was serious about the shape and tone of his writing; and he wanted to work with the real stuff of the world, with marriages and hangovers, with cigarettes and rock bands and junk food and rooming houses, as well as with the bizarre and grotesque materials of our genre. He invested his characters with feeling; he was tender toward them...he was a serious story teller...He, like myself, was doing his damnedest to write books that could be read alongside the best of my contemporaries...[13]

The effect of encountering a storytelling technique so easy and open, so removed from the formal locutions of, say, Henry James, was a profoundly liberating one for Straub. King, he writes,

> ...had shown me how to escape from my own education. Good taste had no role in his thinking; he was unafraid of being loud and vulgar, of presenting horrors head-on, and because he was able to abandon notions of good taste, he could push his am-

> bition into sheer and delightful gaudiness—into the garish beauty of the gaudy. For me, only Todd Browning's film, *Freaks,* had broken through into that realm of the gorgeously overblown and gorgeously garish. For me, this was like a road map of where to go; he armored my ambition.[14]

Thus armed, armored, and equipped, Straub proceeded to demonstrate his instinctive grasp of these newly-discovered narrative principles, and *Ghost Story* was the immediate result.

Like *'Salem's Lot, Ghost Story* opens with an enigmatic prologue which features an adult and a child driving across the country in the wake of an undisclosed, but obviously traumatic, series of events. Straub's version, which focuses on an adult male traveling with an obviously underage female, is charged with a sense of danger and potential perversity, and the scenario itself seems deliberately reminiscent of Humbert Humbert's journeys with Lolita in the Vladimir Nabokov novel. The narrative voice that brings us this scenario is clear and controlled, and establishes its authority in the opening sentence.

> Because he thought that he would have problems taking the child over the border into Canada, he drove south, skirting the cities whenever they came and taking the anonymous freeways which were like a separate country, as travel itself was like a separate country.[15]

The man, we eventually learn, is a writer named Don Wanderley; the girl is named Angie Maule (or Angie Messina or Angie Minoso). Wanderley, who is clearly in desperate circumstances, is simultaneously confused and frightened by the girl. She is a mystery he is unable to solve. At night, in cheap motels they find along their southbound route, he sits over her sleeping form with a hunting knife in his hands, a knife he is finally unable to use. He interrogates her constantly. "Who are you?" he asks her repeatedly, a question which reforms itself, eventually, into "What are you?"[16] Her answer is even stranger than his question. "I am you,"[17] she tells him.

Their journey south, which begins in upstate New York and ends in Panama City, Florida, is filled with references to the writer's past: to his dead brother, David; his former lover, Alma Mobley; a town called Milburn; people with names like Sears James, Ricky Hawthorne, and Edward Wanderley. The journey is also marked by hallucinatory visions of a New York City street scene, by paranoid visions of policemen with nightsticks, by heat, fear, and increasing exhaustion, all played out against a beautifully articulated backdrop of country music, the relentless soundtrack of the south:

> ...for hours they drove south through the songs and rhythms of country music, the stations weakening and changing, the disk jockeys swapping names and accents, the sponsors succeeding each other in a revolving list...but the music remained the same, a vast self-conscious story, a sort of seamless repetitious epic in which women married truckers and no-good gamblers but stood by them until they got a divorce and the men sat in bars plotting seductions and how to get back home, and they came together hot as two-dollar pistols and parted in disgust...The man just drove distracted by the endless soap opera of America's bottom dogs.[18]

The prologue ends with another hallucinatory flash of a New York City street on which Wanderley encounters the image of his dead brother, "his face crumbled and his body dressed in the torn and rotting clothing of the grave."[19] A number of mysteries have been introduced by this point. None have been illuminated. The narrative then abruptly changes course, dropping us into an earlier time and a very different place: Milburn, New York, the source of these unexplained mysteries.

Milburn, a small, well-off, rather isolated town in upstate New York, owes a great deal to the example provided by Stephen King's eponymous town of 'Salem's (i.e. Jerusalem's) Lot. In telling the story of a rural Maine village besieged and ultimately destroyed by a supernatural force (in this case, an ancient European vampire named Barlow), King provided Straub with a working model of a small, highly individualized, convincingly populated community, and showed him how to organize a large cast of characters in a way that deepened, and helped to develop, an ongoing central narrative. Of all the novels directly influenced by *'Salem's Lot* (such as Charles L. Grant's *The Nestling,* David Morrell's *The Totem,* or Robert R. McCammon's *They Thirst*), only *Ghost Story* can be said to have surpassed the original in quality and depth of presentation. Straub's Milburn is a living, breathing, fully realized place, and its people—the drunks and delinquents, bankers and bartenders, doctors, lawyers, adulterers and insurance salesmen—are brought to life quickly and with an almost effortless grace. At the heart of the large cast of characters—and at the heart of the mysteries which form the novel's dramatic center—is a group of aging, haunted, deeply frightened Milburn residents known as the Chowder Society.

The Chowder Society is the nickname—half-affectionate, half-mocking—given to a group of older men—all leading citizens of Milburn—who grew up together and are bound both by common memories and a shared secret. For some years, they have gotten together at regular intervals for semiformal evenings of conversation, storytelling, and moderate drinking. As the novel opens, we are introduced to the four surviving members of the Society: John Jaffrey, a doctor with a drug habit he has thus far successfully concealed, even from his closest friends; Lewis Benedikt, a handsome, aging ladies' man whose wife died in suspicious circumstances several years before; and Sears James and Ricky Hawthorne, Milburn's leading lawyers. A fifth member of the group, Edward Wanderley, died almost one year before, at the climax of a party held at John Jaffrey's house in honor of a visiting actress named Ann-Veronica Moore. His expression, according to a witness, was that of a man who has been frightened to death.

In keeping with the manner of that death, the four survivors have spent the intervening year in a state of steadily increasing anxiety. Tormented by a common nightmare and haunted by a sense of unspecified dread, the four still meet at their accustomed intervals, but the stories they tell have taken on a darker, more oppressive tone, a tone established in the immediate aftermath of Wanderley's death.

> That night, at what looked like being the final meeting of the Chowder Society, [Ricky], inspired, turned to a morose John Jaffrey and asked, "What's the worst thing

> you've ever done?" And John saved them all by answering, "I won't tell you that, but I'll tell you the worst thing that ever happened to me," and told them a ghost story.[20]

Ghost Story is a novel filled with stories, and the opening section, "After Jaffrey's Party," gives us some significant ones. One of its two lengthy chapters, "Jaffrey's Party," is an expository flashback that recreates, in exhaustive detail, the party that ended in tragedy, and that marked the beginning of the Chowder Society's decline into a condition of unrelieved, almost immobilizing terror. It also provides Straub with the opportunity to present a sharply delineated cross-section of Milburn's inhabitants. The remaining chapter is called "The Chowder Society: The October Stories," and it recounts for us the last two undisturbed meetings the Society will ever have.

Ricky Hawthorne is the designated storyteller at the first of these gatherings, although we are never permitted to hear his story. (Had Straub's original impulse held firm, that story would have been a modern-dress version of Nathaniel Hawthorne's "My Kinsmen, Major Molineux.") The evening is largely notable for the group's decision to invite Don Wanderley—nephew of Edward and author of a successful occult thriller called *The Nightwatcher*—to Milburn, in the (admittedly) desperate hope that he might help them understand and dispel the source of their nightmares.

The speaker at the second gathering is Sears James, and we do hear his story: a disturbing account of his early days as a teacher in a small rural community in upstate New York, an account whose characters and events are clearly patterned after Henry James' *The Turn of the Screw*. Sears' version of this story concerns his unsuccessful attempt to save an impoverished, very nearly retarded child named Fenny Bate from the malign influence of his perverse (and, we eventually discover, recently deceased) brother, Gregory. This story, which introduces two characters—Gregory and Fenny—who will play major roles in the subsequent devastation of Milburn, is told at a critical moment in the novel's development: the anniversary of Edward Wanderley's death, a day that is also marked by the not-so-coincidental arrival of an attractive young woman named Anna Mostyn, whose presence will provide the animating force behind virtually everything that happens—to the Chowder Society and to Milburn itself—in the ensuing weeks.

It is the arrival of Anna Mostyn, the mysterious visitor whose initials are echoed throughout this novel, that puts an end to the long period of static, sourceless dread that has haunted the Chowder Society, and initiates the opening movements of an elaborate, carefully designed drama of destruction and revenge. Against the backdrop of an unseasonable October snowfall which starts that night and will continue throughout the book, the haunting of Milburn begins. Images of Fenny and Gregory Bate, who have somehow escaped the confines of Sears James' story, begin to appear, first to Sears, then to others. An eccentric, litigious farmer named Elmer Scales discovers the bloodless, mutilated bodies of several of his sheep, then contacts Sears and Ricky, determined to find someone to sue. Other, similar mutilations, quickly follow. Most significantly, John Jaffrey, responding to the orders of a voice inside his head, climbs to the top of the two-lane bridge that spans the local river and jumps to his death, ironically marking the anniversary of one Chowder Society member's death with the death of another.

With the unannounced arrival of Don Wanderley, who shows up just in time to attend John Jaffrey's funeral, the last critical component of the story locks into place. Wanderley, like virtually every major figure in the novel, has a story to tell. His story, like so many others, centers around his relationship with a woman whose initials have become very familiar: Alma Mobley.

Don first encounters Alma—a pale, lovely woman whose overall "ghostly" pallor suggests a sense of "spiritual blurriness"[21]—during a one-year teaching assignment at the University of California's Berkeley campus. And, as D. H. Lawrence said of the characters in Hawthorne's *The Scarlet Letter,* "the first thing she does is seduce him. And the first thing he does is to be seduced."[22] Don is nearly—but not completely—enraptured by her. For a time, he is consumed in the powerfully erotic spell of their relationship, and soon finds himself ignoring all other aspects of his personal and professional life. Eventually, certain of her less enchanting characteristics—her lies, her claim of friendship with the members of a Manson-like cult called XXX, her insistence on the reality of her communications with the dead, her mysterious relationship with a dangerous looking biker-type named Greg Benton—begin to come between them. In time, a sense of actual, physical revulsion sets in, but before he can formally break off the affair, she leaves him and takes up with his brother David, a successful young lawyer living in New York. Within weeks of this occurrence, David is dead, having thrown himself from the window of an Amsterdam hotel. Alma, his companion on the trip to Amsterdam, has disappeared. This story becomes the basis for *The Nightwatcher*, a novel whose fictionalized resolutions have no equivalent in Don's own life. At the time of his arrival in Milburn, he is still haunted by grief, anger, and a multitude of unanswered questions.

In the aftermath of Don's arrival, events in Milburn escalate to nightmare levels. Animal mutilations are followed by the similar mutilations of a number of townspeople, including Lewis Benedikt, who is trapped within an elaborate hallucination filled with scenes and people from his past, and then savagely destroyed. As a freakish winter storm immobilizes the town, cutting it off from the outside world, corpses accumulate, and chaos overtakes the community. Against this background of panic, confusion, and increasing violence, Sears James and Ricky Hawthorne—the last surviving members of the Chowder Society—at last illuminate the mysteries that lie behind Milburn's present plight. Together, they tell Don Wanderley the final—the ultimate—Chowder Society story: the story of Eva Galli and the lynx that got away.

In 1929, an actress named Eva Galli came to Milburn, and took up a brief but eventful residence. She caught the eye of a gentleman farmer named Stringer Dedham, who promptly asked her to marry him. She also caught the eye of the five young men who would eventually comprise the Chowder Society, and who promptly fell in love with her in a platonic, innocent, intensely vulnerable way. Eva's engagement ended when Stringer unaccountably lost his concentration while operating a threshing machine, and fell in. Later, impatient with her role as fiancee-in-mourning, Eva summoned her five admirers and treated them to a display of unbridled eroticism that shook them to their young and provincial souls. Lewis, panicked, rejected her advances, pushing her away so roughly that she hit her head on the corner of a fireplace, apparently killing herself. The five then came to the anguished decision that they must hide her body or face a scandal that might end their newly launched careers. They placed her body in a borrowed car, and pushed the car into the center of a nearby pond. And then something inexplicable happened. As the car sank, they saw her bloody face grinning at them through the windshield. Seconds later, a lynx appeared out of nowhere on the edge of the pond, then ran away. At the same moment, Eva disappeared from the car.

Fifty years later, with Milburn under siege and their own numbers dwindling, the Chowder Society is reluctantly forced to admit the possibility that Eva, under a different name and in a different guise, has returned. External evidence, together with the first-person account of a boy named Peter Barnes, whose mother and best friend have both been killed by Gregory Bate and who has a great deal of firsthand experience with the supernatural forces abroad in Milburn, leads to an inescapable conclusion: that Eva really has come back, as Anna Mostyn, to exact a protracted vengeance on the town and its citizens.

Armed with this knowledge, the newly-reconfigured Society—Sears, Ricky, Don Wanderley and Peter Barnes—go on the offensive, attempting to track down Eva and her cohorts before Milburn is destroyed completely. Before they can accomplish anything tangible, Sears himself is murdered on Christmas Day, attacked by Gregory and Fenny, the characters from his own story. The three survivors then track the Bate brothers to their hiding place in a local movie theater, and destroy them. The climactic confrontation with Eva Galli comes shortly afterward in an area of Milburn called The Hollow, in the very room where Eva appeared to die in 1929. There, the three fight their way through a barrage of hallucinatory visions and wound Eva/Alma with a hunting knife, only to watch her escape once more, this time in the form of a sparrow.

In the end, the task of watching and waiting for her inevitable reappearance falls to Don Wanderley. In time, he identifies her—tentatively and with great trepidation—as Angie Maule, a nine-year-old schoolgirl whom no one seems willing to befriend. Here, at the point where *Ghost Story* began, he takes her to Florida. There, in an epilogue appropriately entitled "Moth in a Killing Jar," Angie reveals her essential nature, and Don is given a final opportunity to shoot the lynx.

And that, in profoundly simplified form, is *Ghost Story,* a novel formed from the confluence of a vast number of stories, myths, memories, and dreams, a novel whose very title underscores its fascination with the primal power and pervasive presence of narrative—of stories—in our lives. On the most obvious level, *Ghost Story* is a novel filled with interlocking narratives that come together in a kind of ultimate coherence, that connect in unsuspected ways, and are fluid and permeable enough to allow characters like Gregory and Fenny to escape from one story and find their way into others. On a more fundamental level, *Ghost Story* is a novel that is as much about narrative as it is about people. The world, it tells us implicitly, is itself a story. Remove the element of story, and only the void remains.

This concern with narrative is woven into the very fabric of the book, which even makes use of a novelist as viewpoint character, a novelist who has himself written a novel intimately connected with the events of a plot in which he and his dead brother were embroiled, and which connects in turn to events unfolding in Milburn. That same novelist (Don Wanderley, whose name, by the way, deliberately echoes the name of Donald Wandrei, a noted writer of weird tales and the co-founder, with August Derleth, of the Lovecraft-oriented publishing firm of Arkham House) is also in the process of imagining a new, as yet unwritten novel whose subject is

> the destruction of a small town by Dr. Rabbitfoot, an itinerant showman who pitches camp on its outskirts, sells elixirs and potions and nostrums (a black man?) and who has a little sideshow—jazzy music, dancing girls, trombones, etc. Fans and bubbles. If ever I saw a perfect setting for this story, Milburn is it.[23]

Shortly after Don's arrival in Milburn, this imagined image begins to assume an external reality of its own, and Dr. Rabbitfoot—with his music, his smiling, ominous presence, his insistence that he's got "just what your soul needs"[24]—becomes a literal presence on the streets of Milburn, visible (and audible) to a select group of prospective victims. This sense of being caught up in an actual narrative, of traversing "the landscape and atmosphere of...books,"[25] is a recurring one and affects virtually every one of *Ghost Story*'s major characters. For example, Lewis Benedikt, who lives in a big house in the middle of a forest—a kind of faux-Scottish castle that resembles "the end of a quest in a story"[26]—sees the woods around his house lose their accustomed reality and transform themselves into something out of childhood legends.

> ...walking over new snow toward his woods, Lewis had a fresh perception. It

> may have come because he was seeing the woods from an unfamiliar angle, going at them backward...
>
> Whatever the reason, the woods looked like an illustration in a book—not like real woods but a drawing on a page. It was a fairytale woods, looking too perfect, too composed—drawn in black ink—to be real. Even the path, winding off in a pretty indirection, was a fairytale path...
>
> Branches glistened, thorns shone like thumbtacks, implying some narrative on which he'd already closed the book.[27]

The orchestrating force behind this incredibly elaborate assemblage of narratives—the master novelist, so to speak—is Eva Galli, who is also Alma Mobley, Ann-Veronica Moore, and a host of other personas that could almost be viewed as pen names. Eva is a shapeshifter, a Manitou, the vain and hungry prototype of the vampire and the werewolf, the inspiration behind a thousand ghost stories. She is, in a very real sense, a story—a myth—transformed into protean, infinitely mutable flesh. (As Harold Sims, an anthropologist who has a brief affair with Ricky's wife Stella, says, when asked to describe the Manitou: "It's just a story. That's the kind of thing my colleagues are into now. Stories!"[28])

Eva Galli, the embodiment of that story, was directly inspired by another fictional creation: Helen Vaughn, the female nemesis of Arthur Machen's *The Great God Pan.* Helen, as described by Machen, is a hybrid creature, half-human, half...something else, the unexpected result of an experiment aimed at piercing the veil of the visible world and contacting the world beyond: the realm of the great god Pan. Like Eva Galli, Helen Vaughn goes by many names, but none of them are real. As one of the men she destroys comments, "I don't think she had a name. No, no, not in that sense. Only human beings have names..."[29] Like Eva, she is fundamentally corrupt, a seductress capable of driving her victims to suicide and madness. Like Eva's, her outward form is a carefully composed mask covering something strange and indescribable. Here are the words of a witness to the changes "Helen" undergoes on her deathbed:

> I was then privileged or accursed, I dare not say which, to see that which was on the bed, lying there black like ink, transformed before my eyes. The skin, and the flesh, and the muscles, and the bones, and the firm structure of the human body that I had thought to be unchangeable, and permanent as adamant, began to melt and dissolve...Here too was all the work by which mankind had been made repeated before my eyes. I saw the form waver from sex to sex, dividing itself from itself, and then again united. Then I saw its body descend to the beasts whence it ascended, and that which was on the heights go down to the depths, even to the abyss of all being...Then the ladder was ascended again...For one instant I saw a Form, shaped in dimness before me, which I will not farther describe...[30]

And here is a moment from the (apparent) death scene of Anna Mostyn, the penultimate incarnation of Eva Galli:

> For an instant only, as if the corpse of Anna Mostyn were a film, a photographic transparency over another substance, the three of them saw a writhing life through the dead woman's skin—no simple stag or owl, no human or animal body, but a mouth opened beneath Anna Mostyn's mouth and a body constrained within Anna Mostyn's bloody clothing moved with ferocious life: it was as swirling and varied as an oil slick, and it angrily flashed out at them for the moment it was visible; then it blackened and faded, and only the dead woman lay on the floor.[31]

In *Ghost Story*, Straub borrows freely from this basic concept, and then raises the stakes considerably. His Eva Galli is a creature with deeper, more wide-ranging powers. She/it has access to the minds, memories, even the imaginations, of Straub's characters, and can use the information she finds there to further her own ends. She is a master illusionist, and can generate phantasmagorical visions so detailed, so rooted in the psychological predispositions of the viewer, that they achieve their own reality. She is actress and novelist, character and author, and her war against the Chowder Society, which spans continents and decades, comes together like a vast and carefully constructed narrative, a kind of living novel with multiple characters and time frames, interconnected subplots, elaborately detailed histories and settings—all of it motivated by a complex mixture of vanity and anger, and all in the service of a single goal: revenge.

It seems, on the surface, somewhat paradoxical that *Ghost Story,* which may be Straub's most literary novel, is also his most popular, and certainly one of his most accessible. But the fact is that all of the allusiveness and literary gamesmanship at work just below the surface of the text is, finally, of secondary importance. *Ghost Story* is, first of all, a beautifully constructed, compulsively readable book that is at once lively and literate, filled with a sense of mystery and menace, peopled with literally dozens of effectively, often affectionately, rendered characters, and charged with a newly-discovered sense of the extravagant, even garish, possibilities inherent in the tale of supernatural terror. The object lessons embodied in the novels of Stephen King, particularly *'Salem's Lot* and *The Shining,* were clearly well learned, and manifest themselves in the expansiveness, the vitality, and the sheer narrative momentum which inform this novel on virtually every page. The result is a book which can be (and probably has been) enjoyed, appreciated and, in a very real sense, understood by readers who know nothing about the traditions from which it springs.

Much of *Ghost Story*'s appeal arises from Straub's decision to build the novel around the experiences and memories of that group of aging and unlikely heroes, the Chowder Society. This unusual bit of casting gives the book much of its character, and endows it with a singular and refreshing perspective. Although one member, Edward Wanderley, is seen almost entirely through the recollections of his friends, while another, John Jaffrey, is seen only briefly, the three survivors—Sears, Lewis, and Ricky—are complex, empathetic creations, grounded in an unsentimental apprehension of the realities of growing old. Along with the newly-admitted junior members of the Society—Don Wanderley and the teenaged Peter Barnes, who functions as a kind of spiritual older brother to *'Salem's Lot*'s Mark Petrie—they represent the collective human heart of this novel.

Lewis Benedikt, the handsome, aging playboy described as a sort of late-model Cary Grant, is touchingly characterized as a man whose surface gloss conceals unsuspected depths of feeling. Devastated by the death of his wife, Linda (who, we are told, died following a bizarre encounter in a Spanish hotel with "a lovely little girl"[32] named Alice Montgomery some nine years before), he searches, restlessly and without much success, for an acceptable substitute.

> ...Lewis used his comic reputation as a rake to camouflage the seriousness of his heart, and he used his public romances with girls to conceal his deeper, truer relationships with women...He wanted feeling. He wanted emotion—he needed it...Lewis, at the center of his demanding heart, knew that he wanted to recapture the emotions Linda had given him. Frivolous Lewis was Lewis only skin deep.[33]

Sears James, the de facto leader of the Chowder society, is effortlessly rude, formidably intelligent, and constitutionally incapable of suffering fools. If Lewis is the Cary Grant of the Society, Sears is its Orson Welles. His air of native, to-the-manor-born assurance comes dangerously close to insufferability, and he misses more signals than he would ever admit to. (For example, he seriously undervalues Lewis' character and intelligence and, along with every other member of the Chowder Society, completely fails to recognize the signs of morphine addiction in John Jaffrey.) Still, his arrogance has style, his stubborn disdain for the tawdry and the second-rate has a certain nobility, and his eventual death at the hands of Gregory and Fenny Bate is one of the more wrenching moments in a novel filled with images of pain and loss. (Thoughts of Sears and his death bring to mind a moment in 1981 when Straub was being interviewed at NECON, a horror/fantasy convention held annually at Roger Williams University in Rhode Island. The interviewer asked Straub the arch and somewhat overly clever question. "What's the worst thing you've ever done?" Without missing a beat, Straub replied: "The worst thing I ever did was kill off Sears James. I loved him very much."[34])

This unabashed love for his fictional creations is one of the elements that lifts *Ghost Story* above the level of Straub's four previous books, and is one of the more tangible results of the influence of Stephen King. Ricky Hawthorne, "a seventy-year-old lawyer who had lost very little to the years,"[35] and is the only one of the Chowder Society's original members to survive the onslaught of Eva and her familiars, is clearly a reflection of that same authorial affection. Ricky is a figure of quietly deceptive significance, a tolerant husband and loyal subordinate who is also, in the words of Anna/Eva, "a good enemy."[36] Ricky is the quintessential citizen of Milburn, its advocate and conscience. He remembers what the town was like before sidewalks came along to exert their civilizing influence and is attuned, in some fundamental way, to its slow and stately rhythms.

> He had never wanted to live anywhere else, though in the early years of his marriage, his lovely and restless wife had often claimed that the town was boring. Stella had wanted New York—had wanted it resolutely. That had been one of the battles he had won. It was incomprehensible to Ricky that anyone could find Milburn boring: if you watched it closely for seventy years, you saw the century at work. Ricky imagined that if you watched New York for the same period, what you saw would be mainly New York at work.[37]

As the novel opens, Ricky, like his friends, has become the victim of a nameless, precognitive dread, in the face of which he can only wish, fervently and futilely, that "nothing would change,"[38] that he and his community be allowed, simply, "to continue."[39] That, of course, is one wish which will not be granted, and Straub does a superb job of tracing the process of destructive change that sweeps through Milburn, as the interrelated forces of arctic weather conditions and supernatural malevolence settle in on the town, transforming it from a place of rustic, somewhat stodgy charm to an atavistic, frontier version of itself, in which the images framed in the thermopane windows of the attractive houses look "not simply murderous but dead."[40] The last third of the novel takes on a violent and hallucinatory beauty as bodies pile up in the town jail and reality itself grows less and less substantial, disintegrating to the mocking soundtrack of Dr. Rabbitfoot's band.

Straub uses this lurid supernatural drama as a brightly colored backdrop against which to mount a complex account of characters struggling, not merely to survive, but to survive with a measure of grace and dignity in the face of overwhelming catastrophe, and with their fundamental values intact. It is the serious work of a serious novelist and, like all serious and complex works, it is, in the end, "about" many things: community, friendship, and tradition; marriage and infidelity; fear, fate, and the inevitability of change; the power of stories; the nature of romantic and erotic obsession; and, most centrally, the redemptive power of human effort. "Good magic," the novel reminds us, "lay only in human effort, but bad magic could come from around any corner."[41]

The bad magic that Eva Galli and the Bate brothers bring to Milburn manifests itself primarily in an extravagant capacity for destruction, which is a major element of the "fun" that this elaborately created scenario offers them. (And fun, it should be noted—the kind of fun that arises only from the spectacle of suffering and death—is of central importance to these creatures, a fact which says a great deal about their essential natures. "We enjoy entertainment," Gregory tells Don Wanderley. "Only proper, since we have provided so much of it."[42]) But bad magic—that is, evil—also takes the form of hopelessness, of despair, and has about it what Julia Lofting called "the stink of moral failure."[43] It is also powerfully—and paradoxically—seductive, a fact that Peter Barnes is made painfully aware of as he watches his mother die at the hands of Gregory Bate.

> ...the man holding his mother by the throat altered and Peter knew in every cell that what he was looking at was not merely a wolf, but a supernatural being in wolf form whose only purpose was to kill, to create terror and chaos and to take life as savagely as possible: saw that pain and death were the only poles of its being. He saw that this being had nothing in it that was human, and that it only dressed in the body it had once owned...All of this Peter saw in a second. And the next second brought an even worse recognition: that in all of

> this blackness lived a morally fatal glamour.[44]

Earlier in that same scene, Peter asks Gregory what has by now become a familiar question—"What are you?"—and receives an equally familiar reply: "I am you, Peter. Isn't that a simple answer?"[45] The Pogo-like notion that underlies this exchange—that we have met the enemy and that he is, indeed, us—serves a twofold purpose. First, it introduces the legitimate, morally complex notion of our own potential for complicity in the acts that destroy us: our willingness—sometimes even our need—to be seduced. At the same time, the observation "I am you" provides Eva and company with a weapon that takes the form of a lie, a particularly insidious one based, like all the most effective lies, on a measure of psychological truth. Its purpose is to undermine and demoralize, to chip away at the listener's sense of self, to sow doubt, confusion, and despair. In the case of Peter Barnes, the ploy fails utterly, resulting, not in despair or moral confusion, but in anger, and a revitalized sense of purpose.

> "He said he was *me*," Peter said, his face distorting. "He said he was me, I want to kill him."[46]

To which Don Wanderley replies: "Then we'll do it together."[47] And so, with the help of Ricky Hawthorne, they do, in a climactic act of benevolent, communal magic.

Ghost Story's grand design is built on a foundation of closely-observed, lovingly-assembled supporting detail. The novel is filled with incidental flashes of wit and illuminating juxtapositions. For example, a movie poster advertising Brian DePalma's *Carrie* eerily suggests the bloody, smiling face of the Eva Galli wounded by the Chowder Society fifty years before. Another movie image—the shambling zombies of *Night of the Living Dead*—ironically counterpoints the climactic confrontation between the surviving members of the Chowder Society and Milburn's hungry, undead visitors, the Bate brothers. In a similar vein, the allusiveness which informs so much of the novel is often lightly, playfully deployed, as in Straub's decision to call Milburn's one public lodging house The Archer Hotel, in (apparent) acknowledgment of Lew Archer, the detective-hero of a multitude of Ross MacDonald novels centered around a recurring theme: the inevitable reemergence of the haunted, violent past. (Other allusions seem somewhat more private, as in Straub's seemingly deliberate incorporation of certain aspects of Thomas Tessier's novel, *The Fates,* which includes, among other things, cattle mutilation in a small, eastern American town called Millville; or in Ricky Hawthorne's plan to recover from the traumatic events of the novel by traveling with his wife to Arles, France, where the narrator of *Marriages* once chased a ghost across the length of the city.)

Character, as always, is of primary importance to Straub, and he supplements the novel's central figures with his most diverse, highly individualized cast of supporting characters to date. Primary examples include Stella Hawthorne, Ricky's ageless, alluring, compulsively adulterous wife; Jim Hardy, a rebellious, charismatic teenager with more energy than sense; Freddy Robinson, an archetypal insurance salesman whose glad-handing exterior barely conceals his frustration, envy, and fundamental sense of failure; and Elmer Scales, the litigious farmer and would-be poet whose farm is the site of the first wave of animal mutilations, and who is made to pay, in particularly tragic fashion, for a favor that his father did in 1929.

Ghost Story ends on a note of unselfconscious celebration that skirts the boundaries of sentimentality without quite crossing over. Standing at the edge of the Gulf of Mexico, in the triumphant aftermath of his final confrontation with Eva Galli, Don is visited by what he perceives as "a mystical, perhaps a sacred emotion,"[48] a sense of hard-won brotherhood that manifests itself as "a wave of love for everything mortal, for everything with a brief, definite life span—a tenderness for all that could give birth and would die..."[49] The depth of feeling expressed here is, as much as any of the moments of operatic violence or hallucinatory intensity that come before, an indication of the change of direction and intention this novel embodies.

Ghost Story, above all else, represents Straub's commitment to a whole new scale of storytelling, and the resulting sense of grandeur and increased complexity is reflected on every level, from the expansive deployment of plot, incident, and imagery through its highly-charged depiction of the emotional content of the characters' lives. Straub's subsequent career would reflect some dramatic changes—notably a movement away from the overtly supernatural and toward a more realistic, psychologically consistent apprehension of the roots of violence. But this newfound love of the gaudy, the garish, and the extreme marked an early, important turning point in Straub's artistic development, and would continue to animate his fiction for the next several years.

[1] *Ghost Story* (New York: Coward, McCann & Geoghegan, 1979), p. 13

[2] Ramsey Campbell—Forward to the 15th Anniversary Edition of *Shadowland*, p. 25

[3] Ibid., p. 25

[4] *The General's Wife*, p. 12

[5] "Meeting Stevie"—Introduction to *Fear Itself*, edited by Tim Underwood and Chuck Miller (San Francisco, CA/Columbia, PA: Underwood-Miller, 1982), p. 10

[6] *The General's Wife*, p. 13

[7] *Ghost Story* dust jacket material

[8] *Fear Itself*, p. 7

[9] Ibid., p 7

[10] Ibid., p. 7

[11] Ibid., p. 9

[12] Ibid., p. 9

[13] Ibid., pp. 13-14

[14] Ibid., p. 10

[15] *Ghost Story*, p. 13

[16] Ibid., p. 32

[17] Ibid., p. 33

[18] Ibid., pp. 16-17

[19] Ibid., p. 33

[20] Ibid., p. 137

[21] Ibid., p. 183

[22] Ibid., p. 188

[23] Ibid., p. 141

[24] Ibid., p. 142

[25] Ibid., p. 220

[26] Ibid., p. 304

[27] Ibid., pp. 156-157

[28] Ibid., p. 238

[29] Arthur Machen, *The Great God Pan*

[30] *The Great God Pan*

[31] *Ghost Story*, p. 461

[32] Ibid., p. 321

33. Ibid., p. 155

34. Interview with Peter Pautz at Necon (Northeastern Writers' Conference) in 1982

35. *Ghost Story*, p. 37

36. Ibid., p. 137

37. Ibid., p. 38

38. Ibid., p. 47

39. Ibid., p. 47

40. Ibid., p. 416

41. Ibid., p. 421

42. Ibid., p. 436

43. *Julia*, p. 220

44. *Ghost Story*, p. 326

45. Ibid., p. 325

46. Ibid., p. 344

47. Ibid., p. 344

48. Ibid., p. 483

49. Ibid., p. 483

Chapter Six: *Shadowland*

Having achieved, in *Ghost Story,* the rarest kind of success—one that satisfied both the financial expectations of his agent, accountant, and publisher, and the aesthetic demands of his own "internal auditor"[1]—Straub found himself implicitly expected to produce a follow-up novel that would calculatedly replicate the effects and, hopefully, the popularity of its best-selling predecessor. This did not happen. Instead, with typical perversity, the internal auditor grabbed the wheel of the fiction machine, "mashed the accelerator, and went where he wanted to go."[2] The result was *Shadowland*, a complex coming of age novel about magic, illusion, and moral responsibility that is rooted in the imagery and ambiance of one of the oldest literary forms: the fairy tale.

Different as it is, *Shadowland* is nonetheless a logical successor to *Ghost Story,* and its narrative techniques amplify a number of elements already present, to a lesser degree, in the earlier novel. Chief among these is the element of the phantasmagorical: the hallucinatory blending of reality and illusion that gives the last third of *Ghost Story* so much of its power and that becomes, in *Shadowland*, a primary ingredient of the narrative, the medium through which the characters struggle, often futilely, to find their way. Specific influences that underlie and support this hallucinatory superstructure include, in addition to fairy tales, scholarly studies of the history of Renaissance magic by Dame Frances Yates, and the revised, 1978 version of John Fowles' novel, *The Magus*.

Straub's interest in fairy tales, first hinted at in the sequence involving the enchanted woods that surrounded Lewis Benedikt's house in *Ghost Story*, increased dramatically following the birth of his son, Benjamin Bitker Straub, in 1977. By the time young Ben was old enough to understand and respond to stories, he found himself in the day-to-day company of a father with an almost limitless supply of stories to tell. And that, Straub remembers, "is when *Shadowland* really found itself."[3] During this period, he invented literally dozens of stories for his son, spinning them out of the most whimsical of impulses, then following them wherever they led. The results, in his own words, were

> real stories with beginnings, middles, and ends, complete with hesitations, digressions, puzzles, and climaxes. This was thrilling. My little boy was entranced, and I felt as though I had tapped into the pure, ancient well, the source of narrative, the spring which nourished me and everyone else like me.[4]

This creative outpouring affected the evolution of *Shadowland* in some very specific ways. First, a couple of the better stories made their way into the final version of the novel, where they more than hold their own with their classic counterparts. Second, this developing fascination with the actual "taproots of narrative"[5] led Straub to conduct a wide-ranging investigation of the traditional fairy tale. His readings in Perrault, Hans Christian Andersen, and, most significantly, the Brothers Grimm permeate the text, accounting for a large measure of *Shadowland*'s distinctive and idiosyncratic flavor.

Straub's interest in the magical traditions of Renaissance Europe likewise makes a brief appearance in *Ghost Story* when a minor character, a small town curate named Franz Gruber, invites the young Sears James into a book-lined study that contains, among the more standard collections of sermons and Biblical concordances, a small shelf containing works on "Lully, Fludd, Bruno, what you would call the occult studies of the Renaissance."[6] Straub's knowledge of this branch of occult esoterica derives largely from the scholarship of Frances Yates, whose *Giordano Bruno and the Hermetic Tradition* and *The Art of Memory* are among the definitive studies of the impact of hermetic magical practices on sixteenth century philosophy and culture. Straub's Yates studies, together with his readings of such central Gnostic texts as *The Gospel of Thomas* (referred to throughout *Shadowland* as "The Book"), provide his fictional account of magic and magicians with a solid historical underpinning.

Straub's fascination with the magical and mystical is actually a nontraditional reflection of the religious impulse, a way of acknowledging and thinking about the primal forces that govern the universe, and that Tom Flanagan, the young hero of *Shadowland,* thinks of as "the engine"[7] that lies beneath the surface of the visible world. In Straub's view,

> magic, real magic, which could be expressed in stage magic but not confined to it, was connected by the internal resources of the magician to the unseen, subtle, powerful internal structures of the world itself.[8]

The manipulation of these magical forces involves the awareness of certain fundamental principles, the first of which, we are told repeatedly, is "As above, so below."[9] In other words, the elemental nature of the individual soul reflects the elemental nature of the surrounding world. Seen in these terms, the self, like the world it inhabits, is a Gnostic structure, striving, by whatever means are available to it, toward the condition of revelation. Magic, properly used and properly understood, becomes a means of achieving that revelation. In that sense, it is a mirror of those small, daily acts of magic called art. As described in *Shadowland,* magic therefore exists both as a metaphor and as the thing itself, and this underlying metaphorical content connects even the novel's most extravagant acts and images to the more mundane daily realities of the creative spirit.

The third and last of *Shadowland*'s major influences, John Fowles' *The Magus,* was first published in 1965, then republished in 1978 in a revised, expanded, and considerably improved version. *The Magus* tells the story of a shallow, self-deluded young Englishman named Nicholas Urfe who leaves behind the personal and professional dead-ends of his life in England, and takes a position as a teacher at a private boys' school on the fictional Greek island of Phraxos. Once on Phraxos, he encounters a wealthy, charismatic millionaire named Maurice Conchis—the Magus of the title—who subjects him to a seductive and bewildering series of stories, masques, and illusions designed to take him out of his narrow, self-absorbed existence and force him toward a painful reassessment of his life and beliefs, of his fundamental sense of self. This bizarre, incredibly complex experiment is known as The Godgame, and is something of an annual event on Phraxos, shifting its focus each year to accommodate the nature and circumstances of the individual victims, who, like Nicholas, are drawn by the forces of hazard into its field of influence.

The Godgame's operating method reflects a statement made repeatedly throughout *Shadowland:* Everything here is a lie. During the course of the game, Nicholas is presented with a series of elaborate, compelling fictions which give way to a series of equally elaborate fictions which, in turn, conceal more lies, more layers of carefully crafted illusions. By the time Nicholas, and the reader, touch bottom, certainty has all but disappeared, and the universe within which Nicholas struggles to reconstruct himself is revealed as something both coldly indifferent and essentially enigmatic. Fowles' novel, like the "experiment" it describes, is dazzling, maddening, and ultimately quite brilliant. The source of its appeal for Straub is obvious, and manifests itself on a number of levels.

First, *The Magus* is the story of a person forced to change and grow under the pressure of experience, an element common to Straub's fiction, much of which is concerned with the crucibles, supernatural and otherwise, through which his characters pass on their way to larger, often radically different lives. This concern with personal evolution is reflected, less dramatically, on the very first page of Straub's first novel, *Marriages,* when the narrator, Owen, discusses his decision to expatriate himself in terms of his need "to redirect the growth of [his] personality."[10]

The Magus is also, like so much of Straub's work, an extremely literary book, and ranges freely across the length and breadth of its author's vast cultural reserves. Starting out as a kind of modern dress version of *The Tempest,* with Prospero's domain reimagined as a Greek island in 1953, Fowles' story wanders easily and naturally into adjacent realms of myth and legend, echoing first Theseus and the Minotaur, then Orpheus and Eurydice, but never distancing itself from its central philosophical concerns or sacrificing its stylish, decidedly contemporary narrative voice.

Even more significantly, *The Magus* is constructed in a way that reflects Straub's own belief in the pervasive, almost primal importance of narrative. The Godgame to which Nicholas Urfe is subjected is a dense, detailed, multidimensional construction. Like the events of *Ghost Story,* as created by that master novelist, Eva Galli, the events of The Godgame come together to form an actual, living novel in which Nicholas becomes a bewildered, though not unwilling, participant, overpowered by the force of the stories he is constantly being told. Here, for example, is Nicholas at an early moment in the Game, caught in the spell of a thoroughly unreliable account of Maurice Conchis' adventures during World War I:

> He stopped speaking for a moment, like a man walking who comes to a brink; perhaps it was an artful pause, but it made the stars, the night, seem to wait, as if story, narrative, history, lay imbricated in the nature of things; and the cosmos was for the story, not the story for the cosmos.[11]

Later in the story, he even comes to think of Conchis as "a novelist sans novel, creating with people rather than words."[12]

In writing *Shadowland,* Straub drew freely on Fowles' method of creating coherent fiction out of a disorienting combination of lies, illusions, and deliberate misdirection. And though Straub openly acknowledges the influence of Fowles' novel, he also claims, quite correctly, that the influence was essentially liberating. In Straub's words,

> *The Magus* suggested ways to unite the powerful strangeness resulting from the oral tradition with more conventional narrative satisfactions [and] demonstrated how the seductive uncertainty implicit in theatrical illusion and, even more importantly, the emotional effects of this uncertainty, could find expression in a narrative which itself moved through successive layers of surprise, doubt, suspicion, and discovery.[13]

In developing this principle of "seductive uncertainty," Straub added his own distinctive brand of dazzle, extravagance, and narrative ingenuity, and then shifted his story's focus from the realm of trickery and illusion to a realm where trickery and illusion work hand-in-hand with actual magic. The result, *Shadowland,* is a novel that is both like and unlike *The Magus,* that both reflects and transcends its specific influence. Within it, as in *The Magus,*

> a being of overwhelming psychological penetration tells a series of stories. As the stories unfold, they exercise an increasing gravitational power, seeming to speak to the inner life of the listener. Together, put end to end they form a single, unreliable construct, a house filled with hidden passages and trap doors, also an entire wing sometimes but not always entered by a certain flight of stairs.[14]

The "being" in question, Straub's analog of Maurice Conchis, is Coleman Collins, AKA Herbie Butter and Charles Nightingale: master illusionist, Gnostic magician, and reigning "King of the Cats." Collins is the undisputed ruler of a magical realm centered in, but not restricted to, a large Vermont estate called Shadowland, which is located deep within the borders of an enchanted forest. Among the hidden passages and trap doors of this estate, in the recollected summer of 1959, Straub unfolds the central drama of *Shadowland:* a story of the endlessly repeated struggle for power and primacy in the esoteric world of the magician.

In typically tricky fashion, *Shadowland* begins several times, in several different ways. The opening paragraph of the initial prologue, "Tom in the Zanzibar," tells us:

> More than twenty years ago, an underrated Arizona schoolboy named Tom Flanagan was asked by another boy to spend the Christmas vacation with him at the house of his uncle...Tom refused...At the end of the year his friend repeated the invitation, and this time Tom Flanagan accepted. His father had been dead [from cancer] three months; following that, there had been a tragedy at the school; and just now moving from the well of his grief, Tom felt restless, bored, unhappy: ready for newness and surprise. He had another reason for accepting, and though it seemed foolish,

> it was urgent—he thought he had to protect his friend. That seemed the most important task in his life.[15]

That is one kind of beginning, and it encapsulates, in a very literal fashion, the events leading up to Tom Flanagan's climactic summer at Shadowland. But as Tom suggests to the nameless narrator—an old school friend to whom Tom gradually passes on the stories that comprise the bulk of this novel—there is another possible beginning to the book, one that is more mysterious but perhaps more appropriate: the story of the King of the Cats.

In Straub's version of this story, a traveler journeying to the house of a friend stops, late at night, to rest his feet in the courtyard of a ruined abbey. A series of noises from the floor of the abbey catch his attention, and he looks through a window and spies a procession of cats carrying a tiny coffin which they lower, with great ceremony, into an open grave.

> "After that he was so frightened that he could not stay in that place a moment longer, and he thrust his feet into his boots and rushed on to the house of his friend. During dinner, he found that he could not keep from telling his friend what he had witnessed. He had scarcely finished when his friend's cat, which had been dozing in front of the fire, leaped up and cried, 'Then I am the King of the Cats' and disappeared in a flash up the chimney..."[16]

After telling us this story—which opens up, for both the reader and the traveler, a world of previously unsuspected possibilities and at the same time introduces the dominant theme of succession—the narrator reconsiders the story's opening sentence ("Twenty years ago, an underrated schoolboy...") and suggests that a truer, more accurate beginning would include the words: *Once upon a time*...or, *Long ago, when we all lived in the forest...*[17]

Having established, with those words, the peculiar nature of the story that is to follow, the novel proper is almost ready to begin. But first, there is one more prologue, one more beginning to be gotten through: a precognitive dream that comes to Tom Flanagan on the eve of a new school year, a dream which features a dark, threatening figure, a benign and ancient wizard, and a series of hints regarding tests, battles, and future rites of passage which the dreaming boy will be forced to undergo. Having thus reinforced the novel's connection to the world of fairy tales—and having created, also, the sense that the novel's central conflict has been set in motion long before its actual opening moments—Straub takes us into the first of the novel's primary settings: a subdivision of Shadowland called Carson School.

Carson School, a cheerfully libelous reconstruction of Straub's own alma mater, Milwaukee's Country Day School, is an irredeemably second-rate private boy's school that occupies a decaying Gothic mansion somewhere in Arizona. Its headmaster, Laker Broome, is a grimly authoritarian figure who may, in fact, possess literally demonic qualities and whose personal credo, frequently repeated, is: "It is the boy who fails, not the school."[18] Additional staff members include an array of petty bureaucrats and borderline sadists such as "Billy" Thorpe, the dour, humorless Latin Master; and Chester Ridpath, the history teacher and football coach whose failure to understand or control his own son will have disastrous and far-reaching results. The school's motto is "Alis Volat Propriis"[19] (He flies by his own wings), a motto which takes on an increasingly literal meaning as the novel progresses.

Shadowland opens on Registration Day in 1958, a year when "Jack Kennedy was still a senator from Massachusetts and Steve McQueen was Josh Randall and McDonald's had sold only two million hamburgers."[20] Against a candlelit backdrop, the result of a portentous power failure, the staff and a select group of students are quickly introduced and rapidly individualized: Dave Brick, an overweight math prodigy born to be a victim; Bob Sherman, a joker whose native irreverence brings him some immediate and unwelcome attention; and Del Nightingale, a wealthy orphan whose love of magic and illusion provides the basis for his relationship with the boy who will become his protector and best friend: Tom Flanagan. Del lives, in classic fairy-tale fashion, with his remote and quarrelsome stepparents, but his real adult guardian is a manservant named Bud Copeland.

Del is a magician in embryo, and spends most summers at Shadowland, the Vermont estate of his uncle, master magician Coleman Collins, in whose footsteps he plans to follow. Tom, whose father has been recently diagnosed with cancer and who is himself about to become partially orphaned, is underrated in more than one sense: he has a natural aptitude for magic—real magic—of which he himself is largely unaware, but which has already caught the attention of Del's uncle. Through the convergence of these two boys, and the attendant scrutiny of Coleman Collins, Carson School becomes the locus of an extraordinary concentration of forces. For the duration of the 1958-59 school year, its normal mode of pettiness and institutionalized cruelty gives way to something stranger and ultimately more destructive.

Against a backdrop of traditional prep school activities—exams, athletic events, chaperoned dances, compulsory chapel—the narrative slowly darkens, encompassing a series of events that are by turns tragic and inexplicable. Tom's father dies after a painful and protracted illness. Images of a dark, trench-coated figure—evidently Coleman Collins—begin appearing to various Carson students. A valuable glass figurine—an owl—is stolen from its display case at a rival prep school named Ventnor Academy, resulting in an intensification of the totalitarian principles which underlie Carson's disciplinary code. Del Nightingale, who is first presented as a precociously accomplished performer of card tricks and close-up magic, manifests more arcane abilities, once actually levitating in Tom Flanagan's presence. Tom himself causes a pencil to rise up into the air, in an unconscious display of his own latent powers. Reality gradually fractures, dividing into a daylight world where myth, magic, and fairy tales become the subject of lectures and rational discussion, and a considerably less orderly world dominated by dreams, omens, and a persistent sense of the uncanny.

Dreams permeate the first third of *Shadowland,* delivering signs and portents on both an individual and a collective level. Just as Tom Flanagan's initial sense of his peculiar destiny, described in the prologue, comes by way of a dream, so does his first, mysterious lesson in the "economics" of mortality:

> In his dream, which was somehow connected to Bud Copeland, he was being looked at by a vulture...The vulture was gazing at him with a horrid, patient acceptance, knowing all about him. Nothing surprised the vulture, neither heat nor cold, not life or death. The vulture accepted all as it accepted him. It waited for the world to roll its way, and the world always did...First, it had eaten his father, now it would devour him. Nothing could stop it.

> The world rolled its way, and then it ate what it was given. The vulture was a lesson in economics.[21]

Other birds invade Tom's dreams, among them owls, sparrows, and a shadow bird "with huge wings and a tearing beak"[22] which dissolves into the shadow image of a gang of men kicking a boy to death, which dissolves, in turn, into a series of bloody letters that spell out the word "Shadowland." It is this premonitory image that convinces Tom to accompany Del to Vermont, in the vague hope of protecting him from an equally vague danger. At one point, the entire student body of Carson School (which, incidentally, includes the seventeen-year-old Miles Teagarden, caught in a moment between the death of Alison Greening and the disappointments of his later life) is subjected to an epidemic of vivid, often violent nightmares.

> *...a man with no face was chasing me and he was never going to get tired...I was up in the air and no one could get me down and I knew I was going to blow away and be lost...wolves were ripping at me, and I knew I was dying...*[23]

One particular student, Steve "Skeleton" Ridpath, proves more susceptible to the forces at work in Carson than any of his fellows, and acquires a painfully prominent role in the events of this book.

Skeleton, son of the Carson football coach, has moved from "a baffled and empty childhood"[24] into a deeply disturbed adolescence marked by a fascination with violence that borders on the obsessive. A bully and an incipient psychopath, Skeleton spends much of his life in a bedroom whose walls are covered with what he calls his "things:" varnished images of death and torture that form a collage which is an elaborate representation of the state of his own mind. Skeleton not only senses the largely offstage presence of Coleman Collins, but worships and submits himself to it. Like Renfield in *Dracula*, he is a slave in search of a master. Unfortunately for him, he gets exactly what he wants.

Having thus established the characters, the mysteries, and the magical forces which stand at the novel's center, Straub ends Section One—which functions as a kind of extended prologue to subsequent events at Shadowland—on a predictably tragic note. While putting on a magic show for the assembled students, Tom and Del, alias "Flanagini and Night," are approaching the climactic moment of the performance—a moment in which Del plans to levitate above the stage and then disappear—when Tom sees another figure, Skeleton Ridpath, actually levitating near the auditorium's ceiling. At the same moment, smoke from a fire in the adjacent Field House begins pouring into the auditorium. In the ensuing panic, one boy—the perennial victim, Dave Brick—dies, and dozens of others suffer from smoke inhalation. The school year that began with candles in the entry hall ends with a conflagration, and with a host of unresolved questions.

Looking back on that year from an adult perspective, Tom tells the narrator:

> ...there was a mystery in our school, and the end of the mystery was the awful thing that happened when Del and I were doing our magic show. But that wasn't the answer to the mystery, just its conclusion. The real answer was at Shadowland; or the answer was Shadowland.[25]

Shortly after the subdued final ceremonies of the school year, Tom and Del set out, alone, for Vermont, and the answers that wait there. In the course of a two-day train trip, they encounter a number of people and events that will prove to be a part of the story that began at Carson School: a man who bears a disturbing resemblance to Skeleton Ridpath, a private car filled with bearded men in old-fashioned suits, a train wreck that delays their arrival in Vermont. The two also study a document written by Coleman Collins which describes the nine levels of magic to which they will be exposed, a document preceded by the ominous, perhaps threatening statement: Know what you are getting into. Of course, they don't—and can't—know what they are getting into, but they begin to find out almost immediately after their arrival, when an irritable, inebriated Coleman Collins greets them with the premonitory words: "So the birds have come home."[26]

The mysterious house that the birds have come home to occupies the final two sections of the novel, the first of which, "Shadowland," is appropriately preceded by an epigraph from Roger Sales' *Fairy*

Tales and After: "We are back at the foot of the great narrative tree, where stories can go...anywhere."[27] In keeping with this warning, the story that follows, while essentially, even classically, simple, is complicated enormously by the manner in which it is told, a manner in which logic, linear plotting, and conventional literary techniques are subverted by the novel's governing force: magic. The result is a narrative whose eccentric structure reflects the sudden shifts and deliberate discontinuities of the fairy tale, that goes where it needs to go, freely and without restraint.

The centerpiece of that summer at Shadowland—the summer of Coleman Collins' "unburdening"[28]—is a lengthy autobiographical account, told in installments to Del and Tom, of Collins' life as a magician. Like the larger story within which it is nested, this internal narrative concerns one man's discovery of his own essential nature and of his previously unsuspected affinity for magic. It begins, like Maurice Conchis' similar narrative in *The Magus,* on the battlefields of France in World War I, where Collins—then a young doctor named Charles Nightingale with an amateur's interest in magic and obscure magical texts—takes the life of a mortally wounded comrade, an act of mercy which earns him an ironic (and very Fowlesian) nickname: The Collector. Later, after several grueling months as a surgeon in a primitive battlefield hospital, he suffers a breakdown and begins to think of himself as Vendouris, the man he killed, the man whose soul, he believes, appeared to him in the form of a giant white owl. After partially recovering and returning to duty, he experiences one of the defining moments of his life while operating on a Negro soldier who has just been refused treatment by a racist surgeon named Withers.

> I felt a change come over my whole body...My mind began to buzz. My hands tingled. I trembled, knowing what I could do...I could *heal* him. I put down the instrument and ran my fingers along the torn blood vessels. The mess the bullet had caused as it moved from lung to liver to spleen closed itself—all of that torn flesh and damaged tissue; it grew pink and restored, virginal. The nurse backed away, making little noises under her mask. I was on fire...[29]

In the aftermath of that experience, he comes to feel as though he

> had been raised up to a great eminence, and been shown all the things of this world and been told: "You may have what you like."[30]

This "miracle" brings Nightingale to the attention of a young black magician named Speckle John, the King of the Cats. Shortly afterward, Nightingale is inducted—"welcomed"—into a mysterious Order that is ruled by the tenets of an equally mysterious Book. He subsequently apprentices himself to Speckle John, assumes a new identity—as Coleman Collins—and then deserts, as Maurice Conchis once did, heading out into the world to pursue his destiny.

The rest of Coleman's narrative recapitulates his career as a magician, a career which includes encounters with Gurdjieff, Ouspensky, and Alastair Crowley, and which is increasingly marked by ambition, greed, and the desire for dominance. In time, Coleman Collins becomes the King of the Cats, defeating Speckle John and stripping him of his powers. His public career, which ends after a spectacular final performance at a London theater called The Wood Green Empire, gives way to the splendid isolation of his life at Shadowland, a private kingdom built on magic, corruption, and the perversion of the spirit of his ancient Order. For decades, Collins has reigned within this sanctum, consolidating his power and maintaining his position in the face of all competitors, the latest of whom is the underrated schoolboy, Tom Flanagan.

Between installments of this story, Tom and Del find themselves caught up more and more deeply in the tangle of lies, illusion, and trickery that is the essence of Shadowland. Del, the veteran of many summers under the tutelage of his uncle, immediately senses that something is different about this summer, but does not immediately understand that the difference has to do with Tom Flanagan. Del has always considered himself the true heir to Shadowland and its mysteries, but he is, in fact, a journeyman magician whose most impressive feats—such as levitation—are the result of the proximity of his friend. Tom, on the other hand, possesses a gift for magic which he himself scarcely understands, but which declares itself to Coleman Collins across the length of the continent. As Collins tells him:

> At one time, I thought Del would be my successor. It would have been better if he had been. I could control my nephew. But there you were, shining away like the biggest diamond in the golden west.[31]

Not too surprisingly, the bulk of Collins' attention is focused on Tom, a situation which leaves Del puzzled, resentful, and more and more estranged from his friend. This estrangement increases as the two compete for the attention of the same girl, the beautiful and mysterious Rose Armstrong, the employee—and possibly even the creation—of Coleman Collins. Rose initiates Tom into the world of romantic and sexual relationships. Collins, in traditional Biblical fashion, takes him to a great height and shows him a vision of the world that could be his.

> "Look down," the figure behind him commanded. Tom looked over the steaming, foaming horse into a long white vista. The land dropped. The green firs resumed. At the bottom of the valley lay a frozen lake. Above it, on the far end, Shadowland sat on its cliff like a giant dollhouse. Its windows gleamed.
>
> "Pretend that is the world. It is the world. It can be yours. Everything in the world, every treasure, every satisfaction is there..."
>
> "This is your kingdom too, child. Insofar as I make it yours. And insofar as you can accept what you find in it."[32]

As the summer progresses, other forces—forces not under Coleman's control—have their own say. One night, while sleeping in the woods outside of Shadowland, Tom is visited by two mysterious figures—a man in a black cape and a snake—and informed that, on the basis of the "treasure"[33] that is within him, he has been "chosen."[34] Like Collins before him, he is "welcomed" into the ranks of an ancient Gnostic order of which he knows nothing. Some days later, while suffering from a sudden and severe fever, Tom meets the devil in a dream. The devil, who calls himself "M" (Mephistopheles?), offers Tom a simple choice: to take the high road of wealth and power by placing his gifts, as Collins has, in the devil's service; or to take the low road and reject the corrupt kingdom he has been offered. Tom awakens from this dream with a clear sense of purpose, and begins making plans to take the low road out of Collins' domain.

M's offer is central to the concerns of *Shadowland*, which is very much a novel about moral choices. Beneath its dazzle and inventiveness, beneath its gaudy and visionary surface, the novel slowly forms itself around a single, fundamental question: What kind of magician—what kind of man—will Tom Flanagan choose to become? Another key question, which Tom is asked repeatedly and in many forms, is this: Given the opportunity to choose, which gift will you keep: your wings or your song; freedom or the unasked-for burden of your special talent? In the end, Tom chooses his wings, only to find that the gift of song is not so easily put aside. Under the urging of both Rose Armstrong, who pleads with Tom to help her escape, and of his own increasing uneasiness with life at Shadowland, Tom, led by Rose and accompanied by a reluctant Del, attempts to flee. The attempt is curtailed when Rose, in a complex act of betrayal, leads them along an underground passage haunted by the voices of Shadowland's earlier victims, and into the hands of Coleman Collins and his gang of psychopathic associates, The Wandering Boys.

Once back in Shadowland, Collins seizes the opportunity provided by Tom's flight to eliminate his rival and retain his position as "the old king, the only king."[35]

> "Do you understand," the magician said. "I had to see if you'd really try to leave. You don't deserve your talent—but that is academic now, for you won't have it much longer. When it came down to it, you chose your wings."[36]

In an act which is the culmination of the Christian imagery which underlies so much of this novel, and which is prefigured as early as the initial prologue (when the unnamed narrator refers to a card trick as one of "the casual little miracles...that had nailed [Tom] into his life"[37]), Collins crucifies the boy on an X-shaped wooden frame, and leaves him to die.

Once crucified, Tom begins to discover the extent of his powers. With the aid and encouragement of Bud Copeland—who is revealed, at last, as Speckle John, and who is drawn to Shadowland by the sheer force of Tom's internal "battery"[38]—Tom escapes from the cross and goes on the offensive. First, he encounters and defeats Collins' grotesque personal bodyguard, The Collector, a former stage prop now reincarnated as a killing machine. Over the years, The Collector has been inhabited and animated by a number of the magician's victims and enemies, beginning with Withers, a fellow surgeon and rival from the battlefields of World War I. Its current "occupant" is Skeleton Ridpath, the dysfunctional son of the Carson School football coach, who has finally found a purpose commensurate with his own capacity for hatred. In one of the defining moments of his life as a magician, a moment in which he achieves full recognition of his own powers and "welcomes" himself, Tom frees Skeleton from his imprisonment in The Collector, and then arms himself for his final confrontation with the reigning master of Shadowland.

That confrontation is complicated by the fact that Collins is holding Del as his hostage. (Wizards, he reminds Tom, "get the house odds—they use their own decks."[39]) He offers Tom a choice: "Leave magic. Let me have your gifts...walk out of Shadowland and be the boy you thought you were when you came here"[40]; or "Your song against mine. The performance [to] continue until Shadowland has an undisputed master, the new king or the old."[41] The moment Tom accepts the challenge—song against song—Collins transforms Del into a sparrow, and then disappears. At that moment, it seems to Tom as though

> The fairy tales had been blown into each other and got mixed up, so that the old king had a wolf's head under his crown, and the young prince in love with the maiden fluttered and gasped in a sparrow's body...and the wise magician who enters at the end to set everything right was only a fifteen-year-old-boy kneeling on bloodied floorboards and reaching for the transformed body of his closest friend.[42]

In the end, Collins relies on both trickery (reappearing in a multitude of images—one real, the rest shadows) and cruelty (transforming Del, finally and forever, into a glass ornament) to retain his position. Tom, however, has learned a crucial lesson from Collins—the secret of "hating well"[43]—and he uses it, together with a final assist from Speckle John, to trap Collins within the deserted husk of The Collector, and then consign him to the mirror world deep within Shadowland. Tom then uses his newly acquired powers to burn the entire estate to the ground, after which he spends a final night with Rose on the shore of a nearby lake. When he awakens in the morning, she is mysteriously gone, and Tom is left to make his way back to his other life, having lost almost everything he values in exchange for a gift he never wanted to have.

Shadowland is a dark, often troubling morality tale that has much to say about power, loyalty, friendship, responsibility, courage, and ambition, while effectively extending *Ghost Story*'s concern with the power and importance of stories. It is also, despite the extravagance of its subject matter and the often extreme nature of its imagery, a classic example of the Bildungsroman. In its account of the growth and development of an individual soul, it is as much about the inevitability of loss as it is about magic and mystery, and it offers a clear-eyed assessment of the cost implicit in every moment of personal choice. It is a novel which circles relentlessly around the most basic of all questions: How should a man live?

Like so much of Straub's work, *Shadowland* is an intensely personal novel that openly acknowledges a variety of literary sources without ever sacrificing its unique flavor or its complex sense of self. Traces of Stephen King still linger at the edges of the book: Tom Flanagan, with his preternaturally powerful "battery," bears a strong resemblance to *The Shining*'s Danny Torrance, while Coleman Collins occasionally suggests Randall Flagg, the Dark Man from King's 1979 novel, *The Stand*. *The Magus*, of course, provided *Shadowland* with some of its central structural devices, but there are also a number of smaller, deliberately Fowlesian moments along the way. Two sexual encounters involving Rose Armstrong (one in which she participates with Tom; one in which she performs, or is forced to perform, or appears to perform, in front of Tom) reflect similar moments in *The Magus*, while the ultimate destiny of Skeleton Ridpath, who retreats to a monastery in the aftermath of his victimization by Coleman Collins, likewise mirrors the experience of a minor character from *The Magus* named John Leverrier.

Mostly, though, the narrative derives its essential character from the influence of the traditional fairy tale. Just as Collins assures Tom that "everything you...see here comes from the interaction of your mind with mine,"[44] so everything that happens in *Shadowland*—together with the *way* that those things happen—comes from the interaction of Straub's sophisticated, highly informed sensibility with the primitive essence of the fairy tale. The result is an occasionally jarring, deliberately discontinuous narrative in which time is fluid and reality is unstable; where day becomes night and events change course with disconcerting suddenness; where our fundamental assumptions about the nature of the world often prove false and insubstantial. *Shadowland,* in other words, is a novel in which magic, rather than logic, drives the plot, and in which stories can, and usually do, "go anywhere."

Commenting on the novel's relationship to these stories, Straub writes:

> ...I was thinking of fairy tales as the taproots of the great tree of narrative, so part of what I liked—even as it sort of baffled me—in many of the Grimm Brothers' tales was what struck me as a rough, timeworn, disconnected quality, a kind of arrogant, primitive, patchwork narrative authority with no need of smooth, logical, well-motivated and well-prepared connections from part to part...These stories, I supposed, were the oldest and most genuine, the real ancestors of the kind of fiction I was trying to write. They were like pottery shards unearthed at an archeological dig, like fragments of an ancient scroll found within an urn at the back of a cave. They had not been smoothed out and domesticated.[45]

Among the particular tales that find their way into *Shadowland*—sometimes glancingly, sometimes directly, sometimes just as pieces of the general ambiance—are a number of works from the Brothers Grimm, including: "Little Red Riding Hood" (portrayed, early in the novel, by a caped and hooded Rose Armstrong); "The Goose Girl" (subject of a lively classroom discussion about the kinds of stories where the world turns topsy-turvy and the known rules no longer apply, where only magic has the power to set things right); "Hansel and Gretel" (a story of children lost in a hostile wood that comes more and more to reflect the situation of Tom and Del); and "Ashputtle," the original version of "Cinderella" (which, like *Shadowland,* uses birds as "messengers of the spirit").

At least one tale by Hans Christian Andersen bears directly on the novel: "The Little Mermaid." In Andersen's story, a nameless mermaid trades her voice (her song) to a sorceress in exchange for the legs that will allow her to enter the human world and achieve two goals: win the love of a prince and acquire an immortal soul. A further condition of the exchange is the fact that walking will always be painful for her. Her feet will always feel as though they are walking on knives. All of this is reflected in the character of Rose Armstrong, whose essential alienness is made clear to Tom through a brief moment of telepathic contact, in which he feels

> a sense of airlessness, of suffocation, of being in an alien place. His mind made a sudden, shocked withdrawal, having touched for the briefest moment a world in which it knows no landmarks and is queerly cold and lost.[46]

What Tom doesn't know, and cannot perceive, is the pain that the simple act of walking always causes her.

> Rose too was in pain. Rose is always in pain, and only Mr. Collins knows this. For as long as she has walked, she has walked on swords, broken glass, burning coals; the ground stabs her feet. Only Mr. Collins knows how when she walks on her high heels, nails jab into her soles, making every step a crucifixion like Tom's...[47]

She dreams of escaping with Tom, of "going away and away and away"[48] on a train bound for distant places but, like Andersen's mermaid, she is unable to free herself from her native element. At the novel's end, she slips into the water while Tom is sleeping, and disappears forever.

Shadowland is also filled with a great many traditional flourishes and classical fairy-tale motifs which, though largely unconnected to specific sources, are an integral part of the novel's densely detailed atmosphere. Scattered within the larger story are accounts of lost and abandoned children, stolen identities, animals that speak, miraculous transformations, princesses in need of rescue, hidden treasures, magical talismans, and houses with forbidden rooms. (In one of these forbidden rooms, Jakob and Wilhelm Grimm—or, more precisely, Coleman Collins' projections of Jakob and Wilhelm Grimm—hold court, offering their own complex commentary on stories, on choices, and on the nature of life at Shadowland.)

Finally, Straub adds some original stories to the mix, fairy-tale-like narratives which were initially invented for his son and which blend seamlessly into their classical surroundings. One, "The Dead Princess," is a deft little parable about the trickery of wizards that explains why frogs croak and why they hop, and that first raises the recurring question: What will you sacrifice to receive your wish: your wings or your song? A second story, "The Mermaid," revisits the theme of magic and duplicity through its account of an old, lonely king who makes a bad bargain with a wizard, trading his hair and beard for what the wizard calls "the illusion of love"[49] and losing everything he values in the process.

Shadowland also contains an unusual collaboration between Straub and the Brothers Grimm in which Straub adapts and concludes an open-ended little fragment entitled "The Golden Key." In the Grimm original, a poor boy is sent into the forest to gather firewood. While clearing a space in the snow in which to build a small fire for himself, he finds a golden key. Digging down further, he finds a locked iron box.

> "There must be precious things in it," he thought. "If only the key fits!" At first, he couldn't find a keyhole, but then at last he found one, though it was so small he could hardly see it. He tried the key and it fitted perfectly. He began to turn it—and now we'll have to wait until he turns it all the way and opens the lid. Then we'll know what marvels there were in the box.[50]

And so the story, or fragment, ends. In Straub's version, which is called "The Box and the Key," the details of the boy's life in the forest are developed more completely, and the nature of the treasure is revealed:

> Every story in the world, every story ever told, blew up out of the box. Princes and princesses, wizards, foxes, and trolls, and witches and wolves and woodsmen and kings and elves and dwarves and a beautiful girl in a red cape, and for a second the boy saw them all perfectly, spinning silently in the air. Then the wind caught them and sent them blowing away, some this way and some that.[51]

Then, in a moment which prefigures the feeling that will come to Tom when he sees Del transformed into a sparrow, the narrator of the tale—Coleman Collins—speculates on the aftermath of the opening of the box.

> ...I wonder if some of the stories might not have blown into other stories. Maybe the wind tumbled those stories all together and switched the trolls with the kings and put foxes heads on the princes and mixed up the witch with the beautiful girl with the red cape. I often wonder if that happened.[52]

This blurring together of details and discrete narrative lines is typical of both the hallucinatory nature of Shadowland and of the personal proclivities of its master, a man for whom confusion and disorientation are commonplace weapons in his ongoing struggle for supremacy in the world of the magician. But the real underlying premise of this little fable—that stories, rather than riches, are the true undiscovered treasures—is typical of Straub: an affirmation, appropriately couched in the form of a story, of the elemental importance of narrative.

Like *Ghost Story, Shadowland* represented one more turning point in a restless, constantly evolving career. Ramsey Campbell has called it "the first of his books that could have been written only by Peter"[53], and this statement still feels true. Given the opportunity to consolidate his already substantial success, Straub chose instead to confound expectations with this dazzling, intractable, extravagantly complex work that appears to have been written, not out of any commercial consideration, but out of a deep-seated affinity for the adventurous and the idiosyncratic. Like the books that would follow, *Shadowland* is clearly the product of a large spiritual effort. It has about it that sense of internal urgency embodied in the following words from The Gospel of Thomas, words which reflect the governing principle by which Tom Flanagan, and all true magicians, live:

> If you bring forth what is within you, what you bring forth will save you. If you do not bring forth what is within you, what you do not bring forth will destroy you.[54]

The next product of Straub's inner voice—the next bend in a convoluted road—would be *Floating Dragon,* a complex, controversial experiment in deliberate excess that would stand as its author's final statement on the literary possibilities of supernatural horror.

1. Introduction to Gauntlet Press 15th Anniversary Edition of *Shadowland,* p. 14

2. Ibid., p, 14

3. Ibid., p. 16

4. Ibid., p. 17

5. Letter from Peter Straub to the author

6. *Ghost Story,* p. 68

7. *Shadowland* (New York: Coward, McCann & Geoghegan, 1980), p. 61

8. Introduction to Gauntlet Press edition of *Shadowland,* p. 14

9. *Shadowland,* p. 118

10. *Marriages,* p. 3

11. John Fowles, *The Magus: A Revised Version* (New York: Little, Brown and Company, 1978), p. 153

12. Ibid., p. 247

13. Introduction to Gauntlet Press edition of *Shadowland,* p. 18

14. Ibid., pp. 18-19

15. *Shadowland,* p. 3

16. Ibid., pp. 18-19

17. Ibid., p. 9

18. Ibid., p. 46

19. Ibid., p. 23

20. Ibid., p. 27

21. Ibid., p. 43

22. Ibid., p. 111

23. Ibid., p. 90

24. Ibid., p. 55

25. Ibid., p. 59

26. Ibid., p. 146

27. Ibid., p. 129

28. Ibid., p. 255

29. Ibid., pp. 229-230

30. Ibid., p. 230

31. Ibid., p. 347

32. Ibid., p. 194

33. Ibid., p. 277

34. Ibid., p. 277

35. Ibid., p. 384

36. Ibid., p. 346

37. Ibid., p. 7

38. Ibid., p. 355

39. Ibid., p. 383

40. Ibid., p. 382

41. Ibid., p. 382

42. Ibid., p. 383

43. Ibid., p. 197

44. Ibid., p. 288

45. Letter from Peter Straub to the author

46. *Shadowland*, p. 378

47. Ibid., p. 371

48. Ibid., p. 371

49. Ibid., p. 310

50. *Grimm's Tales for Young and Old*, translated by Ralph Manheim (New York, Doubleday, 1977), p. 614

51. *Shadowland*, p. 159

52. Ibid., p. 159

53. Ramsey Campbell, forward to the Gauntlet Press edition of *Shadowland*, p. 26

54. *Shadowland*, p. 291

Chapter Seven:

Floating Dragon

Floating Dragon was published in 1983 to strong sales and a mixed, often puzzled critical response, particularly from that hard-core horror audience for whom the book was chiefly intended. A baroque, unrestrained novel whose governing aesthetic is based on excess and the deliberate cultivation of the gaudy and the extreme, *Floating Dragon* is easily Straub's most controversial work, one that continues, to this day, to generate a divided response. Reviewing it in *Twilight Zone* magazine, Thomas M. Disch savaged the novel for what he perceived as its verbosity, its preposterousness, and its slapdash accumulation of genre clichés, while other genre reviewers took Straub to task for cynically exploiting the methods of his enormously popular contemporary, Stephen King. On the other hand, *Floating Dragon* won the 1983 British Fantasy Award for Best Novel, and has been cited by The Penguin Encyclopedia of Horror as Straub's finest achievement, a "haunting and compelling" work that "speaks of the unspeakable."[1] Straub's old friend Thomas Tessier may have come closer than anyone to capturing the book's peculiar flavor when, with typical acuity, he described it as, among many other things, "the largest sustained *jeu d'esprit* ever written."[2]

That is a useful and perceptive comment. For all its sustained savagery and its steadily intensifying presentation of an affluent community at the mercy of cruel and implacable forces, *Floating Dragon* is animated, in part, by its author's sense of play, and by his obvious pleasure in testing the accepted limits of the supernatural horror novel. Even more than in *Ghost Story,* where Straub's avowed intention was to take the classic elements of the form "as far as they would go,"[3] *Floating Dragon* pushes against the boundaries of good taste and polite literary tradition, goes too far at every opportunity, and has a wonderful time in the process. In this atmosphere of anarchic creative joy, nothing is withheld, suppressed, or saved for another book. As Straub later commented: "If I could think of it, I put it in the novel."[4] An unexpected result of all this creative extravagance was that, having come to the end of the book, Straub found that he had quite literally used up his capacity to write supernatural fiction of this sort and would be forced, from this point forward, to take his fiction in a wholly new direction. *Floating Dragon* is thus notable both for its own intrinsic qualities, and as a watershed moment in the ongoing evolution of its author.

In certain fundamental respects, *Floating Dragon* is reminiscent of both *Ghost Story* and *Shadowland.* Like *Ghost Story,* it is an account of a small, affluent town—Hampstead, Connecticut—besieged by supernatural forces and saved from destruction by the concerted efforts of an unlikely band of heroes. Like both earlier novels, it depicts a world dominated by illusion and by a sense of hallucinatory distortion, a world in which the very fabric of reality proves thin and insubstantial. *Floating Dragon* differs from its predecessors largely in matters of scale and intensity, in its sense of history, in the wider range of its vision of events, in its caustic commentary on the nature of the lives that lie hidden behind the facade of affluence, and in the depth of its focus on the vital but threatened institution of the family. In the world of *Floating Dragon,* families of all sorts—functional and dysfunctional, happy and unhappy, fractured and complete, real and fictional—stand at the heart of a complex design, struggling for survival against a disparate array of destructive forces.

We are introduced to the most powerful of those forces in a deliberately discursive prologue entitled "The Death of Stony Friedgood." Stony, a Hampstead resident married to a corporate executive named Leo Friedgood, is given to periodic adulteries which not only add a sense of adventure to her life, but help her to maintain the delicate balance of her marriage. On May 17, 1980—the day "the Dragon came to Patchin County"[5]—she picks up an unnamed man in a working-class bar called Franco's, and takes him home. Once there, the man accompanied Stony to her bedroom, undresses, and butchers her in her bed. Just before he kills her, the narrative point of view shifts, briefly and abruptly, and we see the world through the newly-awakened perspective of the murderer:

> You were dreaming for a long time and then you were not. You were asleep in a place you did not know, and when you were awakened you were someone else. You had a drink in your hand and a woman was looking at you and Dragon the world was yours again.[6]

Counterpointing the encounter between Stony and her killer is a brief sketch of the troubled family life of Tabby Smithfield, a young boy caught in the crossfire between his wealthy, possessive grandfather and his ne'er-do-well father, a tennis player without quite enough talent for a professional career. On January 6, 1971, while waiting in an airport lounge for a plane that will take him and his father to a new life in Florida, Tabby catches a precognitive glimpse of the murder of Stony Friedgood, nine years, four months, and eleven days before it happens.

A handful of other characters, all centrally connected both to the history of Hampstead and to its immediate future, are brought briefly into the frame of the prologue. Patsy McCloud, née Taylor, has recently returned to Hampstead in the company of her abusive husband Les, a corporate vice-president who has sacrificed his humanity to his ambition, making Patsy his primary victim in the process. Richard Allbee, former child star of a *Father Knows Best* style sitcom called *Daddy's Here,* is likewise returning to his childhood home after spending the last twelve years in England. Richard, who is accompanied by his pregnant wife, Laura, has long since given up acting and has built a second career restoring old, once beautiful houses that have fallen into disrepair. He has given up a burgeoning career in London so that his child—affectionately known as "Lump"—can be born on American soil. The last of the novel's major players is Graham Williams, an aging novelist who has spent most of his life in Hampstead, and is more familiar than anyone with its history, its secrets, and its recurring cycles of violence. Graham is also the secret narrator of the novel, and all of its many stories, however objectively presented, are filtered through his sensibility and organized by him into a complex but ultimately unified narrative.

Most of *Floating Dragon*'s central dramatic events arise out of the unexpected conjunction of specific elements. The simultaneous presence in Hampstead of Patsy McCloud, Graham Williams, Richard Allbee, and Tabby Smithfield—who has recently returned from Florida with his increasingly dissolute father—is the first of these conjunctions. Each of the four is a direct descendent of one of Hampstead's founding families, families that were intimately involved with the first known appearance of a mysterious and malign entity known as the Dragon. The Dragon has reappeared in Hampstead approximately once in every generation, causing varying degrees of destruction with each appearance. Of these four, two—Patsy and Tabby—are connected by a powerful psychic link. One—Graham Williams—has actually encountered the Dragon and defeated it in one of its earlier incarnations. All four, in their very different fashions, reflect or will come to reflect different aspects of the author's vision of the disintegrating family. In time, all of them will come together to form a loose but effective family unit of their own.

The second, and more mysterious, conjunction of events occurs, with exquisite timing, on May 17, 1980, the day of the Dragon's reemergence, of Richard Allbee's return, and of Stony Friedgood's murder. With an irony too great to be accidental, this second series of events involves Stony's cuckolded and slightly kinky husband, Leo. Leo Friedgood is an executive and troubleshooter for the Telpro Corporation, one of whose subsidiaries, Woodville Solvent, has just suffered a fatal and potentially incriminating industrial accident. Woodville Solvent is the innocuous designation of an experimental research center with tenuous and deniable connections to the Defense Department. Researchers at Woodville have been working for many months to refine and quantify the effects of an unstable new biological weapon with the portentous name of DRG-16. At the time of the accident, DRG-16 is still considered a "wildcard," a substance whose effects are unpredictable and only partially understood. On May 17, three Woodville employees die after being exposed to that substance, which is then accidentally vented into the atmosphere. Leo is then contacted by the head of the Special Weapons division, General Haugejas, and sent to Woodville to clean up the mess. This is what he finds when he arrives:

> Leo saw a room within a room, the top half of the inner room lined with glass.

> Stepping in behind Barbara, [his] attention was focused on the three bodies within the glass enclosure. The two farthest from him lay sprawled a few feet apart on a black floor. Their eyes were open, their mouths yawned. They had clean innocent dead faces...The third body in the glass chamber...had bloated. At first Leo thought the body had burst. Lathery white scum coated the hands. The man's head, a white sponge, had seemed to leak toward a drain in the center of the chamber's floor. It took Leo a moment to realize that the lather that had once been skin was moving. As he watched—his eyes incapable of shifting away—the froth of the head crawled into the drain.[7]

This third corpse, all that remains of a research scientist named Tom Gay, is the earliest example of one of DRG-16's more spectacular side effects. Gay, in the terminology that will eventually emerge, is a Leaker—a man whose skin has completely lost its connective integrity and has literally liquefied. In time, as DRG-16 takes hold, Leakers will become commonplace sights on the streets of Hampstead, and in the surrounding areas of Patchin County. For now, however, the late Tom Gay is just another problem to be solved, and Leo Friedgood solves it. He disposes of the liquefied corpse, stages an impromptu press conference in which the two remaining deaths are attributed to carbon monoxide poisoning, completely covers up the Telpro Corporation's involvement in the incident, and returns to Hampstead to find the mutilated body of his wife waiting in his bed.

By this point in the narrative, all major conjunctions have occurred and all key elements are in place. Straub's account of the destruction of Hampstead—an account at once haunting, horrifying and even, at times, grotesquely beautiful—is ready to begin. As noted, the author of that account is Graham Williams, who is himself one of the novel's major participants, but whose reconstruction of events extends well beyond the limits of his first hand experience. Graham, of course, is a novelist, and brings a novelist's resources to the task at hand, alternating between a first-person, eyewitness viewpoint and an omniscient, third-person narrative stitched together from conversations, journal entries, interviews, newspaper accounts, historical research and, in keeping with the narrator's novelistic background, the occasional imaginative leap.

Straub's skillful deployment of this various, constantly shifting perspective, which gives *Floating Dragon* both its range of emotional effect and its impressively varied level of supporting detail, owes much to the influence of the late, unjustly neglected British novelist, Paul Scott. Scott (1916-1987) is best known as the author of *The Raj Quartet,* a magisterial series of novels depicting the last years of British rule in India, whose individual volumes include *The Jewel in the Crown, The Day of the Scorpion, The Towers of Silence,* and *A Division of the Spoils.* And though *Floating Dragon* is, in many respects, the least "literary" of Straub's recent novels—i.e. the least beholden to the works of specific authors and specific literary traditions—Scott's influence, particularly his fluid and dexterous manipulation of point of view, proved both liberating and pervasive. Commenting on this influence, Straub notes:

> Part of what dazzled me about Paul Scott was the surprising and beautiful way he shifted the narrative point of view, moving from the mind of one character to a sort of tender, nostalgic, omniscient pov, then to a different third-person pov centered on the steady flow of perceptions going on in one character's mind, then into a more authoritative, historian-like omniscience, then to sections made of letters or official documents, after that to a conversation between minor league, third-level comic figures which either directly or obliquely refers to the great events at the center of everything...There are brief bursts of internal monologue. There is sometimes a deliberately disjointed quality. Most of the narrative is third-person, but now and then...slides into first-person, from the pov of someone connected to the situation, centrally or not. This lovely, constant movement all but made my head spin around with pleasure and awe.[8]

That sense of "lovely, constant movement" is one of the hallmarks of *Floating Dragon*'s narrative method, as Graham Williams moves swiftly and gracefully from one narrative position to another, offering us a kaleidoscopic series of perspectives that cumulatively illuminate the summer of 1980, when a Dragon by the name of Gideon Winter returned once more to Hampstead.

The story, as Graham presents it, proceeds along three distinct but intertwining lines. First, there is the overarching story of Hampstead itself, of the way the town changes under the relentless pressure of events. This larger story is composed of literally dozens of smaller ones, ranging from quick vignettes to extended set pieces filled with spectacle and a hallucinatory grandeur. Then there are the independent, ultimately interconnected stories of the four principal characters: Richard Allbee, Patsy McCloud, Graham Williams, and Tabby Smithfield. Finally, there are a number of historical accounts which indicate that some form of Hampstead's present plight has recurred with almost monotonous regularity since the area was first settled in 1645.

In that year, the original settlers—settlers whose names included Green (Richard's family), Tayler (Patsy's), Smith (Tabby's), and Williams—encountered a charismatic Englishman named Gideon Winter. While many of the specific details remain unknown, records indicate that, within a relatively short period, Gideon Winter came to own much of the land in what would eventually become Patchin County. Birth records from that time also indicate the possibility that this charming newcomer had seduced and impregnated a number of the settler's wives, most of whom had lost their earlier children under mysterious circumstances, and who would ultimately give birth to other children with names like Darkness, Eventide, and Sorrow. In time, for these and other reasons no doubt lost to history, the founding families banded together and murdered Gideon Winter, whom they called "the Dragon," the Biblical personification of pure evil. Then they buried him in an unmarked grave on a spit of land called Point Winter, which would later be rechristened Kendall Point. That murder marked the beginning of the recurring cycles of violence and destruction that have haunted the area since.

From that point forward, at intervals of approximately thirty years, the Dragon has returned to the scene of his murder, repeatedly taking possession of the mind and body of a local resident, and using that body as a base of operations for his ongoing assault on the citizens of

Hampstead. Once, the Dragon returned as a fisherman named Bates Krell, who was responsible for the murders of several local women before he was discovered and destroyed by the twenty-year-old Graham Williams. Once, he took possession of a lawyer named John Sayre, who retained a strong enough sense of himself to commit suicide before submitting to the Dragon's power. Once, he even returned as a woman. Each of his returns has been accompanied by periods of murder and atrocity. Many, in keeping with the nature of dragons, have been accompanied by fire, while others have resulted in acts of inexplicable natural disaster, such as the incident in 1811 in which the ground opened up and swallowed the entire congregation of the Greenbank Congregational Church. The worst of his visitations occurred in 1873, the legendary "Black Summer"[9] which began with a fire in a local cotton mill and ended with the population of Hampstead cut, quite literally, in half. The Dragon's strength had been mysteriously augmented that summer by the simultaneous presence of members of all four founding families, a circumstance which has repeated itself in the summer of 1980.

During the course of this summer, under the combined effects of the newly resurgent Dragon and the wild card element called DRG-16, Hampstead begins to come apart. Gideon Winter finds a new host in Dr. Wren Van Horne, the town's most prominent gynecologist, who kicks off the summer's activities with the murder of Stony Friedgood. A number of similar murders follow, together with a number of apparently unrelated phenomena. Traffic deaths and heart attacks proliferate. Dead birds begin falling from the sky. Normally respectable citizens engage in bizarre and unlikely forms of behavior: brawling, painting their homes in pastel colors, exposing themselves to local school children. As reality gradually fractures, voices speak from trees and bushes, the dead walk, a bat made entirely of fire becomes visible in the night sky over Hampstead, and Richard Allbee, the former child actor, experiences repeated, and sinister, encounters with his long dead fellow cast members from *Daddy's Here*.

Perhaps the most disturbing manifestation of the crisis in Hampstead is the sudden appearance of "the Lemming Effect,"[10] in which both animals and small children turn suddenly and inexplicably suicidal, throwing themselves in front of moving vehicles and drowning themselves in the waters of Long Island Sound. In the face of these and countless other catastrophic forces, traditional sources of protection prove not only useless, but intensely vulnerable. At one point, the

Hampstead Fire Department is called to the scene of an apparent case of arson on Mill Lane, a fashionable and high-priced residential area known as "Shrinks' Row." Within minutes of their arrival, all of the firemen, both from Hampstead and the adjacent village of Old Sarum, are dead, incinerated by what appear to be thousands of baby dragons, floating in the smoke above the cluster of burning homes. Later in the novel, over one hundred Patchin County policemen come together at a local theater for the Second Annual All Police Screening of *The Choirboys*, an evening intended for drinking beer, raising hell, and blowing off accumulated steam. Instead, something very different happens. The images unrolling on the screen begin to shift, offering new images tailored to the vulnerabilities of the individual viewers. As Graham Williams later learns:

> No two had seen the same thing, but after the first few minutes, none had seen *The Choirboys*. Some had seen their wives and daughters making love with other cops, a few had seen their children's bodies pulled from the gentle surf on Gravesend Beach. A cop named Ron Rice had seen something like a sea monster—a huge underwater reptile with a wide savage mouth—swimming along and biting children in half, tearing their bodies apart and turning the water red. Most saw dead people moving as though they were alive...Many of them saw the drowned children and were chilled by their white cold faces.[11]

In the ensuing panic, someone draws a gun and fires at the screen, killing a young policeman named Larry Wiak, and then, in the words of one of the survivors, "all the guys went stone crazy."[12] "A hundred exuberant cops [become] a hundred hysterics waving pistols,"[13] and, by the evening's end, sixty-eight policemen are dead, victims of the lethal series of illusions that has become the dominant element of life in Hampstead.

Elsewhere in Hampstead, similar distortions prevail. Graham Williams and Richard Allbee are imprisoned in Graham's kitchen by an impossibly large dog that appears out of nowhere. The head of a dragon emerges from the pages of a locally published history of Patchin

County. A young policeman named Royce Griffin gazes into a mirror once owned by Gideon Winter, and loses his hold on reality. (In *Floating Dragon*, as in *Ghost Story*, mirrors are dangerous and untrustworthy objects. Within days of his encounter with the Dragon's mirror, Royce is dead, having killed himself after a particularly gruesome hallucination in which he believes he has defecated hundreds of tiny red spiders.) An elderly Hampstead matron named Hilda du Plessy gazes into that same mirror and is driven first to madness, then to death, by what she sees:

> Something was *happening* inside that mirror, she saw. A face flickered in the gloom of the long corridor. She saw a hand; eyes; teeth. Then she saw this little section of Main Street rotting and decayed, the buildings shuttered, the canopies ripped into flags, garbage blowing onto the steps...Now from within this decaying scene, Dr. Van Horne regarded her. His ears hung below his jaw, his eyebrows twisted into peaks, his nose was a curved beak. His teeth came to points. Hilda screamed without knowing she was going to do it, and found she could not stop.[14]

The message that Hilda reads in that mirror—the message that Gideon Winter has left there for her, and all of Hampstead, to see—concerns the triumph of death, the ultimate primacy of rot and decay. Roughly translated, the message is: Look on me, and despair. Within this atmosphere of induced despair, and against a backdrop of violence, derangement, and increasing disorder, the lives of Graham, Patsy, Richard, and Tabby gradually intersect, both with each other and with the larger pattern currently playing itself out on the streets of their hometown.

Before subjecting them to the rigors of their confrontation with the Dragon, Straub enters deeply into the world of his four central characters, and shows us, with sympathy and precision, the exact conditions of their lives. Of the four, Richard Allbee has come the closest to achieving both happiness and a sense of fulfillment, and his happiness is based on the bedrock principles of love, meaningful work, and a hard-won sense of his proper place in the world. Beneath the culture shock and transitory stresses of his relocation from England, Richard has assembled the elements of a worthwhile life: he loves his wife, is about to become a father, and has found his true calling in the restoration of beautiful, decaying structures. In a sense, Richard's relationship to the "rotting beauties"[15] he restores is not unlike Straub's own relationship with the Gothic literary form.

> He had worked on a dozen large houses in London, starting with his own, and had built a reputation based on care, exactness, and hard work. He took a deep satisfaction in bringing these absurd Victorian and Edwardian structures back to life. What showed in his work was that the man behind it understood where the beauty in such houses lay and knew how to make it shine again. Richard had put himself to school to the buildings an earlier generation had dismissed as monstrosities, and in a short time, guided by an instinct he had not known was his, had learned their secrets.[16]

Of course, having constructed this worthwhile, ultimately fragile life, Richard has more to lose than any of his fellow descendants, and he loses it all with startling, savage abruptness. Returning home from an abortive assignment in Providence, Rhode Island, Richard discovers the dead and mutilated bodies of his wife and unborn daughter, the fourth (and fifth) victims in the series of murders that began with Stony Friedgood. In the devastating aftermath of that discovery, Richard struggles desperately to sustain himself with work and ritual. In the end, he is saved both by his surrogate family and by his discovery of a larger purpose: the destruction of the Dragon.

Sixteen-year-old Tabby Smithfield's life has been marked by a similar pattern of loss and rediscovered purpose. At the age of six, Tabby loses his mother to a drunken auto accident. Shortly afterward, he loses both his grandfather and his familiar place in the world when his father relocates to Florida, where Tabby acquires, and ultimately loses, a goodhearted stepmother named Sherri. In time, following the death of his wealthy, autocratic grandfather, Tabby returns to Hampstead—a town in which families rarely seem to flourish and whose divorce rate is a frequent subject of local humor—where he loses his father twice: once to the effects of alcohol and neglect, and once to the Dragon, who descends on his father in the form of a fire bat, and burns him to death. Like Richard, Tabby is saved from the effect of his losses by discovering his place in the spiritual family that has assembled around him in Hampstead, and by discovering his place in the ongoing story of Gideon Winter and his endless quest for vengeance.

One of the major themes that emerges from Tabby Smithfield's story is that of parental responsibility. Straub's indictment of Clark Smithfield's conduct of his life, and of his failure to be a father to his son, is clear and direct, and is a theme that Straub will revisit in several subsequent works, such as *Koko, Mystery,* and the novella, "Blue Rose." "Happiness," in Clark's view, "can't buy money,"[17] and, in keeping with that philosophy, he has returned to his old home town to drink up his inheritance and indulge his various desires, while leaving his son to his own confused and often impulsive devices. In the end, *Floating Dragon* is as much about small cruelties and distorted values—about modern civilization and its manifold discontents—as it is about the overtly horrific result of the convergence of Gideon Winter with DRG-16.

Patsy McCloud is another victim of quotidian, nonsupernatural abuse. Patsy, the granddaughter of a powerful psychic with the unenviable ability to foresee the deaths of those around her, has inherited at least a portion of her grandmother's gifts, and they have brought her neither pleasure nor satisfaction. She buries these gifts to the best of her abilities, and eventually settles into a loveless marriage with an ambitious young executive named Les McCloud, a marriage in which all true feeling is quickly sacrificed to the overriding dictates of Les' career.

> After they married in 1964, they lived in Hartford, New York City, Chicago, London, Los Angeles, and were transferred back to New York. They bought their home in Hampstead, and Les commuted to New York to, as he put it, "burn ass." Now they never spoke of anything personal. Les, in fact, rarely spoke to her at all. He had started to beat her in Chicago, after his first

> really significant promotion had followed the best efficiency reports of his career.[18]

Straub's investigation of this loveless relationship, in which beatings soon become the only point of contact, physical or otherwise, between Patsy and her husband, is central to the novel's underlying concern with the power of distorted values. Ultimately, Patsy realizes

> that if she never went back to Les McCloud she would not miss him. Les was like someone who had died and was pretending life: no one had killed him, he had killed himself: he had murdered his feelings and intuition and his generosity because he thought his company demanded it.[19]

Just before his death—in a flaming car crash directly connected to the increasing level of violence that is plaguing Hampstead—Les himself experiences brief intimations of his own sad and essentially pathetic nature. Sitting in a bar at the end of a long, bad day, Les listens attentively to a neighbor's emotional account of the recent "suicide" of his cat. At the end of the story, Les smiles, leans forward, and says to the man: "Get stuffed,"[20] a remark which improves his mood enormously, though only for a moment.

> He lifted [his glass] and took a sip of the malt whiskey. As he was appreciating its velvety smoothness, however, an uncomfortable thought penetrated his defenses. If he was such a success, why did he get such pleasure from telling a dork to get stuffed?[21]

Once freed from the small daily horrors of her marriage, Patsy, with the aid of her new, extended family, finds a kind of redemption in her struggle against the larger horrors that surround her. More than any of the other characters, Patsy quite literally transcends herself, moving from a state of abysmal victimization to what, by the novel's end, can only be considered a state of grace.

Finally, there is Graham Williams, who is both narrator and participant, and who may be the novel's greatest living authority on the nature and history of the Dragon. At the time of these events, Graham is seventy-six years old, childless, and twice divorced. He has written over a dozen novels, along with several screenplays and a well regarded memoir about his alcoholic past. He has also survived the attention of the House Un-American Activities committee under Joe McCarthy. In addition to all this, Graham has one great accomplishment to his credit: In 1924, at the age of twenty, he identified and destroyed the current incarnation of Gideon Winter, a fisherman named Bates Krell.

As Graham tells it, his instinctive recognition of the evil embodied by Bates Krell was the single indisputable psychic experience of his life, and it led directly to his single indisputable encounter with the miraculous. After mysteriously "recognizing" Krell, following him at a distance, even sneaking aboard his boat in search of corroborating evidence, Graham received an invitation to accompany his quarry on a lobster run, and rashly accepted. Once out to sea, Krell attacked him with a fisherman's gaff, while Graham was forced to defend himself with an eight inch wooden pin. And then someone, or something, miraculously intervened. The eight inch pin became a shining sword and Graham, in a moment of "crazy radiance,"[22] cut the fisherman in two, bringing the cycle of violence to one more temporary end.

Listening to that story some fifty-six years later, Tabby—who has observed a great deal this summer and who knows what no one else in Hampstead knows: that Wren Van Horne is the latest repository of Gideon Winter's spirit—decides to follow Graham's example, and beard the Dragon in his den. Accompanied by Patsy, who intuitively understands his unspoken plans, he breaks into the Van Horne house, where he is captured and carried away through the Dragon's enchanted mirror. Richard, Graham and Patsy then set out to rescue him, and that rescue attempt precipitates the novel's final, extravagant confrontation.

Stepping through a doorway that suddenly appears in the cellar wall of Bates Krell's deserted old house, they travel down an underground passageway filled with threatening figures from their own past lives: Joe McCarthy, Les McCloud, the ubiquitous cast members of *Daddy's Here,* even Michael Allbee, the absentee father whom Richard has never known. Moving stubbornly ahead, they emerge at last onto the final battleground of Kendall Point, site of the Dragon's burial more than three hundred years before.

There, in a moment of inspired lunacy, they consolidate their sense of unity by singing aloud. The song they choose is the theme song from *Daddy's Here:* "When the Red Red Robin Comes Bob Bob Bobbin' Along."[23] Strengthened by the mystical power of music, by a heightened sense of their common purpose, and—most importantly—by an infusion of psychic energy that passes directly from Patsy's mind and into his, Richard engages the Dragon in battle. The shotgun he has carried with him does, in fact, become a sword and, like the young Graham Williams, Richard rises above himself as he wields it, striking the Dragon with "the strongest backhand of his life,"[24] and destroying him/it in a literal rain of fire.

And that, save for an epilogue entitled "After the Moon," is the story. In the course of this epilogue, which speaks of healing, continuity, and resurrected possibilities, Richard Allbee adopts Tabby Smithfield, Graham completes "the excellent book called *Floating Dragon*,"[25] and Patsy moves away from Hampstead, and either does or does not marry a lawyer named Arthur Powers from Chappaqua, New York. (Patsy's destiny, like her newly discovered sense of self, remains fundamentally unknowable. By the novel's end, she is simply gone, having removed herself to a new and unlocatable region.) Most significantly, Richard eventually remarries and fathers a son, an event which prompts Patsy to contact him from whatever realm she currently inhabits. "You've done a great thing,"[26] she tells him. "We did a great thing once," he replies. And then the novel ends on the triumphant note implicit in these words from the Book of Revelations: "And he laid hold on the dragon, that old serpent, which is the devil, and bound him for a thousand years."[27]

Floating Dragon mingles emotional intensity with hallucinatory spectacle in a manner more consistently over the top than anything Straub had attempted before. The risk inherent in this approach—a risk that Straub assumes with confidence and an almost palpable sense of narrative authority—is that of inducing a kind of overload in the reader, a deadening of the ability to respond appropriately to the almost endless flow of violent and bizarre images. For the most part, though—and this is a viewpoint with which many of the book's more hostile readers will take issue—Straub brings off an almost impossible task with passion, artistry, and control.

More than any of his other books, *Floating Dragon* is structured as a series of escalating, powerfully sustained set pieces, any one of which would stand as high points in the work of lesser novelists. A partial listing of these set pieces would include: the wild night of *The Choirboys* screening, when local police departments are literally gutted by the forces of hysteria and mass hallucination; the collapse and death of Royce Griffin, the policeman whose grasp of reality begins gradually to unravel following his glimpse into the mirror in Wren Van Horne's living room; the death of Leo Friedgood, who, with exquisite irony, has become a "Leaker" and who spends his last, libidinous hours indulging his voyeuristic impulses in the sex-for-sale venues of New York's 42nd Street; Graham Williams' account of the miraculous destruction of Bates Krell; the last hours of Les McCloud, who goes to his death on a rising tide of alcohol, bitterness, and DRG induced hallucinations; the underground journey from Bates Krell's house to Kendall Point; and, of course, the final climactic battle in which a very real dragon is defeated by the combined forces of love, music, and a mysterious, unnamed power.

Floating Dragon derives much of its own power from the care with which Straub connects even his most extravagant inventions to the more commonplace world of human responsibilities and human concerns. The most dramatic of these connections comes, of course, from the conjunction of DRG-16 with the latest visitation of Gideon Winter. The reasons behind this conjunction remain deliberately unclear, and may be the result of chance, of design, of some unknown dimension of Gideon Winter's power, or of some natural affinity arising from the ironic similarity of names. Whatever the reasons, the addition of this wild card element provides the novel with one of its most distinctive elements: that sense of a fluid, infinitely malleable reality against which the activities of that other dragon are played out to such disturbing, even haunting, effect. As the story progresses, it becomes increasingly difficult to determine just which of the two linked forces are responsible for a particular atrocity. The devil is never permitted to assume full responsibility for the devastation of Hampstead. Human actions, in the form of reckless experimentation, ecological irresponsibility, and military and governmental arrogance, are bound up inextricably with Gideon Winter and his works.

Floating Dragon is, of course, very much concerned with evil in the broadest, most Biblical sense. But finally, beneath its gaudy surface and its cruelly elaborate funhouse effects, the evil that comes to Hampstead on such a regular basis is stupid and limited, which is to say: fundamentally unimaginative. So many of the things that happen in this latest Black Summer are extensions, or perverse reflections, of tendencies that are very much a part of day-to-day life in Patchin County. As the epigraph from Frederick K. Price reminds us: "The devil is a dumb spirit. All the devil knows is what you tell him with your own big fat mouth."[28] In a very real sense, Hampstead under the Dragon's influence is merely Hampstead writ large, its worst aspects ratified and extended, its gentler aspects trampled underfoot. The end result of all this is a world given over to chaos and disorder, a world that is devoid of love, joy, or grace. Beyond its affluent facade, Hampstead, even without the hyperbolic aftereffects of biological weapons and ghostly revenants, hides more than its share of greed, lovelessness, and overweening ambition, and houses more than its share of civilized monsters who abuse their spouses, mistreat their neighbors, and ignore their most fundamental responsibilities: their children. Beneath the violence, the horror, and the relentless melodrama of the supernatural, *Floating Dragon* never loses sight of its real world correlatives, and this intensely maintained double focus accounts for much of its capacity to move and to illuminate, even as it dazzles us with outrageous and extraordinary visions.

In the end, even more than most novels of horror and the supernatural, *Floating Dragon* is also a novel about mystery, about our relationship to the nameless forces that govern so much of our lives. As the history of Gideon Winter makes clear, within everything that is known, there is much that is unknown, and possibly unknowable. The story of the Dragon goes all the way back to the seventeenth century, and a large number of stories, legends, and descriptive details have accumulated in that time. But virtually nothing is known about his origins, his essential nature, or the source and scope of his powers. At one point, a feisty local reporter named Sarah Spry even suggests that the cycles of violence associated with the Dragon might be a fundamental element of the land itself, predating the existence of all human inhabitants.

> ...she knew that if she looked back onto the records she would find the pattern repeating and repeating itself, going back as far as the records themselves went...and before that, in a time when man did not inhabit the Connecticut coast, did the animals insanely attack and kill one another, bear against bear and wolf against wolf, every thirty years?[29]

The idea that Gideon Winter may have represented the first human manifestation of an ancient and implacable power is as valid as any other, but it remains simply one more interpretation of events, unproved and unproveable.

Then, too, there is evidence of another sort of power, one that shows itself only on rare and extreme occasions: the power that transformed an eight inch wooden pin into a sword in 1924, then transformed Graham Williams into a man capable of wielding that sword; that performed a similar feat for Richard Allbee in 1980, before fading away into silence and mystery. Years later, walking with his newborn son down the streets of Paris, Richard concludes: "If some malevolent power had given him the summer of 1980, other forces had given him this."[30] Straub never attempts to name those forces, nor does he attempt to explain or define them, or connect them in any way to conventional religious beliefs. He merely lets us know that they are there, lurking enigmatically beneath the surface of the visible world.

Its extravagance, its passion, and its stubborn determination to summarize and encompass everything its author understood about the nature of the supernatural horror novel have made *Floating Dragon* one of the unique and frequently misunderstood books in the recent history of horror literature. Nevertheless, it continues to find an audience, and seems destined to outlive the carpings of its original critics. Commenting on the novel some seventeen years after its initial appearance, Straub continues to regard it with affection and a justifiable pride.

> I know what I did [in writing *Floating Dragon*] and I know what it cost to do it. I'll never try to write another book like it, for the same reason I'll never write another *Shadowland*. I am far too aware that both of these novels are deeply flawed, but I'm also aware that a similar spirit propels them, and that the spirit in question [is] recklessly expansive and generously, wildly exploratory.[31]

More than five years would pass before the next solo expression of Straub's exploratory spirit, *Koko*, would see print. Before that, however, one more long-standing commitment remained to be met: a much publicized, much anticipated collaboration with the world's most popular novelist: Stephen King.

[1] *The Penguin Encyclopedia of Horror and the Supernatural*, edited by Jack Sullivan (New York, Viking Press, 1986), p. 408

[2] Thomas Tessier, Afterword to the Gauntlet Press edition of *Shadowland*, p. 598

[3] *Ghost Story*, dust jacket material

[4] Letter from Peter Straub to the author

[5] *Floating Dragon* (New York, G. P. Putnam's Sons, 1983), p. 21

[6] Ibid., P. 26

[7] Ibid., p. 43

[8] Letter from Peter Straub to the author

[9] *Floating Dragon*, p. 220

[10] Ibid., p. 207

[11] Ibid., p. 353

[12] Ibid., p. 353

[13] Ibid., p. 348

[14] Ibid., p. 159

[15] Ibid., p. 61

[16] Ibid., pp. 61-62

[17] Ibid., p. 372

[18] Ibid., p. 113

[19] Ibid., p. 150

[20] Ibid., p. 207

[21] Ibid., p. 208

[22] Ibid., p. 425

[23] Ibid., p. 486

[24] Ibid., p. 495

[25] Ibid., p. 512

[26] Ibid., p. 515

[27] Ibid., p. 515

[28] Ibid., epigraph

[29] Ibid., p. 295

[30] Ibid., p. 512

[31] Letter from Peter Straub to the author

Chapter Eight:
The Talisman

In 1966 or 1967, while still an undergraduate at the University of Maine's Orono campus, Stephen King conceived and began an intriguing little story fragment called "Verona Beach." This fragment concerned a woman—a failed actress—living with her son in a deserted resort hotel on the Atlantic seacoast. The woman is dying, and the story, if completed, would have examined the day-to-day realities of this situation while focusing on the son's desperate desire to prevent his mother's death. Eventually, King abandoned the story because, as he later stated, "I wasn't capable of handling it at that time."[1] Years later, in 1980, the idea resurfaced during a conversation with Peter Straub and, after some crucial modifications, became the basis for their mammoth, perennially popular collaboration, *The Talisman.*

The idea of a collaboration between these two different and distinctive figures had its origin in their very first face-to-face encounter, which took place in London in 1977. At the time, Straub was still a London resident while King, who had yet to settle on a permanent home, had just arrived in England for an extended visit. According to Straub, King arrived "in sections, like a caterpillar:"

> First, his wife, mother-in-law and new baby, at a party in my agent's office. I remember a vast crowd, a fog of smoke, cheap wine, a crazy meal in a Greek restaurant—also Tabitha King's wit and intelligence. Then a series of telephone calls from the man himself, first from Maine and

> then from London hotels, as we tried to arrange a meeting. It was raining, and he couldn't find a cab. When he did find one, the driver didn't want to come all the way north to Crouch End...Finally, we made an afternoon appointment at the bar in Brown's Hotel, the most English and restrained, the most Agatha Christie-like, of London hotels.[2]

There, over drinks and during the course of a conversation that included comments on the exorbitant British taxation policy currently in force ("Like any writer I knew," Straub notes, "he talked a lot about money"[3]), King asked Straub if he would like to consider collaborating on a novel. The conversation was resumed, a week or so later, during a dinner party at the Straub house. The two agreed that, yes, the prospect of collaborating was an exciting one, but would have to be delayed for some years until a number of contractual obligations had been met. Still, the idea had been put forward and, over the course of time, gradually took hold.

The project, as King has noted, became "a little more serious"[4] as the dialogue continued at various fantasy conventions over the next few years. A major breakthrough occurred when King sold the paperback rights to *Danse Macabre*, his nonfictional reflection on the place of horror in popular culture, to Berkeley Books, giving the two novelists a common publisher and eliminating many of the larger logistical difficulties at a stroke. In 1980, following Straub's return to America after a decade abroad, a storyline based on a modified version of the "Verona Beach" scenario began to emerge, with ideas and details added to the mix whenever time and circumstances permitted. In the spring of 1982, with *Floating Dragon* still only two-thirds written, King and Straub got together in Westport, Connecticut for an intense joint planning session that resulted in the creation of a detailed, ultimately unwieldy outline that would, before the end, be halved, and then halved again, in order to keep the already long and complex narrative within publishable limits. In 1982, with *Floating Dragon* completed and all other commitments met, the actual process of writing *The Talisman* finally began.

For the majority of the writing, the two authors worked from their respective homes, each, in turn, taking up a narrative thread and carrying it forward to a logical, but unspecified, stopping point. The completed pages would then be transmitted, via modems attached to compatible word processors, to whichever writer was currently on deck, at which point the process would start all over again. The bulk of the manuscript was written to this repetitive, systolic/diastolic rhythm, supplemented by the occasional face-to-face strategic conference. (One of these, a lengthy working session which took place on Thanksgiving Day in 1982, was the occasion for the final, ruthless streamlining of the overly ambitious outline, and would be fondly memorialized by both authors as "The Great Thanksgiving Putsch."[5])

As the story neared completion, the rhythm of the collaboration changed. King and Straub came together at King's summer home on Lake Kezar, Maine, for what Straub described as "one of the greatest experiences of my life, an extended period of blissful concentration...when King and I literally took turns at the keyboard and spurred ourselves on, each marveling at what the other was doing."[6] Finally, with a completed manuscript in hand, each writer undertook to edit and revise the sections written by the other. That, too, according to Straub, was a rewarding, surprisingly benevolent experience. Throughout the actual writing, he remembers, each one

> accepted whatever the other guy did...Then in the final editing, we each took a free hand with the other's stuff. And there were times when I wished we could have done the whole book that way, because it was a wonderful and profound experience, and something very few writers ever get the chance to have. It's like having an X-ray of someone's mind when you review his material that way.[7]

Finally, after a protracted, cumulatively exhausting creative effort that ended nearly seven years after the initial suggestion in the bar of Brown's Hotel, *The Talisman* was published—to an atmosphere of intense anticipation—in the fall of 1984.

Critical response, unsurprisingly, ran the proverbial gamut. *Publisher's Weekly* praised the book for its suspense, energy, and imaginative warmth. *Newsweek,* on the other hand, published a gratuitously insulting interview/review which not only panned the book, but stopped just short of vilifying its authors as commercial parasites. In the end, reviews—whether good or bad—had little to do with the novel's performance in the marketplace. People wanted to read *The Talisman* and they did, in record-breaking numbers. An initial printing of 900,000 copies swept into bookstores in November of that year, and *The Talisman* immediately proceeded to dominate the nation's bestseller lists. Fourteen years later, the novel not only remains popular but appears, from the evidence, to occupy a special position in the affections of many of its readers. Looking back on the book from his current, and considerably altered, aesthetic perspective, Straub notes that

> I've never known quite what to make of the book since [its original publication]. It was so unlike anything I'd ever done and so much of it was King's. I loved certain passages in that book, while others, as often or even more often mine as...his, didn't seem to come off to me. Almost all of the reviewers lambasted it. Later on, I found that many readers cherished it and had taken it to heart, which helped to reconcile me to what we had done.[8]

What they had done, in *The Talisman,* was to create an odd and uneven amalgam of road novel, Bildungsroman, and heroic fantasy. The result is an eccentric hybrid of a book that is frequently vital and moving, and occasionally attenuated and overlong. It is also, in its reliance on myth, magic, and the trappings of traditional quest literature, deeply uncharacteristic of the works of either of its authors, and seems particularly uncharacteristic of Straub. Unlike King, who would return to this sort of unabashed fantasy in works like *The Eyes of the Dragon* and the ongoing series of *Dark Tower* novels, Straub's only subsequent use of heroic fantasy would come, many years later, in *The Hellfire Club,* where it enters the novel in a more typically Straubian fashion: in the form of a book, an imaginary fantasy novel that has a profound and lifelong effect on the lives of a number of characters. The fantasy elements of *The Talisman*, by contrast, are naked and unfiltered, untouched by the distancing effect of literary devices, and the story that they help to tell is, at bottom, straightforward and almost classically simple.

As *The Talisman* begins, a twelve-year-old boy named Jack Sawyer is standing on a deserted stretch of beach in New Hampshire, "looking out at the steady Atlantic."[9] Jack's life, we soon discover, has been recently and violently disrupted. His father, a Hollywood agent named Phil Sawyer, has been shot to death in a hunting accident; his mother, a former second-rank movie actress named Lily Cavanaugh—AKA The Queen of the Bs—is mysteriously ill and possibly dying, and has retreated with Jack to this remote New Hampshire resort to console herself in a setting filled with pleasant personal memories, and to escape from the harassment of her husband's former partner, an avaricious entrepreneur named Morgan Sloat. In the opening pages, Jack moves listlessly through a world filled with ominous, inexplicable signs: a rainbow that appears and disappears over the roof of his hotel; a weathervane that seems to fly; a disembodied voice crying "Come to me;"[10] a funnel that opens in the sand and speaks, in a familiar voice, about his mother's death. In the midst of all this escalating strangeness, Jack makes an unexpected friend: an old black man named Speedy Parker who works as a repairman at a local amusement park. Speedy invites Jack—whom he pointedly rechristens Travelin' Jack—to his hole-in-the-wall of an office. There, hanging on a wall and surrounded by a constellation of overripe centerfolds, Jack finds a picture that speaks, directly, to his most secret self:

> It too was a photograph; and it too seemed to reach out for him, as if it were three-dimensional. A long, grassy plain of a particular, aching green unfurled toward a low, ground-down range of mountains. Above the plain and the mountains ranged a deeply transparent sky. Jack could very nearly smell the freshness of the landscape. He knew that place. He had never been there, not really, but he knew it. That was one of the places of The Daydreams.[11]

Speedy has a name for the place in that photograph, a place that Jack has known since early childhood and has always thought of as The Daydreams. Speedy calls it "the Territories,"[12] and he has much to say to Jack about the nature of that place; about its relationship to our own world; and about the dramas unfolding simultaneously in both. He also has a job for Jack—a quest—whose outcome will determine both the fate of Jack's mother and the related fates of the interconnected worlds through which Jack must travel.

The Territories, as described by Speedy Parker and then elaborated on as the novel progresses, is a parallel world adjacent to our own, the first, perhaps, in an infinite series of parallel worlds—what Jack comes to think of as "the Territories' Territories" or the "Daydreams' Daydreams."[13] It is an agrarian society, primitive and utterly devoid of technology, animated more by the principles of magic than of science. It is smaller than, and roughly analogous to, our own world, and contains within its borders numerous distorted reflections of the people, places, and things that populate our own society. A hotel in this world becomes a castle in the Territories; an amusement park becomes a rural county fair. Many of the people from the "real" world also have doppelgangers of a sort in the Territories. They are called "Twinners" and, for the most part, they lead autonomous existences that never intersect directly with their real world counterparts. (There are, however, exceptions. Morgan Sloat, who was educated in the nature and idiosyncrasies of the Territories by Jack's late father, has established a corrupt alliance with his own Twinner, Morgan of Orris, and has become a man of power in the Territories.)

Jack himself is uniquely "single-natured"—able to flip back and forth between worlds even though he has no Twinner in the Territories. (His own Twinner, Jason de Loessian, was murdered in infancy, just as Jack himself was very nearly murdered.) Jack's mother, however, does have a Twinner, a figure of enormous significance in the Territories: Queen Laura de Loessian. The queen, like Lily Cavanaugh (The Queen of the Bs), is dying, and her death will provide Morgan Sloat and his counterpart with the opportunity to consolidate their power by importing into the Territories the most advanced examples of twentieth century weaponry. According to Speedy, there is only one chance to prevent the deaths of Lily Cavanaugh and Laura de Loessian and, by extension, the ultimate deaths of the endless chain of interconnected worlds: Jack must travel from New Hampshire to the West Coast—"to the other ocean"[14]—where he must locate and retrieve a magical device—a Talisman—from the "scary place, the bad place"[15] in which it has been hidden for many years. He must then return with the Talisman to the East Coast and use its power both to heal his mother and to eliminate the threat of corruption that Morgan and his Twinner represent. As Speedy tells Jack in his gravelly, blues singer's voice:

> "Talisman be given unto your hand, Travelin' Jack. Not too big, not too small, she looks just like a crystal ball. Travelin' Jack, ole Travelin' Jack, you be goin' to California to bring her back. But here's your problem, here's your cross: drop her, Jack, and all be lost."[16]

Jack accepts the terms of this quest and sets out immediately from New Hampshire (whose last syllable, as Tolkien fans will no doubt recognize, is the word "shire") for California, traveling sometimes in the Territories, sometimes in the "real" world. (Jack's dormant ability to flip back and forth between these two worlds is strengthened by the bottle of placebo-like "magic juice"[17] that Speedy gives him, a substance that works like Dumbo's magic feather, helping him, for a while, to perform a function he is perfectly capable of performing on his own.) Alone and frightened, Jack slowly makes his way westward, pursued both by Morgan and by assorted representatives, human and otherwise, from each of the parallel realms. After many weeks and many life-altering hardships, he reaches that other ocean, locates the Talisman in the ballroom of a "black hotel"[18] called the Agincourt, rescues it from its otherworldly guardians, uses its power to repel the assaults of Morgan and his minions, and returns in triumph to the place from which he started, the place at which the full healing power of the Talisman is finally, successfully, released.

And that, minus most of its supporting detail, is the essence of this novel. *The Talisman* is, of course, a quest story—a grail story, if you will—and its long, winding narrative arc recapitulates, in contemporary terms, the kind of story that Tolkien himself loved to tell, the kind whose nature is encapsulated in the subtitle that Tolkien provided for *The Hobbit: There and Back Again*. In *The Talisman,* the long and dangerous journey There—which is followed by a considerably simpler journey Back—is described through a series of extended set pieces, each marking a different geographical stage of the journey. The first of these set pieces takes place in the Territories, where Jack chooses to begin the journey west. There, against the colorful and discordant backdrop of an outdoor country market on the outskirts of Queen Laura's Summer Pavilion, Jack crosses paths with two very different types of men.

Farren, the brusque but sympathetic Captain of the Queen's Guards, becomes Jack's first ally in the Territories. Farren, a friend and associate of Speedy Parker (known, in the Territories, as Parkus), allows Jack his first glimpse of the dying, comatose Queen (who is indeed a near duplicate of Jack's own terminally ill mother). He also gives Jack a coin engraved with the image of the Queen, a coin which will have some talismanic significance of its own for Jack as the novel progresses. While still in Farren's company, Jack encounters Osmond ("the Great and Terrible"[19]), right hand man of Morgan of Orris and a psychopath with a whip. Jack manages, without much difficulty, to offend Osmond, and earns himself a whipping that very nearly proves fatal. With Farren's help, he escapes and sets out on the Western Road toward the Outposts of the Territories, and the Blasted Lands that lie beyond. Once on the road, two events of a particularly Tolkienesque nature take place.

First, a giant horse-drawn carriage carrying Morgan of Orris to the Queen's Pavilion passes Jack on the highway. He hides in the woods, but not before he is somehow "recognized" by Morgan, whose sorcerous scrutiny seems deliberately reminiscent of the Eye of Sauron. Moving deeper into the forest to escape that scrutiny, Jack finds himself in another kind of danger entirely.

> Something slithered over his foot...and up his ankle. Jack screamed and floundered backward, thinking it must be a snake. But when he looked down, he saw that one of those gray roots had moved...and now it ringed his calf...The grayish roots of those fir-fern hybrids were all moving now—rising, falling, scuttling along the mulchy ground toward him. *Ents and Entwives,* Jack thought crazily. *BAD Ents and Entwives.* One particularly thick root, its last six inches dark with earth and damp, rose and wavered in front of him like a cobra piped up from a fakir's basket...Tolkien had never been like this.[20]

Trapped by a tree root, Jack takes the only escape route available to him: he flips, returning to the questionable safety of a familiar world. Shortly after returning, he finds himself in a little corner of redneck hell called Oatley, somewhere in upstate New York.

In the words of a friendly motorist, Oatley is "the sort of place where they eat what they run over on the road."[21] To Jack, Oatley is the urban personification of the pitcher plant, the sort of place it's easy to get into and almost impossible to escape. Jack's troubles in Oatley begin when he goes to work for Smoky Updike (sic), the sadistic and parsimonious proprietor of the Oatley Tap, who hires him to swab out the toilets and hump heavy kegs of beer for a dollar an hour, minus the cost of his meals. Jack, who is obviously a runaway, attempts to quit, but is blackmailed into staying by his employer, who knows good cheap labor when he finds it. A bad situation quickly becomes critical when a newcomer to Oatley—a Randolph Scott look-alike named Ellroy—reveals himself as a shapeshifting were-creature—half goat, half human—who has come from the Territories in search of Jack. Moments before falling victim to the now fully transformed Ellroy, Jack once again exercises his only method of escape, and flips into the Territories.

And so it goes. Jack continues his steady westward movement, switching from one world to the other whenever danger threatens. Once, after narrowly avoiding Morgan Sloat in a rest stop on the Ohio/Indiana border, Jack flips and finds himself in the presence of an old friend of his father's, a benevolent werewolf named, simply, Wolf. Wolf, who may be the most vividly imagined of the novel's supporting characters, is a shepherd as well as a shapeshifter, and is perfectly capable of balancing the animal side of his nature with the moral responsibilities implicit in his role as Protector of the Herd.

> "Wolf," [Jack asked], "do you really change into an animal when the moon is full?"
>
> "'Course I do!" Wolf said. He looked astounded, as if Jack has asked him something like *Wolf, do you really pull up your pants after you finish taking a crap?* "Strangers don't, do they? Phil told me *that.*"
>
> "The, uh, herd," Jack said. "When you change, do they..."
>
> "Oh, we don't go *near* the herd when we change," Wolf said seriously. "Good Jason, no! We'd eat them, don't you know that?

> And a Wolf who eats of his herd must be put to death. *The Book of Good Farming* says so. Wolf! Wolf! We have places to go when the moon is full. So does the herd. They're stupid, but they know they have to go away at the time of the big moon..."[22]

Shortly after they meet, Jack and Wolf find themselves under attack by Morgan Sloat, whose sudden entry into the Territories constitutes a kind of rape, a tearing of the membrane between the worlds. When Jack flips back to the normal world to escape from Sloat, Wolf flips with him. The two travel together briefly before being captured and incarcerated in The Sunlight Home, a repressive institution for difficult, delinquent and runaway youths run by a crazy fundamentalist preacher named—in a puzzling allusion to novelist John Gardner, author of *The Sunlight Dialogues*—Sunlight Gardener. Shortly after his arrival at the Home, Jack recognizes Gardener as the Twinner of Morgan of Orris' psychopathic associate, Osmond.

The Sunlight Home exists for two primary purposes: to break the spirits of its inmates and to profit from their suffering. Sunlight Gardener, convinced that he and Jack have met before, but unable to remember where, attempts to break Jack's spirit by first breaking his friend's. Gardener imprisons the powerfully claustrophobic Wolf in a squat, three foot high chamber called the Box, and leaves him there for several days. Wolf's subsequent panic triggers a premature Change. He escapes from the Box and, fully transformed now, decimates The Sunlight Home. In the ensuing slaughter, Gardener himself escapes, while most of his disciples are killed. Wolf himself dies while protecting Jack, who, in Wolf's terms, now represents the Herd. His body dissolves at the moment of his death, and is transported back to the Territories.

Desolate and weary, Jack hits the road once more, still heading westward, stopping, this time, at Thayer Academy in Illinois. Here, Jack links up with his oldest friend, Richard Sloat, only son of Morgan Sloat. Richard is a bedrock rationalist whose rationalism was constructed as a kind of bulwark against the nightmare memories of his childhood. Now in the throes of a buttoned down adolescence, he believes only in science, in order, and in the immutable physical laws of the universe. His beliefs will be strained past the breaking point by the impossible series of events that follows in Jack Sawyer's wake.

Thayer Academy, we are told, is one of the thin places between the worlds, a former railhead that played a critical role in the great westward migration of the nineteenth century. Jack's arrival unleashes a flood of inexplicable occurrences, as creatures from the Territories—many of them Twinners of Thayer students and staff members—take over the campus in an all-out effort to track Jack down. In typical fashion, Jack flips, this time with Richard, into the Territories, where he finds himself in sole possession of a train filled with modern weapons—grenades, Uzis, plastic explosives—that have been imported there to support the ambitions of Morgan Sloat. The two then simply hijack the train, which takes them from the Outpost—the outermost settled areas of the Territories—through the Blasted Lands—poisoned analogues of the nuclear test sites of the American West—and on to that "other ocean" where the Talisman lies hidden.

The westward journey ends with a Ramboesque battle in which Jack and Richard wipe out an entire brigade of Morgan's handpicked mercenaries: renegade Wolfs (corrupted creatures who have Eaten of the Herd); Ellroy the were-goat, returned from Oatley; a nameless creature that is part human, part alligator; and "Assorted Geeks and Freaks"[23] including Sunlight/Osmond's monstrous, wildly mutated child, Reuel (whose name, incidentally, represents one more tip of the hat to the works of John Ronald Ruel Tolkien). The prose in this sequence is overheated and often crude, straining much too hard to achieve its pedestrian, pulp-fictional effects:

> Most of Morgan's carefully culled Wolf Brigade...were wiped out in one spitting, raking burst of the machine gun in Jack's hands. They went stumbling and reeling backward, chests blown open, heads bleeding...[24]
>
> Bullets also tore open the whitish-green belly of the alligator thing, and a blackish fluid—ichor, not blood—began to pour out of it...[25]
>
> He looked up and saw that the engine, boxcar and flatcars were covered with hot guts, black blood, and shreds of...flesh...A vile dark fluid, the color of overbrewed

> tea, ran out of Reuel's head and over Jack's wrist. The fluid was hot. There were tiny worms in it. He felt them biting.[27]

And so on. Following this protracted bloodbath, the boys make their way northward to the town of Point Venuti, where the Talisman begins to call to Jack from its place of concealment in the Agincourt Hotel. There, in a sequence which reflects the classical nature of his knightly quest, Jack defeats the five armored guardians who stand in his way, passes through the doorway of the Agincourt ballroom, and receives the Talisman:

> "Come to me!" he shouted to it as it had sung to him, "Come to me!" It was three feet above his hands, branding them with its soft, healing light; now two; now one. It hesitated for a moment, rotated slowly, its axis slightly canted, and Jack could see the brilliant, shifting outline of continents and oceans and icecaps on its surface. It hesitated...and then slowly slipped down into the boy's reaching hands.[28]

At this point, having achieved his goal, and having survived, as well, a final desperate attack by Morgan Sloat and Sunlight Gardener (an attack in which the participants flip back and forth, in a rapid series of jump cuts, between this world and the Territories), Jack is faced with one more, seemingly insurmountable problem: how to get back home. Having spent several hundred pages getting Jack to the Agincourt Hotel, the authors wisely decide to cut through the Gordian knot of narrative and send Jack home in style. In a small northern California town appropriately called Storeyville, Jack and Richard meet up with another Wolf—the considerably less claustrophobic "litter brother"[29] of Jack's dead friend—who drives them to New Hampshire in a black El Dorado Cadillac "as big as a house trailer and as dark as death."[30]

Jack arrives at his dying mother's bedside with very little time to spare. By this point, some three months after the beginning of Jack's quest, Lily Cavanaugh weighs seventy-eight pounds, is suffering from pneumonia as well as cancer, and has slipped into her final coma. In a moving, lyrically composed conclusion, Jack stands by and watches while the Talisman—whose vast, primal power extends well beyond its capacity to heal the sick—restores his mother's health:

> The green golden cloud from the heart of the Talisman was lengthening over his mother's body, coating her in a translucent, delicately moving membrane...Lily's eyes opened wide. They stared up into Jack's face with a startled where-am-I expression...Then she jerked in a startled breath—and a river of worlds and tilted galaxies and universes were pulled up and out of the Talisman as she did. They were pulled up in a stream of rainbow colors. They streamed into her mouth and nose...They settled, gleaming, on her sallow skin like droplets of dew, and melted inward...All the disease fled from her face.[31]

At the same time, Queen Laura of the Territories opens her eyes and emerges from her own extended coma, ending this novel of parallel worlds with the perfectly balanced image of parallel resurrections.

Commenting on *The Talisman* in 1984, Stephen King noted that "You've got to put an asterisk by it" when viewing it in the larger context of either writer's work. In Straub's case, it is, as noted, particularly anomalous, especially in light of the kind of fiction he would subsequently produce: fiction which would become less and less fantastic, and more and more concerned with the realistic exploration of extreme and violent behavior. Straub himself has commented on the uncharacteristic nature of so much of this book:

> The fact that we were writing such a big book, spending so much time on individual episodes, forced a kind of simplicity of narrative on me that I would not otherwise have had. It's much simpler than the things I normally do—that is, it's not compiled in fragments from a bunch of seemingly unrelated stories, which is the way I tend to write. Because Steve was my collaborator, it is much more openhearted. I

> think you can find warmth and generosity in my books, but not normally expressed so openly.[32]

That said, there are a number of recognizably Straubian riffs scattered throughout, although they tend not to dominate the narrative the way King's more straightforward, headlong narrative style does. For instance, jazz music and jazz musicians are featured with characteristic frequency throughout the text. (However, given the nature of this collaboration, a soundtrack for the novel would necessarily contain a fair amount of rock 'n' roll, particularly Credence Clearwater's "Running Through the Jungle.") *The Talisman* is also filled with a sense of that all-encompassing mystery within which we live out our lives; and is distinguished, at certain key moments, by a lovingly articulated sense of rapture, that feeling of rightness and grace that enters into the characters' lives at unexpected moments, and is reflected in the frequent repetition of Elizabeth Bishop's beautiful incantation, "rainbow, rainbow, rainbow."[33] Then, too, there is the recurring theme of children damaged by parental irresponsibility, as embodied by the relationship between Morgan Sloat—a man perfectly willing to sacrifice his son if it gains him the world—and his obsessively rational son, Richard, whose ability to continue loving his father depends on his simultaneous ability to ignore the evidence of his own senses.

Finally, *The Talisman* reiterates Straub's ongoing concern with the primal importance of narrative—of Story—in our lives. The Territories, as described in this book, is both a literal world filled with dangers and uniquely beautiful visions, and a gigantic metaphor for the world of the imagination; a metaphor, in fact, for fiction itself. Jack Sawyer, though only twelve years old, understands this instinctively, and acknowledges it explicitly while reflecting on rational Richard's utter inability to take pleasure in fantasy—in fiction—of any kind:

> Richard's dislike of fantasy was so deep that he would not pick up any novel unless it was an assignment—as a kid, he had let Jack pick out the books he read for free-choice book reports, not caring what they were, chewing them up as if they were cereal. It became a challenge to

> Jack to find a story—any story—which would please Richard, divert Richard, carry Richard away as good novels and stories sometimes carried Jack away...the good ones, he thought, were almost as good as the Daydreams, and each mapped out its own version of the Territories.[34]

As always, in Straub's work, other fiction by other writers lurks just below the surface of the story. Tolkien is here, of course, as well as C. S. Lewis, whose Narnia books lend the Territories something of their distinctive flavor. *Le Morte D'Arthur,* together with the many versions of the Arthurian legend that Mallory inspired, underscore the novel's radical recasting of the Grail quest. A more recent work of fantasy, Stephen R. Donaldson's *The Chronicles of Thomas Covenant, Unbeliever* also finds its way into the text by way of Richard Sloat's absolute refusal to acknowledge the reality of the Territories, even as he travels through them. Another major influence—in both its book and film versions—is L. Frank Baum's *The Wizard of Oz,* echoes of which are littered throughout the text: in the recurrent rainbow imagery; in the ability of the characters to flip back and forth between magical and mundane realms; in the creation of the great Western Road, an obvious variant of the Yellow Brick Road; in half a dozen overt textual references (Osmond the Great and Terrible, et al); even, though this is admittedly speculative, in the choice of the principal villain's name, Morgan Sloat, which calls to mind the name of Frank Morgan, the actor who played the fraudulent wizard in the 1939 film.

Another major, and very obvious, influence, is Mark Twain, whose work provides Jack Sawyer with his famous surname and the novel as a whole with its opening and closing passages. Twain, of course, was the author of the quintessential novel of American boyhood, *The Adventures of Huckleberry Finn,* which, as Douglas E. Winter has pointed out[35], was serendipitously published in 1884, exactly one hundred years before *The Talisman.* Beyond the more obvious similarities—the picaresque nature of the two books, the way in which both Jack and Huck "light out for the Territories"[36] in response to the pressure of external events—the central moral concerns of *Huckleberry Finn* permeate *The Talisman* in subtle but fundamental ways. Huck, in one of the more indelible moments of nineteenth century American literature, vows that he will "go to hell"[37] rather than reveal the whereabouts of Nigger Jim, a runaway slave, to Jim's owner, Mrs. Watson. Huck's friendship with Jim, and the choices which result from that friendship, cast an ironic and critical light on the monolithic institution of slavery. *The Talisman*, in its way, is also about slavery and, by extension, slavery's opposite number: power.

The Talisman signals its concern with these issues in the very first chapter, in the course of a brief description of the Alhambra Hotel, where Jack and his mother have just taken up residence.

> The formal gardens on its landward side were barely visible from Jack's beachfront angle...The brass cock stood against the sky, quartering west by northwest. A plaque in the lobby announced that it was here, in 1838, that the Northern Methodist Conference had held the first of the great New England abolition rallies. Daniel Webster had spoken at fiery, inspired length. According to the plaque, Webster had said: "From this day forward, know that slavery as an American institution has begun to sicken and must soon die in all our states and Territorial lands."[38]

Jack's wanderings across both worlds bring him into continuous contact with the realities of slavery, in both its literal and more socially acceptable forms. From Smoky Updike's Oatley Tap—where Jack is coerced into performing the most demeaning and backbreaking labors for obscenely low wages—to the Sunlight Home—where the adolescent inmates provide the workforce and Sunlight Gardener receives the profits—the underlying principles of slavery are alive and well. And in the Territories—which is repeatedly depicted as a good place, brighter, cleaner, *purer* than its real world counterpart, outright slavery has gained a foothold, largely through the poisonous intervention of Morgan Sloat. For example, the Ore Pits of the East, which are the Territories analogue of the Sunlight Home, are presented as Dante-esque visions in which naked prisoners are harnessed like animals to heavy carts and are presided over by monstrous figures with metal-tipped whips. And the railroad tracks which carry Jack, Richard, and Morgan Sloat's trainload of weapons from the Outposts to the ocean are also the product of slave labor, which is represented both as an autonomous manifestation of evil, and as an aspect of a larger issue that informs this book on every level: the corruption of the land, and of all its inhabitants, by the unrestrained pursuit of power and profit.

The final words of *The Talisman* are also the final words of *The Adventures of Tom Sawyer,* and they lead directly to the consideration of one more thematic thread:

> So endeth this chronicle. It being strictly the history of a *boy*, it must stop here; the story could not go much further without becoming the history of a *man*. When one writes a novel about grown people, he knows exactly where to stop—that is, with a marriage; but when he writes of juveniles, he must stop where he best can.[39]

By the end of this novel, Jack has just turned thirteen, but is no longer a child in any recognizable respect, having evolved from a twelve-year-old boy who cries in the dark at the prospect of traveling through a hostile world—a boy who often needs to be carried on his friend Wolf's shoulders—to a young man of heightened spiritual awareness and luminous physical beauty who is capable, when circumstances demand it, of carrying his friend Richard on his own shoulders. The physical, mental, and moral toughening that Jack undergoes is a function of more than just the rigorous nature of his quest. As Jack comes to recognize,

> ...he had been trying to do more than simply save his mother's life: from the beginning he had been trying to do something greater than that. He had been trying to do a good work, and his dim realization now was that such mad enterprises must always be toughening.[40]

In at least one respect, then, *The Talisman* stands squarely in the tradition of Straub's—and King's—previous fiction: its extravagant inventions are grounded, always, in the moral and psychological realities of everyday life. It's epic structure is inextricably entwined with the simpler, classically familiar story of the growth and development of an individual human soul.

Seen in its entirety, *The Talisman* is rambling but extremely readable, moving and occasionally annoying, ambitious but ultimately overlong. It seems likely that future readers and reviewers will continue to follow King's advice and put an asterisk beside it. The virtues of the novel are the virtues that had long been evident in the works of both its authors: warmth; narrative energy; a sense of personal engagement with the material at hand; an almost unerring eye for the accurate detail and appropriate phrase; a willingness to follow and fully develop every branch of the narrative, never skimping or holding back; the ability to enter directly into the emotional centers of a variety of characters; together with an almost palpable sense of affection for those same characters.

Set against these virtues are a couple of crucial problems that seem connected, at least partially, to the basic nature of collaboration. There are, despite the authors' avowed intention to create a single, seamless narrative voice for this novel, two distinct voices at work here, and it is frequently possible to make a reasonable guess as to which writer actually wrote a particular section of the book. This isn't a huge problem, and the two voices are by no means incompatible with each other but, still, the line of division shows through a bit more clearly than it should. A second, and more significant, problem is the fact that many of the individual episodes that make up the novel simply run on too long, as though each writer, having finally been handed the baton of the narrative by the other, is reluctant to give it back. The impact of this problem is cumulative, and by the latter stages of the story a sense of strain has set in, along with the desire to see this lengthy narrative move more quickly toward its promised denouement.

In the aftermath of this complex act of collaboration, Straub's pen fell temporarily silent. Having produced four large, increasingly ambitious works of the fantastic in just under six years, he found himself suffering from creative exhaustion, compounded by the belief that his capacity to produce this sort of fiction had finally played itself out. Yielding to necessity, he retreated into a year-long period of silence, reflection, and renewal. At the end of this period, he began the slow, painstaking process of redirecting his fiction into vital new areas. With the publication of *Koko,* in 1988, he demonstrated his immediate mastery of the mainstream thriller and succeeded, once again, in reinventing his own career.

1. "Stephen King, Peter Straub, & the Quest for The Talisman" by Douglas E. Winter, *Twilight Zone Magazine*, Fall, 1984
2. *Fear Itself*, p. 11
3. Ibid., p. 11
4. Douglas E. Winter, Op. Cit.
5. Ibid.
6. Letter from Peter Straub to the author
7. Douglas E. Winter, Op. Cit.
8. Letter from Peter Straub to the author
9. *The Talisman* (New York: Viking Press, 1984), p. 3
10. Ibid., p. 6
11. Ibid., p. 30
12. Ibid., p. 30
13. Ibid., pp. 165-166
14. Ibid., p. 54
15. Ibid., p. 54
16. Ibid., p. 54
17. Ibid., p. 46
18. Ibid., p. 556
19. Ibid., p. 106
20. Ibid., pp. 115-116
21. Ibid., p. 123
22. Ibid., p. 232
23. Ibid., p. 492
24. Ibid., p. 490
25. Ibid., p. 490
26. Ibid., p. 491
27. Ibid., p. 494
28. Ibid., p. 582
29. Ibid., p. 629
30. Ibid., p. 628
31. Ibid., p. 642
32. Douglas E. Winter, Op. Cit.
33. *The Talisman*, p. 622
34. Ibid., p. 412
35. Douglas E. Winter, Op. Cit.
36. Mark Twain, *The Adventures of Huckleberry Finn*
37. Ibid.

[38]. *The Talisman*, p. 4
[39]. Ibid., p. 646
[40]. Ibid., p. 503

Section III

Blue Roses and Buffalo Hunters

Chapter Nine:
Koko

The long, arduous process of creating *Koko* began in the summer of 1983, early in the course of Straub's one-year, self-imposed sabbatical. At that time, Straub still owed Putnam Books the second novel in a two book contract that had begun with *Floating Dragon*, but had no concrete ideas for that novel until, crossing the lawn of his Westport home one day, he was visited by the following notion: what if a group of Vietnam veterans, former members of the same combat unit, discover that one of their platoon mates has gone crazy and is murdering people in the Far East? And what if, having made that discovery, they decide to travel to the sites of those murders, and track the killer down? The idea, in this undeveloped form, seemed a bit like the premise of a made-for-TV movie but, as Straub has noted, "it was the only idea I had,"[1] so he filed it away in the hope that it would develop enough complexity and emotional resonance to support a novel. Eventually, it did.

The first major step in the process began that fall, when Straub, sitting in his office making notes for the novel he was still utterly unprepared to write, watched a PBS documentary on the dedication of the Vietnam War Memorial in Washington, DC. What he saw affected him profoundly, and forced him to confront, with unprecedented immediacy, the emotional realities of the men who survived the war. Commenting on his response to the program, Straub notes that

> one reason for my being so affected was that the men in the documentary were

> themselves so moved, so wide-open emotionally, so rawly, centrally, beautifully engaged and reawakened by what they were doing. I could see them open themselves to an enormous grief, part of which was grief for themselves. The magnitude of what they felt healed them, or was helping them to heal—they were forced to inhabit the incredible pain at the center of their lives, in the face of which almost everything else was shallow, superficial, in a way trivial. The other reason for my response was that I felt I understood them because I identified with them. Then, I had no idea why this should be, but I knew it was true. If I were going to write about anything at all, it would have to take this reality into account, or be condemned to triviality.[2]

At the same time, Straub concluded that the kind of supernatural elements employed so freely in his earlier novels could have no place in the story now unfolding in his imagination. To commemorate and underscore that realization, he opened his notebook to a fresh page and wrote down the following phrase: "Never write anything you don't believe in."[3] And then he wrote the phrase again. Afterward, guided by this newly minted aesthetic manifesto, he began the protracted process of researching, absorbing, and coming to terms with the reality of Vietnam. For several months, Straub's research proceeded along two basic lines. He met and talked with a great many veterans—including his brother John, who served in Vietnam as a lieutenant—and immersed himself in the voluminous literature of the war, searching for the kinds of details—about "weapons, smells, terrain, helicopters, uniforms, food, villages, military units, behavior, camps, LZs"[4]—that would give his projected fiction the necessary sense of unobtrusive authenticity. In May of 1984, he visited those Far Eastern landscapes—Singapore, Bangkok, Penang, Taipei, and Hong Kong—through which characters—still unnamed, still just vague shapes on the fictional horizon—would eventually make their way. After this, he retreated to Barbados for a ten-day stint of concentrated work, in the course of which a number of the novel's central elements began to take on a coherent form. Straub then returned to Westport, determined to begin the novel whose gestation had already occupied one full year. Before he could start, however, one more preliminary project announced itself to him, and occupied his attention for the next three months: a novella entitled "Blue Rose."

"Blue Rose" represents the attempt of one of *Koko*'s principal characters, Tim Underhill, to imagine his way into the violent and disordered childhood of another of the characters, Harry Beevers, "the world's worst lieutenant."[5] In addition to its very considerable intrinsic merits, "Blue Rose" helped, in a couple of ways, to prepare Straub for the larger task of writing *Koko*. First, it introduced the central thematic notion of childhood traumas and their relationship to the later crises of adult life. Second, it forced him to examine his most fundamental writer's tool—his style—and refine it to meet the very different requirements of a new, and very different, sort of fiction.

> I wanted transparency, which meant I had to approach my style, formerly a source of considerable pride, with a meat-axe. The story wouldn't work at all if the style were conspicuous, because the point was to erase all friction between the reader and the subject so that the reader would look straight through the sentences and see, with absolute clarity, what was being described. My word for this aesthetic was "presentational." I wanted the reader to see what was going on as if it were right before her, without mediation.[6]

This "transparency" was achieved through a process of constant revision, and by a rigorous attention to the most basic elements of every sentence.

> To be transparent, the sentences had to put the right words in the right order, to employ pungent, accurate active verbs and shun passive ones, to maintain an unobtrusive musical cadence and avoid repetition, awkwardness, and flaccid rhythms. I'm not saying that I managed to accomplish all this, because I did not, merely that

> I first became aware of such principles while I was writing "Blue Rose," and that what I learned seemed vitally important, eye-opening to me.[7]

The result of this Flaubertian obsession with exactness was a quietly powerful novella written in a clean, deceptively effective voice. (A second related novella, "The Juniper Tree," would soon follow, and would bring the same stylistic rigor to its graphic presentation of childhood trauma and long-buried secrets.) Finally, having established the novel's basic nature and having created, as well, a kind of small-scale model of its presentational aesthetic, Straub gathered his courage, turned on his word processor, and began to write *Koko.*

This was in the autumn of 1984, a particularly hectic time for Straub. *The Talisman,* with its attendant demands for interviews, autographings, and all manner of public appearances, was just then being published. At the same time, Straub and his family had begun the long, drawn-out process of relocating from Westport to Manhattan. Most significantly, Straub had just embarked on what he called "an instructive, in fact revelatory ten-year journey through a classic psychoanalysis"[8] conducted under the guidance of Dr. Lila Kalinich, to whom *Koko* (and, subsequently, *Mystery* and *Mrs. God*) would be dedicated.

> Four days a week, I stretched out on the couch, opened my mouth to address the ceiling and the unseen figure seated behind me and sailed into the unknown, a process that did exactly what it was supposed to do: made it impossible for me to avoid seeing what was right in front of me. Over time, I came to understand both myself and other people in far greater depth than ever before, also now and then to apprehend certain nearly mystical and ever-present realities.[9]

Against this clamorous background, Straub embarked on the opening sentences. The immediate results were, to say the least, disheartening. Four or five hours of intense effort resulted in the production of a single, unusable page. Reading it over, Straub recalls, he very nearly fainted. All of it, in his judgment, was "humiliatingly badly written,"[10] the work of a man who "couldn't write for beans."[11] Details were presented in the incorrect order. Adjectives were overused. The entire day's output lacked clarity and focus. The lessons learned during the writing of "Blue Rose" seemed useless in the face of the very different requirements of a novel. Finally, after the initial shock had passed, Straub went back to work on the offending paragraphs, rewriting, reorganizing, pushing them at last into something resembling acceptability. And so it went, day after day: writing, cringing at the finished pages, and then endlessly, patiently revising. At the end of that first year, he had completed approximately 150 manuscript pages, or one-sixth of the final total, all of it the result of the most intense, exhausting labor.

At least two specific problems lay at the root of Straub's difficulties during this period. First, he was writing to the new, even more exacting standards set by his vision of a pure, perfectly transparent style, and these standards were difficult to meet. Second, he was suffering from the aftereffects of his year long layoff, and was facing the single largest artistic challenge of his career with a set of badly atrophied literary muscles. The single bright spot in that long, dreary year lay in Straub's increasing ability to subject his sentences to a merciless, objective scrutiny, to revise, scrutinize and then revise again until all traces of slackness and imprecision had been effectively eliminated. This capacity for tireless, ruthless revision quickly became habitual and continues, to this day, to inform Straub's approach to the art—and craft—of fiction.

In time, Straub's characteristic fluency began to return, and that agonized sense of constriction—of being "hobbled to progress made one step at a time"[12]—gradually subsided. In the second year, Straub's output literally doubled. In the third and final year, it very nearly doubled again. According to Straub, that third year,

> particularly its latter half, was sort of like going to heaven. I felt all of my imaginative resources come back to me, and I moved into the heart of my story, fully understanding why it was important to me...By the end, I was up to fifteen pages a day, writing by hand in big journals. We were back in Westport for another summer, and one morning I met Robert

> Ludlum...at the little Greens Farm post office used by both of us...He asked how my work was going, and I could not help saying, "Bob, I put down my smoking pencil just long enough to pick up the mail." Little candle flames appeared in his eyes, and he said, "Me, too!"[13]

Racing along behind that furiously smoking pencil, Straub reached the end of the novel in state of controlled ecstasy that felt, he said, "like music,"[14] like a long-delayed reward for the pain and misery of that initial year. One year later, in the fall of 1988—following another intense period of editing and revision—*Koko* was published to strong sales and general acclaim. Ironically, this most realistic of Straub's mature fiction went on to win the World Fantasy Award for Best Novel. More significantly, it established its author as a man willing to confound fixed expectations, and follow his vision into new and unexpected areas.

After the comparative simplicity of *The Talisman, Koko* marked a return to a more complex, typically Straubian interplay of narrative elements. *Koko* tells the related stories of several haunted veterans of Vietnam, all of them affected in different ways by their memories of the war; all of them concerned, for a variety of reasons, with tracking down the former fellow soldier they believe to be responsible for a series of recent murders in Singapore and Bangkok. Straub uses multiple viewpoints, multiple settings both exotic and familiar, and multiple time frames ranging backward from 1982 to the war years of the sixties, and then further back to what Tim Underhill would eventually call "the Vietnam before Vietnam"[15] of childhood. All of these elements come together to create a moving meditation on individual grief and individual healing set against the larger source of an entire nation's grief: the Vietnam War.

The novel opens, appropriately, with the dedication of the Vietnam War Memorial in the fall of 1982. It's worth taking a look at the opening sentences—those same sentences Straub labored over so despairingly—to see how swiftly and cleanly they carry us into the peculiar ambiance of that event.

> At three o'clock in the afternoon of a gray, blowing mid-November day, a baby doctor named Michael Poole looked down

> from the window of his second-floor room into the parking lot of the Sheraton Hotel. A VW van, spray-painted with fuzzy peace symbols and driven by either a drunk or a lunatic, was going for a ninety-eight point turn in the space between the first parking row and the entrance. As Michael watched, the van completed its turn by grinding its front bumper into the grille and headlights of a dusty little Camaro. The whole front end of the Camaro buckled in. Horns blew. The van now faced a stalled, frustrated line of enemy vehicles...[16]

After catching our attention with this sharply observed comic contretemps, *Koko* sideslips effortlessly into a rounded, wide-ranging re-creation of that day, as seen from the perspective of Michael Poole, a discontented pediatrician from the affluent Westchester community of Westerholm. Poole attends two very different reunions on the day of the Dedication: one with the dead, whose names are memorialized on the Wall; another with the surviving members of his combat platoon: Conor Linklater, a down-on-his-luck carpenter who drifts from one temporary job to the next; Tina Pumo, embattled owner of a trendy New York restaurant called Saigon; and Harry Beevers, the manipulative former platoon leader who has recently lost both his wife and his job, and who thinks he sees the opportunity for the one big score that has always eluded him.

Beevers has stumbled upon a series of newspaper accounts—from *The Stars and Stripes*, *The Bangkok Post*, and *The Straits Times* of Singapore—describing a number of unsolved murders in which playing cards bearing the handwritten word "Koko" were stuffed into the mouths of the mutilated victims. This bizarre detail speaks immediately to Poole, Pumo, and Linklater. Each of them—in an uncharacteristic act that arose out of the specific circumstances of their lives in Vietnam, and out of the pervasive Conradian darkness that came to dominate those lives—once committed an atrocity on the dead body of an enemy soldier, removing the corpse's ears and placing a card marked "Koko" in its mouth. Those acts, whose symbolism remains obscure even to the participants, were part of an arcane act of solidarity, the nature of which becomes clearer as the long and winding narrative unfolds. It is quite clear to all four survivors, though, that the

Koko reference points directly back to Vietnam, and to the activities of their own platoon.

Beevers thinks he knows the identity of the killer: Tim Underhill, who disappeared into Singapore some time after the war, and became, for a time, a moderately successful crime novelist. Underhill is one of only two possible candidates for the role of Koko. The other, Victor Spitalny, is believed to have deserted under cover of a Bangkok street riot in 1969, the same riot believed to have claimed the life of another platoon mate, the much missed, much admired M.O. (Manny) Dengler. Beevers, with visions of book deals dancing in his head, wants to lead the others on a "mission" to the Far East to track down Underhill and bring him back alive. Pumo, who has enough problems to deal with in New York City, refuses to go. Poole and Linklater eventually agree, though for distinctly different reasons of their own.

In the interim between the dedication in Washington and the departure for Singapore, Straub takes us into the daily routines of his four principal characters, and shows us quite a bit about the disordered nature of their lives. Harry Beevers, once known as "the lost boss," is now just an unemployed lawyer living off the charity of his wealthy ex-wife. He drinks too much, often in the bar of Tina Pumo's restaurant, and spends his time indulging in infantile fantasies out of Ian Fleming. Harry is greedy, desperate, and utterly without empathy, a combination of qualities that makes him both dangerous and faintly ridiculous.

Conor Linklater is a goodhearted working stiff—a kind of latter day Mr. Malaprop—who can't quite get it together. He, too, drinks too much, and tends to lose his temper when he does. He lives alone, and owns almost nothing. He is a talented carpenter, but can't hold on to a job. As with his companions, images and memories of Vietnam are never very far from his thoughts.

Tina Pumo, on the other hand, is more of a traditional success story. His restaurant, Saigon, has been written up in *New York* magazine and has grown into one of the city's more popular sources of exotic cuisine. Beneath the surface, however, elements of Tina's life are beginning to crumble. His restaurant has encountered problems with the Board of Health and his relationship with a beautiful young Chinese woman named Maggie Lah is in a state of continual disarray. Tina believes, quite honestly, that he emerged unscarred from his experiences in Vietnam, but he did not. He has simply kept certain forms of self-knowledge at arms length, and has never acknowledged a basic truth that most people know, and that is central to the meaning of this novel: that "deep down, the things that happened to you never stop happening."[17]

For a long time, Michael Poole's life seemed like the embodiment of order and coherence. He survived Vietnam, finished medical school, fathered a son—a "dear tender dull beautiful"[18] child named Robbie—and became a pediatrician with an affluent Westchester practice. And then Robbie died, eaten up by a series of wildly metastasizing tumors that Poole associated, immediately and instinctively, with his own exposure to Agent Orange many years before. In the aftermath of Robbie's death, order and coherence fled. Poole's marriage lapsed into painful habit, and his interest in his upscale medical practice gradually faded. By 1982, when *Koko* begins, he cares deeply about only one person—a twelve-year-old girl named Stacy Talbot who, like Robbie, is dying of cancer—and wants only one thing: to leave Westerholm and recover what he thinks of as the "real raw taste" of the medical profession by establishing a practice in some squalid, poverty-stricken corner of the Bronx. It is against this backdrop of stasis and confusion that Michael heads for Singapore, grateful for the opportunity, however temporary, to step outside the confines of his increasingly untenable life.

This being a Peter Straub novel, there are, of course, other elements, other threads of narrative, weaving their way through the story. By the time Beevers, Poole and Linklater leave on their "mission," we have been exposed to several. Among them are a couple of very distinctive new viewpoints that periodically interrupt the larger narrative, leaving new mysteries and new questions behind them. One of these, eventually identifiable as Tim Underhill, speaks in a series of Socratic dialogues about what he calls "the nearness of ultimate things"[19] suggested by his recurring vision of a dying Vietnamese girl, and about the presentiment of death and violence arising from the resurrected presence of "the usual subject, my subject. Koko. More than ever now."

> *Why more than ever now?*
>
> Because he has come back. Because I think
> I saw him. I know I saw him.
>
> *You imagine you saw him?*

> It is the same thing.
>
> *What did he look like?*
>
> He looked like a dancing shadow. He looked like death.
>
> *Did he appear to you in a dream?*
>
> He appeared, if that is the word, on the street. Death appeared on the street. Tremendous clamor accompanied the appearance of the girl, ordinary street noise, that earthly clamor, surrounded the shadow. He was covered, though not visibly, with the blood of others. The girl, who was visible only to me, was covered with her own. The Pan-feeling poured from both of them.
>
> *What feeling is that?*
>
> The feeling that we have only the shakiest hold on the central stories of our lives.[20]

Underhill's voice, allusive and enigmatic, is the voice of a man slowly coming back to life, fueled by visions, and by his awareness that a story rooted in his own past—the story of Koko—has reappeared in the world, bringing with it "terror...chaos, and night."[21] Straub counterpoints this voice with the equally idiosyncratic perspective of Koko himself, that embodiment of death who stands at the center of his own delusional universe. Koko's world is almost entirely self-referential, a closed system filled with demons, totemic images of elephants, visions of dying children, stern patriarchal figures, and voices that speak to him in a private, indecipherable code. It is the manifestation of an intensely individual pathology, and Straub takes us deeply into the heart of it. Here, for example, is our first glimpse of Koko, standing over the trussed-up bodies of two of his victims in a deserted bungalow in Singapore.

> The man in the first of the two heavy chairs now grunted and stirred, or pushed his

arms against the ropes. The woman did not move because the woman was dead. Koko was invisible but the man followed him with his eyes. When you knew you were dying, you could see the invisible.

If you were in a village, say—

If the smoke from the cookfire rose straight into the air again. If the chicken lifted one foot and froze. If the sow cocked her head. If you saw these things. If you saw a leaf shaking, if you saw dust hovering—

Then you might see the vein jumping in Koko's neck. You might see Koko leaning against a hooch, the vein jumping in his neck.

This is one thing Koko knew: there are always empty places...Rich people leave the empty places behind, as
the city itself leaves them behind...

...and at night eternity quietly breaks in with Koko.

His father had been sitting in one of the two heavy chairs the rich people had left behind. *We use everything*, his father said. *We waste no part of the animal.*

We do not waste the chairs.

There was one memory he had seen in the cave, and in memory no part of the animal is wasted.[22]

In addition to the primary present day narratives and the periodic appearances of Underhill and Koko, Straub includes a fragmentary re-creation of significant moments from the platoon's experience in Vietnam. Included among them are a vivid account of an ambush in a place called Dragon Valley, where the arrogance and inexperience of Harry Beevers very nearly destroys the platoon; stories of a relentless, swivel-hipped North Vietnamese sniper named Elvis, who has made Beevers' platoon his particular target; and, most memorably, the story of Ia Thuc, and of the thirty children who may or may not have been murdered there.

Ia Thuc, before the army descends upon it and makes it "unhappen,"[23] is a small, unimportant village believed to be sympathetic to the Viet Cong. It is also believed to be the home base of Elvis the sniper, who has recently demoralized Beevers' platoon by wounding one of its most vital members, Manny Dengler, who, along with Tim Underhill, has done more than any other individual to help the platoon maintain both its sanity and its humanity in the face of the war and its daily helping of horrors. The unit therefore arrives at the village in a state already bordering on homicidal mania. Responding to a burst of machine gun fire from a nearby forest, Beevers snaps and orders the entire village destroyed. In the ensuing chaos, Beevers murders an injured little girl, Victor Spitalny turns a flamethrower on a group of children hiding in a ditch, and Michael Poole accidentally shoots and kills a little boy. In the midst of his shock, he realizes that the worst aspect of the entire situation is its absolute lack of consequences.

> In the next instant he realized that absolutely nothing was going to happen to him because of what he had done...Unless the entire platoon was court-martialed nothing was going to happen. This too was terrible. There were no consequences. Actions that took place in a void were eternal actions, and that was terrible.[24]

Then, in the midst of the sudden, violent unhappening of Ia Thuc, Harry Beevers discovers a cave set at the base of a hill on the outskirts of the village, and decides to investigate. Two men, first Dengler and then Spitalny, follow him in. After that point, nothing that happens is ever entirely clear. Poole and Underhill hear a rattle of gunfire from the mouth of the cave. Moments later, Spitalny runs out screaming, covered with welts and eruptions that appear to be wasp stings but which fade away to nothing within minutes. Dengler exits next, dazed and apparently in shock. Poole and Underhill then enter the cave and encounter a deranged, jubilant Harry Beevers, whose subsequent statements indicate that he has just executed, or believes he has executed, perhaps thirty children who had hidden themselves in an inner chamber of the cave. When Poole and Underhill enter that chamber, they see "blood...disappearing into the bullet-pocked walls the way Spitalny's skin eruptions...had faded back into his body."[25] But there are no children and no dead bodies. And no satisfactory explanations.

Beevers' unchecked rantings to the visiting press corps ("There are no children in war!"[26]) put him on the covers of *Time* and *Newsweek* under headlines that read: "Ia Thuc: Shame or Victory?"[27] It also earns him a court-martial for war crimes. (Dengler, who had been with him in the cave, is also court-martialed, which precipitates the brutal acts of solidarity in which his comrades place "Koko cards" in the mouths of mutilated North Vietnamese soldiers, thereby joining him in his role as "war criminal." The full significance of this action is deliberately unexplained. We are left only with the implicit assumption that the word "Koko" has some meaning or some association that Dengler will understand.) In the absence of any bodies, or of supporting evidence of any kind, the accused are acquitted and the incident, real or imagined, gradually fades from public memory. But it is still very much a part of the personal histories of the men flying to Singapore to bring Tim Underhill home.

These are among the elements at play as the plane touches down in Singapore, at which point the primary storyline once again branches, dividing into three alternating narrative lines. One follows the progress of Koko who, using the identity and passport of his most recent victim, travels from East to West, away from Poole, Beevers, and Linklater, and toward New York City, and an unsuspecting Tina Pumo. Tina, meanwhile, has looked up from his own troubles long enough to do some research, and has discovered something Harry Beevers missed: that the recent victims of the Koko murders were largely journalists who had covered the incident at Ia Thuc, thirteen years before. Armed with the knowledge that Ia Thuc and its mysteries are somehow at the heart of events, and that people associated with Ia Thuc are dying violently, Tina attempts to contact the three travelers but is himself murdered—and, in typical Koko fashion, mutilated—before he can tell them what he knows.

Meanwhile, on the other side of the world, Poole, Beevers, and Linklater have scoured the blandly commercial city of Singapore to no avail, and have moved on: Beevers to Taipei, Poole and Linklater to Bangkok. Once in Bangkok, Poole and Linklater pick up Underhill's trail and follow it in different directions. Conor Linklater discovers a bizarre private "club" in which sex and death are bound inextricably together. Michael, more by luck than by design, discovers Tim Underhill.

Underhill, as Poole understands almost immediately, is not Koko. He is merely a tired, burned-out writer slowly emerging from his own history of personal disorder, and trying to reconstruct his life through the exercise of his one indisputable gift: his imagination. He is, as his dialogues indicate, aware of Koko and his atrocities, and will soon become aware that many of Koko's actions have been carried out under the name "Tim Underhill," underscoring a complex connection that has always existed between the two. Any doubts regarding Underhill's innocence are removed when news of Tina Pumo's murder finally reaches them. Shaken by the news, Poole and Linklater, with Underhill in tow, return to America, rejoin Harry Beevers, and resume their hunt for the man they now believe must, by default, be Koko: Victor Spitalny.

Back in America, events move quickly toward their open-ended resolution. Koko goes to ground in an appropriately cavelike dwelling in New York's Chinatown. Beevers posts open letters to Koko all over the city, in an elaborate attempt to lure him into the open and trap him in a "killing box"[28] of Beevers' choosing. A little bit of Vietnam thus resurfaces in the New York City of 1982. In order to clear the field for this grandstand climax, Beevers sends Underhill and Poole, in the company of Maggie Lah, to Victor Spitalny's hometown, Milwaukee, to learn whatever they can about his life, habits, and personal history.

The scenes set in Milwaukee are brilliant, surreal evocations of what Conrad would immediately have recognized as one of the "dark places" of the earth. Against a backdrop of almost Arctic severity, an irate driver attacks a bus with a tire iron; a man stands on a street corner and "plays" with his dog by smashing the animal repeatedly in the face; a cab driver taking Maggie, Poole, and Underhill to the Spitalny home threatens to throw them out for asking "smartass" questions about the city. Their visit with the Spitalnys provides the three with an object lesson in the art of destroying children. George Spitalny, whose initial reaction to his newborn son ("I couldn't get over how goddam ugly the kid was. Right away, I saw he was never going to measure up to me."[29]) set the tone for Victor's childhood, is a man too enamored of himself to provide any love for his disappointing son. His wife, Margaret, is too cowed and subservient to provide an effective counterpoint. By the end of a very long evening at the Spitalny's, Poole and his companions believe they have confronted the forces that helped create Koko.

Before leaving Milwaukee, however, they stumble across an unexpected piece of information. Manny Dengler, who served with such distinction in Vietnam and who was last seen in the company of Victor Spitalny during the chaos of a Bangkok street riot in 1969, was a resident of that same Milwaukee neighborhood, and was generally believed to be the only kid who was "more of a loser"[30] than Spitalny. Puzzled and curious, they visit Dengler's childhood home and interview his half-demented mother. What they learn, both there and in the microfilmed files of the local newspapers, drops them through the novel's last false bottom and leads them to the ugly, unpalatable truth.

Dengler, they discover, was the orphaned son of a murdered Nicaraguan woman. Three weeks after his mother's death, he was adopted by the man who may have been both his biological father and his mother's killer: a deranged street-corner preacher named Karl Dengler, proprietor of Dengler's Blood of the Lamb butcher shop. ("We Waste No Part of the Animal."[31]) Dengler's childhood was a catalog of large and small cruelties, among them beatings, confinement, sexual abuse and, perhaps most centrally, the suppression of his natural imaginative faculties. ("Imagination," his stepmother Hilda categorically states, "has to be stopped...You have to put an end to that. That's one thing I know."[32])

When Dengler was thirteen, a visiting social worker found him badly beaten and shut up in the shop's meat locker. The subsequent police investigation uncovered an entire history of abuse, and resulted in Karl Dengler's arrest, conviction, and eventual death in prison. A local judge then reaffirmed Hilda Dengler's status as Manny's guardian, and he spent the next four years in her dour company. In time, the arrival of his draft notice released him into the paradoxical freedom of Vietnam, where he flowered, briefly, before the enigmatic horrors of Ia Thuc trapped him in a "backwards and forwards"[33] universe in which the events of his childhood and the events of Ia Thuc endlessly recur, turning him into an "agent of eternity"[34] and an avatar of death.

Even in the face of these revelations, Poole and Underhill fail to make the final leap—to understand that Dengler, not Spitalny, is Koko—until they discover, among his few remaining effects, a sacred text of his childhood, *Babar the King*. Maggie Lah, for whom Babar was also a sacred text (just as it was for Poole's son Robbie), then reads them the following words from Babar's Song of the Elephants:

Patali Di Rapato
Cromda Cromda Ripalo
Pata Pata
Ko Ko Ko[35]

Armed with Koko's name, they return to New York, where a subsequent excursion into Chinatown leads them—with an instinctive certainty that overrides logistical probability—to the latest of Koko's caves. There—in a room whose walls are covered with images of dying children; and where a mutilated Harry Beevers, caught in his own killing box, lies trapped and bleeding, waiting to die - Poole and Underhill descend into the cave and confront Manny Dengler for the first time since Vietnam. Dengler, who never once relinquishes his control of the situation, shatters the overhead light and escapes under cover of darkness, slipping through a waiting police cordon by means of a ruse that has worked for him many times before: pretending to be Underhill. With an almost supernatural facility, he eludes one police dragnet after another, ending up, eventually, in Honduras, where he disappears from view forever. Our final glimpse of Koko—of "a small lean figure...moving, one step now at a time"[36] toward the covering darkness of the Honduran jungle—comes to us through the redemptive imagination of his eternal counterpart, Tim Underhill.

Seen in its broadest, most fundamental terms, *Koko* is a novel about the immense fragility of human life in a world that is alternately wonderful and terrible, beautiful and cruel. Its most emphatic illustration of that principle comes through its obsessive, endlessly repeated vision of the vulnerability of children. *Koko* is very much a novel about children at risk in an inimical universe. Images of children abused and abandoned, warped and destroyed, brutalized by forces both random and deliberate, are scattered throughout the text. Robbie Poole and Stacy Talbot, dead of cancer; Victor Spitalny and Manny Dengler, victimized in childhood by ignorant and deranged parents;

the vanished children of Ia Thuc, victimized by Harry Beevers; the victims of anonymous news reports found drowned, burned, and sexually abused—these and countless similar images are part of the emotional fabric of this novel, part of its inner life.

At the same time, *Koko* directly addresses the corollary issue of survival in such a world, and correctly identifies the most essential of all survival tools: imagination, a quality which reflects more than simply the capacity to create. True imagination, in the terms of this novel, also manifests itself as empathy, love, responsiveness to beauty, and the ability to step outside the narrow framework of the self and view the world from a deeper, broader perspective. If, as Straub later suggests, Tim Underhill is really the "secret hero"[37] of *Koko*, it is because he has retained his imaginative integrity in the face of debilitating and traumatic memories, and uses it to find his way back into the everyday human world. Manny Dengler, on the other hand, has been subjected to the systematic suppression of his imaginative capacity, and can't quite find the strength to escape from the caves of Milwaukee and Vietnam. In support of this vision of the primal power of imagination, Underhill tells the story of a dream that came to Henry James in the last years of the novelist's life. In this dream, James is awakened by a dark, threatening figure battering at his bedroom door. Terrified, James at first attempts to bar the door against the intruder. Then, in an extraordinary reversal, he throws the door open and turns on his attacker, who flees, defeated, into the distance. It is, as Underhill tells us, "a dream of elation and triumph,"[38] the triumph of the imaginative spirit, and it provides the novel with an appropriate metaphor for its closing pages.

There, in a first-person epilogue, narrated by Underhill and played out against the strains of Charlie Parker's 1945 rendition of "Koko"—music in which "fear is dissolved by mastery,"[39] and urgency by a Mozartean sense of "beauty and great calm"[40]—we learn something of the later lives of *Koko*'s principal characters. For the most part, they have found their way back into sane, reasonably coherent lives. Michael Poole abandons his lost marriage and meaningless career, falls in love with Maggie Lah, and establishes his front-line medical practice in a Bronx storefront. Conor Linklater likewise recovers his life through a similar combination of love and work, and Underhill himself successfully resumes his literary career. Only Harry Beevers, deprived of his "destiny," utterly loses his way. Six months after his encounter with Koko in the killing box, Harry enters a luxurious hotel in Times Square and checks into an expensive suite where, according to Underhill,

> he undressed...removed the .38 Police Special which...he had carried from his apartment, put its barrel against his temple, and pulled the trigger. He died four hours later. A playing card was found on the sheet beside his bed...The force of the bullet had knocked the card out of his mouth. His life had become useless to him and he threw it away.
>
> Harry opened the door and stepped back to let the dark figure enter. He had no job, little money, and his imagination had failed him. His illusions were all the imagination he had—a ferocious poverty.
>
> Perhaps in despair like Harry's, Koko once opened the door, stepped back, and let the dark figure enter.[41]

Koko is written with a force and freshness, an absolute clarity of intention and expression, that belie the difficulties that attended so much of its composition. And despite the fact that it represents a clear departure from the extravagantly imagined supernatural fictions that preceded it—despite the fact that it is in every way a more "realistic" novel—*Koko* remains, in many respects, the clear product of the sensibility that produced *Ghost Story, Shadowland,* and *Floating Dragon.* The "realism" of this novel is the realism of a man who believes that the world is filled with strange corners and unresolved mysteries, and that any attempt to convey the essential reality of the world must take into account the tangential, periodic presence of the numinous and extraordinary, or risk being considered both narrow and incomplete. In the course of this novel, the invisible world asserts itself in a number of ways. Dead children disappear from the site of their apparent murder, while their blood dissolves into the walls. Dozens of wasp stings appear and then disappear on Victor Spitalny's body. A dead girl from the distant past shows herself to Underhill, warning him of the approach of "ultimate things."[42] A giant cockroach appears out of nowhere in the kitchen of Tina Pumo's restaurant. And, in one of

Koko's most effective scenes, a vision of Michael Poole's dead son Robbie appears to him—fully grown and shining "like a god"[43]—in the aftermath of Tina Pumo's funeral.

A number of other characteristic Straubian concerns find their way into *Koko*, all of them looking perfectly at home in their new aesthetic surroundings. Straub's recurring concern with the often tawdry values that govern so much of contemporary life surfaces once more, largely through Straub's remorseless portrait of the doomed and infantile Harry Beevers. Straub's bedrock belief in the absolute necessity of meaningful work is likewise in evidence, particularly in the account of Michael Poole's transformation from discontented suburban baby doctor to useful practitioner of front-line medicine in the world of the urban poor. The past, always a powerful, even dominant, element in Straub's fiction, is particularly *present* in *Koko*, coloring the lives, beliefs, and personalities of virtually every major character. Raw, undigested memories—of childhood, of Vietnam, and of a variety of random, senseless personal tragedies—lie just below the surface of this vast complex of interconnected narratives. *Koko*, like so much of Straub's work, brings the words of William Faulkner forcibly to mind: "The past isn't dead. It isn't even past."

At the same time, books and music—the eternal influences—continue to help shape and characterize Straub's narratives. Two classic thrillers, Graham Greene's *The Third Man* and Eric Ambler's *A Coffin for Demitrios*—each of which is built around the central image of a criminal who has falsified his own death—helped Straub to flesh out a key element of the plot, while two works by Joseph Conrad provided major thematic inspiration. *Heart of Darkness*, with its grim vision of the human capacity to descend, under the proper circumstances, to unsuspected levels of savagery, is an obvious influence; while *The Secret Sharer*, the story of a sea captain who encounters his "double" in the Gulf of Siam, stands loosely behind the series of lies, misunderstandings, and false perceptions that connect Tim Underhill with his own hopelessly damaged double, M.O. Dengler.

Music, jazz especially, has always had an influence on Straub's life and writing but, in *Koko*, that influence seems more central, more directly connected to the way the characters think and feel and respond to the world. Music, in Poole's view, is a manifestation of the miraculous. ("Like a magic light that could pass through stone, brick, lead, wood, and skin, music streamed through the world on its way to somewhere else."[44]) It is also a useful metaphor for the process of discovery to which art, at its best, always aspires. Here, for example, is Michael Poole reflecting on his memories of a performance by jazz pianist Hank Jones, some years before:

> Poole knew very little about jazz, and now he could remember none of the actual music that Hank Jones had played. But what he did remember was a grace and joy that had seemed abstract and physical at once. He could remember how Hank Jones, who was a middle-aged black man with grizzled hair and a handsome, devilish face, had tilted his head over the keyboard, purely responsive to the flow of his inspirations...Poole had felt as though he were watching an old lion filled with the essence of lionhood.[45]

This wide-open, nothing-withheld response to what Poole calls the "blazing inner weather"[46] of the imaginative act reflects a fundamental belief in the existence of the sacred, and its presence in the novel is symptomatic of Straub's increased ambition, and of his increasing ability to articulate the most complex, inexpressible conditions.

Koko also continues Straub's ongoing presentation of the universe as Story, as the endless source of narratives that impinge on and affect the inner life of the novel. In *Koko*, Straub approaches this theme through the symbiotic relationship between Tim Underhill's novels and Manny Dengler's life. Dengler borrows the details of his escape from the war—i.e., murdering and mutilating Victor Spitalny, then switching identities—from the central plot device of an Underhill story initially called *The Running Grunt*, later published as a novel entitled *A Beast in View*. Underhill, in his turn, borrows the details of the Milwaukee setting of his second novel, *The Divided Man*, from the stories and anecdotes of Manny Dengler. He also, through an unconscious, utterly intuitive process of imaginative empathy, "invents" for his protagonist a tortured childhood remarkably similar to Dengler's own childhood. Dengler then borrows other elements of *The Divided Man*—notably its account of a murderer who leaves behind calling cards inscribed with the words "Blue Rose" at the scene of each murder—and uses them to create the template for the series of murders that he himself will commit. Thus, life imitates art and art imitates life in an alternating rhythm, as fact and fiction, the actual and the imagined, twine and intertwine. In a limited but very real sense, Dengler becomes a character in Underhill's books, and Underhill becomes the author of Koko's life, and the line of division between what is real and what is written become increasingly hard to discern.

Elsewhere in *Koko*, Narrative asserts itself in a variety of ways, even, on occasion, entering the novel in the form of dreams. Returning home from Bangkok after successfully locating Tim Underhill, Michael Poole dreams that he is a character in a non-existent Underhill novel called *Into the Darkness*. In that dream, which features Babar the Elephant and his own dead child, Robbie, Poole very nearly grasps something crucial about Koko, but the understanding fades when he startles himself awake. Life, messy and incoherent, aspires to the condition of fiction, the formal perfectibility of Stories.

Koko continues to stand as one of the artistic milestones of Straub's career, a book that is in every way deeper, richer, more stylistically assured than the novels that preceded it. In turning away from the admittedly grand visions of external evil that informed these novels, and toward a more balanced, judicious vision of evil as a human creation, Straub accomplished several things at once. First, he escaped from the very real dangers of typecasting, of finding himself trapped within a set of narrow, constricting expectations. Second, he began, in direct response to the stylistic requirements of *Koko*, the lifelong process of redefining his relationship to the language of the novel. Third, through the act of writing *Koko*, and through the parallel process of psychoanalysis that accompanied it, he put himself—and his fiction- more directly in touch with the central emotional issues of his life.

Finally, although Straub himself was unaware of this at the time, certain elements of *Koko*—the character of Tim Underhill; the plot of Underhill's novel, *The Divided Man*—would find their way into two subsequent novels: *Mystery* and (most particularly) *The Throat*. Along with *Koko*, these books would form a set of independent, loosely connected narratives commonly referred to as "The Blue Rose Trilogy," an ambitious exploration of related themes that would occupy Straub's attention for the next five years.

1. Letter from Peter Straub to the author
2. Ibid.
3. Ibid.
4. Ibid.
5. *Koko* (New York: E. P. Dutton, 1988), p. 4
6. Letter from Peter Straub to the author
7. Ibid.
8. Ibid.
9. Ibid.
10. Ibid.
11. Ibid.
12. Ibid.
13. Ibid.
14. Ibid.
15. *The Throat*, p. 3
16. *Koko*, p. 3
17. Ibid., p. 143
18. Ibid., p. 81
19. Ibid., p. 243
20. Ibid., pp. 125-126
21. Ibid.,p. 126
22. Ibid., pp. 98-99
23. Ibid., p. 331
24. Ibid., p. 331
25. Ibid., p. 336
26. Ibid., p. 337
27. Ibid., p. 189
28. Ibid., p. 511
29. Ibid., p. 449
30. Ibid., p. 454
31. Ibid., p. 99
32. Ibid., p. 473
33. Ibid., p. 343
34. Ibid., p. 554

Chapter Ten:
Mystery

Mystery appeared in January of 1990, just sixteen months after the hardcover publication of *Koko*. Considering the book's length and complexity, that is a remarkably short interval and seems to indicate that, this time out, Straub had managed to avoid many of the difficulties that attended the creation of *Koko*. That is a logical enough assumption, but one that is only partially accurate. Much of *Mystery* was, in fact, written at the same rapid-fire pace that characterized the final year of work on *Koko*, a period in which an average day's output ranged between ten and fifteen pages. However, the first few months of writing proved typically frustrating and difficult, and the story never really solidified until Straub forced himself to accept a painful but inevitable fact: that the novel he had planned to write was fundamentally different from the novel that wanted to be written.

As originally conceived, the novel that eventually became *Mystery* concerned the very different lives of a pair of identical twins. This notion was loosely inspired by Daphne Du Maurier's 1957 novel, *The Scapegoat*, in which a traveling Englishman meets his double, a dissolute French nobleman, and foolishly agrees to trade identities, thereby earning himself a great deal of unanticipated trouble. Straub's version of this story focused on teenaged twins, one of whom, Tom, is raised in a big house in a wealthy, privileged community while his brother, Mat, is imprisoned in a shed behind a squalid little house, and is subjected, throughout his childhood, to torture and harassment by a group of local delinquents known as the Corner Boys. The planned dramatic centerpiece involved Mat's escape from his prison, and his subsequent, violent acts of retaliation.

In an attempt to duplicate a method that had proved so effective during the preliminary planning of *Koko,* Straub retreated to Jumby Bay, a Caribbean resort located just off Antigua, to work out the details of his embryonic plot. Ironically, the tropical setting, which featured "frequent appearances by hummingbirds and lots of bougainvillea,"[1] soon insinuated itself into the novel, presenting Straub with a brand new notion that seemed to him both interesting and comic: translating the novel's original Midwestern setting into the radically altered ambiance of a Caribbean island. The city of Milwaukee is thus relocated to the tropical island of Mill Walk. Its various social milieus (its slums and tenements, the mansions of its wealthy Eastern Shore Road); its solidly Germanic heritage (manifested here in places like Goethe Park and in streets with names like Calle Berlinerstrasse, Calle Drosselmayer and An Die Blumen); its peculiarly Straubian landmarks (such as the Pforzheimer and St. Alwyn Hotels, which are featured prominently in both *Koko* and *The Throat*)—all of these elements are freshly reimagined and presented to us from a startling new perspective. The resulting transformation of a gray, somber city into its colorful Caribbean equivalent suffuses *Mystery* with a quality that is both familiar and exotic, and sets it apart from everything Straub had written up to that point, and everything that he has written since.

Having established the characters, the setting, and a general sense of the novel's direction, Straub returned to Manhattan, set to work, and ran into problems almost immediately. Most of these problems had to do with his plans for Mat, the beleaguered and imprisoned twin. After a couple of months of intensive work, he recalls,

> the ground seemed to be shifting beneath me. No matter how much I resisted, the book seemed far more interested in dealing with Tom's peculiar old neighbor, von Heilitz, than with Mat, although most of the best pages thus far concerned Mat...I hated cutting this material from the manuscript, but in the end I had to. It simply had no place in the real direction of the narrative. I spent about a week or two being deeply depressed, just dragging

> around in a sort of murky, underwater gloom, and then finally bit the bullet and accepted what I had to do.[2]

The character who usurps Mat's place in the novel is Lamont von Heilitz, which is also the name of a character who appears in *Under Venus* as the central figure in a couple of Denmark family anecdotes, but who bears no real relationship to the von Heilitz of *Mystery*. The new Lamont von Heilitz is a detective. More specifically, he is a Great Detective: a brilliant, eccentric, erudite figure set squarely in the tradition of such mythical and cerebral forebears as Sherlock Holmes, Nero Wolfe, Lord Peter Wimsey, and Hercule Poirot, all of whom are invoked during the course of the narrative.

The von Heilitz of *Mystery* is a dandyish, reclusive figure who dresses in almost comically old-fashioned three-piece suits (all with matching gloves); lives in a large expensive house just across the street from the novel's surviving protagonist, Tom Pasmore; and rarely shows himself in public. Although retired and now largely forgotten, he has solved over two hundred cases, beginning with the murder of his own parents some fifty years before. During his active career, he worked primarily in the background of events, solving many of his cases through deductions drawn from his study of newspapers, legal documents, real estate transactions, etc.: the endless array of paperwork that surrounds acts of violence. As a young man, he became popularly known as The Shadow, and was the direct inspiration for that other, "fictional" Shadow named Lamont Cranston, who always knew what evil lurked in the hearts of men. Von Heilitz's presence in *Mystery*—his interest in and connection with events on Mill Walk, together with his undisclosed relationship to his teenaged neighbor, Tom Pasmore—altered the nature of the book, leading Straub to reshape the narrative around a formal puzzle that was unlike anything he had attempted before. The result is a novel that is both a mystery, in the classical sense, and a contemplation of those larger mysteries that have occupied a place in virtually all of Straub's mature fiction.

Like *Shadowland*, the Straub novel it most resembles, *Mystery* offers us a number of significant preliminary scenes before proceeding to the main line of its narrative. In the first of these, we are introduced to the mythical island of Mill Walk, a place, the narrator assures us, that cannot be found on any map; that exists, rather, in "another continent of feeling, one layer beneath the known."[3] We are then presented with an enigmatic image: a small boy fleeing in terror from one of the emblematic sounds of his childhood. The nameless boy

> is fleeing down the basement stairs, in so great a hurry to escape the sounds of his mother's screams that he has forgotten to close the door, and so the diminishing screams follow him, draining the air of oxygen. They make him feel hot and accused, though of an uncertain crime—perhaps only that he can do nothing to stop her screaming.[4]

Moving through the basement in a blind panic, the boy—who appears to be about five years old—stumbles on a stack of old, yellowed newspapers with headlines that he can read, but cannot begin to understand.

> JEANINE THIELMAN FOUND IN LAKE,
>
> LOCAL MAN CHARGED WITH THIELMAN
>
> MURDER, MYSTERY RESOLVED IN TRAGEDY[5]

Of these last four words, we are told, the boy understands only "in." Other words—"wife," "children," "Shadow"—stare out at him alongside pictures of people he does not know. With an irony that is not immediately apparent, the boy then gathers up the papers and offers them to his mother, in a futile attempt to divert her from the source of her screams.

The following section, "The Death of Tom Pasmore," takes place several years later. Tom—who is, of course, the nameless boy in the basement—is now ten years old and has just hitchhiked from his family's mansion on Eastern Shore Road to a decidedly less affluent part of the island, driven by a compulsion he cannot explain. The impetus behind Tom's journey is a recent encounter with a figure he calls "The Chaos Man"—actually a disgruntled drunk named Wendell Hasek who has had a long-standing, and rather shady, relationship with Tom's grandfather, Glendenning Upshaw, who is one of the leading players in the social, political, and economic life of Mill Walk. Hasek, nursing an obscure grievance, had arrived at the Pasmore's door two days before, hurling rocks and shouting obscenities before being forcibly ejected by Glen Upshaw. Shortly afterward, Tom discovered Hasek's address and is now on his way there, responding to his newly awakened need to uncover the answers to unknown things.

Tom's decision to follow his instincts—to become, in effect, a detective—puts him in direct contact with the first of the novel's underlying spiritual mysteries.

> A sense of urgency, of *impendingness,* had awakened him with the screams that came from his mother's bedroom and clung to him during the whole anxious, jittery day, and when he waved his thanks to the driver, the feeling intensified like a bright light directed into his eyes...Tom squinted into the dusty haze through which passed a steady double stream of bicycles, horse carts, and automobiles. It was late afternoon and the light had a reddish, faintly molten cast...
>
> In the next moment this busy scene seemed to suppress beneath it another, more essential scene, every particle of which overflowed with an intense, unbearable beauty. It was as if great engines had kicked into life beneath the surface of what he could see. For a moment, Tom could not move. Nature itself seemed to have awakened, overflowing with being.[6]

Tom's contemplation of this hidden, vital, *invisible* world is shortly interrupted by a confrontation with Jerry Hasek—the Chaos Man's son—and two of his companions, Corner Boys named Robbie and Nappie. After a scuffle in which Tom breaks Jerry's nose, knives are drawn and the Corner Boys chase Tom into the stream of rush hour traffic, and into the second of the novel's fundamental mysteries.

> Tom knew that the car was going to hit him...then at last it did...and a series of irrevocable events began happening...Searing pain enfolded and enveloped him as

> the impact snapped his right leg and crushed his pelvis and hip socket. His skull fractured against the grille, and blood began pouring from his eyes and nose...Almost instantly unconscious, Tom's body hugged the grille for a moment, then began to slide down the front of the car...His right shoulder snapped, and the broken femur of his right leg sliced through muscle and skin like a jagged knife...At some point during the next few moments, while the driver moved reluctantly toward the front of his car, another event even more irrevocable than anything else that had occurred in the past sixty seconds, happened to Tom Pasmore. The accumulation of shock and pain stopped his heart, and he died.[7]

Tom's death—a very real, very literal death—lasts for only a few minutes, but before his spirit is returned to his broken body, he experiences a classic after-death interlude in which he views both himself and his surroundings from a suddenly detached perspective, and experiences a feeling of great peace—of "absolute rightness"[8]—that is abruptly curtailed when "a filament attaching him to his old life"[9] catches him like a hook, and returns him to the world.

Straub, who was himself the victim of a similar near-fatal accident, handles the details of Tom's subsequent recovery with the intimate familiarity of a survivor. Tom spends several months in Shady Mount Hospital and several more months recuperating at home, missing an entire year of school in the process. This experience goes a long way toward defining his essential character, and separates him, subtly but permanently, from the attitudes and beliefs of his peers. During the course of this year, he learns a great deal about pain and endurance. He learns to live with solitude and isolation, and learns to trust his own judgments regarding the character and ability of the people around him. (For example, he acquires a lifelong antipathy toward the hospital's glad-handing, incompetent medical director, Dr. Bonaventure Milton, and develops a lasting admiration for two tough-minded nurses from the wrong side of the island, Nancy Vetiver and Hattie Bascombe.) Most fundamentally, he learns to love and depend upon the company of books. "Before the accident," we are told, "books had meant the safety of escape; for a long time afterwards, what they meant was life itself."[10] Straub devotes a great deal of time and attention to the books in Tom's life—books that run the gamut from Shakespeare to Sax Rohmer, from Edgar Rice Burroughs to Edgar Allan Poe—and demonstrates, with absolute authority, the vital, sustaining power of the imaginative life.

Straub passes quickly from the year of Tom's "death" to the point, seven years later, when he discovers his true self by engaging those interconnected mysteries that form the centerpiece of this convoluted narrative. During those years, Tom's idiosyncratic development proceeds steadily and inevitably against the grain of the unwritten rules that govern behavior among Mill Walk's upper crust. The people who inhabit that upper crust form a reflexively conservative society governed by a handful of ruling dynasties. Chief among them are the Redwings, a pompous, dissolute family that has dominated Mill Walk society for nearly fifty years. The Redwings, and the vast majority who think like the Redwings, have built their lives around an immutable set of received standards which reflect a sort of cheerful, morally superior Philistinism that is uncorrupted by ideas or unusual points of view. Tom Pasmore, by contrast, has been shaped both by his experiences and by a heritage he does not yet understand, and has become a natural outsider, a boy whose deepest beliefs fly in the face of the prevailing social codes. Tom has been educated by the books he has read. He believes in "the melody of the English language"[11] and in the "idea of eloquence as mysteriously good and moral in itself."[12] Books connect him to that sense of a hidden, unacknowledged beauty that first appeared to him on the day of his accident.

> At times, deep in a book, he felt his body begin to glow; an invisible but potent glory seemed to hover just behind the characters, and it seemed as if they were on the verge of making some great discovery that would also be his—the discovery of a vast realm of radiant meaning that lay hidden just beneath the world of ordinary appearances.[13]

Tom's fascination with the world of hidden meanings and vast, imminent discoveries manifests itself as a fascination with murder, specifically with Mill Walk's own sketchy history of murder. For reasons that he himself does not entirely understand, he fills a scrapbook with newspaper clippings recounting various acts of violence and mayhem. Murder calls to him, and he is helpless to ignore that call. He is particularly intrigued by the island's most recent homicide, in which a woman named Marita Hasselgard—sister of the island's Finance Minister, Felix Hasselgard—is shot, supposedly by political opponents of the Minister, and dumped in the trunk of her brother's car. Dismayed by his unseemly interest in such matters, Tom's mother asks an English teacher named Dennis Handley to "have a talk" with Tom, and to persuade him to return to the world of socially acceptable obsessions.

The ploy fails utterly. Tom, in his turn, persuades Handley to drive him around the native sections of the island until he locates the bloodstained car in which Marita Hasselgard was murdered. Once there, two significant things happen. First, Tom's assessment of the physical evidence revealed by the car leads him to a new and ultimately dangerous theory: that Felix Hasselgard—for reasons that are not yet known but are probably related to some form of official corruption—murdered his sister and doctored the evidence to point to the involvement of an unknown political enemy. Second, Tom encounters another observer at the crime scene: his eccentric neighbor, Lamont von Heilitz, who is conducting an independent investigation that will lead him to an identical conclusion.

Shortly afterward, Tom writes an anonymous letter to Mill Walk's police chief, Fulton Bishop, in which he describes both his findings and his beliefs. Within days of the letter's arrival, the powers that govern Mill Walk respond in unexpected ways. A recently released convict named Foxhall Edwards is accused of murdering Marita Hasselgard. Edwards is then shot to death in a pitched battle in which two dissenting police officers are also fatally wounded. At about the same time, Felix Hasselgard "disappears" at sea, having apparently committed suicide in the face of recently discovered "irregularities" in the conduct of the Finance Ministry's affairs. Thus, in one massive act of damage control, scapegoats are found, witnesses are eliminated, and the case of Felix Hasselgard—who was once the political protégé of Tom's influential, and sinister, grandfather—is formally closed, safely written off before it can be tied into any wider, more established patterns of governmental corruption.

The Hasselgard investigation and its convenient, violent aftermath are played out against the more quotidian events of Tom Pasmore's life, events that help to illuminate both the varied nature of life on Mill Walk, and the particular relationships which will prove most crucial to Tom's own spiritual development. Through Tom, we see both the upper levels of Mill Walk society—as embodied by the Founder's Club, the ruling class enclave where Tom's dour, implacable grandfather holds court—and the lower depths, as represented by Elysian Courts, a rambling, organically evolved tenement built, some fifty years before, by the construction company owned by Glendenning Upshaw, and which is described by Straub with an almost Dickensian sense of detail.

Of the relationships which dominate Tom's life at this time, three stand out. The most problematic of the three is his relationship with his parents. His mother, Gloria Pasmore, is a helpless, badly damaged woman who appears to be in full retreat from some powerful but unspecified trauma, and whose screams have reverberated throughout Tom's life. Victor Pasmore, Tom's father, is a bitter, loveless man who spends most of his life numbed by the combined effects of alcohol and television, and who regards his son as a puzzling, inescapable annoyance. On a brighter note, Tom's childhood friendship with a beautiful, intelligent and witty young woman named Sarah Spence shows signs of becoming something more substantial, despite the fact that Sarah has been earmarked for Mill Walk's version of a royal marriage: her loutish boyfriend, Buddy Redwing, is the heir apparent to the ruling dynasty of the island. Finally, and most significantly, Tom enters into a secret compact with Mill Walk's most reclusive figure, Lamont von Heilitz, and that, more than anything, is the relationship that changes his life.

Von Heilitz first enters Tom's life in the days following his accident, when he appears to Tom as "a slim, fantastic figure...with webs of shadowy darkness dripping from his shoulders."[14] Later, he reenters Tom's life as a figure bearing books, all of them of a certain distinct type: Rex Stout, Arthur Conan Doyle, Josephine Tey, E. C. Bentley, etc. Eventually, after their encounter at the site of Marita Hasselgard's murder, he invites Tom into his house and offers him the first in an ongoing series of personal revelations.

Like Tom, von Heilitz keeps a scrapbook filled with newspaper accounts of murder investigations, but these accounts deal with cases von Heilitz himself participated in and, for the most part, solved. The first of these cases concerned the murder of his own parents, which occurred when von Heilitz was twelve years old, and which he solved several years later. Like the Hasselgard affair, that double murder was intimately bound up with the "irregularities" so prevalent in the highest levels of Mill Walk's government. In all, von Heilitz's scrapbook contains the records of several dozen murder investigations, and constitutes a kind of spiritual memoir that opens up, for young Tom Pasmore, a world of previously unsuspected possibilities. Von Heilitz quickly draws Tom's attention to one particular case, the same case that caught Tom's baffled attention when he was five years old: the murder of Jeanine Thielman.

Von Heilitz had "solved" this case many years before, but has since grown uncertain as to the justice of that solution. The facts of the case, briefly stated, are these: Jeanine Thielman, wife of wealthy Mill Walk contractor Arthur Thielman, had been murdered in a Wisconsin resort called Eagle Lake in 1925. (Eagle Lake is a privately owned vacation spot where many of Mill Walk's wealthier residents spend their summers. Tom's own grandmother, Glendenning Upshaw's wife, died in that same lake—an apparent suicide—in 1924, one year before the Thielman murder.) Jeanine, whose Eagle Lake cottage bordered the property owned by Tom's grandfather, had been shot in the back of the head, wrapped in a length of curtain, and then dropped into an isolated section of the lake.

Von Heilitz's investigation led him, eventually, to a likely suspect: a shady hotel business associate of Upshaw's named Anton Goetz, who had been conducting a clandestine affair with Jeanine. In time, von Heilitz confronted Goetz and accused him of the murder. Hours later, Goetz was found dead, hanging by a length of fishing line from the crossbeams of his cottage. In the face of what appeared to be a clear indication of guilt, the case was closed, and the Shadow was credited with one more deductive triumph. But now, forty years later, von Heilitz is still obsessively circling the events of that summer, convinced that there is much that remains undiscovered, and that the Thielman case is somehow vitally connected to the ongoing history of personal and institutional corruption that is so much a part of Mill Walk's history, and that has found its latest manifestation in the Felix Hasselgard affair.

By telling this story, von Heilitz has, in effect, enlisted Tom Pasmore's assistance in reinvestigating an ancient, largely forgotten crime. Tom receives an unexpected opportunity to participate in that investigation when his grandfather, alarmed by Tom's propensity for asking embarrassing and inappropriate questions, shunts him off to Eagle Lake for a summer of innocuous pleasures.

As things turn out, the events of that summer prove anything but innocuous. Obeying von Heilitz's injunction to "ask questions and stir things up,"[15] Tom manages, within the space of two or three weeks, to alienate, offend and unsettle the majority of Eagle Lake's summer residents. He begins by entering into a sexual relationship with Sarah Spence, thus earning the undying enmity of the Redwings, who believe, quite literally, that Sarah belongs to them. At about the same time, Tom once again encounters Jerry Hasek and his Corner Boys, Robbie and Nappie, who had last entered his life just seconds before his near-fatal accident. The three are now employed as glorified bodyguards for the Redwings, and are augmenting their income through a lucrative sideline in housebreaking, a sideline that Tom will discover and expose before his "vacation" is over.

And, of course, Tom continues to pursue all available sources of information on the Thielman murder, ransacking old newspaper files and interviewing anyone with any connection to, or memory of, that event. The elderly Kate Redwing, a relative by marriage who had been present at the discovery of Jeanine Thielman's body, fills in some of the background of that summer, and provides some additional indications of Anton Goetz's probable innocence. She also introduces Tom to one of Eagle Lake's other persona non grata, a gay pediatrician named Buzz Laing. Laing, although not present during that crucial summer, holds a critical element of the puzzle: his familiarity with the medical records of an unnamed patient exhibiting classical symptoms of sexual abuse. This last fact, not revealed until later in the novel, ties in directly with Tom's final discovery: a series of notes which appear to have been written by Jeanine Thielman to her killer. The notes state: *I know what you are and you must be stopped.* And *This has gone on too long. You will pay for your sin.*[16]

In the course of his investigation, Tom is very nearly killed on three occasions. Once, in a moment of ironic deja vu, he is pushed in front of a moving vehicle, which passes harmlessly over him. Another time, while talking on the phone with his grandfather, he leans toward the window in response to his grandfather's question ("What do you see when you look out the window?"[17]) and is nearly shot by a high caliber bullet that shatters the window and misses him by inches.

The third occurrence follows his discovery of Jeanine Thielman's notes. He is asleep, with Sarah, in the bedroom of his grandfather's cottage when a fire breaks out on the ground floor. Tom saves both himself and Sarah, but the remaining occupant of the cottage, a former nurse and midwife name Barbara Deane, burns to death. When her charred body is discovered the next morning, she is mistakenly identified as Tom. Tom, officially regarded as dead, is spirited back to Mill Walk by Lamont von Heilitz, who, just hours before the fire, had met with Tom at Eagle Lake and presented him with another vital revelation: that he, not Victor Pasmore, was Tom's biological father. Together in Mill Walk, still tentatively exploring the boundaries of this newly acknowledged relationship, father and son reexamine the pieces of the forty year old puzzle, reassess the personalities involved and come to a new, mutually agreed upon conclusion: that Jeanine Thielman's murderer was—must have been—Glendenning Upshaw.

The Glen Upshaw who is cumulatively revealed in these pages is, in von Heilitz's words, a man with "a special kind of mind,"[18] one utterly lacking in the most fundamental qualities: empathy and imagination. Von Heilitz, who has known Upshaw since childhood, remarks that "other people were never very real to him. They never have been."[19] Upshaw's essential soullessness allows him to function with a chilling indifference to all humane standards, an indifference that is reflected in both his private and professional lives. A master manipulator who knows where all of Mill Walk's bodies are buried, he is as responsible as anyone for the corruption endemic to his native island. His abuse of the public trust is echoed by another form of abuse, one alluded to by Buzz Laing and recognized, forty years before, by Jeanine Thielman: the sexual abuse of his daughter, who has spent the bulk of her lifetime screaming at shadows and hiding from the world.

Tom and von Heilitz decide to test their theory—and provoke a reaction—by sending Upshaw exact duplicates of the notes for which Jeanine was murdered in 1925. The reaction, like the one that followed Tom's earlier letter to Police Chief Fulton Bishop, is violent and immediate. Von Heilitz, on his way to a meeting with one of Mill Walk's uncorrupted policemen, a homicide detective name David Natchez, is intercepted and murdered by a pair of policeman in Glendenning Upshaw's pay. Tom, suddenly fatherless, meets with Natchez himself. Together, they track Upshaw to his hiding place in the rambling tenement that he himself built—Elysian Courts—and lure him into the open by shouting the by now talismanic words: *I know who you are. You must be stopped.* As Tom and his grandfather come face to face, Upshaw draws a pistol, fires at Tom, and misses. Natchez then kills Upshaw with a single shot to the head. Afterward, Tom and the detective move the body to the study of Upshaw's house, surround it with Jeanine Thielman's accusing letters, and restage the killing as a suicide, an elaborate piece of fiction which leads Tom to remark that "Sometimes life is like a book."[20]

Afterward, in the uproar that follows both Upshaw's death and the scandalous revelations found in his private papers, the political machine that has governed Mill Walk for almost fifty years collapses, and Tom is left to face some fundamental questions about his own destiny and identity. In a final meeting with Sarah Spence—a meeting that takes place in Goethe Park Zoo, beneath the gaze of a prowling panther—Tom comes to terms with the fundamental condition of his life: that he is a detective, and that what he is and what he must do are one and the same thing. In the end, he turns his back on the seductions of ordinary life, and accepts his role as Lamont von Heilitz's son.

Despite the fact that it is a serious novel dealing with some of the darkest aspects of human nature, much of *Mystery* has a buoyancy, a comic lightness of tone, that sets it apart from the majority of Straub's fiction, particularly the intense and disturbing *Koko*. This relative lightness comes, for the most part, from two elements. One is the degree of informed, satirical social observation that permeates the book, particularly in its view of the follies and foolishness of life in the upper levels of Redwing Society. The other is Straub's decision to build his plot, or much of his plot, around certain aspects of the traditional detective story.

Straub has always been concerned with the values that underlie the actions of both individuals and the societies they represent. In *Mystery*, the closed, self-contained society of the Redwings provides him with the perfect opportunity to examine and deflate the pretensions of a life style that is both stifling and comically self-absorbed.

> Tom had no interest in being an imitation Redwing, though that was the goal of most of what passed for society on Mill Walk. Redwing reliability consisted of thoughtlessness, comfortable adherence to a set of habits and traits that were generally ac-

> cepted more as the only possible manners than as simple good manners.
>
> One arrived at business appointments five minutes late, and half an hour late for social functions. One played tennis, polo and golf as well as possible. One drank whiskey, gin, beer, and champagne—one did not really know much about other wines—and wore wool in the winter, cotton in summer...One smiled and told the latest jokes...one never publicly disapproved of anything, ever, nor too enthusiastically gave public approval, ever. One made money (or, in the Redwing's case, conserved it) but did not vulgarly discuss it. One owned art, but did not attach an unseemly importance to it: paintings, chiefly landscapes or portraits, were intended to decorate walls, increase in value, and testify to the splendor of their owners.[21]

Straub has a great deal of fun delineating the complete awfulness of this society, creating, in the process, a gallery of characters who are vivid embodiments of its most absurd, inbred characteristics: Ralph and Katrinka Redwing, for whom the world is divided into two groups: "our people" and everyone else; Buddy Redwing, the teenaged heir who is characterized both by his absolute uselessness and his unshakable sense of inherited privilege; Victor Pasmore, Tom's "official" father, who is galvanized by the prospect of receiving a crumb from the Redwing table; and Mr. and Mrs. Spence, who would gladly sell their daughter into white slavery if doing so would gain them access to the Redwing inner circle.

The detective story element of the novel—the mystery behind *Mystery*—derives much of its essential nature from the presence of Lamont von Heilitz, a certified Great Detective in the grand tradition. Von Heilitz evokes, and is meant to evoke, certain aspects of his legendary predecessors. Like Poirot, he is dandified, cerebral, and eccentric. Like Nero Wolfe, he is a recluse who prefers to deal with criminal matters at a distance, solving many of his cases at home through research and ratiocination. Like Holmes, he is, when circumstances require, a master of disguise. Like Holmes, he has a crew of

Irregulars, street people who run errands and perform discreet, highly specialized services whenever the Great Man calls on them. A certain sense of fun, of narrative joie de vivre, attaches almost automatically to this sort of story. Despite the stark facts of pain and loss that are inevitable elements of what von Heilitz calls the obscenity of murder, the formal detective story, as practiced by such writers as Agatha Christie, Rex Stout, and Dorothy Sayers, is a kind of airily exhilarating adventure, one in which both reader and detective travel from darkness into light, from obscurity toward the intellectual satisfaction of a logical, rational resolution. Through Tom Pasmore, who relaxes from the rigors of Eagle Lake by reading Agatha Christie's *The ABC Murders,* Straub reflects on the nature of the form, in terms of both the satisfactions that it offers, and the more profound satisfactions that it usually withholds. In one of his more dissatisfied ruminations, Tom notes that detectives like Hercule Poirot

> were abstraction machines, and you never had any idea at all what it felt like to be them, but by the last chapter they could certainly tell you who had left the footprint beneath the Colonel's window, and who had found the pistol on the bloody pillow and tossed it into the gorse bush. They were walking crossword puzzles, but at least they could do that.[22]

On the other hand, and within certain strict limits, the classic puzzle offers certain very comfortable pleasures, pleasures Tom acknowledges later on in the story.

> He stretched out again and read a few more pages of *The ABC Murders.* He remembered being dissatisfied with it yesterday, but could not remember why—it was a perfect book. It made you feel better, like a fuzzy blanket and a glass of warm milk. A kind of simple clarity shone through everything and everybody, and the obstacles to that clarity were only screens that could be rolled away by the little grey cells. You never got the feeling that a real dark-

> ness surrounded anyone, not even murderers.[23]

That last, of course, is the major problem with such books: their refusal to acknowledge the pervasive darkness that accompanies the act of murder. Straub, by contrast, does believe in acknowledging the darkness, and does believe that death and grief are profoundly powerful things, incapable of being sublimated beneath the quaint surface of an elaborate puzzle. As a consequence, *Mystery* is never more than partially indebted to this sort of cozy, Golden Age confection and evolves, instead, into something darker and more ambitious.

Just as there is more than one type of detective in this book (von Heilitz, of course, and the grim, incorruptible Mill Walk homicide detective, David Natchez), so there is more than one type of influence lurking behind the scenes, including: Raymond Chandler (whose *The Lady in the Lake* provides the novel with one of its central images); Dashiell Hammett (who, in novels like *Red Harvest,* which is mentioned in the text, virtually created the archetypal image of the corrupt community); and Ross MacDonald (whose recurring vision of the connection between the violent, unresolved past and the traumas of the present seems to bear a profound relationship to so much of Straub's work, *Mystery* included.) Influences like these help Straub ground his story in the emotional realities of his characters' lives, returning it to the sort of artistic first principles Chandler had in mind when he praised Hammett for taking murder out of the drawing room and giving it back "to the sort of people that commit it for reasons, not just to provide a corpse; and with the means at hand, not hand-wrought dueling pistols, curare, and tropical fish."[24] In the end, one of *Mystery*'s most significant accomplishments is the way in which Straub opens up the form of the detective novel, widening it to permit seemingly incompatible elements to coexist, and to maintain their claim on both our emotional and intellectual attention.

All in all, the detective novel proved to be a remarkably effective vehicle for Straub's particular purposes, allowing him to experiment freely with the conventions of the form, and providing him with a forum within which to continue working out a number of obsessively recurring themes. Many of the animating ideas last seen in *Koko* are revisited here, reinforcing certain of that novel's most fundamental concerns. For instance, Straub's vision of the vulnerability of children in a harsh, inimical universe is once again centrally present, this time through the character of Gloria Pasmore, who, as the four year old Gloria Upshaw, was abused and very nearly destroyed by her own father, and left with a legacy of nightmares that would never go away. Gloria's predicament also embodies that recurring, Ross MacDonald-like notion that the past is always with us, and that the things that happen to us, whether in childhood or in later life, never stop happening.

The act of detection also ties in neatly with the idea of narrative as an actual, palpable element of our day-to-day lives. Detectives—certainly the detectives of *Mystery*—do more than simply solve crimes or dazzle the reader with ingenious deductions. They unearth *stories*—revising and completing them, teasing coherent narratives out of disconnected clues, making narrative sense out of the scattered and intractable material of human lives. It is no accident that when von Heilitz presents Tom Pasmore with the memories of his professional life, he presents them in the form of a book; or that the Lamont von Heilitz once known as the Shadow should be so easily transmuted into Lamont Cranston, the fictional centerpiece of an ongoing series of popular stories. Life aspires to the condition of fiction, and the detective, even more than most of us, lives very close to that invisible line where life and narrative meet.

Like *Koko*, *Mystery* is also a novel about the consolations of art—books and music in particular—and the fundamental importance of imaginative empathy to the growth of the human soul. Tom learns, at the age of ten, that books are necessary to the survival of the spirit. He also learns, in the moments following his temporary death, that "in the end, music did explain everything,"[25] a piece of hard-won wisdom that will find its way into his later life. From von Heilitz, he learns another fundamental lesson: that what we think of as intelligence is really just imaginative empathy, and that imaginative empathy is the essential element of a worthwhile life. The people who inhabit *Mystery* are characterized, finally, by the degree to which they possess this one overarching quality. The most extreme example of the absence of empathy is found in Glendenning Upshaw, who is not, in any recognizable way, human. Less lethal examples of this imaginative poverty include the Redwings and their circle, people who have willingly sacrificed their best selves for the banal and trivial rewards of social and financial success.

Two more uniquely Straubian themes stand at the heart of *Mystery*, and they are of primary importance. One, logically enough, concerns the pervasive presence of mysteries in and around the world of human affairs. The other, a recurring concern with the importance of meaningful work, is here broadened and deepened, and helps to transform *Mystery* into a meditation on the existence, and importance, of "callings," of vocations so perfectly aligned with one's nature and gifts that they seem to possess aspects of the sacred; seem, in fact, to be directly connected to the hidden mysteries of the world.

Early in the novel, just before the accident that puts him in touch with the fundamental mysteries of life and death, Tom Pasmore encounters another mystery. As he jumps down from the milk cart that has carried him to a strange section of the island, he experiences an almost miraculous heightening of the senses, together with the feeling that, in another minute, he will see the world suddenly open itself up to him, revealing its secrets, showing him "the engines" that lie beneath the surface of things, driving the world. Tom, of course, is ten years old, and doesn't understand that he has just experienced the holy sense of connection to the vital center of things, a connection that can only come—if it comes at all—when one has yielded to the dictates of one's essential self, and found a calling.

Lamont von Heilitz, who experienced a similar feeling when he began the investigation that confirmed him in his own calling, might have been able to explain this to Tom. Several years later, he does, describing to Tom the feelings that accompanied the initial stages of his investigation into Jeanine Thielman's murder:

> "...I want you to consider my state of mind. Once the body had been discovered, I noticed a change in everything about me. I could say that I had become more alert, more involved in things, or that Eagle Lake had become more interesting. But it was more than that. Eagle Lake had become more *beautiful.*"
>
> Tom wanted to shake him. "How did you get him to confess?"
>
> "Listen to me. The solution is not what I'm talking about here. I am describing a sudden change in my most basic feelings. When I walked beside my lodge and

> looked at the lake and the lodges scattered around it, at the docks, at the pilings outside the Redwing compound, the tall Norwegian pines and enormous oaks, it all seemed—changed. Every bit of it *spoke* to me. Every leaf, every pine needle, every path through the woods, every bird call, had come alive, was vibrant, full of meaning. Everything *promised.* Everything *chimed.* I knew more than I knew. There was a secret beating away beneath the surface of everything I saw."
>
> "Yes," Tom said, not knowing why this raised goose bumps on his arms.
>
> "Yes," the old man said. "You have it too. I don't know what it is—a capability? A calling?"[26]

Earlier, speaking of his very first case—the murder of his parents—von Heilitz remarks that, through the frustrating and often tedious process of investigation, "I was saving my own life."[27] Later in the novel, Tom Pasmore comes to understand that his own investigation into the Thielman murder has become the source of his personal salvation. These moments call to mind the Gnostic gospel of St. Thomas that Tom Flanagan discovers in *Shadowland.*

> If you bring forth what is within you, what you bring forth will save you. If you do not bring forth what is within you, what you do not bring forth will destroy you.[28]

Both Tom and von Heilitz have yielded to the most compelling of their inner voices, and have, in their idiosyncratic fashions, become artists, just as anyone—whether poet, novelist, magician, or musician—whose work is intimately involved with the process of discovery is, in a sense, an artist. And the reward—the rare and occasional reward—for such occupations is this sense of *immanence,* the feeling that "a great unconscious paradise"[29] lies just beneath the surface of the ordinary world.

Mystery is a novel that, in *Koko*'s words, looks backwards and forwards at once: obsessively reworking themes and situations from earlier novels—particularly *Shadowland*—and anticipating the revelations of Straub's subsequent fiction. The connection with *Shadowland*, already implicit in the lines from the Gnostic gospel, is clear and direct. Both novels feature teenaged boys—Tom Pasmore and Tom Flanagan—who apprentice themselves to the master of an arcane art; travel to a kind of enchanted forest filled with mysteries and unforeseen dangers; fall hopelessly in love with girls who have been "claimed" by opposing powers; experience both the wonder and the terror of encountering the underlying forces of the world; escape from the forest on the heels of a climactic fire; and return to the "normal" world altered and enhanced, having discovered something essential about their lives and natures; having discovered, in fact, just who they are and what they must become. The following passage—which happens to come from *Shadowland*—could have appeared, exactly as written, in either novel.

> Every night I had terrible dreams...but the oddest feeling I had in these dreams, no matter how bad they were, was that I was somehow seeing how things really were. It was like the world had split open, and I was part of the engine of things—or not seeing as much as feeling it there. As scared as I was, there was this funny kind of satisfaction, the satisfaction of knowledge. As if without at all understanding it, I was at least seeing how the mystery worked. Suppose the skies opened and you saw a great wheel, the wheel that turns us round the sun—that is the kind of feeling I had.[30]

At various points in the narrative, Straub foreshadows the central subject matter of his next novel by revisiting a subject first raised in *Koko:* the Blue Rose murders. First, he recapitulates the plot of Tim Underhill's "fictional" recreation of those murders, *The Divided Man*, a book which provides its own provisional solution to a series of killings that took place in and around the St. Alwyn Hotel in 1950. He then introduces a startling new element by informing us that Buzz Laing, the pediatrician who provided Tom with the first indication that his mother had been sexually abused, had himself survived an attack by the Blue Rose killer. Later, during the course of his final confrontation with Glendenning Upshaw, Tom presents his grandfather with an enigmatic accusation consisting of two words: Blue Rose. We are thus permitted to draw the inference that Upshaw was responsible for the attack on Buzz Laing, an attack that may have been motivated by the desire to prevent Buzz from revealing his suspicions of sexual misconduct.

Once the Blue Rose case is connected, however tentatively, to Glendenning Upshaw, new possibilities present themselves, including the possibility that Buzz Laing was the real—the only—target, and that the other murders were simply smoke screens, a scenario made famous by a book that is referred to repeatedly throughout the novel: Agatha Christie's *The ABC Murders*. (Life, as Tom has reminded us, really is "sometimes like a book.") But that, of course, is just one more provisional solution, one more way of looking at an elusive series of events we cannot yet fully understand. Three years later, those events would form the centerpiece of Straub's longest, most ambitious, most labyrinthine creation to date: *The Throat*.

1. Letter from Peter Straub to the author
2. Ibid.
3. *Mystery* (New York: E. P. Dutton, 1990), p. 1
4. Ibid., pp. 1-2
5. Ibid., p. 2
6. Ibid., pp. 7-8
7. Ibid., pp.25-26
8. Ibid., p. 33
9. Ibid., p. 33
10. Ibid., p. 54
11. Ibid., p. 56
12. Ibid., p. 56
13. Ibid., p. 56
14. Ibid., p. 39
15. Ibid., p. 243
16. Ibid., p. 388
17. Ibid., p. 346
18. Ibid., p. 457
19. Ibid., p. 457

[20]. Ibid., p. 541

[21]. Ibid., p. 58

[22]. Ibid., p. 307-308

[23]. Ibid., p. 344

[24]. Raymond Chandler, *The Simple Art of Murder* (New York, Houghton Mifflin, 1950)

[25]. *Mystery*, p. 32

[26]. Ibid., p. 98

[27]. Ibid., p. 89

[28]. *Shadowland*, p. 291

[29]. *Mystery*, p. 187

[30]. *Shadowland*, pp. 60-61

Chapter Eleven:
Houses Without Doors

Before turning his attention to *The Throat*, Straub gathered together a number of shorter pieces and published them, in 1990, under the title *Houses Without Doors*. A distinguished, ambitious collection that remains, justifiably, one of Straub's own favorite books, *Houses* gathers together two novellas (both of which have deep connections to Straub's ongoing series of Blue Rose novels), two short stories, and two short novels. In addition, the book contains seven short, loosely connected vignettes whose themes, scenes and subjects—childhood, Vietnam, resurrected memories—echo and amplify the central concerns of the stories that surround them, giving the collection an overall sense of cohesiveness and thematic unity that is both unusual and effective. Together, these thirteen pieces create a composite portrait of a violent, claustrophobic universe whose essence is suggested by the Emily Dickinson epigraph that gives the book its title.

> Doom is the house without the door—
> 'Tis entered from the sun—
> And then the ladder's thrown away,
> Because escape—is done—

Following a brief vignette in which a woman sees what just might be an angel on the streets of New York City, the collection opens with "Blue Rose," a novella whose title unambiguously announces its relationship to the world of Straub's novels. Written while *Koko* was still in the planning stages, "Blue Rose" is connected to that novel in at least two ways. First, its central character is the ten-year-old Harry Beevers, who will grow up, go to Vietnam, and become the world's worst lieutenant. Second, its "author" (though this particular conceit is never made explicit in the text itself) is Tim Underhill, the Straubian alter ego who appears in *Koko* and narrates *The Throat*. Straub decided to attribute both "Blue Rose" and "The Juniper Tree," his subsequent novella, to Underhill because, on reflection, the stories seemed, quite naturally, to be "a part of [Underhill's] moral world, part of his process of exploration."[1] The two stories represent what Straub called "the first part of Underhill's efforts to comprehend violence and evil by wrapping them in his own imagination."[2]

The germ of "Blue Rose" came to Straub by way of a book called *The Freudian Fallacy* by E. M. Thornton, a rather "contentious"[3] attempt to discredit certain of Freud's theories on neurological grounds. At one point in the book, Thornton noted that the effects of epilepsy on the brain were remarkably similar to the effects of hypnosis. At about the time he encountered Thornton's book, Straub also came across an essay published in *The New York Review of Books* which discussed the fact that many seriously disturbed people—some of them murderers—come from families in which the mother sees herself as someone higher on the social scale than her husband. These two notions, combined with the emerging character of Harry Beevers, provided Straub with the central elements of his first published novella.

"Blue Rose" takes place in Palmyra, New York, in what is "usually but wrongly called a simpler time"[4]: the mid-1950s. With great clarity and economy, Straub takes us into the troubled home life of the Beevers, a deeply unhappy, fully dysfunctional American family. Maryrose Beevers, Harry's mother, is a figure out of Tennessee Williams, constantly bemoaning the reduced circumstances of her life with Edgar Beevers, a borderline alcoholic who has all but abdicated in the face of Maryrose's relentless unhappiness. The Beevers have five sons. The two oldest, George and Sonny, left home at the first available opportunity. Both, significantly, have become soldiers. Three sons remain at home: Albert, a sullen, brutish thirteen-year-old; Little Eddie, the youngest, a whiny nine-year-old with a full complement of incipient neuroses; and Harry, the "smart one," the one who is destined to go places.

The story begins when Harry, rummaging through an attic filled with the symbols of his mother's superior past, discovers a do-it-yourself book on hypnosis. Harry, who is already a natural manipulator, begins to develop his hypnotic technique by practicing on Little Eddie. The results are immediate and astonishing. The first time out, Harry succeeds in putting his brother into a deep, highly suggestible trance state. At one point, they practice a standard hypnotic set piece called "the chair exercise," in which Eddie puts his head on one chair and his feet on another, forming a human bridge between the two. At Harry's command he becomes so rigid that Harry can literally bounce up and down on his brother's frail, suspended body. Slightly drunk with power, Harry ends the session by implanting a posthypnotic suggestion: whenever Eddie hears the words "blue rose," he will revert immediately to that same, deeply acquiescent trance state.

At the next session, which takes place a few days later in the same crowded attic, disaster strikes. Harry has spent the intervening period reading books on Murder, Incorporated and the Nazi concentration camps, and their imagery has begun to infect him. After hypnotizing Eddie and telling him that his body has become completely numb and impervious to pain, Harry produces an eight-inch hat pin stolen from Maryrose's bedroom and, in the story's most visceral sequence, stabs Eddie deeply and repeatedly, first in the forearm, later in the abdomen. At some point in the process, Harry crosses over into a state of scarcely controlled mania.

> I can do this every night, he thought. I can bring Little Eddie up here every single night, at least until school starts.[5]

In a final experiment, Harry forces Eddie to regress through earlier stages of his brief life. The regression proceeds smoothly until Eddie returns to the age of three, and to the memory of a painful confrontation with Maryrose. Faced with a memory that frightens him, Eddie goes into a blind, windmilling panic, pulling down racks of dresses, shattering his mother's prized mirror, damaging or destroying some of her most treasured possessions. Stunned and terrified, Harry see only one way to deflect his mother's anger. Uttering the control phrase, "blue rose," he puts Eddie back into a hypnotic trance and, calling to mind the details of an epileptic seizure that a former classmate once suffered, he coerces Eddie into duplicating the symptoms of a grand mal seizure, at the end of which, on command, Eddie swallows his tongue and chokes to death.

In the aftermath of Eddie's death, the Beevers' family rapidly disintegrates. Thirteen-year-old Albert begins a long, slow slide into mental and emotional instability. Edgar Beevers descends further into an alcoholic haze, eventually deserting his family. Maryrose continues to hide behind the unbreachable facade of her illusions. Harry, by contrast, thrives, moving from this crucial formative experience through a life that will include college, law school, and a bizarre, violent apotheosis in Vietnam.

"Blue Rose" is notable for the clarity and unadorned precision of its prose. This "presentational" effect is one that Straub labored to achieve, and it brings the people, places, and events of this story—particularly the scenes in which Harry uses the power of hypnosis to torture and then murder his little brother—into sharp relief. It is also notable for its subtle prefiguring of the peculiar role that military service will eventually play in Harry's life.

To begin with, the Beevers' household is, in effect, a war zone, marked by carefully defined territorial divisions and scattered pockets of neutral ground, the domestic equivalent of No Man's Land. Harry's two oldest brothers are both soldiers, while Albert is counting the days until he, too, can enlist and escape. And Edgar Beevers, Harry's drunken, defeated father, is a World War II veteran who once participated in the liberation of Dachau. Early in the story, Edgar recounts to Harry his single most memorable wartime experience: shooting an escaping concentration camp guard in the back.

This story has a profound effect on Harry. It feeds his fantasies and—together with the books he has just read on the atrocities perpetrated both in the death camps and in the world of organized crime—colors his mental and emotional landscape, contributing the power of its imagery to Harry's already violent and disordered inner world. Here, for example, is Harry, standing in the devastated attic with his brother just minutes before uttering the words that will trigger the fatal seizure.

> He saw himself, a man in another life, standing in a row with men like himself in a bleak gray landscape defined by barbed wire. Emaciated people in rags shuffled up toward them and spat on their clothes. The smells of dead flesh hung in the air. Then the vision was gone, and Little Eddie stood

> before him again, surrounded by layers of glittering light.[6]

Immediately afterward, he retreats down the stairs, while his brother begins to thrash around on the attic floor.

> Harry went across the hall and into the "dormitory" bedroom. There seemed to be a strange absence of light in the hallway. For a second he saw—was sure he saw—a line of dark trees across a wall of barbed wire.[7]

The central events of Harry's life are thus inextricably connected to the events and images of two different wars. One involves his active, adult participation. The other invades his childhood imagination, and helps to shape the course of his subsequent history. In the end, "Blue Rose" works equally well as a self-contained account of savagery and childhood trauma, and as a kind of supplementary text that illuminates certain hidden, subterranean aspects of the novel that would follow it some three years later: *Koko.*

The collection's second novella is "The Juniper Tree," and it, too, is concerned with the revelation of deeply buried, subterranean events. The title, and much of the relevant imagery, is taken from the folktale by the Brothers Grimm, which concerns a young boy who is murdered, cut to pieces, and buried beneath a juniper tree. But in the world of Straub's story, as in the world of Jacob and Wilhelm Grimm, "dismembered children...can rise and speak, made whole again."[8]

"The Juniper Tree" is also the second and last of the stories attributed to Tim Underhill. Again, nothing in the text explicitly connects the story to Underhill, and the nature of that connection will not be revealed until the closing chapters of *The Throat,* which would appear some ten years later. Both novel and novella deal with the revelation of a long-buried secret. In both cases, the secret has to do with a brief, deeply repressed history of sexual abuse.

"The Juniper Tree" contains very little in the way of a formal plot, but is built, instead, around a series of brief, shabby sexual encounters that are described with a pitiless, unflinching directness. Like "Blue Rose," the story is set in the American Midwest of the early 1950s. It is narrated by a successful, middle-aged novelist who has only recently recovered the memory of an event that occurred when he was seven years old, and that boiled throughout his subsequent life with "underground explosions and hidden fires."

The story begins with an act of deceit. The seven year-old hero, adrift in the middle of a solitary summer vacation, has deceived his parents into thinking that he spends his days in the supervised setting of a Summer Play School. Instead, he goes to a local movie theater—the Orpheum Oriental—and spends countless hours "in the rapture of education" that movies, and only movies, can provide him.

> I watched Alan Ladd and Richard Widmark and Glenn Ford and Dane Clark. *Chicago Deadline*. Martin and Lewis, tangled up in the same parachute in *At War with the Army*. William Boyd and Roy Rogers. Openmouthed, I drank down movies about spies and criminals, wanting the passionate and shadowy ones to fulfill themselves, gorging themselves on what they needed.[9]

Part of what the boy finds at the movies is respite from a world dominated by his loveless, eternally disappointed father, a carpenter who "spent whatever love he had in the rented garage that was his workshop,"[10] and who is completely unable to control his temper in the face of his son's ineptitude at sports. "What the hell do you think you're going to do when you grow up?" he rages, after a particularly dispiriting hour of batting practice.

> "I wonder what you think life is all *about*. I wouldn't give you a job, I wouldn't trust you around carpenter tools, I wouldn't trust you to blow your nose right—to tell you the truth, I wonder if the hospital mixed up the goddamn babies."[11]

The movies, by contrast, offer paternal images like Alan Ladd, star of *Chicago Deadline*, a neat, solicitous figure who walks off the screen and into the boy's imagination, telling him what he desperately needs to hear.

> "You okay, son?"
>
> I nodded.
>
> "I just wanted to tell you that I like seeing you out there every day. That means a lot to me."[12]

Of course, the boy never encounters an Alan Ladd in real life. Instead, he encounters Frank—who sometimes calls himself Stan and sometimes Jimmy—an unemployed, alcoholic pedophile whose vestigial resemblance to Alan Ladd gives him a kind of seedy glamour, and helps him to establish a claim on the boy's attention. Frank/Stan/Jimmy meets the boy at the popcorn stand during the second week of *Chicago Deadline*'s run. With a predator's unerring instinct, he zeroes in on the boy's loneliness and vulnerability—his need to matter to *someone*—and induces the boy to cooperate in his own seduction.

That seduction takes place swiftly and brutally. By the end of their second day together, this "interesting new friend"[13] has coerced the boy into masturbating him. Straub's description of that act—which ends with an ejaculation that is described in clinical detail—is one of the more disturbing and horrific moments in the entire body of Straub's fiction.

The next few days pass in a blur of movies, newsreel footage, and alien sexual encounters that leave the boy devastated and longing for death.

> I thought: I have already forgotten this, I want to die. I am dead already, only death can make this not have happened.[14]

The process of forgetting, itself a kind of death, begins almost immediately. The weekend passes in a dream, a jumble of disconnected images. By the following Monday, the details of the encounter in the theater have faded, have been reduced to the primal images of a fairy tale.

> From the last row of seats on the other side of the inner door...a shapeless monster whose wet black mouth said *Love me, love me* stretched yearning arms toward

> me. Shock froze my shoes onto the sidewalk and then shoved me firmly in the small of the back, and I was running down the block, unable to scream because I had to clamp my lips against the smoke and fire trying to explode from my mouth.[15]

By the time the boy returns to the Orpheum-Oriental, the man is gone, and the boy understands that he has killed the monster by forgetting him, and then proceeds to forget him once again.

But, as the folktale reminds us, the pieces buried beneath the juniper tree eventually speak. Returning, years later, to his father's house, the man who was once that seven-year-old boy is blindsided—just as Tim Underhill, who is writing this story, will later be—by the reemergence of those buried moments in a darkened theater. Being a novelist, he responds to those memories in the only way he can: by writing a story that partially illuminates the central questions of his life ("What I am, what I do, why I do it..."[16]), and recreates the portrait of "a boy of seven before whose memory I shall forever fall short."[17]

"The Juniper Tree" is a compact, multilayered novella, dense with levels of meaning. On the most obvious level, it is a story about the victimization of children, and the effects—both long-term and immediate—of sexual abuse. It is also about the world as viewed through the sensory apparatus of a child, for whom all the elements of the world, even the inanimate ones, are sources of meaning, trembling forever on the edge of speech.

> While I read, everything in the house seems alive and dangerous. I can hear the telephone in the hall rattling on its hook, the radio clicking as it tries to turn itself on and talk to me. The dishes stir and chime in the sink. At these times, all objects, even the heavy chair and sofa, become their true selves, violent as the fire that fills the sky I cannot see...I walk swiftly through the kitchen and the living room to the front door, knowing that if I look too carefully at any one thing, I will wake it up again..."I'm leaving," I say to no one. Everything in the house hears me.[18]

Most centrally, "The Juniper Tree" is a story about memory: the persistence of memory, the relationship between memory and love, the power that memory has either to sustain or obliterate the people, places, and objects within its keeping. At the same time, it is about the power of subterranean events, and about the fact that our lives are often shaped and directed by forces we understand either imperfectly, or not at all, a theme that will find its way into much of Straub's subsequent fiction, including *The Throat*, *Mr. X*, and "Mrs. God." "The Juniper Tree" is an early and particularly powerful treatment of the theme, and it remains one of Straub's central texts, a milestone in his evolution from supernatural horror novelist to a novelist whose work is powered by a sympathetic apprehension of the spiritual and psychological causes of human suffering.

"A Short Guide to the City"—which, true to its title, is one of the two shortest pieces in this collection—had its origins in an essay by Joseph Brodsky called "A Guide to a Renamed City." Brodsky's essay is a witty, deeply informed attempt to analyze those elements—history, climate, geographical peculiarities—which helped to form the essential character of the twice-christened city of Leningrad/St. Petersburg. Straub's story borrows much of its form, and something of its tone, from Brodsky, and then uses these elements to create a surreal portrait of a modern American city that is drawn, irresistibly, to violence.

The nameless city that the nameless narrator takes us through is clearly Milwaukee, but a Milwaukee not found in any of the traditional guides. The first thing we learn about the city is that it is currently beset by a series of unsolved murders, all the work of the same man, who has been dubbed "The Viaduct Killer" for his habit of leaving the bodies of his victims—all adult females—near the concrete supports of a local bridge. Once the fact of these murders has been established, the narrator takes us on a guided tour of the city's various social, ethnic, and economic sectors, any one of which might have produced the murderer.

The tour begins with the mansions of the rich in the eastern precinct of the city, then moves around the points of the compass, taking us through an increasingly strange series of neighborhoods largely defined by their individual "relationships to violence."[19] In the working class district known as The Valley, tourists are advised to dress inconspicuously and carry only small amounts of cash. In the mercantile district at the city's heart, bands of ragged, near-feral children live in "tree houses" built atop mountains of tires, and wage private, internecine war against their tree house neighbors. In "the ghetto," an entire section of the city has cut itself off from its neighboring sections, and has evolved into a self-sustaining society in which outsiders of any sort are no longer welcome. (Its relationship to violence is therefore difficult for any of these outsiders to judge.) And in the highly ethnic Polish/Estonian district, the residents, we are told, have a "profound relationship to violence,"[20] one that tends to turn inward, resulting both in instances of self-mutilation and in the periodic murders of entire families, murders almost always committed by a family member.

The reigning symbol—and unifying image—of this violent, variegated city is the great, unfinished bridge that stands in the southeast corner of the city, its giant span reaching halfway across to its neighboring cities, and then abruptly ending. To the residents of the city, the abandoned bridge directly reflects the condition of their own lives. This "Broken Span," as they call it,

> has the violence of all unfinished things, of everything interrupted or left undone. In violence, there is often the quality of *yearning*—the yearning for completion. For closure. For that which is absent and would if present bring fulfillment. For the body without which the wing is a useless ornament. It ought not to go unmentioned that most of the city's residents have never seen the bridge, except in its representations, and for the majority, the "bridge" is little more or less than a myth, being without any actual referent. It is pure idea.[21]

And that is what this story is: pure idea, an interesting but minor footnote to Straub's ongoing investigation of the phenomenon of violence. Unlike Straub's more characteristic explorations of this theme, "A Short Guide to the City" deliberately sacrifices the light and heat of fully imagined experience for the colder, more intellectual satisfactions of literary pastiche.

The remaining short story, "Something About a Death, Something About a Fire," is the oldest entry in the collection. (It is, Straub tells us in his Author's Note, one of his very first stories, and the only that he still likes well enough to preserve.) Like "A Short Guide to the City," "Something About a Death..." is something of an intellectual exercise, a brief, mock-documentary account of an imaginary cultural phenomenon known as "Bobo's Magic Taxi."

The history of Bobo's taxi is the history of an enigma that, despite the efforts of a variety of experts, has never been satisfactorily explained. Bobo's "act," which takes place within a seedy, circus-like setting, goes like this: Bobo (who has no last name) sits behind the wheel of "an ordinary taxi, long, black, squat as a stone cottage."[22] As the performance begins, Bobo drives (or, some say, is driven) into the center of the circus tent, where an elusive and variable miracle takes place, a miracle that assumes one general form for children, another for adults.

The performance that children see begins with a fireworks display that emanates from the taxi itself. Unlike traditional fireworks, the exploding patterns linger in the air, and begin to enact a "drama" that cannot be coherently described.

> When pressed by adults, the children merely utter some few vague words about "The Soldier" and "The Lady" and "The Man with a Coat." When asked if the show is funny, they nod their heads, blinking, as if their questioner is moronic.[23]

Adults—meaning everyone over the age of eighteen—see something that is different, but equally difficult to describe. The adult performance falls into three stages (The Great Acts) that correspond to the three great waves of emotion that invariably overwhelm the audience during the course of Bobo's act. The first stage is "The Darkness," a preliminary period of sorrow and inescapable gloom in which, the narrator tells us, "we remember ours sins, our meagerness, our miseries."[24] This is followed by "The Falling," in which a drama that differs from one person to the next is projected, like a beam of light, from the taxi. Within this drama, there is "something about a death, something about a fire."[25] The members of the audience travel backwards in time to the world of their ancestors and find themselves immediately welcomed, immediately "at home." Each person has the sense of being granted "a brief moment to be heroic, a long lifetime to be moral."[26] The exhilaration of that moment prepares them for the final stage of the performance, "The Layers."

The Layers—which also varies in its effects from person to person—takes the audience on a dreamlike progression through layers of experience; through layers of color and light; through geological strata of stone, earth and gravel; through different stages of civilized development—cave dwellers, hut builders, iron makers; and, on occasion, through different layers of an individual life, from childhood through the various stages of maturity. None of this is ever successfully analyzed or explained away. None of it is ever really understood.

"Something About a Death, Something About a Fire" is, like Bobo's taxi, infinitely open to interpretation. As much as anything, it is "about" the consolations of art, and the infinite range of responses that exist between artist and audience. It is also about the sorrow and splendor of ordinary life, the existence of the sacred, the possibility of miracles, the imminence of transcendence, and the constant capacity of the universe to present us with images that "astonish, delight, and terrify,"[27] and that, however temporarily, illuminate and enlarge our lives.

"The Buffalo Hunter" was one of two last minute additions to *Houses Without Doors.* (The other was the series of vignettes that connect the longer stories.) The inspiration for the story—which evolved, eventually, into a forty thousand word short novel—was an exhibit of Rona Pondick's sculptures called *Bed Milk Shoe,* which was held at a gallery on Manhattan's Upper East Side in 1989. Pondick's work makes frequent use of primitive Freudian material, and *Bed Milk Shoe* was no exception. A couple of the pieces on exhibit consisted of "long beds made of some kind of metal cast to look like silken sheets and fluffy pillows, upon which rested lumpy, irregularly cylindrical bronze objects bearing an unmistakable resemblance to human feces."[28] Some of these beds featured genuine baby bottles, most of them painted an opaque white on the inside.

> The most striking of these beds was lashed down with ropes that went through the centers of the bottles, one of which was black, not white. When I woke up the next morning, I started thinking about what it would mean if someone did the same kind of thing in his own home, without any ar-

> tistic impulse behind it. Pretty soon, Bobby Bunting started to take shape, and I thought I had the beginnings of a pretty interesting story.[29]

He was right. Starting with a single central image—a Manhattan apartment festooned with baby bottles—Straub developed one of his most striking stories, the bizarre account of an intensely solitary young man trying desperately to reestablish an element of the sacred within his disordered life.

The young man in question is the aptly named Bobby Bunting. As "The Buffalo Hunter" opens, Bobby is celebrating his thirty-fifth birthday by climbing into his bed with a Luke Short western, and guzzling vodka through the modified rubber nipple of a baby bottle. To a large degree, this image sums up Bobby's existence. At the Biblical midpoint of his life, he is a data entry clerk for a company with the generic name of DataComCorp; has no social life (and has never, in fact, had a real date); lives in a dingy, one-room Manhattan efficiency; and spends the bulk of his free time reading and rereading the same limited group of mystery novels and pulp westerns. He has also developed a detailed, ongoing fantasy centered around his romantic relationship with a mythical DataComCorp executive named Veronica. He uses this fantasy (which he himself has come more and more to believe in) to regale his one friend (a younger coworker named Frank Herko) with salacious lies, and to provide ready-made excuses to avoid visits to his dismal childhood home in Battle Creek, Michigan.

As with so many Straub heroes, the defining elements of Bunting's life and character are located in his childhood. The most significant of these forces is his judgmental, domineering father, whose general contempt for his son (who was always, he declares, "a fuckup"[30]) set the tone for much of Bobby's life. The second element is more elusive, and Bobby has buried it deeply beneath his own version of the juniper tree, where it stirs and quickens, gathering itself to speak. A photograph of his parents standing before their drab, Battle Creek home, looking for all the world like the rural couple in American Gothic, triggers the following enigmatic occurrence.

> Distant white lights wheeled above him, and he was falling through space. Some massive knowledge moved within him,

> thrusting powerfully upward from the darkness where it had been jailed, and he understood that his life depended on keeping this knowledge locked inside him, in a golden casket within a silver casket within a leaden casket. It was a wild beast with claws and teeth, a tiger, and this tiger had threatened to surge into his conscious mind and destroy him.[31]

The event that finally allows the tiger to surface is both innocuous and comic. Having decided to buy himself a thirty-fifth birthday present, Bobby wanders into a local drugstore and, motivated by forces he cannot quite comprehend, buys an entire assortment of baby bottles and rubber nipples (the first of several such purchases.) Once these talismanic objects are present in his home, a door that was slammed shut long before begins to open, with astonishing results. Late that evening, Bobby begins his fourth or fifth reading of Luke Short's *The Buffalo Hunter*, and suddenly finds himself pulled—quite literally—into the physical reality of the story and its world. For the duration of the evening, he lives in the American West of the 1870s, smelling the smells, enduring the dangers, and participating fully in "a flawless narrative of what it mean[t] to be alive at this moment."[32] When the book is finished, he returns, shaken, to the "shrunken and diminished world"[33] of modern Manhattan.

A short while later, he begins to reread Raymond Chandler's *The Lady in the Lake*, and the same thing happens. Bunting is transported into the Los Angeles of 1944, where his life, history, and personality merge with those of Philip Marlowe, and he finds himself able to share in the dangers and complex satisfactions of Marlowe's world. For Bunting, this experience is a grace note, pure and simple, a way of experiencing, without mediation, the full weight and potential of the written word. This "incredible state of grace"[34] is, he knows, connected to the buried world of his childhood. The newly purchased collection of baby bottles has somehow helped him to reestablish contact with a miraculous feeling-state that once animated his life, and that was crushed, derided, and almost destroyed by his blunt, impatient father.

Having stumbled into this strangely vibrant relationship with the world of the word, Bunting soon finds himself experiencing a similar, but temporary, relationship with the quotidian reality of life in New

York City. In one of the story's central passages, he finds himself caught in a sudden thunderstorm, a storm which leaves behind it an unexpected, equally sudden feeling of transcendence.

> People thrust past him to get into doorways and beneath the roof of the bus shelter, but he neither could, nor wanted, to move. It was as if all of life had gloriously opened itself before him. If he could have moved, he would have fallen to his knees with thanks. For long, long seconds after the lightning faded, everything blazed and burned with life. Being streamed from every particle of the world—wood, metal, glass, or flesh. Cars, fire hydrants, the concrete and crushed stones of the road, each individual raindrop, all contained the same living substance that Bunting himself contained, and this was what was significant about himself and them. If Bunting had been religious, he would have felt that he had been given a direct, unmediated vision of God: since he was not, his experience was of the sacredness of the world itself.[35]

This is one of the clearest, most naked expressions found anywhere in Straub's work of a belief in the existence of sacred, transcendental mysteries, mysteries that have been ignored, forgotten, or utterly misrepresented by the bureaucratic machinery of organized religion. Everything that happens in "The Buffalo Hunter," all of the events that drift within the frame of Bunting's circumscribed life—an abortive first date, his mother's newly discovered health problems, the ongoing conflict with his abrasive father, his growing inability to concentrate on his job, his continuing and obsessive accumulation of baby bottles—happens against the backdrop of a single, central thesis: that everything in the universe has meaning. Everything is an aspect of the sacred.

In a sense, "The Buffalo Hunter" is an account, told in strictly secular terms, of the individual struggle for salvation. (To emphasize this point, a bloody, irascible Jesus makes occasional appearances, lecturing Bobby on the inability of the human species to see what is in front of its face.) In Bobby Bunting's case, the quest for salvation centers around a simple, overwhelming question: will he, in the end, be forced to inhabit the banal, heartless world that his father represents, a world that is "a testament to ignorance, incompatibility, resentment, violence, and disorder,"[36] or will he find his way back to that higher level of perception in which everything is alive and "overflow[ing] with meaning?"[37]

In the end, a book provides Bobby with his ticket out of his father's world. (Books may be imperfect vehicles of enlightenment, but they are sometimes all we have. As Jesus tells Bobby, "Go home and read a book. That'll do. It's a piss-poor way to get there, but I guess it's about the best you can do."[38]) Continuing the steady upward progress of his literary standards, Bobby moves from Luke Short to Raymond Chandler to Leo Tolstoy. He buys a battered copy of *Anna Karenina* from a street vendor, who charges him a dollar and offers him a succinct and useful critical evaluation as an added bonus.

> "World's greatest realistic novel, hands down...Anybody says different, he's out of his fuckin' mind." He wiped his nose on his sleeve. "One dollar."
>
> Bunting fished a dollar from his pocket and leaned over the rows of bright covers to give it to the man.
>
> "What makes it so great?" he asked.
>
> "Understanding. Depth of understanding. Unbelievable responsiveness to detail linked to amazing clarity of vision."[39]

That, of course, is a recommendation Bunting can appreciate. He takes the book home and, after hovering around the edges of the story for a day or so, begins to read. In a risky but ultimately triumphant conclusion that allows the story's implicitly fantastic elements to take center stage, Bunting falls into the world of Tolstoy's novel, places himself in the path of the same train that kills Anna at the novel's end, and dies with a smile on his face, having found his way back to that luminous world that most of us never see.

Straub's exploration of that world, and of Bunting's relationship to it, is equally luminous and unexpectedly affecting. Even by the standards of the present collection, "The Buffalo Hunter" is an eccentric, deeply satisfying story that comes right out of that imaginative left field from which the best fiction always seems to emerge. With clarity of vision and responsiveness to detail, it illuminates some of the most fundamental concerns of Straub's life and work, opening up the world from a startling, and wholly original, perspective.

"Mrs. God," a fifty thousand word short novel written under the enigmatic influence of Robert Aickman, is unique among Straub's fiction in at least two respects. First, it is the only one of his novels or stories that exists in two substantially different versions: the longer, slightly more opaque version published as a limited edition hardcover by Donald M. Grant; and the shorter, somewhat less obscure version that was rewritten—at the request of Straub's consternated publishers at Penguin/Dutton—for inclusion in this collection. Second, "Mrs. God" is, as the publisher's reaction implies, arguably the most "difficult" of Straub's fictions: i.e., the most dreamlike and elusive, the most deeply, intractably mysterious. It is governed, more than anything else that Straub has written, by deliberately withheld explanations, and by a refusal to accommodate itself to the expectations of readers in search of more conventional, more linear, narratives.

"Mrs. God" was written in the immediate aftermath of *Koko,* and much of Straub's psychological condition at this time found its way into the story. Having invested so much time, effort, and emotion in *Koko,* Straub found himself literally bereft by its completion, a feeling complicated by the sense that he had just placed his baby, his "Real Baby,"[40] into the keeping of strangers, and he "did not know how they would care for it."[41] To combat this feeling, he needed to begin writing again, but was completely unprepared to begin working on a new novel. Instead, he embarked on a longish story patterned, as he later realized, much too closely on *The Turn of the Screw.* Not surprisingly, given Straub's emotional condition at the time, the story that eventually evolved from this initial notion had at its center the recurring image of a lost—in this case, aborted—child.

At about the same time, Straub agreed to write an introduction to an omnibus edition of Robert Aickman stories called *The Wine-Dark Sea.* Aickman (1914-1981) was one of the greatest and most original practitioners of the twentieth century tale of terror. His stories—which he referred to, simply and precisely, as "strange stories"—are perverse, eccentric, often willfully obscure, and absolutely unlike anyone else's. Writing, in a British anthology called *Dark Voices*, about Aickman's 1957 story "Ringing the Changes," Straub noted that

> the real oddness of most of Aickman's work is related to its psychological, even psychoanalytic, acuity. Unconscious forces move the stories...as well as the characters, and what initially looks like a distressing randomness of detail and events is its opposite—everything is necessary, everything is logical, but not at all in a linear way. To pull off this kind of dreamlike associativeness, to pack it with the menace that results from a narrative deconstruction of the nature of "ordinary reality," to demonstrate again and again...that our lives are literally shaped by what we do not understand about ourselves, requires a talent that yokes together an uncommon literary sensitivity with a lush, almost tropical inventiveness.[42]

The process of reading a great many Aickman stories in a short period of time helped Straub solidify his notions about Aickman and his work. It also helped him to solidify certain notions about narrative, and the ways in which narrative can be deepened and enhanced by subverting conventional expectations, and by denying readers the comforts of neat conclusions, sequential plot development, traditional climaxes and, above all, rational explanations. The most enduring result of this extended encounter with Aickman and his work was "Mrs. God." And though there are a number of other influences discernible in the story—traces of Ramsey Campbell, himself an Aickman devotee, can be found here, along with traces of Stephen King *(The Shining)*, Shirley Jackson *(The Haunting of Hill House)*, and Carlos Fuentes *(Aura)*—Aickman is the major force behind this strange, extreme "meditation on sex, violence, and the sacred."

On its simplest level, "Mrs. God" tells the story of William Standish, a second-rate academic from Zenith, Illinois, who travels to England to do some research in the library of Esswood House, an English Stately Home which, earlier in the century, had opened up its doors to a number of England's more prominent literary figures: Henry James, E. M. Forster, Virginia Woolf, T. S. Eliot, etc. Standish hopes to save his flagging academic career by resurrecting the obscure (in both senses) poetry of Isobel Standish, his grandfather's first wife and a frequent visitor to Esswood House. Standish, both literally and figuratively, is bringing a great deal of baggage with him on this trip. At his previous teaching post—Popham College, fictional home base of fictional Straub critic Putney Tyson Ridge—he had discovered his wife's adulterous affair with a fellow academic named Smith ("like the cough drop"[43]). In the ensuing scandal, which ultimately forced him to leave the college, he coerced his then pregnant wife into aborting a child that was, in all probability, his own. That lost, aborted child is the central image of "Mrs. God," and finds its way into the text with a surreal, obsessive frequency.

After landing at the tiny airport in Gatwick, he endures a hallucinatory, totally disorienting journey by car to Esswood House. Deeply shaken by the difficulties of adapting to the British style of driving, he gets lost; meets a vaguely menacing vagrant with a penchant for quoting nineteenth century poetry; sees, or seems to see, a child with its frightened face pressed against the window of a passing house; and stops to eat in a pub called The Duelists, whose occupants bear an eerie resemblance to the principal figures in a recent scandal involving adultery and murder. (At this point, Standish know nothing about that murder, but he soon will, and the details of the murder will be ironically reflected in the violent, hallucinatory conclusion to this story.)

Exhausted, hungry, and confused, Standish eventually finds his way to Esswood House, and falls immediately in love with it. Just as quickly, he becomes infatuated with the woman who greets him at the door, a nameless, alluring figure he rapidly begins to think of as his "beloved."[44] She passes him into the keeping of the Esswood Foundation's director, Robert Wall. Wall, by his own autobiographical account, must be over eighty years old, but appears to be perhaps fifty; and has about him an indefinable aura of "hunger."[45] After serving Standish his dinner (loin of veal with morel sauce, Isobel Standish's favorite meal and the same meal Standish will be served over and over while at Esswood, a detail suggested by the Carlos Fuentes novella, *Aura*), Wall helps Standish acclimate himself to his new surroundings, and then leaves him to his work.

Once Standish enters the library and begins to pursue his research, linear reality rapidly breaks down. Standish quickly comes to realize that living at Esswood is very much like living within an Isobel Standish poem: obscure, quirky, pregnant with undisclosed meanings, as in "Rebuke," the only poem of Isobel's we are permitted to see.

> Neither found he any, the vagrant said
> Under the moldering eaves of the house
> Full of heaviness and no one to comfort,
> No one wavering up to say
>
> "Put on your indiscretions, little fool,
> After you take your glasses off. Why, Miss
> Standish..."
>
> This glowing moon. The crowd
> Has already gathered on the terraces.
>
> The history of one who came too late
> To the rooms of broken babies and their
> toys
>
> Is all they talk about around here,
> And rebuke, did you think you'd be left
> out?[46]

Standish's exploration of Isobel's poetry broadens almost immediately to become an exploration of the nature—the history beneath the history—of Esswood House. From a variety of sources, he pieces together an unsettling portrait of what Isobel—who saw in Esswood the living embodiment of the sacred—referred to, simply, as The Land. His own dreams bring him disturbing images of violence, of ritual murder reduced to a sort of bureaucratic routine. Photographs reveal the existence of Esswood residents who, like Robert Wall, appear never to have aged in the normal fashion. A visit to the local churchyard reveals that the owners of Esswood—a family named the Seneschals, a word which means stewards or guardians—have been anathema to local townsfolk for generations. During his own subterranean wandering through the cellars of Esswood, he discovers what Isobel called "the rooms of broken babies": miniature replicas of Esswood within which damaged, afflicted children once lived, children whose mother—Edith Seneschal—loomed above their lives like the dim, distant, matriarchal divinity of the title.

Most of what he learns, though, comes from an unpublished memoir by Isobel Standish enigmatically entitled "B. P." ("Birth of the Poet," perhaps, or even "Birth of the Past.") The memoir illuminates Esswood's early history as a minor league literary colony to which distinguished visitors left small offerings in the form of stories, poems, and variant versions of their best known works. None of these gifts have ever been offered to the outside world. They remain Esswood's private property, and are the primary lures which have induced generations of scholars—"Esswood Fellows"[47]—to visit The Land. "B. P" also recounts Isobel's gradual seduction by the forces which animate The Land, forces represented by its reigning matriarch, Edith Seneschal.

Through the journal, and through the occasional reminiscences of Robert Wall—who, he comes to realize, is actually Robert Seneschal, Edith's son—Standish learns about Isobel's affair with her "gypsy-vagrant,"[48] a minor poet named Theodore Corn. As a result of this affair, Isobel became pregnant. Eventually, she died in childbirth, along with her child, and was buried on the grounds of Esswood. In the words of "Robert Wall," repeated over and over throughout "Mrs. God," "It is better never to leave Esswood."[49] And Isobel never did. Standish, following clues from Isobel's journal, discovers her gravesite, which is also the gravesite of numerous other visitors who sacrificed themselves so that Esswood and its inhabitants might continue. At Isobel's grave, which is surrounded by the sub-audible humming of imprisoned souls, Standish experiences his final epiphany, and comes to an understanding of the true nature of Esswood House, a place which is eternally, unassuageably hungry.

> Standish exhaled, understanding everything at last, and heard the sound disappear into the broader but still inaudible sound of the soul traffic that was the sound of the hive. *Magickal*, Isobel had written, using the old spelling, and for once she had been right. It had always been a sacred place, probably, for that was one way to put it, but now it was more so because of the people they had used and buried here. Edith was not buried here, and neither were any of her children, for none of

> them were dead. Others were...Down in the soil with Isobel lay a lost child who screamed for release with all the others, screaming like a pale creature pressed against a window.
>
> What power a lost child has, what a lever it is, what a battery of what voltage.[50]

Fueled by this comprehension, which is itself fueled by the lost child who speaks to him so powerfully across the intervening years, Standish returns to the main house, and destroys Esswood, its library, and its mysterious remaining inhabitants, setting everything and everyone alight in a giant conflagration which he himself barely escapes, and which scorches the hair from his body, turning him into "a totally new being, bald, covered with grease and blood, pink and blue-eyed...his own baby."[51] As the story ends, the deranged and reborn Standish is standing alone beneath "the great sentence"[52] that is the universe itself, a "poor Baby"[53] now ready to resume his journey into "the wide desolation"[54] of the world.

Essentially, "Mrs. God" is a story about hunger, about people sacrificed to the endless hunger of whatever entity animates Esswood (whose name itself deliberately suggests "eating") and its guardian family, the Seneschals. This particular theme—supernatural hunger—manifests itself across the length of Straub's career, ranging backward in time to *Ghost Story* ("Ghosts are always hungry"[55]) and forward to his most precise exploration of this idea, the bluntly titled novella, "Hunger."

Still, despite the fact that—in its broadest outlines, at least—the meaning and general movement of the narrative are clearly discernible, "Mrs. God" remains very much a dreamlike, mysterious, open-ended work that draws a great deal of its power from the enigmatic details out of which the story is constructed. In the end, despite everything we know—or think we know—about Esswood and its history, there remains much that we do not—cannot—know for certain. Who, and what, are the Seneschals? Are they the guardians that their same suggests, or the presiding spirits of Esswood? And if they are simply guardians, what power do they serve? What is the fundamental nature of the force that made Esswood into a sacred, or apparently sacred, place? What happened to the children—"the broken babies"—

who inhabited the miniature Esswoods that Standish finds in the cellar? What is the nature of their "affliction?" What is the connection between these broken babies and the older, more arcane secrets which bind the Seneschals to The Land they inhabit? And what were the fates of the various scholars—the Esswood Fellows—lured to Esswood by the magnetic attraction of its incomparable library? These are only some of the many questions that haunt "Mrs. God," giving this dense, compact narrative the kind of disconcerting power so characteristic of Robert Aickman and his strange, uncomfortable fictions.

Ultimately, despite its immersion in the literary techniques and emotional terrain of its principal model, "Mrs. God" remains very much a Peter Straub story, and its obsessions are familiar ones. A concern with the sacred, unknowable mysteries at the heart of human experience; a fascination with buried, subterranean secrets; a belief that lost and broken children, buried beneath their own particular versions of the juniper tree, will find a way to speak—all of these elements are part of the emotional and intellectual fabric of this story. So, too, is the notion that the terrors and vicissitudes of existence find their truest expression, their purest form of redemption, through stories. In the case of "Mrs. God," Straub tells us, the troubled past of Esswood, altered by and filtered through the artistic imagination, found its way into the subsequent creations of writers who once spent time under Edith Seneschal's roof: *The Turn of the Screw*, *The Wasteland*, and E. M. Forster's "The Machine Stops" all have their mythical origins in the mythical history of Esswood.

Taken all together, *Houses Without Doors* is notable for its vigor and variousness, and for its willingness to experiment with eccentric, even bizarre, images and ideas that might not have been sustainable at novel length but prove perfectly suited to the mid-range fictional forms that dominate this collection. Complementing those longer fictions, and illuminating them from oblique angles of their own, are the seven short prose pieces that begin and end the volume, and serve as connecting material between the major narratives.

The idea for these little vignettes came to Straub at the eleventh hour, just as he was preparing to turn the completed manuscript over to his editor at Dutton. Straub's immediate inspiration came from a collection of brief, one or two page stories called *The Assignation* by Joyce Carol Oates. After purchasing the Oates book, Straub recalls,

> I started walking home and read two of them before I got to Amsterdam Avenue, one block east. It suddenly struck me that I could use pieces of that length to create a kind of unity of *Houses Without Doors,* to tie it all together by slipping them in between the stories. Some of them could be only a paragraph or two long, but all of them would be variations on the central themes of the longer stories in the collection, so as to keep these themes in the foreground of the reader's imagination.[56]

At a deeper level, however, the real inspiration behind this notion was Ernest Hemingway's great collection, *In Our Time,* which used a similar device, linking its fifteen stories together through quick, evocative fragments called chapters, many of which resonated with painful memories of the recently concluded Great War.

In the opening vignette of *Houses Without Doors,* a woman spies a luminous young man—possibly an angel—on the streets of New York, just as the first hint of winter is settling in on the city. This angel, which calls to mind the rumored appearance of an angel in "A Short Guide to the City," will appear, in some form, in two or three subsequent vignettes, each time at the same moment of seasonal change, each time lending a sense of the miraculous to the settled lives of Straub's often troubled characters.

Visitations—miraculous and otherwise—form the substance of all of these brief pieces, and the visitations come in a variety of forms: as buried memories of childhood, as echoes of the Vietnam War, as fantasies, visions, and dreams whose primary images—subterranean fires, blood swirling down the drain of a bathroom shower—are direct reflections of similar images from the surrounding stories. In the final piece, the nameless woman from the opening paragraph once again spies her "angel" on the streets of New York. It is one year later. The weather has turned "misty gray,"[57] and the air is now chilly. Spotting the luminous young man in faded jeans and black sweater—a being she has neither thought of nor forgotten in the intervening months—she yields to an unarticulated desire for change, for transformation. In the lovely final paragraph, she steps outside the frame of her ordered life, acknowledges the sudden, unexpected presence of the sacred, and follows her angel into an unforeseen, and unforeseeable, future.

> She walked down the avenue half a block behind the man. Her life had changed, it came to her, it would never again be what it had been, and with every step she took the change deepened. She had been set free: this was what had been promised, it was this she had anticipated. An entire year had been wasted in the realm of the ordinary, and now she was slipping away from the ordinary altogether. The air darkened around her, and she followed the man out of everything she had ever known.[58]

1. Interview with Michael Berry, *Horror Magazine*, January 1994
2. *Houses Without Doors*, p. 357
3. Interview with Michael Berry
4. *Houses Without Doors*—"Blue Rose"—p. 14
5. Ibid., p. 32
6. Ibid., p. 37
7. Ibid., p. 39
8. Ibid.—"The Juniper Tree"—p. 72
9. Ibid., p. 62
10. Ibid., p. 63
11. Ibid., p. 73
12. Ibid., p. 73
13. Ibid., p. 73
14. Ibid., p. 81
15. Ibid., p. 88
16. Ibid., p. 90
17. Ibid., p. 90
18. Ibid., p. 66
19. Ibid.—"A Short Guide to the City"—p. 100
20. Ibid., p. 100
21. Ibid., p. 104
22. Ibid.—"Something About a Death, Something About a Fire"—p. 216
23. Ibid., p. 217
24. Ibid., p. 217

25. Ibid., p. 217
26. Ibid., p. 218
27. Ibid., p. 215
28. Letter from Peter Straub to the author
29. Ibid.
30. *Houses Without Doors*—"The Buffalo Hunter"—p. 206
31. Ibid., p. 118
32. Ibid., p. 147
33. Ibid., p. 147
34. Ibid., p. 151
35. Ibid., p. 163
36. Ibid., p. 183
37. Ibid., p. 144
38. Ibid., p. 183
39. Ibid., p. 195
40. *Mrs. God* (Hampton Falls, NH: Donald M. Grant, 1990), p. 203
41. Ibid., p. 203
42. Introduction to "Ringing the Changes"—*Dark Voices*, Edited by Stephen Jones and Clarence Paget (London: Pan Books, 1990), pp. 191-192
43. *Mrs. God*—Grant edition—p. 205
44. *Houses Without Doors*—"Mrs. God"—p. 295
45. Ibid., p. 261
46. Ibid., p. 235
47. Ibid., p. 227
48. Ibid., p. 310
49. Ibid., p. 267
50. Ibid., p. 331
51. Ibid., p. 350
52. Ibid., p. 351
53. Ibid., p. 352
54. Ibid., p. 352
55. *Ghost Story*, epigraph
56. Letter from Peter Straub to the author
57. *Houses Without Doors*—"Then one day she saw him again"—p. 355
58. Ibid., p. 356

Chapter Twelve:
The Throat

The Throat, more than any of Straub's previous novels, is the literary equivalent of an extended jazz solo: a long, sinuous composition that circles and recircles a familiar series of themes, scenes, and characters, improvising its way toward a number of revelations that retrospectively illuminate the central events of both *Koko* and *Mystery.* In fact, the primary impetus behind the writing of *The Throat* was Straub's belief that he had not yet exhausted the emotional content of those books, and that their central elements—the war in Vietnam, the auto accident, his concern with the grief, bitterness and buried rage that are the frequent aftereffects of childhood traumas—virtually demanded further elaboration. Added to this was Straub's obvious affection for the characters he had lived with for the past five years, particularly that battle-scarred survivor, Tim Underhill.

Underhill, Straub has noted, is a character whose nature and experience allowed his creator access to "all sorts of material I did not otherwise know how to approach."[1] Having already identified Underhill as the author of those brutal novellas of childhood, "Blue Rose" and "The Juniper Tree," Straub found it was a simple enough matter to further identify Underhill as his "collaborator"[2] on the previous two novels. This relationship enabled Straub himself to appear as a secondary character in the opening pages of *The Throat,* where Underhill, the narrator, describes him as "a nice enough kind of guy" who lives "in a big, gray Victorian house in Connecticut, just off Long Island Sound. He has a wife and two kids, and he doesn't get out much."[3] Freed from his role as Straub's anonymous collaborator, Underhill now speaks to us, directly and in his own distinctive voice, about the unfinished business that lurks in the background of both *Koko* and *Mystery:* the Blue Rose murders.

Having decided to use Underhill as his viewpoint character, and having developed an effective voice for that character—a voice inspired, in part, by his reading of John Irving's 1989 novel, *A Prayer for Owen Meany,* a novel whose precise, unhurried, deeply responsive "feeling tone"[4] provided a useful model for Underhill's own first-person ruminations—Straub set to work immediately. He began writing in July of 1990, days before he and his family departed for a month's vacation in Mondelieu, a town just outside of Nice on the French Riviera. Straub recalls being so charged up, so ready to write, that he actually completed a couple of pages in the departure lounge at John F. Kennedy airport, while his family looked on in amazement and his ten-year-old daughter Emma shouted "Go, Daddy!"[5] Straub kept that momentum going throughout the vacation, and returned to New York with a substantial section of the novel—more than one-hundred-fifty handwritten pages—already complete.

Much of this was prefatory material. *The Throat,* even more than most Straub novels, takes a long time getting to the main line of its narrative, and most of what Straub wrote during his sojourn in Mondelieu concerned critical moments in Tim Underhill's traumatic past. Included is an account of Underhill's adolescent encounter with a young football rival named John Ransom, whose character will be permanently formed by his experiences in Vietnam, and whose involvement in a bizarre reenactment of the Blue Rose murders of forty years before provides the catalyst for most of what follows. In addition, Straub takes us through some emblematic moments from Underhill's own experience in Vietnam; and reveals some previously undisclosed information regarding the original Blue Rose murders, which took place in Millhaven (Straub's latest fictional portrait of Milwaukee) in 1950.

The opening sections of *The Throat* deal with Underhill's arrival in Vietnam, and his subsequent, temporary assignment to a Graves Registration detail known as the Body Squad, whose function is to verify the identities of the newly dead before shipping them back to their families in the states. Underhill's companions on the Body Squad are a group of combat-hardened misfits with names like Scoot, Attica, Pirate, and Ratman. They are not, in Underhill's words, "ordinary people—the regiment had slam-dunked them into the Body Squad to get them out of their units."[6] Most members of the squad have stories to tell, and most of these stories concern death.

The majority of those stories, even those not concerned directly with death, tend to reflect the infinite strangeness of day-to-day life in the quagmire that was Vietnam. The Vietnam that Straub describes in both *Koko* and *The Throat* is one of the "thin places" of the world, a place where the world's invisible "engine"—the same engine sensed by both Tom Flanagan and Tom Pasmore—can sometimes be heard. Describing to Underhill the psychological and sensory effects of spending extended periods out on patrol in hostile territory, Ratman has this to say:

> "Every sense you got is *out* there, man, you hear a mouse move...hear the dew jumpin' out of the leaves, hear the insects movin' in the bark. Hear your own fingernails grow. Hear that thing in the ground, man."
>
> "Thing in the ground?" Pirate asked.
>
> "Shit," said Ratman. "You don't know? You know how when you lie down on the trail you hear all kinds of shit, all them damn bugs and monkeys, the birds, the people movin' way up ahead of you...all kinds of shit, right? But then you hear the *rest*. You hear like a humming noise underneath all them other noises like some big generator runnin' way far away underneath you."
>
> "Oh, *that* thing in the ground," Pirate said.
>
> "It *is* the ground," said Ratman. He stepped back from the truck and gave Pirate a fierce, wild-eyed glare. "Fuckin' ground makes the fuckin' noise by *itself*. You hear me? An' that engine's always on. It never sleeps."[7]

Later, Pirate describes one of his own experiences while on a marathon, twenty-day patrol, a patrol that ends when his unit encroaches on the private preserve of a legendary Special Forces captain named Franklin Bachelor, a rogue soldier clearly patterned after Joseph Conrad's Kurtz. One man, Bobby Swett, trips a land mine set by Bachelor's men and is blown into "a red fog."[8] Pirate himself is transformed into " a walking bruise"[9] by the subsequent concussion. Shortly afterward, Pirate and his unit gather up their wounded and head back to the "civilized" world of Headquarters, leaving Bachelor and his followers to continue conducting their private war in the wilds of Dar Lac province. This little vignette is notable both for its grunts-eye-view of the ground war in Vietnam, and for its introduction of a character who will haunt this long narrative under a variety of names: Franklin Bachelor.

Other crucial sequences set in Vietnam include Underhill's first exposure to addictive drugs, which results in a dependency that continues for several years; a pair of enigmatic encounters with John Ransom, himself a Special Forces captain whose destiny becomes inextricably entwined with Franklin Bachelor's; and a bizarre, inexplicable encounter with the "ghost village" of Bong To.

The incident at Bong To occurs after Underhill's release from the Body Squad and before the arrival of the world's worst platoon leader, Harry Beevers. Its strangeness, its sense of a connection with another, *invisible* world, prefigures the events that will later occur in the cave at Ia Thuc. Bong To is a tiny Vietnamese ville that appears to be completely deserted. Underhill's platoon—which includes Michael Poole, Tina Pumo, Victor Spitalny, and " a wonderful soldier named M. O. Dengler"[10]—arrives there on the heels of a firefight in which two other platoon members, Tyrell Budd and Thomas Blevins, have been killed. While searching the empty buildings, Poole and Underhill discover an underground chamber equipped with a blood covered chain set three feet off the ground: a torture chamber suitable for monkeys, or for children. The walls of the chamber are covered with thick, absorbent paper that is covered in turn with Vietnamese script, reminding Underhill of "the left-hand pages of Kenneth Rexroth's translations of Tu Fu and Li Po."[11]

Although Underhill understands nothing of the ville's true nature, he senses that he has stumbled on a mystery that "had nothing to do with the war, a *Vietnamese* mystery."[12] Moments after leaving the chamber, with the strains of Frederick Delius' "A Walk to the Paradise Garden" playing in his head, transporting him briefly to a saner world, something of the essence of that mysterious village declares itself to him.

> If nothing else had happened, I think I could have replayed the [Delius] piece in my head. Tears filled my eyes, and I stepped toward the door of the hut. Then I stopped moving. A boy of seven or eight was regarding me with great seriousness from the corner of the hut. I knew he was not there—I knew he was a spirit. I had no belief in spirits, but that's what he was...I wiped my eyes with my hand, and when I lowered my arm, the boy was still there. I took in his fair.hair and round dark eyes, the worn plaid shirt and dungarees that made him look like someone I might have known in childhood...Then he vanished all at once, like the flickering light of the Zippo.[13]

That vanishing boy, who first appears to Underhill in this wildly incongruous time and place, is one of the central images of this novel, an image that will appear and reappear in one form or another throughout Underhill's life; that is, in effect, his muse. Before leaving Bong To and its mysteries behind, Underhill sees two more ghosts, familiar figures who have recently been killed in combat: Budd and Blevins, his former platoon mates. No one else can see these figures, although Dengler, always more observant than his comrades, knows that something mysterious has happened, and presses Underhill for an explanation he cannot provide.

> I could not speak. I could not tell Dengler in front of Spanky Burrage that I had imagined seeing the ghosts of Blevins, Budd, and an American child. I smiled and shook my head. It came to me with a great and secret thrill that someday I would be able to write about all this, and that the child had come searching for me out of a book I had yet to write.[14]

The rest of *The Throat*'s prefatory matter takes place a long way from Vietnam, in the Millhaven of 1950, site of the two defining events of Underhill's childhood. Both of these events are intimately connected to the Blue Rose murders, which Underhill reconstructs for us in considerable detail. In October of that year, a prostitute named Arlette Monaghan was murdered in an alcove outside the St. Alwyn Hotel. The words "Blue Rose" were written on the wall above her body. Five days later, a jazz musician named James Treadwell was murdered in room 218 of the St. Alwyn. Five days after that, a man named Monte Leland was murdered outside of the Idle Hour tavern, just down the street from the St. Alwyn. Two weeks later, an anomaly occurred when a young pediatrician—Buzz Laing—survived an attack that took place in his house on Millhaven's wealthy East Side. Five days afterward, the final murder occurred when Heinz Stenmitz, a butcher with a long history of sexual misconduct and a pronounced affinity for little boys, was found dead outside his shop. In his case, as in all the others, the words "Blue Rose" appeared on the wall alongside his corpse.

The investigation ended when the chief detective, William Damrosch, was found dead in his hotel room, with a bullet in his head, a gun in his hand, and the words "Blue Rose" scrawled on a piece of paper. Damrosch, an alcoholic with a history of blackouts, had been violently abused by his foster father, Heinz Stenmitz, and had connections of some sort with all of the other victims. His death was viewed as suicide, and as an implicit admission of guilt, in the face of which the case was officially closed. Underhill, like almost everyone else in Millhaven, accepted the official solution and used the case as the basis for his novel, *The Divided Man*. This much is already "known." But, as the events in both *Koko* and *Mystery* indicate, what is known or believed is not necessarily what is true, and *The Throat* proceeds almost immediately to demonstrate that fact.

Underhill's revised version of these events centers around his previously undisclosed conviction that the Blue Rose killer had claimed one additional victim: his nine-year-old sister, April. Five days before the first officially recorded Blue Rose murder, April had left her home and begun walking toward a friend's house, following a route that led through the alcove outside the St. Alwyn Hotel. Underhill, then seven years old, was listening to his favorite radio program, "The Shadow," when a premonition of danger caused him to leave the house and follow his sister. While he was still some distance from her, she passed into the shadows of the alcove just as a large, indistinct figure appeared, moving in her direction. Panicked by this dimly glimpsed vision, Tim ran toward his sister, stepping blindly into the rush hour traffic of Livermore Avenue. At that point, the "real" version of the accident ascribed to *Mystery*'s Tom Pasmore occurred. Tim was hit by a car, dragged more than thirty feet, and "killed," though only for a time. In the moments after his "death," he experiences that sense of being "accelerated into another, utterly different dimension"[15] that deliberately echoes *Mystery*'s earlier, "fictional" account of the same experience.

Afterward, Underhill spent months in the hospital and many more months recovering at home. His parents, numb with shock, struggled to adjust to the simultaneous traumas of their son's accident and their daughter's death. (April was found, brutally murdered, in the alcove adjacent to the hotel. Probably as a result of the furor that accompanied Tim's accident, the words "Blue Rose" did not appear at the crime scene. Her death was therefore never officially connected to the subsequent series of murders.)

In *Mystery,* the accident is kept at arm's length by the mediating presence of Tom Pasmore, while the story of April's death has never, up to this point, been mentioned at all. But it is the secret heart of Tim Underhill's ongoing obsession with the Blue Rose case and is, along with his memories of Vietnam, a large part of the emotional and psychological baggage that is firmly in place by the time the primary narrative begins. That beginning occurs when Underhill, now a successful novelist living in New York, receives a call from his old friend John Ransom, who has some startling news: his wife, the ironically named April Ransom, is in a deep coma, having been stabbed, beaten, and left for dead in room 218 of the St. Alwyn Hotel. On the wall above the bed were written the familiar and enigmatic words: "Blue Rose."

Underhill returns to Millhaven immediately, to provide aid and comfort to Ransom as he stands his deathwatch, and to try to learn why the distant past has suddenly resurfaced in the present. The Millhaven that he returns to is at once familiar and deeply strange, a place where new structures and old landmarks stand side by side; and where old, often dangerous memories, are never far away. In the same sense, Ransom himself is both familiar and strange. The son of a well-to-do businessman who once owned the St. Alwyn Hotel, Ransom survived a harrowing tour of duty in Vietnam, in the course of which he was once listed as officially dead. After the war, he traveled to India in search of spiritual enlightenment, joined an ashram, returned to America, received a Ph. D. in the arcane field of religious thought, and apprenticed himself to a nationally known religious scholar named Alan Brookner. Eventually, he married Brookner's daughter April, a successful stockbroker and a bright, multifaceted woman with a wide range of aesthetic interests. Ransom, on the other hand, has retained no apparent interest in either scholarly or spiritual pursuits. He is now sullen, defensive, and prone to violence, and is more interested in maintaining his expensive, well-stocked "vodka library"[16] than in pursuing a career as writer, teacher, or scholar.

Shortly after his arrival, Underhill learns that the attack on April Ransom was actually the second installment in the re-creation of the Blue Rose murders. Five days earlier, an unidentified man was found, stabbed to death and then disfigured, in the alcove outside of the St. Alwyn. All too aware that an old, familiar pattern is reasserting itself, Underhill begins to investigate, searching for answers in both the past and the present. At this point, *The Throat* threatens, briefly, to become a conventional serial killer/detective story with a single, fairly conventional question at its core: has the original Blue Rose killer decided, for some unknown reason, to return to the game; or are the present day killings simply the work of a well-informed copycat?

As the investigation proceeds, it becomes clear that Straub is not at all interested in producing a neat, conventional detective story with a neat, conventional solution. Instead, *The Throat* casts its net over a much wider area, becoming a kind of meditation on violence itself: its nature, its causes, its effects. There are, it turns out, a great many crimes of violence lying just beneath Millhaven's placid, middle class surface, some related to the Blue Rose killings, many not. The result is a portrait of a twentieth century American city in which monstrous crimes give rise to other monstrous crimes, in which buried rage always finds an eventual outlet, in which false and frivolous values proliferate, poisoning the spirit.

In *The Throat,* questions tend to have more than one answer, mysteries more than one solution. For example, according to one of the returning characters, *Mystery*'s Tom Pasmore, the original Blue Rose murders involved three separate solutions: one that was false but convenient, one that was true but essentially incomplete, one that is still totally unknown. The Pasmore we encounter in *The Throat* (who never experienced the auto accident described in *Mystery* but whose history remains, in most respects, essentially the same) believes that his grandfather, Glendenning Upshaw, attacked Buzz Laing under cover of the unsolved murders in order to prevent the pediatrician from revealing Upshaw's deepest secret: that he had been systematically molesting his own daughter since she was two years old. He then, in Pasmore's view, staged the suicide of detective William Damrosch in order to provide an acceptable scapegoat, thus closing the case and preempting further investigation.

That solution, of course, fails to account for the other murders that occurred in and around the St. Alwyn. And though Pasmore has no idea who the killer is (or was), he does share with both Underhill and Ransom his long held belief that the killings were somehow connected to the place at which they occurred; that someone with a grudge against the St. Alwyn or its owner had used these murders as a way of striking out at the hotel itself.

In a parallel development, April Ransom, who has started to show signs of emerging from her coma, is murdered in her bed at Shady Mount Hospital, beaten to death by an unknown assailant. Then, on the morning of her murder, an event occurs which throws the entire city into a frenzy of violence and recrimination. Walter Dragonette, a mild-mannered accountant who has lately been the subject of numerous complaints—his house smells; screams and strange sounds emanate from it late at night—finally receives a visit from the Millhaven police, and what they discover defies rational explanation. Walter's house contains a grotesque assortment of severed heads, headless torsos, and amputated genitalia. Confronted with all this, Walter, a fictional analogue of that other Milwaukee serial killer, Jeffrey Dahmer, meekly—even cheerfully—surrenders, and proceeds to confess to a multitude of unsolved murders, including the murder of April Ransom.

Although as stunned as everyone by the horrors unearthed in the Dragonette house, Underhill finds himself unable to accept Walter's statements regarding April Ransom's death. His confession seems too convenient, too unlikely, too filled with inconsistencies. Convinced that April's murderer is still at large, Underhill continues his independent investigation and, following Tom Pasmore's suggestion, focuses on people connected with the St. Alwyn Hotel. That suggestion, which brings a fresh sense of direction to a moribund investigation, eventually breaks the forty-year-old case—and its modern reenactment—wide open.

An extensive series of interviews with older Millhaven residents leads Underhill to a long forgotten name: Bob Bandolier. Bandolier, a harsh, humorless religious fanatic believed by his neighbors to have beaten his own wife to death, had a violent temper, a tendency toward alcoholism, and an obsessive interest in roses. He had also been fired from his job as manager of the St. Alwyn Hotel in the fall of 1950, just before the Blue Rose murders occurred. In the face of all these corroborating circumstances, Underhill understands that he is now in possession of the unprovable truth; that he has at last identified his sister's killer.

The discovery of the now deceased Bob Bandolier leads, in short order, to a series of interconnected discoveries. The first of these concerns the existence of Bob Bandolier's son, Fielding—"Fee"—Bandolier, a damaged child who watched his mother die at his father's hands, was battered by his father and, in all probability, sexually molested by Heinz Stenmitz, the Millhaven butcher who was William Damrosch's foster father and Bob Bandolier's final victim.

Fee's trail leads from Millhaven to a series of Midwestern foster homes, and from there to Vietnam, where he served under the "borrowed" name of Franklin Bachelor. As Bachelor, his path connected tangentially with Underhill's but directly—and violently—with John Ransom's. Ransom, forced to play Marlowe to Ransom's Kurtz in a surreal reenactment of Conrad's *Heart of Darkness,* was sent by his superiors to track down the renegade Bachelor and return him to the control of his Special Forces masters. That mission, naturally, ended badly for everyone involved.

Like Ransom, Bachelor was, at one point, believed dead. Like Ransom, he survived, and returned to America under the first in a series of assumed names. Various bits of evidence—which include an incriminating diary entry found in a deserted Millhaven taproom—lead, in time, to the following conclusion: that Bachelor is both a policeman and a secret, phenomenally successful serial killer, callings he has pursued under a variety of false identities. Further evidence eventually suggests that he is now a member of the Millhaven police force, and that he has recently begun to re-create the Blue Rose murders of 1950, in an apparent effort to punish the man who had once been his adversary in Vietnam: John Ransom.

Having narrowed the list of possible suspects down to a finite number of policemen, *The Throat* proceeds through a series of false conclusions to a climactic encounter in a Millhaven movie theater called the Beldame Oriental, where Fee Bandolier—revealed at last as a charismatic homicide detective named Michael Hogan—is shot and killed by a reluctant Tim Underhill. Together with Tom Pasmore, Underhill then alters the details of the shooting so that it appears to be a suicide, prints the words "Blue Rose" on the wall above the corpse, and waits for the body to be discovered. Sometimes, life is like a book.

Devious to the end, Straub withholds his last surprise, his last reversal, until the final pages, reinforcing the notion that the questions posed by *The Throat* have more than one answer, and the mysteries more than one solution. Underhill—whose musings on events in Millhaven have led him to a radical new interpretation of certain key occurrences—confronts John Ransom, accusing him of murdering his wife and of manipulating Underhill into placing the blame on the deranged Fee Bandolier. Ransom's motive: to prevent his wife from leaving him for someone else; to preserve his comforts, his way of life, and his inalienable right to three-hundred-dollar bottles of hyacinth vodka. The relentless pursuit of the trivial, and the simultaneous rejection of the spiritual, can have murderous results.

In the aftermath of this bizarre series of interrelated cases, Tom Pasmore retreats into the von Heilitz-like solitude of his Eastern Shore mansion, and resumes his search for cases of comparable intellectual interest. Tim Underhill returns to New York and finally completes a novel called *The Kingdom of Heaven*, a book he has been struggling with throughout the long, complex narrative. John Ransom, on the other hand, chooses a more tragic ending. Some months after his final confrontation with Tim Underhill, he dies in an auto accident, driving his car at high speed into a highway abutment. The postmortem examination reveals a blood alcohol level three times greater than the legal limit. Like *Koko*'s Harry Beevers, his life has become useless to him, and he throws it away.

The destruction of John Ransom is one of the central tragedies in a book so filled with competing tragedies—and filled, as well, with such a profusion of ideas, characters, details, subplots, and internal narratives—that it resists easy summary. Ransom is a man who could have become someone special but who is poisoned by the nature of his experiences in Vietnam and trapped, in his own way, by that same heart of darkness that captures and then destroys Fee Bandolier. In the end, he abandons his spiritual quest—his quest for personal peace—and settles for a lifestyle, rather than a life.

Ransom's primary literary antecedent is Terry Lennox, a pivotal character from Raymond Chandler's most personal, least conventional detective novel, *The Long Goodbye,* a man whose friendship with Chandler hero Philip Marlowe ends in a welter of lies and betrayal. Chandler's novel is deliberately evoked early in *The Throat,* through Ransom's account of his initial encounter with his future wife.

> April wandered off toward her father's fiction shelves. She stretched up to take down a book. Ransom had not been able to take his eyes off her. "I'm looking for a work of radically impure consciousness," she said. "What do you think, Raymond Chandler or William Burroughs?" The title of Ransom's dissertation had been *The Concept of Pure Consciousness,* and his grin grew wider. *"The Long Goodbye,"* he said. "Oh, I don't think that's impure enough," she said. She turned over the book in her hands and cocked her head. "But I guess I'll have to settle for it." She showed him the title of the book she had already selected: it was *The Long Goodbye.*[17]

While the Burroughs reference is an interesting and even relevant one—once, in Vietnam, Ransom tells Underhill that, under certain conditions and certain states of consciousness, "everything is permitted,"[18] a comment which brings Burroughs' *Naked Lunch* deliberately to mind—April's choice of *The Long Goodbye*, with its numerous correspondences between Ransom and Terry Lennox, is preternaturally appropriate. Both men survived traumatic wartime experiences, and both, for a time, were believed to have been killed in action. Both married women wealthier and more successful than themselves, developed serious problems with alcohol, and emerged into middle age with a kind of moral emptiness as their dominant characteristic. In Tim Underhill's final "goodbye" to John Ransom, Straub implicitly acknowledges his debt to Chandler. Here is a moment from Philip Marlowe's last conversation with Terry Lennox.

> "I'm not sore at you. You're just that kind of guy. For a while I couldn't figure you at all. You had nice ways and nice qualities, but there was something wrong. You had standards and you lived up to them, but

> they were personal. They had no relation to any kind of ethics or scruples. You were a nice guy because you had a nice nature. But you were just as happy with mugs or hoodlums as with honest men. Provided the hoodlums spoke fairly good English and had fairly acceptable table manners. You're a moral defeatist. I think maybe the war did it, and again I think maybe you were born that way."[19]

And here's Straub's version of a similar moment, Underhill's final confrontation with John Ransom.

> "No matter what you say, we used to be friends. You had a quality I liked a lot—you took risks because you believed that they might bring you to some absolutely new experience. But you lost the best part of yourself. You betrayed everything and everybody important to you for enough money to buy a completely pointless life. I think you sold yourself out so that you could keep up the kind of life your parents had, and you have scorn even for them. The funny thing is there's still enough of the old you left alive to make you drink yourself to death. Or destroy yourself in some quicker, bloodier way."[20]

Other, by now familiar literary influences discernible in *The Throat* include Joseph Conrad and Ross MacDonald. Conrad's influence is powerfully reflected in the Vietnam sequences, in which the *Heart of Darkness* material is recast—much in the manner of Francis Ford Coppola's *Apocalypse Now*—through the surreal account of John Ransom's search for the legendary "Last Irregular," Franklin Bachelor. The investigation that dominates the contemporary sections of the novel owes a great deal to MacDonald's Lew Archer series. MacDonald's persistent concern with the effect that past crimes have on present-day events makes him an ongoing, almost archetypal influence whose effect is apparent in almost all of Straub's novel length fiction.

In addition to the extravagant complexities of its plot, *The Throat* is a dense, thematically rich book that obsessively recapitulates Straub's characteristic ideas and beliefs. Like *Koko* and *Mystery, The Throat* is an extended consideration of the mysteries that surround and suffuse the visible world, and that appear to Straub's characters in a variety of forms: as ghosts, as sudden flashes of awareness, as transcendental glimpses of larger, more luminous realms. *The Throat* also revisits the idea of Life as Narrative, largely through the progress of Underhill's current project, a novel entitled *The Kingdom of Heaven,* the events of which are so bound up with the events of Underhill's own life that each becomes a part of the other. When Underhill first sees the room in which Fee Bandolier spent his childhood, he recognizes it immediately—not because he has ever seen it but because, as he understands an instant later, "I had written it."[21] On another occasion, Underhill becomes lost in Millhaven's early morning fog, wandering in circles until he comes upon the impossible figure of a young boy, who appears and then disappears in the window of a deserted house. Later in the book, Maggie Lah explains this incident with absolute accuracy: "You walked into your book. You saw your character, and he was yourself."[22]

More than anything, though, *The Throat,* like the novels that preceded it, is concerned with the fundamental importance of the imaginative life. *That* is its theme. *That* is its deepest level of meaning. Intelligence—as von Heilitz told us in *Mystery,* and as Underhill tells us again—is really just "sympathetic imagination,"[23] the indispensable quality out of which all worthwhile things arise. Alan Brookner (who is John Ransom's father-in-law, and a wonderfully vivid character whose descent into Alzheimer's Disease is powerfully described) puts it somewhat differently. "There is another world," he tells Underhill, "and it is *this* world."[24] Which is to say: the world that we move through, and that moves through us, can only be perceived—can only be fully *seen*—through the filter of a functioning imagination.

Straub's belief in the power of the imaginative impulse is visible on every level of this novel, and manifests itself in a variety of ways. Witness, for example, the number of artistic responses generated by the Blue Rose murders themselves, the number of ways in which the novel's more creative characters struggle to interpret that event, to understand its essential nature, and to memorialize its victims. Underhill's own novels, *Koko, Mystery,* and *The Divided Man,* are based, in part, on their author's obsessive need to come to terms with the meaning of those murders. April Ransom is motivated by a similar need. At the time of her death, she leaves behind an uncompleted manuscript called *The Bridge Project*, which is a kind of empathic history of the killings and of the personalities associated with them, particularly investigating detective William Damrosch.

In the area of nonverbal art forms, Glenroy Breakstone, a legendary saxophone player who makes his home in the St. Alwyn Hotel, creates a famous jazz album called *Blue Rose* to honor the memory of his friend and fellow musician James Treadwell, murdered in room 218 of that same hotel. That album, with its complement of classic ballads ("Stardust," "My Funny Valentine") serves as a kind of ghostly soundtrack that plays in the deep background throughout long stretches of this book.

And Byron Dorian, a young painter whose father worked with Damrosch on the original Blue Rose investigation and whose love affair with April Ransom helps precipitate her murder, exorcises his own lifelong fascination with the case by creating a series of paintings depicting scenes from the life of William Damrosch, paintings which are themselves inspired by an Edmond Vuillard canvas called, with exquisite irony, *The Juniper Tree*.

The central figure of Vuillard's painting is a lonely, obviously troubled young boy who stands, surrounded by his family, beneath the spreading limbs of a juniper tree. The Vuillard, together with a Byron Dorian painting of a barroom scene featuring an isolated, intoxicated Damrosch, eventually finds its way into Tim Underhill's New York City loft, where it inspires the following reflection:

> The Vuillard was a much greater painting than Byron Dorian's, but by whose standards? John Ransom's? April's? By mine, at least at the moment, they had so much in common that they spoke in the same voice. For all their differences, each seemed crammed with possibility, with utterance, like Glenroy Breakstone's saxophone or like the human throat—overflowing with expression. It occurred to me that for me, both paintings concerned the same man. The isolated boy who stared out of Vuillard's deceptively comfortable world would grow into the man turned toward

> Byron Dorian's despairing little bar. Bill Damrosch in childhood, Bill Damrosch near the end of his life—the painted figures seemed to have leapt onto the wall from the pages of my manuscript, as if where Fee Bandolier went, Damrosch trailed after.[25]

Underhill's manuscript, the novel entitled *The Kingdom of Heaven,* is very much a part of the imaginative inner life of this book. Underhill is at work on this novel throughout *The Throat*'s considerable length, sometimes actively, sometimes simply on a subconscious level. The plot, which concerns a deranged killer named Charlie Carpenter who is stalking a potential victim named Lily Sheehan, is constantly being impinged upon by Underhill's exposure to the various dramas playing themselves out in Millhaven. At one point, the revelations regarding the secret life of Walter Dragonette—together with Walter's glib, unsubstantiated assertion that all of his crimes were the direct result of his childhood history of sexual abuse—find their way into the novel, which suddenly takes form around Underhill's densely detailed vision of the damaged childhood of Charlie Carpenter. Thinking about Walter Dragonette's claims, Tim realizes that, if he could describe the world through the eyes of the young Charlie Carpenter, he could

> begin to work out what could make someone turn out like Walter Dragonette. The Ledger had tried to do that, clumsily, by questioning sociologists, priests, and policemen; and it was what I had been doing when I put the photograph of Ted Bundy's mother up on my refrigerator...I saw five-year-old Charlie Carpenter in my old bedroom on South Sixth Street, looking at the pattern of dark blue roses climbing the paler blue wallpaper in a swirl of misery and despair as his father beat up his mother...I saw the child walking along Livermore Avenue to the Beldame Oriental, where in a back row the Minotaur waited to yank him bodily into a movie about treachery and arousal. Reality flat-

> tened out under the Minotaur's instruction—the real feelings aroused by the things he did would tear you into bloody rags, so you forgot it all. You cut up the memory, you buried it in a million different holes. The Minotaur was happy with you, he held you close and his hands crushed against you and the world died.[26]

This crucial passage, with its deliberate restatement of the themes and imagery of the earlier Underhill novella, "The Juniper Tree," crystallizes within itself many of *The Throat*'s most essential concerns. First, it represents an implicit statement of faith: faith in the capacity of the novel—and of all forms of art that are deeply imagined and honestly rendered—to tell us what we need to know about the condition of being human; to say, in its idiosyncratic fashion, what cannot be said in any other way. Art, in a sense, is "the throat" reflected in the title of this book, a vehicle for expressing the most complex, inexpressible states.

Second, it gives a name—one of many possible names—to that nameless boy who first appeared to Underhill some twenty years before in the deserted ghost village of Bong To, and whom he has seen many times since, stepping out of the "imaginative space" from which all of Underhill's novels have emerged. That boy is Fee Bandolier, Charlie Carpenter, M. O. Dengler, William Damrosch, Walter Dragonette and Hal Esterhaz. He is also, of course, Tim Underhill, a fact which Underhill himself both knows and does not know, at one and the same time. ("Behind every figure stood another, insisting on being *seen*."[27])

Third, it introduces the subject of buried secrets, secrets too painful to be borne, but too potent to be suppressed forever. Once again, the words of the Gnostic injunction that informed both *Shadowland* and *Mystery* find their way into the text.

> If you bring forth what is within you, what you bring forth will save you. If you do not bring forth what is within you, what you do not bring forth will destroy you.[28]

This time, though, the words take on an altered meaning, implying that salvation lies not only in recognizing and employing our most essential gifts, but in recognizing and confronting our most essential secrets. Tim Underhill—author of "The Juniper Tree," the painful and beautiful story of a young boy molested in a movie theater in a nameless Midwestern city; creator, as well, of Charlie Carpenter, whose childhood harbors a similar, and similarly buried, encounter—has a buried secret of his own, and he brings it forth, without preamble or preparation, on a New York City street. Passing the window of his local video store, he notices that a film entitled *From Dangerous Depths*—a wholly invented example of 1950s' noir—has been recently reissued. Moments later, standing outside a Spring Sreet. cafe with a copy of John Ashbery's *Flow Chart* in his hands, he watches a Mercedes pull into a parking space across the street. The man who gets out of the Mercedes is big, blonde, bearded; is, in a generic sort of way, *familiar.* Suddenly, the conjunction of that particular movie and that particular man triggers a kind of mental seizure, and Underhill finds himself torn from the world of contemporary New York, and abruptly faced with the darkest, most deeply buried memory of his childhood.

In memory, Underhill is once again a seven-year-old boy, trapped in a movie theater—the Beldame Oriental—while *From Dangerous Depths* unfolds on the screen. He is kneeling between the legs of a big, blonde, bearded man—the Millhaven butcher, Heinz Stenmitz—who forces him to perform an act of oral sex. Blindsided by the memory, Underhill vomits, then staggers home, where he tries to come to terms with the reality of an act he has thus far confronted only within the fictional worlds of his own characters.

> When I got back to Grand Street, I fell into a chair and began to cry, as if I needed the safety of my own surroundings to experience the enormity of whatever I felt—shock and grief. Anger, too. A glance in the street had just unlocked a moment, a series of moments, I had stuffed into a chest forty years ago. I had wrapped chain after chain around the chest. Then I had dropped the chest down into a psychic well. It had been bubbling and simmering ever since. Among all the feelings that rushed up from within was astonishment—this had happened to me, to *me*, and I

> had deliberately, destructively forgotten all about it. Memory after memory came flooding back. Partial, fragmentary, patchy as clouds, they brought my own life back to me—they were the missing sections of the puzzle that allowed everything else to find its proper place. I had met Stenmitz at the theater. Slowly, patiently, saying certain things and not saying others, playing on my fear and his adult authority, he had forced me to do what he wanted. I did not know how many days I had met him to kneel down before him and take him in my mouth, but it had gone on for a time that the child-me had experienced as a wretched eternity—four times? Five times? Each occasion had been a separate death.[29]

Having finally confronted the body buried beneath the juniper tree, Underhill can now begin to understand the shape of his own life, and the nature of the obsessions that have dominated so many of his novels, from *The Divided Man* to *The Kingdom of Heaven*. He can also understand his affinity, and affection, for the nameless boy who has emerged so often from the imaginative space within himself, and into both his life and his books.

In an ironic final revelation, Underhill at last watches *From Dangerous Depths*, which is described as "a Hitchcock version of Fritz Lang's *M*,"[30] and which revolves around a detective (played by Robert Ryan) searching for the man (William Bendix) who has murdered a number of local school children. Watching the credits, Underhill realizes that he has just discovered the source of the pseudonyms (Franklin Bachelor and Michael Hogan, among many others) that Fee Bandolier used throughout his various careers. Fee's use of the names of characters—of a detective, a murderer, and a variety of victims—from this particular movie places his seduction by Stenmitz at the same time and at the same place as Underhill's: Millhaven's Beldame Oriental Theater, where *From Dangerous Depths* played a two week engagement in the summer of 1950. Together with that earlier victim, William Damrosch, Tim Underhill and Fee Bandolier are part of a procession: children of the night, all of whom "had passed through the filthy hands of Heinz Stenmitz."[31] After calling Tom Pasmore to deliver this latest piece of news, Underhill watches the movie once again. As the novel ends, he is sitting in front of his television,

> thinking of Fee Bandolier, the man I had known and the first Fee, the child Fee, my other self, delivered to me at so many times and in so many places by imagination. There he was, and I was there too, beside him, crying and laughing at the same time, waiting for the telephone to ring.[32]

The Throat—both by itself and in conjunction with the first two novels in the Blue Rose sequence—constitutes a kind of magnum opus, a summing up of Straub's primary beliefs about the nature of stories, the importance of art, the power of the imagination, and the simultaneous beauty and terror of the world. Despite the fact that all three novels revel in complexity, and are among the most rigorously intellectual suspense novels of recent years, they are also, in the end, very moving books, treating the most lurid and violent material with sensitivity, intelligence, and compassion—treating it, in other words, with the full force of Straub's own capacity for imaginative empathy—and bringing an informed and unsentimental sympathy to that most volatile and delicate of subjects: the infinite vulnerability of children.

In the aftermath of this massive project, Straub stopped, took a metaphorical breath, and then turned his attention to a very different sort of book: a suspense story patterned, in its original conception, on Geoffrey Household's classic novel of hunter and hunted, *Rogue Male,* and provisionally entitled *American Nights.* Nearly three years later, after more than the usual number of false starts, wrong turns, and unanticipated travails, a very different novel with a very different title appeared in stores, confounding expectations once again.

1. Letter from Peter Straub to the author

2. Ibid.

3. *The Throat* (New York: E. P. Dutton, 1993), p. 3

4. Letter from Peter Straub to the author

5. Ibid.

6. *The Throat*, p. 12

7. Ibid., p. 14
8. Ibid., p. 18
9. Ibid., p. 18
10. Ibid., p. 63
11. Ibid., p. 61
12. Ibid., p. 62
13. Ibid., p. 62
14. Ibid., pp. 65-66
15. Ibid., p. 39
16. Ibid., p. 472
17. Ibid., p. 84
18. Ibid., p. 231
19. Raymond Chandler—*The Long Goodbye* (New York: Houghton Mifflin, 1953)
20. *The Throat*, p. 675
21. Ibid., p. 490
22. Ibid., p. 597
23. Ibid., p. 4
24. Ibid., p. 237
25. Ibid., p. 611-612
26. Ibid., p. 217-218
27. Ibid., p. 414
28. Ibid., p. 140
29. Ibid., p. 605
30. Ibid., p. 688
31. Ibid., p. 637
32. Ibid., p. 689

Section IV

The End of the Century Is in Sight

Chapter Thirteen:
Uncollected Short Fiction

In addition to the stories gathered together in *Houses Without Doors,* Straub has written enough uncollected short fiction to fill another substantial volume. Most of these uncollected pieces are novella-length stories that take their inspiration from some familiar themes and sources: Vietnam, fairy tales, childhood traumas, music, influential works of literature, etc. One novella, "The General's Wife," was inspired by Carlos Fuentes' *Aura* and was originally intended as an extended flashback to the main narrative of *Floating Dragon.* (See Appendix B.) Another, "Hunger," was written as an "introduction" to *Ghosts,* an anthology of supernatural fiction that Straub edited in 1995. (See Appendix A.) And the stories "The Kingdom of Heaven," "The Ghost Village," and "Bunny is Good Bread" are either excerpts from or offshoots of the final Blue Rose novel, *The Throat.*

"The Kingdom of Heaven," which appeared originally in Patrick McGrath and Bradford Morrow's 1991 anthology, *The New Gothic,* is directly excerpted from *The Throat,* and recounts Tim Underhill's early experiences in Vietnam as a junior member of the Body Squad. "The Ghost Village" takes as its centerpiece another of Underhill's Vietnam adventures: the visit to the haunted village of Bong To, where Underhill encounters the spirit of a murdered Vietnamese child, along with the ghosts of two recently deceased platoon mates. Straub's account of Bong To and its aftermath is reshaped for inclusion in this novella and is framed by a story that does not appear in the original novel: the story of Private Leonard Hamnet and his desperate attempts to return home to "take care"[1] of his wife and young son, who has been sexually molested—"messed with"[2]—by the leader of the local church choir. The central matter of the story is identically recounted in *The Throat* (see Chapter Twelve), but is given heft and resonance by the additional material. It works quite effectively as an independent narrative. In fact, "The Ghost Village," which first appeared in Dennis Etchison's original anthology, *Metahorror*, went on to win the 1993 World Fantasy Award for Best Novella.

The third *Throat*-related story, "Bunny is Good Bread," differs from the first two in that it consists entirely of material that was excised from the final version of the novel. First published in Thomas and Elizabeth Monteleone's anthology, *Borderlands Four,* under the title "Fee," "Bunny is Good Bread" brings together elements from *Koko, The Throat,* "Blue Rose" and "The Juniper Tree" to create a genuinely wrenching portrait of the damaged childhood of Fielding "Fee" Bandolier, only child of Bob Bandolier, perpetrator of the original series of Blue Rose murders that swept through Millhaven in 1950.

Fee is five years old as the story begins, and is about to be subjected to a simultaneous series of pressures that will shape—and warp—his character forever. To begin with, his mother is dying, having been recently beaten into a coma by the drunken, brutal Bob Bandolier.

> Two weeks ago, when everything had changed, Fee had heard his father smashing...bottles, raving, smashing the chair against the wall. It was as if a monster had burst from his father's skin to rage back and forth in the bedroom. The next morning, his father said that Mom was sick. Pieces of the chair lay all over the room, and the walls were covered with explosions.[3]

Fee's mother is hidden from the world in the Bandolier bedroom, and never provided with any form of medical treatment. Her death comes slowly, gradually, and is accompanied by hemorrhages, convulsions and the sickly sweet smell of gangrenous bedsores, which pervades the apartment and enters Fee's dreams.

At the same time, Bob Bandolier loses his job as night manager of the St. Alwyn Hotel, ostensibly for excessive absences resulting from his need to care for his ailing wife. In a demented act of revenge against the hotel and its owners, Bandolier then plans and executes the series of "Blue Rose" murders that take place in and around the St. Alwyn, murders that are eventually attributed to Millhaven detective William Damrosch, and whose real solution will remain unknown until their latter day reenactment forces Tim Underhill to reopen the case.

The third element in Fee's moral and psychological disintegration comes when Bob Bandolier takes a temporary job in another Millhaven hotel, and forces Fee to spend entire days, alone, in the nearby Beldame Oriental movie theater. There, against the garish noir backdrop of the film called *From Dangerous Depths,* Fee is systematically—and repeatedly—molested by Millhaven's resident predator, Heinz Stenmitz. Like Underhill, and like the nameless narrator of "The Juniper Tree," Fee does his best to bury the memory, but buried memories always find a way to speak. In Fee's case, they speak in dreams—hallucinatory montages in which the events of his life and the events of the movie blend inextricably together—and in a series of drawings in which people, houses, whole cities are crushed beneath the feet of an impossibly large, absolutely indifferent being. Bob Bandolier discovers these drawings and demands an explanation. Forced to speak, Fee tells the entire story of Heinz Stenmitz and the events that occurred in the Beldame Oriental. It is the only time in his life he will ever speak in this fashion.

> An unprecedented thing happened...he opened his mouth and spoke words over which he had no control at all. Someone else inside him spoke these words. Fee heard them as they proceeded from his mouth, but forgot them as soon as they were uttered...Finally, he had said it all, though he could not have repeated a single word if he had been held over a fire.[4]

In the aftermath of this revelation, two things happen. First, Bob Bandolier kills Heinz Stenmitz, whose death marks the end of the initial series of Blue Rose murders. Second, unable to face the sight of his tainted, corrupted child, Bandolier sends Fee away, placing him in the care of his dead wife's relatives in Azure, Ohio. There, in a succession of foster homes, Fee develops his own capacity for cruelty and sexual violence. He also learns to dissemble, to conceal his nature beneath an acceptably "normal" facade. In time, he leaves Ohio, joins the army, and is accepted into the Special Forces program. This is the point at which his real life begins, a life which will carry him from the Conradian darkness of Vietnam to the American Midwest of his childhood. There, under a series of false identities, he will maintain two spectacularly successful careers as a policeman and as an itinerant serial murderer, careers which will proceed along parallel tracks until his eventual unmasking in the closing chapters of *The Throat.*

"Bunny is Good Bread" is the definitive treatment of one of Straub's classic themes: the making of a monster through the unremitting application of violence, abuse, and neglect. Like "Blue Rose," and "The Juniper Tree," it is the secret history that illuminates the known history, the story beneath the story that has already been told. It is also, perhaps, the single most desolating piece of fiction that Straub has ever written, a naked, absolutely unmediated account of the systematic destruction of a child's spirit. "Bunny is Good Bread" is chilling, memorable, and beautifully constructed. It is also, in its darkest moments, almost too painful to bear.

A very different sort of serial killer inhabits the pages of "Ashputtle," a story whose title and primary imagery are taken from a story by the Brothers Grimm, which was itself the precursor to a gentler, and much more famous, fairy tale, "Cinderella."

The serial killer in question is Mrs. Asch, a hugely overweight kindergarten teacher who has organized her life around three central beliefs. She believes that she is an artist, although of a highly unusual type. She believes that the events of the original "Ashputtle"—the story of a disenfranchised child, her widowed father, and her callous stepmother—reflect the overarching pattern of her own life. And she believes, finally, that "what [people] need, they get from their own minds."[5] What Mrs. Asch derives from her own deeply disturbed mind forms the substance of this bizarre, artfully constructed account of art, mania, and murder.

According to her own version of events, Mrs. Asch spent a small portion of her childhood living within a "golden time,"[6] in which both her parents still lived, and in which their love for their only daughter created, briefly, the illusion of a perfectible universe. But then her mother died, and everything, both within Mrs. Asch and in the wider world outside, suddenly changed.

> Every day the little girl watered her mother's grave with her tears. But her heart was dead. You cannot lie about a thing like this. Hatred is the inside part of love. And so her mother became a hard cold stone in her heart. And that was the meaning of her mother, for as long as the little girl lived.[7]

"Ashputtle" recounts, from deep within the twisted perspective of its narrator, the progress of a life whose defining characteristics are a dead heart and an underlying hatred of the world. Mrs. Asch (that is, the little girl who will become Mrs. Asch; we never know her by any other name) believes she has been betrayed by her mother's death. She is further betrayed when her father remarries, choosing for his second wife a beautiful, exotic Chinese-American woman named Zena, who is quickly cast in the archetypal role of wicked stepmother. And she may, for all we know for certain, really be a wicked stepmother. But we only know what Mrs. Asch chooses to tell us, and only see what she lets us see. And so the portrait of Zena that emerges from these pages is of a grasping, avaricious woman whose role in life is to provide fuel for the narrator's endless supply of bitterness, misery, and rage.

In time, the narrative solidifies around Mrs. Asch's "artistic" responses to her situation, and around her discovery that she is capable of generating in others a wide range of responses to her own actions, because people always take what they need from the things they see. In her own words,

> I thought of myself as a work of art. I caused responses without being responsible for them. This is the great freedom of art.[8]

At the age of twelve, she further tells us, "misery and anger made me a great artist."[9] Her art, at this stage, takes a bizarre and pathetic form. She embarks on a series of eating binges that will turn her into the "pathetic old lumpo"[10] she eventually becomes. She takes the products of those binges—large vividly described bowel movements that she smears all over her naked body—and stands beneath a hazel tree on a nearby hill, a self-created work of art that reflects what she sees as the true condition of the natural world. This piece of primal performance art brings her to the unwanted attention of a series of therapists, all of whom are cast in the roles of wicked stepsisters, all of whom prove incapable of understanding the nuances of her singular form of artistic expression.

Over the years, Mrs. Asch tells us, she became "a much greater artist."[11] In her career as a kindergarten teacher, she is able to elicit a satisfying range of responses from the children under her care—children she alternately terrifies and beguiles—and from their heedless, well-to-do parents, all of whom take what they need—pity, usually, and an unacknowledged contempt—from their encounters with the fat, smiling lady who teaches their kids to read.

The apotheosis of Mrs. Asch's artistic career takes a much more dramatic form. Every now and then, when the compulsion becomes too great to resist, she murders one of her charges, and buries the body in the nearby woods. In these moments, which occur at cautious intervals and have taken place in several different states, Mrs. Asch achieves her most indelible effects. Local newspapers devote endless columns of print to the event. Classmates of the missing child "suffer nightmares and recurrent enuresis."[12] In the classroom, they begin to exhibit "lassitude, wariness, a new unwillingness to respond, like the unwillingness of the very old."[13] And the grieving parents slowly come apart, moving from a state of desperate, distracted optimism to a new and unwelcome realization: that hope is not, as they have always believed, "an essential component of the universe."[14] The range of reactions, in cases like these, is virtually endless. As Mrs. Asch tells us,

> Works of art generate responses not directly traceable to the work itself. Helplessness, grief and sorrow may exist simultaneously alongside aggressiveness, hostility, anger, or even serenity and relief. The more profound and subtle the work, the more intense and long-lasting the response it evokes.[15]

And Mrs. Asch, from her privileged position as caretaker to the local children, gets to witness—and feed off—all of these responses, as she counsels and comforts the children, listens to the parents, joins the search parties and, in the end, attends the funerals, after which, eventually, she moves on, bringing her art to the attention of a new and unsuspecting audience.

Straub has written frequently about the consolations of art, but "Ashputtle" may be the first time he has addressed so explicitly the destructive power of art, or dramatized the ways in which the artistic impulse can be corrupted when it is fueled, not by creative ambition, but by bitterness, misery, and rage. This is a strong, strikingly original story, one that renders, with uncomfortable acuity, the inner workings of a powerful, but deeply disordered, imagination.

"Pork Pie Hat," a novella about music, murder, and childhood memories, was originally commissioned for an anthology called *Murder For Halloween,* edited by Michele Slung and Roland Hartman (better known to mystery aficionados as Otto Penzler). "Pork Pie Hat" is actually several stories at once, and uses the framing device of a Columbia University grad student's brief relationship with a legendary jazz musician—referred to, simply, as "Hat"—to unearth its central story: a Gothic, deliberately enigmatic account of a young boy's Halloween adventure in rural Mississippi in the mid-1920s.

As the story opens, the unnamed narrator has just arrived in New York City from Evanston, Illinois with two purposes in mind: to earn an M.A. in English from Columbia, and to avail himself of the "unimaginable wealth"[16] of cafes, bars, restaurants, record stores, bookstores and jazz clubs that the city offers. One evening, he notices an advertisement for a live performance featuring jazz pianist John Hawes—a longtime favorite of the narrator—and the legendary tenor sax player called Hat. Driven mostly by the desire to hear John Hawes play, he attends the performance. Midway through the set, Hat—who appears to be affectionately based on jazz great Lester Young—shows up, late and a little drunk, and begins to play.

> What happened next changed my life—changed me, anyhow. It was like discovering that some vital, even necessary substance had all along been missing from my life. Anyone who hears a great musician for the first time knows the feeling that the universe has just expanded. In fact, all that happened was that Hat started playing "Too Marvelous For Words," one of the twenty-odd songs that were his entire repertoire

> at the time...Halfway through Hat's solo, I saw John Hawes watching him and realized that Hawes, whom I all but revered, revered *him*. But by that time, I did, too.[17]

The narrator attends every one of Hat's New York performances, and eventually musters the courage to ask him for an interview. Hat agrees, and they meet on the evening of October 31—Halloween—in the musician's dingy room in Manhattan's Albert Hotel. There, they conduct a rambling, marathon, all-night interview that is really a series of monologues in which Hat blithely ignores the prepared set of questions and talks about whatever comes to mind. Part of the interview—heavily edited—eventually appears in *Downbeat.* Another part—Hat's reminiscence of a Halloween night nearly forty years before—forms the substance of this story.

Hat begins by describing life in "Woodland," Mississippi, a typical small town in the segregated South where strange things are reputed to occur. For example, a "witch-lady"[18] named Mary Randolph lives in the town, and legends claim that she once brought a murdered man—a local lowlife named Eddie Grimes—back from the dead. On Halloween night of his eleventh year, Hat, together with his best friend, a preacher's son named Dee Sparks, decides to explore a rough, forbidden section of Woodland called the Backs. As Hat explains, "No matter where you live, there are places you're not supposed to go. And sooner or later, you're gonna wind up there."[19]

In the course of their brief, hallucinatory visit, the boys encounter an unsettling series of images and events they are unable to comprehend completely. While still en route, they are nearly run down by a Model-T Ford driven by the alcoholic town doctor, who appears to be deeply frightened, and is driving frantically away from the Backs. Once at their destination, they nearly stumble into the recently resurrected Eddie Grimes, who is tending an illegal still. While trying to avoid Grimes, they hear a woman screaming, apparently in great pain, somewhere nearby. While trying to locate the source of the screams, they become separated, and Hat endures a disconcerting few minutes in which—to the incessant accompaniment of screaming—he sees what he believes is a ghost, and has a brief, face-to-face encounter with an obviously frightened Eddie Grimes. Eventually, he links back up with Dee Sparks, and they find their way to a tarpaper shack which houses the screaming woman.

Once there, they see a man—who appears to be both white and well-dressed—leaving the shack, carrying a small, wrapped bundle. Inside the shack, they see a naked white woman whom Dee identifies as Abbey Montgomery, a local philanthropist, and whose lower body is covered in blood. (Hat assumes the woman is dead. Dee, who is a sharper observer than Hat, disagrees.) Beside Abbey Montgomery, holding her hand, is Mary Randolph, the local witch-lady.

Not understanding that what they have seen is the aftermath of a difficult—and illicit—birth attended by a local midwife, the boys return home, frightened and confused. Hat is convinced that the sight of the bloody white woman spells trouble for the black community. He is right. Within days, Eddie Grimes is shot and killed by Woodland police officers. Shortly afterward, Mary Robbins is also killed, murdered in her own home. And Abbey Montgomery, older, thinner, makes a brief public appearance, delivering Thanksgiving food baskets to the local Baptist church. It is her last such appearance. When it is over, she disappears into the solitude of her family mansion, and is never seen again. She dies just a few years later.

That is Hat's story, an enigmatic, unresolved tale that appears, to Hat's interviewer, to have "two separate meanings, the daylight meaning created by sequences of ordinary English words, and another night-time meaning, far less determined and knowable."[20] In the aftermath of their night-long interview, Hat and the narrator go their separate ways. Two months later, Hat is killed by an internal hemorrhage. "Miss Rosemary"[21] (as Hat affectionately dubs him) completes his M.A., then slides into an ordinary, slightly disappointing career in corporate America, settling for a life without "a perpetual soundtrack."[22] But Hat's story continues to nag at him and, some years, later, he attempts to pursue the hidden truth.

A brief conversation with John Hawes, a reference in a biography of dead jazz musician Grant Kilbert—a long time disciple of Hat's—and a series of articles resurrected from the pages of two defunct Mississippi newspapers lead "Miss Rosemary" to a tentative identification of the "white man" who carried the bundle away from the Backs, and a tentative explanation of Hat's seep-seated, long-standing dread of Halloween. Rumor, supposition and circumstantial evidence point, in the end, to a disturbing possibility: that Hat's light-complected, womanizing, musician father—a man with a marked propensity for violence—may have been the "white man" that Hat and his companion saw that night. Given the fact that two "witnesses" to events in the

Backs were subsequently murdered, the possibility alone would serve as an enormous, life-long weight on Hat's spirit. In the narrator's words,

> I wonder if Hat saw more than he admitted to me of the man leaving the shack where Abbey Montgomery lay on bloody sheets; I wonder if he had reason to fear his father. I don't know if what I'm thinking is correct—I'll never know that—but now, finally, I think I know why Hat never wanted to go out of his room on Halloween nights.[23]

Our final image of Hat is of a gifted, haunted man forced by circumstances to spend much of his life alone in hotel rooms, drinking gin "until he obliterated the horror of his own thoughts."[24] "Pork Pie Hat" is an effectively open-ended mystery that is deeply informed by Straub's love and understanding of the music that is Hat's primary legacy. Straub's responsiveness to jazz, together with his ability to articulate the actual experience of listening, really *listening,* to music gives this story a great deal of its distinctive flavor. More than anything, though, it is the character of Hat—an enormously dignified figure who has been marked, but not disfigured, by sadness—that provides the story with its emotional center.

During the course of "Pork Pie Hat," we see Hat's life from a variety of viewpoints: through his own words; through the recollections of fellow musician John Hawes; and from the evolving perspective of the callow young grad student who meets and interviews Hat in the early 1960s, and the older, sadder, more settled man who reflects on that meeting, and who may have identified the central source of Hat's quiet, characteristic grief. Of course, as the older Miss Rosemary reminds us, "most of what is called information is interpretation, and interpretation is always partial."[25] "Pork Pie Hat," filled as it is with speculations and provisional interpretations, makes art out of uncertainty. In the process, it gives us a moving portrait of the nature and meaning—"the whole long curve"[26]—of a master musician's life.

In late 1995, Straub—together with friend and fellow novelist Lawrence Block—joined the Adams Round Table, a Manhattan-based writers group that meets, for dinner and conversation, on the first Tuesday of every month. Its members—which include Mary Higgins

Clark, Whitley Strieber, Justin Scott, Susan Isaacs and Dorothy Salisbury Davis—have, in addition to their social activities, produced a series of members-only theme anthologies, the latest of which, *Murder on the Run*, appeared in 1998. Straub's contribution—his first as a Round Table member—was a novella-length tale entitled "Isn't It Romantic?" In keeping with the theme implied by the anthology's title, it is the story of an itinerant professional assassin attempting to complete the final assignment of his career.

As the story opens, the assassin—whom we know only as N—has just arrived in the tiny village of Montory in the Basque region of France. Once there, he settles into a small local hostelry, makes contact with his "divisional regional controller,"[27] and proceeds—with the caution that has kept him alive and active in an extremely high-risk profession—to familiarize himself with his surroundings and to prepare the way for a clean hit on his latest, and last, target: an antique dealer and small-time arms trader named Daniel Hubert, who is about to consummate a big-money, major league arms deal with a group of Middle Eastern terrorists.

N is a legend in his profession, a consummate contract killer who has been everywhere and done everything. His instincts are nearly flawless, and he has trained himself to take note of the slightest anomaly. The moment he begins his surveillance of Hubert, he encounters one such anomaly: a beautiful blonde woman who is constantly in Hubert's company, and who represents a serious "glitch in the data flow."[28] N learns from his controller—Charles Many Horses, a Lakota Sioux with a Harvard MBA—that the woman is an undisclosed "background resource"[29] also working for N's unnamed employers. In other words, she is an apprentice assassin being given the opportunity to watch N in action, and to learn the trade at the feet of the master.

N then flashes back to an incident from the early years of his own career. He himself had been briefly apprenticed to a master assassin named Sullivan. Sullivan, like N, was then one final assignment away from retirement. Their joint assignment was carried out flawlessly, but Sullivan, in the words of his controller, "never came back."[30] He died in France, an apparent suicide. N, however, has always believed that a second, hidden "background resource" eliminated Sullivan, violently terminating a career from which no one ever really retires. Believing, as he does, that "in institutions, patterns had longer lives than employees,"[31] N suddenly, intuitively understands that he himself is the intended final victim of the operation currently in progress.

The bulk of "Isn't It Romantic?" concerns N's attempts to subvert that operation, to identify and eliminate his hidden executioner, and to survive long enough to enjoy a comfortable—and lucrative—retirement. En route to the story's ironic, but not unexpected conclusion, N murders a street thief unlucky enough to catch his attention and then, in the course of fulfilling his assignment, takes out not only his scheduled target, but his beautiful blonde apprentice and the two Middle Eastern arms buyers as well, after which he hijacks a suitcase full of cash and heads into the future he believes he has secured for himself. Unfortunately, he stops along the way for one last romantic liaison and learns, too late, the identity of his final, elusive adversary. By the final moments of the story, N lies dead, the victim—like Sullivan before him—of a fatal short-sightedness. In institutions, patterns have longer lives than people.

The oddest thing about this story is its relative lack of oddness or narrative eccentricity. Straub's fiction, particularly his shorter work, tends toward the adventurous and experimental. This one, by contrast, is kind of experiment in reverse: a deliberate attempt to work within a conventional narrative framework. It is a cool, assured, ironic tale that is filled, to an unusual degree, with details of tradecraft, weaponry, professional and procedural data. More than any of Straub's other stories, long or short, "Isn't It Romantic?" feels as though it could have been written by someone else.

Which is not to say that the final product is bad or even second-rate. It's not. It is an intelligent, thoroughly professional piece of work that accomplishes its purposes with great precision and an exacting eye for detail. Straub has great fun, for example, with the way jargon has invaded virtually every profession, including that of contract killer.

> [N] traveled three cars behind the Mercedes...wishing that his employers permitted the use of cell phones, which they did not. Cell phones were "porous," they were "intersectable"—they were even, in the most delightful of these locutions, "capacity risks..." In order to inform his controller of M. Hubert's playmate, he would have to drive back to the "location usage device," another charming example of

> bureaucratese, the pay telephone in Montory. You want to talk capacity risks, how about that?[32]

In addition, the ambiance of the Basque countryside is vividly evoked; the dialogue is consistently fresh and often funny (dialogue continues to be an area of steadily increasing strength for Straub); and the characters—including, in addition to N himself, the long-departed Sullivan, the cynical regional controller Charles Many Horses, and an attractive female assassin with a world-class case of body odor—are uniformly distinctive and convincing. The problem with the story lies in its essential remoteness, its deliberate failure to engage the sort of personal, emotional issues that underlie Straub's best, most characteristic fiction. Despite its many virtues, it lacks the obsessional power of stories like "Blue Rose," "The Juniper Tree," or "Bunny is Good Bread," all of which have both a tragic dimension and an emotional immediacy that are missing this time out. In the end, "Isn't It Romantic?" succeeds, but only on its own circumscribed terms: as entertainment that never really aspires to the condition of art.

Straub's next novella, "Mr. Clubb and Mr. Cuff," was written in the interval between *The Hellfire Club* and *Mr. X*, and it raised the stakes considerably. A long, strange, extremely dark story loosely patterned after Herman Melville's "Bartleby the Scrivener," "Mr. Clubb and Mr. Cuff" was originally published in another Otto Penzler theme anthology, this one entitled *Murder for Revenge*. It went on to win both the International Horror Guild Award as Best Novella of 1998, and the Horror Writers of America's Bram Stoker Award for Best Long Fiction. The awards were well deserved.

The original Melville story is narrated by a pedantic, self-congratulatory Wall Sreet lawyer who—after being awarded a political patronage position known as Master in Chancery—finds himself in need of additional help, and augments his clerical staff by hiring a scrivener (i.e. copyist) named, simply, Bartleby. Bartleby, like his fellow scriveners, is expected to perform a variety of tasks, but "prefers" to restrict his activities to copying legal documents. Eventually, he stops doing even that, preferring not to take orders of any kind from his employer. As the story progresses, he withdraws more and more into his own private universe, his stillness and impassivity an implicit rejection of the driven, newly industrialized society of nineteenth century New York.

Straub's story—which borrows several elements from the original and takes them in directions that Melville would never have dreamed of—concerns the "great journey"[33] undertaken by the nameless narrator, who has exchanged the pieties of his provincial upbringing for a successful career as a financial adviser in the cutthroat world of modern Wall Street. Much of his success is attributable to his flexible moral standards. His chief assistants—"Gilligan and the Captain"—were chosen because of their intelligence, lack of imagination, and "slight moral laziness,"[34] while his most lucrative clients are hardened criminals with complex financial requirements and "subterranean floods"[35] of illegitimate cash.

Trouble begins when the narrator learns that his wife—a beautiful ex-singer named Marguerite—is having an affair with his principal business rival, Graham Leeson. Driven past endurance, and not yet aware of the fact that revenge inexorably exacts its own revenge, he enlists the aid of an ex-convict from his old home town of New Coventry in securing the services of "serious men"[36] willing to serve as agents of his vengeance. The very next morning, two short, stout, bowler-hatted men named Mr. Clubb and Mr. Cuff—"Detectives Extraordinaire"[37]—show up at his office, offering him their highly specialized—and very expensive—services.

Clubb and Cuff, whose names suggest the nature of the services they provide, are dark angels of vengeance who offer the narrator a Faustian bargain. (After "Bartleby," the Faust legend is the story's primary literary influence, an allusion which is reinforced by Straub's decision to name the adulterous wife Marguerite.) The two begin their relationship with their new "employer" by intercepting his breakfast of high cholesterol comfort food and eating it themselves. (Clubb and Cuff seem to subsist on things that contain varying levels of poison: steak, eggs, butter, bacon, alcohol and tobacco.) Like Bartleby, they successfully resist all directives and displays of authority, "preferring" to do things according to their own established principles.

During the course of a long afternoon, Clubb and Cuff ensconce themselves, like Bartleby, behind a gilded screen in their employer's private office. Chaos seems to emanate from them, and quickly insinuates itself throughout the entire suite of offices. The narrator watches incredulously as life puts the lie to his frequently stated belief that "all is in order, all is in train."[38] First, the long-standing No Smoking rule is suspended, then a supply of alcoholic beverages is delivered to the two intruders, who find the "sacred properties"[39] of alcohol essential to the completion of their assigned tasks. Suddenly, what starts as an unaccustomed lapse in discipline begins to assume orgiastic proportions, and life within the dignified precincts of the office begins to slide into chaos and disorder. Before the afternoon is over, the firm has lost both its collective dignity and its most lucrative client, a garrulous Mafioso named Arthur "The Building is Condemned" C_____, who is unaccountably terrified by his brief encounter with the firm's bowler-hatted new "consultants." It is the first in a series of similar, equally catastrophic financial setbacks.

Hours later, after a drunken interlude with the girlfriend of one of the firm's rock star clients, the narrator is roughly awakened by his new employees, who have spent the intervening hours carrying out their assignment, with devastating results. While their employer lay in a semicomatose state in his Manhattan townhouse, Clubb and Cuff journeyed to "Green Chimneys," his country estate, captured and subdued both Marguerite and her lover, and prepared to embark on the penultimate stage of their "great journey," a process that began with the rape of their intended victims and culminated, or was intended to culminate, with a highly refined series of "non-terminal" punishments. At several points along the line, things went badly wrong, and both Marguerite and Leeson were murdered. (Leeson, whose will to resist proved virtually limitless, was butchered in spectacularly brutal fashion.) Afterward, Mr. Clubb and Mr. Cuff destroyed all forensic evidence by setting the entire house on fire, reducing it to ashes with the practiced efficiency of professional arsonists.

All of this is contained in the "report" that Clubb and Cuff deliver to the narrator. In the aftermath of the report, and in keeping with the notion that vengeance always exacts its own form of vengeance, the story takes a dark, strangely appropriate turning. Forced to face the terms that were always implicit in his Faustian compact—the fine print, so to speak—the narrator himself becomes the victim of his two employees, who rigorously pursue his continuing education—taking him, in effect, on the final stages of the "great journey"—by subjecting him to the same sort of punishments he had hired them to perform on his wife. At the end of a month that has about it a timeless, eternal quality, he reenters the world with one hand and one eye missing, with a newly created host of patchwork scars hidden beneath his clothing, and with the bulk of his fortune transferred to the accounts of Mr. Clubb and Mr. Cuff. In the final pages, newly shriven and fundamentally altered by the process of his "education," he leaves

New York forever, and takes up a modest, anonymous, ultimately more ascetic life in his childhood home of New Coventry.

"Mr. Clubb and Mr. Cuff" is a strange, funny, graphic, and disturbing story that is both a Mystery (in the truest, most Capitalized sense of the word) and a morality tale. At the heart of the Mystery, of course, are Mr. Clubb and Mr. Cuff themselves. Like Bartleby, they have no known antecedents and no discernible relationships or associations, save with each other. They are simply *there,* inexorable and immutable, embodiments of the darkest human impulses. Their natures, their powers, their uncomfortably acute perceptions, their paradoxical sense of the sacred nature of their ancient calling—all of these elements are part of their essential mystery, and can neither be rationalized nor fully understood. In their own view, which is as tentative and unsupported as any other, they are merely the agents of a vast, unknowable Plan.

> "A great design directs us," said Mr. Clubb..."We poor wanderers, you and me and Mr. Cuff and the milkman, too, only see the little portion right in front of us. Half the time we don't even see that in the right way. For sure we don't have a Chinaman's chance of understanding it. But the design is ever present, sir, a truth I bring to your attention for the sake of the comfort in it...[40]

Seen from a less cosmic perspective, "Mr. Clubb and Mr. Cuff" is also a story about values: about greed, corruption, and the poisoning of the spirit. The narrator, who has earned enough money through questionable means to lead a pointlessly sybaritic life, willingly sacrifices the remnants of his soul for the dubious, and very expensive, comforts of revenge. In a fit of rage composed of equal parts jealousy, wounded vanity and childish pique, he yields to the urgings of his reptile brain—the dark subcellar of consciousness which is entirely devoid of empathy, or of humane considerations of any kind. In doing so, he opens himself up to the darkness at the heart of things, a darkness that manifests itself in the bowler-hatted figures of Mr. Clubb and Mr. Cuff, enigmatic representatives of the invisible Design.

[1] "The Ghost Village"—*Metahorror* ed. by Dennis Etchison (New York, Dell Abyss, 1992), pp. 336

[2] Ibid., p. 334

[3] "Bunny Is Good Bread" (Originally published under the title "Fee")—*Borderlands 4* ed. by Elizabeth E. Monteleone and Thomas Monteleone (Brooklandville, MD: Borderlands Press, 1994), p. 270

[4] Ibid., p. 323

[5] "Ashputtle"—*Black Thorn, White Rose* ed. by Ellen Datlow and Terry Windling (New York, Avon Books, 1994), p. 299

[6] Ibid., p. 285

[7] Ibid., p. 292

[8] Ibid., p. 294

[9] Ibid., p. 295

[10] Ibid., p. 284

[11] Ibid., p. 295

[12] Ibid., p. 302

[13] Ibid., p. 302

[14] Ibid., p. 299

[15] Ibid., pp. 302-303

[16] "Pork Pie Hat"—*Murder for Halloween* ed. by Michele Slung and Roland Hartman (New York: Mysterious Press, 1994), p. 301

[17] Ibid., p. 303

[18] Ibid., p. 303

[19] Ibid., p. 320

[20] Ibid., p. 351

[21] Ibid., p. 313

[22] Ibid., p. 352

[23] Ibid., p. 362

[24] Ibid., p. 362

[25] Ibid., p. 315

[26] Ibid., p. 299

[27] "Isn't It Romantic?"—*Murder on the Run: An Adams Round Table Anthology* ed. by Lawrence Block (New York, Berkley Prime Crime, 1998), p. 228

[28] Ibid., p. 225

[29] Ibid., p. 227

[30] Ibid., p. 231

[31] Ibid., p. 232

[32] Ibid., p. 225

[33] "Mr. Clubb and Mr. Cuff"—*Murder for Revenge* ed. by Otto Penzler (New York, Delacorte Press, 1998), p. 305

[34] Ibid., p. 267

[35] Ibid., p. 268

36. Ibid., p. 272
37. Ibid., p. 264
38. Ibid., p. 277
39. Ibid., p. 305
40. Ibid., p. 330

Chapter Fourteen:
The Hellfire Club

In 1992, as his three book contract with Penguin/Dutton was drawing to a close, Straub signed another multi-book contract with a brand-new publisher: Random House. The first book that Straub proposed to write under this new contract was the novel that would eventually be called *The Hellfire Club*, and which provided its author with the single most harrowing writing experience of his twenty-five-year career.

The deal with Random House was signed before Straub had even begun writing *The Throat*, the last book called for by the earlier contract. The protracted process of writing that big, ambitious novel prevented Straub from addressing his new obligations for nearly two years. As a result, the contractual due date for his first Random House novel arrived while *The Hellfire Club*—then called *American Nights*—was still in the planning stage. Having been assured that delivery dates were pro forma matters, and never intended to be taken seriously, Straub ignored the date and kept on working. As things turned out, however, the "brisk new boys"[1] who had recently taken the helm at Random House had a more stringent regard for dates and deadlines than their predecessors had ever had. In time, this new regime, with its rigorous—even ruthless—insistence on the primacy of the bottom line would take note of Straub's delinquent status and call him forcibly to account.

Straub's deadline problems, initially the result of his unexpectedly late start, were compounded by the painfully slow evolution of the novel's central plot. Originally, Straub had planned to write a straightforward chase novel—something along the lines of Geoffrey Household's *Rogue Male*—in which a woman discovers that her husband is a murderer and then runs for her life, closely pursued by the husband. On reflection, Straub found this notion too simple, too "programmatic,"[2] to accommodate his affinity for big, wide-ranging narratives, and he quickly scrapped it in favor of a more complex scenario involving the intersecting lives of two imperiled women.

In this version, which still carried the provisional title of *American Nights,* two women from vastly different social and economic backgrounds, both of whom are on the run from violent, abusive marriages, meet, talk, and agree to switch identities, after which they continue moving in separate directions. This plan, whose basic structure described a kind of giant X, appealed to Straub, who then put together a detailed, six-page outline and sent it to his editor at Random House, Joe Fox. Fox, a legendary figure in American publishing, read the outline and informed Straub that it would inevitably result in an eight-hundred-page manuscript, which was larger than Random House's current, restrictive standards would permit. Could he (Straub) somehow simplify the story? Straub, motivated by the desire to be as reasonable and cooperative with his new publisher as circumstances would allow, yielded to this request, with disastrous results. "Having apparently lost my mind,"[3] as he later recalled, he suggested to Fox that removing one of the women might do the trick. Fox, unfortunately, agreed and the narrative, bereft of its original X-like structure, began almost immediately to founder.

Straub built his new, simplified design around the figure of Nora Chancel, a nurse who has endured a traumatic tour of duty in Vietnam; who now lives in the affluent Connecticut community of Westerholm; and who is married to the handsome, ineffectual scion of a successful—and somewhat sinister—New York publishing house. All of this was viable. All of it would find its way into the final product. The problem was that, try as he might, Straub found himself unable to attach this promising material to an equally viable plot. For an alarmingly long period of time, the novel went nowhere.

> I worked away for a long time, six months, nine months, a year, becoming increasingly desperate as I became increasingly aware of my novel's essential lack of direction. Daily, I found new things to write, I kept

> producing pages, but the story had no center, it just wandered along through descriptions of interiors, meals, the awfulness of the Chancel family. A terrible circumstance that had befallen a dear cousin of mine suggested a secret part of Davey Chancel's history, but after something like sixteen to eighteen months, I still had no real handle on the story.[4]

At his absolute low point, convinced that ruin was imminent and that his willingness to eviscerate his proposed plot in the name of good-hearted cooperation had ultimately undone him, Straub and his family departed, somewhat gloomily, for a planned vacation in Puerto Rico. Midway through the flight—exotic vacations seem to have a salutary effect on Straub's creative powers—help appeared from a most unexpected direction. A minor character from the novel, then still nameless but soon to be known as Dick Dart, began metaphorically tapping Straub on the shoulder, clamoring for a larger role in the proceedings.

> A character too minor to be called minor, a nameless extra drifting through the background of a single scene, [Dart] wanted to carry the ball. This spear-carrier's ambition was ridiculous, but I pulled the notebook out of my carry-on bag, uncorked a pen and listened to him. At this point, I was so desperate that I would have listened to Minnie Mouse if she thought she had a worthwhile idea. Old Dick thought his idea was more than merely workable, he thought it was great. His talents were being wasted, he said—he was lively, funny, and really perverse, qualities I should be smart enough to find useful, especially when I needed them most. Fine, I said, OK, but what do you think you can do for the so-called plot, at that point merely a vapor. I can save your sorry ass, he said, and leaned forward to whisper a couple of details in my ear. I wrote them down...[5]

Throughout the vacation, Straub continued to heed that inner voice, listening, taking notes, finding doors suddenly opening in his previously closed off narrative. "Despair," he remembers, "yielded to [his] more familiar companion, Resolve,"[6] and by the time he and his family returned to New York, he had the makings of a workable plot. After doing some revisions to accommodate the novel's sudden change of direction, Straub plunged into his revitalized narrative, which began to develop a miraculous and steadily increasing momentum.

That was the good news. The bad news came three months later, when a Random House executive conducted an audit of outstanding contracts, and discovered that Straub's problematic new novel was now two years past its original due date. Meeting were held. Ultimatums were issued. Straub was granted two brief extensions and then, in early January of 1995, an unhappy Joe Fox was forced to deliver the following edict: Straub was to deliver a completed, publishable manuscript by March 1 (then some six or seven weeks away) or face cancellation of the entire contract. Despite his rapid progress in the past few months, hundreds of pages—more than one-third of the entire book—remained to be written. In the words of *Night Journey*, the fantasy novel that stands at the heart of *The Hellfire Club*, Straub "understood the nature of the task. That was not the problem. The problem was that the task was impossible."[7] He asked Random House for one more month, and his request was turned down. At that point, armed with a kind of angry determination, he resolved to ignore the impossible nature of his task, and to deliver the manuscript on time.

Straub then shifted into a brutal daily regimen in which, for seven days a week, he began writing at eleven in the morning and continued, with only the most necessary interruptions, until three (or four, or five) o'clock the next morning. It was, he recalls, "a period of total immersion, like trying to learn Czech by holing up in a Prague hotel room and speaking only to Czechs."[8] During the course of those frantic seven weeks, events within the novel unrolled, characters revealed their essential natures, mysteries of many kinds resolved themselves, and the entire complex structure of the book came gradually into view. As Straub later commented, "It was kind of like watching a movie and writing down whatever I saw on the screen."[9] Finally, in late February, he reached the point at which Nora Chancel knocks on the door of a woman named Natalie Weil, discovers the novel's final secret (a secret to which Straub himself had not, to that point, been privy) and *The Hellfire Club* rolled to its conclusion. After a furious period of trimming and revision, the completed manuscript was printed, boxed, and delivered to Joe Fox on March 1, one day before Straub's fifty-second birthday.

The novel that resulted from this painful process was, in more than one respect, a personal triumph for its author. First, it proved to Straub that, pushed to the wall, he was capable of performing creative feats that would have seemed impossible under normal circumstances. Second, the novel itself is a remarkably successful creation, a complex, hugely entertaining affair that is filled with mysteries, surprises, and hidden turnings; and charged with a highly developed sense of the infinite variety of human nature. Most significantly, *The Hellfire Club* delivers its effects with a confidence and authority that give no hint of the struggles and uncertainties that underlay its composition. In the end, it rises above its hectic origins and achieves the vital, independent existence of a good story skillfully told.

That story, like so many Straub stories, is deeply rooted in the novel's past. It's therefore no surprise that *The Hellfire Club* opens with an enigmatic flashback which takes place in a writer's colony called Shorelands in 1938, on the very day that one of the residents, a poet by the name of Katherine Mannheim, disappears for good. Without pausing to explain the significance of that disappearance, or to elaborate on any of the other characters who are briefly introduced in this prologue, Straub then jumps ahead some fifty years, taking us to Westerholm, Connecticut, and into the troubled life of his remarkable heroine, Nora Chancel.

When we first meet Nora—who is described, ominously, as a woman "soon to be lost"[10]—she is deep in the heart of a recurring nightmare. Nora is another of Straub's haunted veterans, a former operating-theater nurse who spent a hallucinatory tour of duty in Vietnam, where she tended to an endless procession of the wounded, the mutilated, and the dying. Most of Nora's nightmares arise directly out of her memories of the war. Her "better nightmares"[11] are inhabited by images of dying soldiers, like "the boy on a gurney, his belly blown open and his life slipping out through his astonished eyes."[12] Her other nightmares come from someplace deeper, and are much, much worse.

Straub places Nora directly at the center of a complex web of interconnected elements. All of these—the characters, events, stories, and rumors that populate this book—impinge on each other in various ways. Included among them are an unsolved series of murders—all of single, independent women—currently taking place in Westerholm; the history of the Chancel family, publishers of Hugo Driver's phenomenally popular fantasy novel, *Night Journey;* and the Driver novel itself, which has taken on an astonishing life of its own, a life that is reflected in a number of ways throughout the primary narrative. Other significant elements include the events that occurred at Shorelands in 1938, which are intimately connected both to Hugo Driver and to the early history of the Chancel family; and, finally, the painful personal history of Nora herself, a history that has left her with a legacy of nightmares and a deep-seated belief in the existence of demons.

By the time the novel begins, Westerholm has developed a kind of siege mentality, a result of the unsolved murders of four middle-aged business women and the disappearance of a fifth, a local real estate agent named Natalie Weil whose deserted bedroom is found covered in blood. Nora, who knows far more than most Westerholm residents about the reality of violence—particularly violence against women—is deeply affected by the murders. She begins to think of the unknown killer as "the Wolf of Westerholm,"[13] a reference to a character—portentously named Lord Night—from the ubiquitous Hugo Driver novel, *Night Journey*. She senses, in his predatory presence, an echo of the world she left behind in Vietnam.

> Some renegade part of Nora had overlooked the savagery of the unknown man to remark on his reality. The unknown man strolled here and there on Westerholm's pretty, tree-lined streets, delivering reminders. He was like the war.[14]

Nora knows—has known since the war—that there are no safe places, and the Wolf of Westerholm simply reinforces that belief. Demons and monsters are real, and nothing—certainly not her troubled home life with handsome, ineffectual Davey Chancel—can keep them away for long.

Davey, Nora's husband, is the son of Alden and Daisy Chancel, and the grandson of Lincoln Chancel, the brutal, legendary founder of Chancel House Publishers. Alden is a vain, self-important bully who disapproves of his son's marriage and will use anything—threats, lies, blackmail—to bring that marriage to an end. Daisy is an alcoholic former novelist who has spent years composing a bloated, unpublishable manuscript aimed at venting her rage at her adulterous husband and her deceased, neo-Nazi father-in-law. Lincoln Chancel, the neo-Nazi in question, was a twentieth century robber baron who, in Straub's carefully chosen phrase, "raped his way into a huge fortune,"[15] most of which has since dwindled away. All that now remains of Lincoln's fortune is the publishing firm of Chancel House, a venture funded and maintained by the incredible success of Hugo Driver's novels.

Night Journey—and, to a lesser extent, its two sequels, *Journey into Light* and *Twilight Journey*—permeates this novel. Characters, events, and images from these three books are endlessly reflected in the "real world" of *The Hellfire Club,* whose own inner movement is intended to echo the structure and inner movement of *Night Journey. Night Journey,* a fairly traditional example of the heroic quest novel, features a young boy, Pippin Little, who succumbs to a mysterious illness, awakens into a death-haunted landscape, then travels from scene to scene and character to character, searching for some large but unspecified Truth about himself and his world. Over the years, cults of varying degrees of derangement have formed around this book. Its fans include a couple of bona fide serial killers, who have found in its pages an elaborate justification of their own actions; and a great number of average, unexceptional people like Davey Chancel, who finds in those same pages "the code to his own life."[16]

Whatever else it might be, *Night Journey* is also the source of an immense amount of money. Therefore, when two sisters of Katherine Mannheim, the poet who disappeared from Shorelands in 1938, bring suit against Chancel House, claiming that Katherine, not Hugo Driver, was the author of *Night Journey,* the issue of the novel's provenance becomes more than merely academic; becomes, in fact, the central mystery in a novel filled with mysterious, unresolved events. As the story progresses, it becomes more and more obvious that the answer to the mystery lies at Shorelands where, in the eventful summer of 1938, Lincoln Chancel met Hugo Driver, and Katherine Mannheim disappeared from the face of the earth.

These are some, though not all, of the elements at play in *The Hellfire Club,* elements which form the essential backdrop to the story which follows. There is, however, one more crucial element which must be understood, that is central to the novel's meaning, and to an understanding of Nora Chancel and her fragile emotional state. The key to that understanding lies, unsurprisingly, in Nora's experience in Vietnam.

In Vietnam, Nora worked in what she called a "flesh factory,"[17] an evacuation hospital in which she assisted in twenty to thirty operations a day. At some point, the experience took on a kind of "exalted" quality, and the procession of quotidian horrors was transformed into something sacred, into what she would come to call " an education in the miraculous."[18] There were a couple of reasons for this. One was her relationship with a brilliant, resourceful surgeon named Dan Harwich, who, over time, would assume a larger and larger role in her memories of that period, and who would come to occupy a special position in her small, private pantheon. The second reason—a particularly Straubian reason—was the unsought happiness she found through "usefulness," through immersion in important and meaningful work.

> She had won a focused concentration out of the chaos around her, and every operation became a drama in which she and the surgeon performed necessary, inventive actions which banished or at least contained disorder.[19]

This period of exaltation was a brief one, and ended in a particularly brutal way.

> After three months she was raped by two dumbbell grunts who caught her as she came outside on a break. One of them hit her in the side of the head, pushed her down, and fell on her. The other kneeled on her arms...The rape was a flurry of thumps and blows and enormous reeking hands over her mouth; it was having the breath mashed out of her while grunting animals dug at her privates. While it went on, Nora was pushed through the bottom of the world. This was entirely literal. The column of the world went from bottom to top, and now she had been smashed through the bottom of the column along

> with the rest of the shit. Demons leaned
> chattering out of the darkness.[20]

Once admitted, the demons become a part of Nora's life. They return, again and again, as memories, and as the substance of her most extreme nightmares. In moments of extremity, they are as real—as visible and audible—as any other aspect of her surroundings. (Hallucinations, as the Louis Althusser epigraph informs us, are also facts.[21]) The Nora Chancel we encounter at the novel's outset is thus a particularly vulnerable woman, beset by demons and isolated from the world in a number of ways. Her marriage is failing, and her husband has recently admitted to an affair with the missing Natalie Weil. Her father-in-law has virtually ordered his son to divorce her. She is no longer employed, having left her latest nursing position when her attempt to rescue an abused child from his abusive father nearly resulted in a kidnapping charge. Even her own body has begun to betray her. As the story opens, she is beginning to experience the unexpected onset of early menopause.

Having established so much of Nora's—and the novel's—essential background, Straub, with the inspirational assistance of former spear carrier Dick Dart, is ready to unleash the narrative, which is galvanized by the confluence of two unrelated events. First, the missing Natalie Weil, generally believed to be dead, returns to Westerholm, frightened, disheveled, largely incoherent. During the course of her muddled, often contradictory interviews with the Westerholm police, Natalie astonishes her interrogators by accusing Nora of kidnapping her at knife point and locking her away in an abandoned nursery. The motive: uncontrolled anger over Natalie's affair with Davey Chancel. Given the fact of Nora's prior involvement in a kidnapping incident, the police take Natalie's story seriously, and Nora—now more isolated than ever—is summoned to police headquarters, where she is faced with the prospect of imminent arrest.

At about the same time, police finally arrest a suspect in the string of killings that has paralyzed the town. The suspect is Dick Dart, who is both a lawyer and the son and employee of local lawyer Leland Dart, who manages the legal affairs of many of Westerholm's most prominent citizens, including the Chancel family. Dart's arrest has resulted in the inevitable media circus, and Nora's own arrival at the station only adds to the overriding feeling of chaos. At one point, in a badly timed attempt to relocate Dart from his holding cell to an interrogation room, the two parties—Nora and her interrogators, Dart and his entourage of lawyers and guards—come face-to-face in a crowded hallway. Dart, always prepared to exploit an opportunity, steals a gun from a distracted policeman, grabs Nora, and then cheerfully escapes—hostage in tow—through a nearby office window.

Nora's ensuing night journey, which lasts for ten days and occupies the remainder of the novel, breaks down into three distinct phases. In the first, she and Dart—her gabby, grinning, lunatic Lord Night—careen wildly from place to place, easily eluding police and effortlessly stealing a series of cars in the process. Dart, who is a whole new breed of villain—serial murderer as stand-up comic—has an agenda of his own for the journey, an agenda that ties in closely with the personal affairs of the Chancel family. Dart, like so many other deeply deranged people, has an obsessive regard for *Night Journey*. (He describes it as "one twisted motherfucker of a book. Whole thing takes place in darkness. Almost everything happens in caves, underground. All the vivid characters are monsters."[22]) Dart has learned through his father that Driver's authorship of the novel has been disputed, and that Leland Dart—who is surreptitiously betraying his own client, Alden Chancel—has entered into negotiations with the Mannheim family, and stands to make a lot of money if the Mannheim claim can be proven. Driven as much by the desire to cause his father trouble as by his desire to protect Hugo Driver's reputation, Dart sets out to locate and destroy any potential witnesses against the established provenance of *Night Journey*.

Along the way, Dart—"a fun guy,"[23] in Nora's words—takes whatever pleasures he can find. These include re-creating Nora's outward appearance by applying his amazingly elaborate knowledge of make-up, hair styling, and women's fashions; delivering nonstop monologues on subjects ranging from the duplicity of women to the poetry of Emily Dickinson (which, by the way, he loathes); stealing, and then dissecting, the recently deceased corpse of a heart attack victim, a procedure he performs with the skill and confidence of a natural-born surgeon; and, in the novel's single most painful sequence, tying Nora to the bed of their rented room, and raping her.

Nora's rape is described in a carefully controlled prose that is both graphic and reticent; that says what it must in order to convey the full enormity of the event, and then looks away, refusing to linger over the humiliating details. The rape returns Nora to a place she has visited before: the bottom of the world, where the demons she encountered in Vietnam gather around her once again.

> She heard them rattling up to her, whispering to her in their rapid-fire voices, and drew into herself as tightly as possible, though she knew that the elated demons would never touch her. If they touched her, her mind would shatter, and then she would be too crazy to be interesting.
>
> A demon who looked like a rat with small blue wings and granny glasses whispered, *You can't get out of this one, is that clear? You passed through and now you're on the other side, is that clear?* When she nodded, the demon said, *Welcome to the Hellfire Club.*[24]

There is, however, another voice that speaks to Nora in the aftermath of the rape: the voice of her survivor self. This voice comes to her through the image of her dead father, Matthew Curlew, engaging her in a dream dialogue that counteracts and contradicts the message of the demons; that tells her, in one of the novel's most crucial passages, the things she most needs to hear.

> Nora began to cry. *I need you.*
>
> Honey, the person you need is Nora. You got lost and now you have to find yourself again.
>
> I don't even have a self anymore. I'm dead.
>
> Listen to me, sweetie. That pile of horse manure did the worst thing to you he could think of because he wants to break you down, but it didn't work, not all the way...You're going to get through it, but to do that, you have to go through it...
>
> I can't.

> He folded his hands on top of his raised leg and leaned forward.
>
> Okay, maybe I can. But I don't want to.
>
> Of course not. Nobody wants to go all the way through. Some people, they're never even asked to do it. You might say those are pretty lucky people, but the truth is, they never had the chance to stop being ignorant. You know what a soul is, Nora? A real soul? A real soul is something you make by walking through fire. By keeping on walking, and by remembering how it felt.
>
> I'm not strong enough.
>
> *This time you get to do it right. Last time you got hurt as bad as this, you closed your eyes and pretended it didn't happen. Inside you, there are a lot of doors you shut a long time ago. What you have to do is open those doors...*[25]

From this point forward, *The Hellfire Club* follows Nora's gradual ascent from the bottom of the world toward a renewed sense of self. The process by which she reclaims her soul and reopens its doors begins with her escape from Dick Dart. While Dart is preoccupied with dissecting the heart attack victim whose car he has just stolen, Nora grabs a hammer, smashes Dart repeatedly in the side of the head, jumps behind the wheel of the stolen car, and lights out for the territories.

Nora's escape from her demented Lord Night ushers in the second stage of her night journey. This stage takes her, first, to Springfield, Massachusetts, home of wealthy neurosurgeon Dan Harwich, Nora's former lover and an emblematic figure in her memories of Vietnam. Harwich is, to put the matter mildly, a disappointment. Whatever he may have been—whatever Nora believes him to have been—he has since dwindled into a warier, more cynical, more self-absorbed version of the man she remembers. He is, in fact, something of a sexual predator himself, and he has more in common with Dick

Dart than he would ever willingly acknowledge. Beneath the sympathy, the surface solicitude, with which he welcomes Nora, he has one thing and one thing only on his mind: getting Nora into his bed and then out of his house before his latest fiancee returns. Nora, who has spent enough time in the company of corrupt, self-serving men to know one when she sees one, quickly assesses the situation and just as quickly departs, on a wave of bitterness and mutual recriminations. Her abortive visit to Harwich simply reinforces the lesson from the dream dialogue with Matt Curlew: That the one person she must learn to rely on is Nora herself.

Nora is not entirely without friendship or support, of course. A Westerholm detective named Holly Fenn takes her side in the Natalie Weil affair; and Jeffrey Deodato, a Harvard-educated manservant who, for reasons of his own, has chosen to work for the Chancel family comes to her aid at a number of critical moments. Mostly, though, she is forced to become the agent of her own salvation. Shaken—nearly shattered—by her encounter with Dart, disillusioned by her reunion with Dan Harwich, and sick to death of being lied to and manipulated by the men in her life, Nora turns her back on Westerholm, where, even now, police are waiting to arrest her for a crime she did not commit. She then sets out to illuminate the unresolved mystery that stands at the heart of the Chancel family history: the real origin of *Night Journey*.

Nora's investigation is motivated by her desire for clarity, and by her need to understand the full truth behind the events which have affected three generations of Chancels; events that, without her consent, have involved her in the obsessive, even crazed, agendas of other people.

> From the beginning, she had been forced to concentrate on a matter far more important to everyone else around her than to herself. A cyclone had smashed her life and whirled her away. The cyclone was named Hugo Driver, or Katherine Mannheim, or *Night Journey*, or all of these together, and even though Dick Dart, Davey Chancel [and others] cared enough about the cyclone to open their houses, ransack papers, battle lawsuits, drive hundreds of miles, risk arrest in its name, it

> had been she, who cared not at all, who
> had been taken over.[26]

The notion that truth is worth pursuing for its own sake becomes increasingly important as the narrative—and Nora's investigation—unfolds. One of the most important things that Nora learns about herself in this novel is that truth really does matter to her; that the endless process of distinguishing what is true from what is not is of fundamental importance. A woman named Helen Day—who is Jeffrey Deodato's mother, Katherine Mannheim's sister, and a former employee of both Lincoln and Alden Chancel—tells her:

> You're a person who wants to know what's true. When I look back, it seems to me that most of what I learned when I was little was all wrong. Lies were stuffed down our throats day and night. Lies about men and women, about the proper way to live, about our own feelings, and I don't believe too much has changed. It's still important to find out what's really true, and if you didn't think that was important, you wouldn't be here now.[27]

The truths that Nora painstakingly unearths come from a variety of sources, including manuscripts—among them novels, diaries, memoirs, and literary histories, both published and unpublished—and interviews, which she conducts with a variety of people familiar either with the Chancel family history or the events that occurred at Shorelands in 1938. Like Pippin Little, whose quest carries him from character to character and story to story, and who learns, in the end, that truth is like "a mosaic, to be assembled over time and at great risk,"[28] Nora slowly uncovers the disconnected fragments of a larger truth.

In the course of her researches, Nora learns a great deal about the rapacious, essentially predatory nature of the crypto-fascist publishing magnate, Lincoln Chancel; about Hugo Driver and his propensity for petty thefts; about the fragile, acerbic Katherine Mannheim and her scarcely concealed contempt for Shorelands and its many pretensions; about the astonishing number of violent deaths visited upon the other writers invited to Shorelands that eventful summer. She is even able to identify Daisy Chancel as the author of *Night Journey*'s two sequels, and to look through their thinly disguised storylines to the biographical revelations encoded within. Ultimately, Nora comes to realize that the answers to *The Hellfire Club*'s remaining mysteries—the provenance of *Night Journey* and the disappearance of Katherine Mannheim—can only be found at Shorelands, which has recently been renovated and opened to the public. She makes plans to visit Shorelands with Jeffrey Deodato, but her plans are interrupted by the sudden reappearance of her personal Lord Night, the battered but still boisterous Dick Dart.

A hostage once again, Nora does eventually arrive at Shorelands, accompanied by Dart, for the final stage of her ordeal. Once at Shorelands—which is the real world equivalent of *Night Journey*'s Mountain Glade, the place where secrets are finally revealed—events proceed toward a parallel series of resolutions. First, Nora and Dart encounter the "golden key"[29] to the mystery of Katherine Mannheim's fate. The key comes in the form of an aging servant named Agnes Brotherhood, who reveals to Nora the tawdry—and, in retrospect, inevitable—account of Lincoln Chancel's rape and inadvertent murder of the invalid Mannheim; and the subsequent, frantic efforts of Chancel and Hugo Driver to bury her body within Shoreland's sprawling forest. Second, Nora manages, once again, to escape from Dart, stealing a revolver in the process. Against the vibrant Gothic backdrop of a summer thunderstorm, Nora confronts Dart and, in Straub's word, "puts him to death,"[30] saving not only herself, but the entire female staff of Shorelands, all of whom have been tied to chairs in the living room of Shoreland's Main House, in anticipation of a leisurely evening of rape and murder.

In a brief epilogue, Straub answers the novel's remaining questions, revealing Alden Chancel's behind-the-scenes involvement in the Natalie Weil "kidnapping" (which was never more than a desperate attempt to discredit Nora in the eyes of the community and of her husband); and showing us, finally, the process by which *Night Journey* came into being. (It existed, initially, as a series of notes for an unwritten novel that Katherine Mannheim was contemplating at the time of her death. Hugo Driver, of course, stole those notes and transformed them, through his own fatuous prose style, into the only novel he would ever publish.)

Mostly, though, the epilogue presents us with a lovingly rendered portrait of the Nora Chancel (now Nora Curlew) who has emerged from the crucible of the previous ten days. Surrounded by the kind of media storm that inevitably arises from our tabloid culture's morbid fascination with the violent and the grotesque, she undergoes an intense, uncomfortable period of public scrutiny in which she is lionized by the media as "the woman who...killed Dick Dart."

> If she had agreed, Nora could have appeared on a dozen television programs of the talk-show or tabloid variety, sold the rights to her story to a television production company, and seen her photograph on the covers of the many magazines devoted to trivializing what is already trivial. She did none of these things, considering them no more seriously than she considered accepting any of the sixteen marriage proposals which came to her in the mail. When the public world embraced her, its exaggerations and reductions of her tale made her so unrecognizable to herself that even the photographs in the newspapers seemed to be of someone else.[31]

The Nora who walks out of Shorelands is a woman who has rediscovered her long-lost self, who has recovered her own soul by walking through the fire and "remembering how it felt." In a matter-of-fact, nondramatic fashion, she returns (briefly) to Westerholm, terminates her marriage, confronts the two people—Alden Chancel and Natalie Weil—whose collusion placed her in harm's way, and then quietly avenges both herself and Katherine Mannheim by sending a letter on the true origins of *Night Journey* to *The New York Times.* Her transformation from a woman constantly acted upon by external forces to a woman ready to reengage the world on her own terms is credible and moving, a grace note that brings the novel to an effective, perfectly judged conclusion.

On the way to that conclusion, *The Hellfire Club* recapitulates a number of Straub's primary concerns. It is, first of all, a novel rooted in the past, a perfect embodiment of Miles Teagarden's dictum that "the past of a story is what enables us to understand it."[32] Nora Chancel's life and character have been indelibly marked by events that occurred in Vietnam some twenty-five years before; while the history and fortunes of the Chancel family are inextricably linked to events that took place a generation earlier, in 1938. The mysteries that haunt this novel, mysteries in which Nora is caught up and carried away, all have their origins in a violent past, whose unresolved secrets have never ceased to impinge on present day events.

The Hellfire Club is also one of the purest examples of Straub's ongoing fascination with the complex interrelationship between narrative and life; and it approaches its subject from a couple of directions. First, Straub once again creates a world in which stories—independent, internal narratives—reflect and intersect with the lives of his characters. The primary example, of course, is *Night Journey,* whose account of its hero's epic quest for self-knowledge comes more and more to echo Nora's own private quest. In addition, the three novels written by Daisy Chancel—her unpublished work-in-progress and her pseudonymous sequels to *Night Journey*—are actually thinly veiled autobiographies that illuminate some of the hidden corners and closely guarded secrets of a corrupt and decadent family.

Second, Straub examines the peculiar, often powerful bond that exists between books and their readers. *Night Journey,* the fictional McGuffin that animates this novel, is a particularly extreme example of that bond, a book that has entered the culture and taken on an autonomous, and often disturbing, life of its own. Rabid fans like Davey Chancel reread the book regularly, internalizing its characters, imagery, and vocabulary, finding within it the encoded messages that illuminate and explain their lives. In some cases, Moonie-like cults have formed around the novel, cults peopled by "Driverites" who never read anything but *Night Journey* and its sequels, who come together in deranged little communities where everyone pretends to be a character from one of the novels. In the most extreme cases, Bundy-like serial killers take their inspiration directly from its pages, in much the same way that the Manson Family found hidden meanings and private directives in Robert A. Heinlein's *Stranger in a Strange Land.* Even "normal" readers like Nora Chancel, who dislikes both *Night Journey* and its effect on susceptible readers, finds herself vulnerable to its surprising, but undeniable, power.

> She opened *Night Journey,* leafed past the title page...and began grimly to read...The landscapes were cardboard, the characters flat, the dialogue stilted, but this time she wanted to keep reading. Against her will

> she found that she was *interested.* The hateful book had enough narrative power to draw her in. Once she had been drawn in, the characters and the landscape of stunted trees through which they wandered no longer seemed artificial.[33]

More than anything, though, *The Hellfire Club* is, in the truest sense, a novel of character, a novel whose deepest, most fundamental concerns arise directly from its consideration of the natures and circumstances of its central characters. Straub's ability to populate a story with vital, fully realized people, together with his increasing ability to write pungent, accurate dialogue, distinguish the novel at every level. The supporting characters—among them the increasingly *diminished* generations of surviving Chancels; Dan Harwich, who has allowed himself to dwindle into an unrecognizable shadow of his former self; Holly Fenn, the Westerholm detective who maintains his belief in Nora's innocence in the face of continuing opposition—are all, along with more than a dozen others, substantial presences in this book. And so are a number of characters from the novel's past, characters like the predatory robber baron, Lincoln Chancel; the shifty, compulsive sneak thief, Hugo Driver, and the commanding, enigmatic poet, Katherine Mannheim; all of whom come to us through the varied, sometimes conflicting reminiscences of the people who survived them.

Mannheim, in particular, is an imposing offstage presence, a quietly charismatic figure who haunts the background of this novel. The Katherine Mannheim who comes gradually into focus is a gifted, acerbic, solitary figure who is absolutely unconcerned with the judgments or opinions of anybody but herself. She is also a frail, physically vulnerable woman whose heart condition keeps her from participating fully in the "normal" activities of the world. She believes, for example, that sexual intercourse would probably kill her, an assessment which proves tragically correct. She evokes—and seems deliberately intended to evoke—that iconic American recluse, Emily Dickinson, another figure who hovers at the edges of the novel, and whose own words, ironically quoted by Dick Dart, speak to Nora, piercing her "like an inexorable series of waves."[34]

"There's a certain Slant of light
Winter Afternoons—
That oppresses, like the Heft
Of Cathedral Tunes.

Heavenly Hurt it gives us—
We can find no scar,
But internal difference,
Where the Meanings, are—"

The man who recites those lines, Dick Dart, is something new in Straub's fiction: a genuine monster, a living embodiment of the predatory impulse. Dart is, at bottom, a rapist and murderer who goes about his business with an unquenchable sense of joie de vivre and a bottomless self-regard. He is enormously intuitive, is capable of the most amazing feats of mental gymnastics, but is utterly devoid of kindness or empathy. He hates his father, professes to adore women, but believes that they are, without exception, manipulative and corrupt. He regards his abduction and violation of Nora as part of a "reality lesson"[35] that he alone is qualified to teach. He is a vital, vile, brilliantly realized character.

In the end, though, it is Nora Chancel who provides *The Hellfire Club* with its moral and emotional center. Nora, too, is a brilliantly realized character: a lost, troubled, essentially valiant woman whose journey through the flames toward a newly refined sense of self gives the novel much of its capacity to enlighten and move us. Straub's ability to organize a complex narrative around the perceptions of an intelligent, damaged woman surrounded by hostile and inimical forces—a woman who has been raped, abducted, devalued, mistreated, and isolated from the human community—transforms the novel from the generic hostage drama it might have become into a novel that is, in itself, an act of imaginative empathy. Through Nora, we are made to experience the world from the perspective of the victimized and the powerless. Through Nora, Straub finds his way into the true heart—and the real thematic center—of his story.

It is hardly an exaggeration to say that *The Hellfire Club* is a novel *about* rape. Certainly, rape is a key image and a recurring act throughout the book. Nora is raped both in Vietnam and during the course of her night journey with Dick Dart. When she kills Dart during their climactic confrontation at Shorelands, she is actually interrupting a rape in progress. In fact, the entire saga of the Chancel family's relationship with the so-called Hugo Driver novels begins with Lincoln Chancel's rape of Katherine Mannheim, which is followed both by Mannheim's death and by the subsequent theft of her notes for the unwritten novel that would eventually become *Night Journey*.

Within the world of *The Hellfire Club*, the various acts of rape are viewed on two levels: as the obscene, egregious acts of violence that they are; and as aspects—the most brutal and traumatizing aspects—of a more fundamental sort of moral and spiritual malaise: unbridled greed. Straub explicitly connects these two issues—rape and rapacity—when, early in the novel, Davey talks to Nora about the exploits of his piratical grandfather, Lincoln Chancel.

> "He was a tremendous crook, I'm sure. It's like the big secret in my family—the thing we don't talk about. On the way up, my dad's dad obviously stabbed everybody he met in the back, he must have stolen with both hands whenever he had the chance, he raped his way into a huge fortune...[36]

Lincoln Chancel's compulsive need to own, to control, to accumulate—to take what he wanted whenever he wanted it—provided both the inspiration for his business success and the motivation for his rape of Katherine Mannheim. It's no accident that Dick Dart, who has a great deal in common with Lincoln Chancel, equates sex with ownership and ownership with rape. Every sexual experience of his life, Dart tells Nora, was a form of rape. "And do you know why? Because when it was all over, I owned them. That's the secret."[37]

Seen in this light, many of the novel's less overtly violent incidents take on a more sinister, *rapacious* aspect. When Dick Dart subjects Nora to a thoroughgoing makeover that alters her appearance to suit his own tastes; when Dan Harwich views Nora's sudden reappearance in his life as a sexual opportunity and nothing more; when Alden Chancel attempts to blackmail his son into a quick divorce, or coerces his wife into producing the sequels to *Night Journey*, or purchases the collusion of Natalie Weil in a desperate bid to discredit his own daughter-in-law—when we witness these or any of a dozen other examples of callous manipulation, we are actually witnessing that same predatory impulse that, in its most extreme form, underlies the act of rape.

In confronting that predatory impulse so directly, *The Hellfire Club* evolves into a novel that is very much about values, about the need for civilized and humane standards of conduct in an increasingly rapacious world. At the same time, it implicitly raises the most fundamental of all moral questions: how should a person live? When Nora turns her back on the talk shows, the book deals, and all the lucrative accoutrements of an innately acquisitive culture, she is answering that question in her own fashion. For Nora, as for so many of Straub's battle-scarred protagonists, the key to the treasure is the treasure. The qualities of courage, independence, and imaginative empathy she is forced to develop in order to survive are the intangible treasures that she most needs to own; that she will carry with her into the uncertain future that lies beyond the boundaries of this book.

1. Letter from Peter Straub to the author
2. Ibid.
3. Ibid.
4. Ibid.
5. Interview with Paula Guran for Omni Online
6. Ibid.
7. *The Hellfire Club* (New York, Random House, 1996), p. 221
8. Letter from Peter Straub to the author
9. Ibid.
10. *The Hellfire Club*, p. 3
11. Ibid., p. 7
12. Ibid., p. 7
13. Ibid., p. 12
14. Ibid., p. 12
15. Ibid., p. 77
16. Ibid., p. 29
17. Ibid., p. 47
18. Ibid., p. 48
19. Ibid., p. 48
20. Ibid., p. 49
21. Ibid., epigraph
22. Ibid., p. 189
23. Ibid., p. 219
24. Ibid., p. 181
25. Ibid., p. 204
26. Ibid., pp. 288-289

27. Ibid., p. 314
28. Ibid., p. 317
29. Ibid., p. 267
30. Ibid., p. 448
31. Ibid., p. 447
32. *If You Could See Me Now*, p. 25
33. *The Hellfire Club*, pp. 265-266
34. Ibid., p. 190
35. Ibid., p. 170
36. Ibid., p. 77
37. Ibid., p. 179

Chapter Fifteen:

Mr. X

The eight or nine months following the completion of *The Hellfire Club* were largely devoted to rest and recuperation. Although he did write one piece of fiction during this period—the Bartleby-inspired novella, "Mr. Clubb and Mr. Cuff"—Straub did not begin seriously contemplating his next book until the spring of 1996. At that point, he embarked on a novel about a series of murders in New York's Central Park, a novel that—ironically continuing his recent run of creative difficulties—ultimately went nowhere.

Central Park is a place where something is always happening, and the idea of using it as the setting for a novel appealed to Straub. For several weeks, notebook in hand, he made daily excursions into the park, familiarizing himself with its geography, absorbing its atmosphere, and trying, with minimal success, to attach his impressions to a workable plot. By summer, he had accumulated a great many notes, but had failed to work out the basic story. Then August came, and Straub and his family left New York for a month's vacation in the Sag Harbor home of composer David Del Tredici. Here, Straub hoped, the traditional stimulus of pleasant new surroundings would enable him to work through his difficulties. This time, however, it didn't happen, for a number of different reasons. First of all, as Straub recalls,

> I so much wanted the feeling of writing again that I tried to jump in immediately, without enough preparation. Besides that,

> it was one of the hottest and most humid Augusts since the beginning of time, and I became completely enervated. All I did was write and rewrite the same ten pages, utterly stumped as to where they were going. August ended, and we came back to New York. I tried to keep writing, but it felt like walking through quicksand. Another couple of months flew by while I did nothing.[1]

Finally, Straub decided to step back, stop writing, and attempt to create a detailed description of the story that would serve as a kind of outline. Unfortunately, this didn't work either. The outline, which Straub spent weeks putting together, was unwieldy, overly complicated, and filled with plot lines that failed to converge. At that point, Straub stepped back even further from the project, and asked himself a question: What would happen if he suddenly attempted a completely different story? Much to his surprise, a brand new story did announce itself, and quickly developed an unexpected momentum. Before too long, he found himself with detailed plans for the first two or three hundred pages of the novel that would eventually be published as *Mr. X.*

Mr. X is a doppelganger story. As such, it embodies an impulse that had been present in Straub's fiction for a number of years and in a number of ways. For example, Straub himself has existed in a doppelganger-like relationship with certain of his own creations, among them Putney Tyson Ridge, his mythical childhood buddy and eternal critic (see Appendix C); and Tim Underhill, narrator of *The Throat* and Straub's "secret collaborator" on *Koko* and *Mystery.* Underhill, in turn, finds his own secret sharer in *Koko*'s Manny Dengler. In addition, one of Straub's earlier novels, *Mystery,* started life as a very different sort of book called *Family Romance,* which, had its original impulse endured, would have invoked the doppelganger theme through the story of two brothers who are separated and then raised under radically different circumstances. Clearly, the theme has great resonance and psychological significance for Straub, who has spent many years reflecting on the subject and familiarizing himself with the literature of the double.

> Secret sharers, unknown brothers, shadow selves, with their inevitable suggestion that the truly dangerous adversary has stepped out of the mirror, had always appealed to me. They had a lovely eeriness combined with great psychological suggestiveness. Poe, Stevenson and Dostoyevsky had written doppelganger stories, and so had Daphne du Maurier, Christopher Priest, Orhan Pamuck and lots of other people. Wilkie Collins, one of my ancestral spirits, had virtually built his career on the conceit, continuing to draw upon it well past the point at which he degenerated into unwitting self-parody.[2]

Having decided, once again, to attempt his own version of this peculiar archetype, Straub made two preliminary decisions which, taken together, had an enormous effect on the novel's essential character. First, he decided—in the face of his own repeated pronouncements—to return to a type of fiction he had turned his back on almost fifteen years before: supernatural horror. This decision, which would come as a surprise to many of Straub's readers, was a logical outgrowth of the type of story he had decided to tell. The concept of the doppelganger, with its innate sense of mystery, of shared, otherworldly connections, of "lovely eeriness,"[3] stands naturally outside the borders of traditional realism, inviting the kind of phantasmagorical treatment that characterized Straub's earlier, overtly supernatural novels. Once he decided to readmit this element into his fiction, Straub kicked the door wide open and had a field day, populating his novel with all manner of strange and extravagant phenomena, including time travel, lucid dreaming, telekinetic manifestations of various sorts, and one of the wittiest, most original appropriations of H. P. Lovecraft's Mythos that has ever appeared in print.

Straub's second major decision concerned the ethnic background of his narrator and hero, Ned Dunstan, and of the entire bizarre, larger-than-life Dunstan family. The Dunstans, middle-class residents of the small Midwestern city of Edgerton, are black people. Straub's decision to place a black family at the center of the narrative—an idea that came to him late in the development of his initial outline—helped extend the basic metaphor of the doppelganger. As Straub put it,

> It occurred to me that the story would have more weight if the characters were black. Black people would then be present as a sort of doppelganger to the white world, an unacknowledged other self.[4]

While the decision to present the bulk of the novel from the perspective of a young black man is politically risky, it is by no means revolutionary. In fact, it falls directly into the main line of Straub's aesthetic philosophy, which holds that the novel, like all other forms of genuine art, is an act of imaginative empathy, capable of going anywhere and assuming whatever narrative perspective the circumstances require. (A case in point, of course, is Straub's deeply sympathetic portrait of the abused and violated Nora Chancel in *The Hellfire Club.*)

There is, however, one aspect of *Mr. X*'s presentation of character that *is* unique, and that is Straub's deliberate refusal to limit our perceptions by telling us, directly, that the Dunstans are black. The information is there, of course, embedded in the details of the text: in the speech patterns of the Dunstans, in descriptions of food, in the social dynamics at work in several of the scenes, in the edgy bits of dialogue that only make complete sense when seen in the context of racially motivated tensions. But none of this is ever made explicit. We are permitted, in a sense, to create our own versions of the Dunstans by filtering the details through our own individual assumptions and largely unexamined preconceptions. Commenting on this unusual narrative tactic, Straub notes that

> I was interested in making use of the white reader's assumption that every character in a novel is white unless it is made clear that he or she is not, an assumption that embodies a cheerful, ignorant, status quo sort of racism; and I liked the idea of presenting Ned and his family as human beings first...A common humanity is the point, despite the fact that the Dunstans are anything but normal people. And I also liked the linkage between Black Americans and what is in shadow, i.e., essential but un-

> seen or ignored. The issue of race is like a sort of time bomb located just under the surface of the book, whether anyone sees it or not...[5]

Interestingly, the overwhelming majority of the novel's early readers fell into the trap and, in the absence of any specific statements to the contrary, assumed that they were reading a novel about middle-class white people. But *Mr. X* is a bit like one of those children's pictures in which a design lies hidden within the larger, more obvious pattern. Once that design has been pointed out, it becomes impossible, from that point forward, not to see it.

Once its various elements had been established, *Mr. X* moved steadily forward. Straub spent about a year writing the first third or so of the book, then found himself confronted by a deadline which bitter experience had taught him to take seriously. To expedite the writing, he developed an outline so detailed that it amounted to a speeded-up version of the rest of the book. Although he was ultimately forced to request a three month extension (which Random House granted), the outline enabled him to progress rapidly through the final five hundred pages, and he reached the finish line in March of 1998, having managed, for the most part, to avoid the traumas that attended the creation of *The Hellfire Club*.

After the usual intensive period of cutting and revision, *Mr. X* was published in the summer of 1999, and it was immediately apparent that Straub had produced one of his most striking and original works, a book that establishes its authority immediately through its distinctive deployment of two radically different narrative voices. Here are the opening sentences of the first narrator.

> Stupid me—I fell right into the old pattern and spent a week pretending I was a moving target. All along, a part of me knew that I was hitching toward southern Illinois because my mother was passing. When your mother's checking out, you get yourself back home.[6]

And here are the opening words of the second.

> O Great Old Ones, read these words inscribed within this stout journal by the hand of Your Devoted Servant and rejoice![7]

The first voice belongs to Ned Dunstan, a young man who is hitchhiking from New York to Edgerton because a peculiar, Dunstan-like ability that he does not understand has told him that his mother is about to die. The baroque second voice belongs to another of Edgerton's residents, a being who has haunted Ned since childhood, and whom Ned has always thought of as "Mr. X." Despite their individual differences in style, the two are connected in fundamental ways, and those connections stand at the heart of this formidably complex book.

Mr. X is a novel about family legacies, and its intricate structure encompasses a great many individual stories, most of which—to borrow one of the novel's recurring images—are nested within each other like Chinese boxes. The early sections recount the formative, eerily mirrorlike experiences of Ned Dunstan and the mysterious Mr. X, and those experiences are essential to an understanding of everything that will follow.

The earliest of these experiences belong to Mr. X, a man who will go by many names, none of which are immediately revealed. Mr. X's story begins a generation or so before Ned Dunstan's, and is the step-by-step account of the creation and evolution of a monster. The boy who will become this monster is the oldest son of an affluent Midwestern family, and his entire childhood is marked by an escalating propensity for violent acts, which include shooting animals with a BB gun, pounding a schoolmate's forehead into the concrete pavement, and tying his eleven-year-old neighbor to a birch tree and then threatening her with Indian-style tortures. In time, the boy—who has all the earmarks of a potential serial killer—finds himself irresistibly drawn to a nearby stretch of forest known as Johnson's Woods. Here, a disembodied voice seems to speak to him, saying *Come to me. You need me. You are mine*[8]. Once in the forest, the boy experiences the immediate sense of coming home, of arriving, for the first time in his life, at "the right place,"[9] a place that is deeply, mysteriously connected to the secret sources of his own bitterness and rage. He also begins to acquire unprecedented new powers, such as the ability to kill birds through the unassisted power of his own thoughts.

Eventually, he stumbles into the secret heart of Johnson's Woods, a clearing that contains the burned-out ruins of an ancient house. There, he receives the revelation that will dominate his life, a revelation that has about it a distinctly familiar ring.

> It was within [this] sacred enclosure that the Great Old Ones imbued my early torments and humiliations with the Salvific Splendor of Preparation. An Elder God spoke, and I learned...the Mighty Tasks for which I had been placed upon this Earth. My Role came clear, my Nature given Explanation. Half-human, half-God, I was the Opener of the Way, and my task was Annihilation. After me, the Apocalypse, the entry through a riven sky of my leathery, winged, beclawed ravenous Ancestors the Elder Gods, the Destruction of mankind, Your long-awaited repossession of the earthly realm.[10]

He also learns that he will eventually father a traitorous shadow—a "hidden double self"[11]—who will oppose the grand design, and whom he must therefore eliminate. Thus armed with a newly acquired sense of destiny, he begins, from that point forward, to devote his life to the service of the nameless Old Ones.

Years later, while enrolled as a cadet at Pennsylvania's Fortress Military Academy, the other shoe finally drops and he learns the identity of the Old Ones. He spies a book called *The Dunwich Horror* in the possession of a fellow cadet and "borrows" it, murdering the cadet in the process. The book, particularly the title story, galvanizes him, ratifying his deepest beliefs, confirming him in his mission, and giving names to his nameless Masters: Nyarlathotep, Yog-Sothoth, Shub-Niggurath and great Cthulhu. *The Dunwich Horror* becomes, in Mr. X's words, "my Genesis, my Gospels, my gnosis,"[12] and H. P. Lovecraft, thereafter known as The Providence Master[13], becomes his personal prophet, and the source of his most secret knowledge.

Straub then quickly sketches in the highlights of Mr. X's subsequent career, a career which includes a lengthy stint as a Lord of Crime, a term or two in prison, and a brief period spent writing fiction in (of course) the Lovecraftian mode. Most significantly, his short-lived relationship with aspiring singer Valerie "Star" Dunstan produces a son, the "traitorous shadow" he is obligated to destroy. As the novel opens, Ned Dunstan, the elusive son, is returning to Edgerton, where the father he has never met is waiting to fulfill his destiny.

Ned Dunstan's story also begins in childhood and is marked by a similar series of unresolved mysteries. Star Dunstan is eighteen years old when she gives birth to Ned, who describes her as "a generous, large-souled girl with no more notion of a settled life than a one-eyed cat."[14] As a result of Star's incurable rootlessness, Ned spends most of his childhood in a series of largely benign foster homes, while his mother serves as a loving but peripatetic presence in his life. Ned's childhood is marked by two recurring events, each of which helps to set him apart from the "normal," everyday world.

One of these is a recurring dream which begins when he is seven and "wreck[s] his sleep"[15] for two or three nights each month. The dream always begins with Ned's panicked pursuit of his own shadow, and always ends with a dialogue concerning his unresolved need for reconciliation with this shadow self.

> "You seem to be trying to catch me," my shadow said...
>
> "We need each other," I said. "We're the same thing."
>
> "You are me, and I am you, yes," said the shadow. But only in the sense that we each have qualities that the other lacks..."[16]

The second event begins on Ned's third birthday, and manifests itself as a kind of epileptic fit which signals the onset of a peculiar and terrifying vision. With certain variations, the vision always centers on a single basic scenario. Ned follows an unnamed being through walls of blue fire into "the ordinary world."[17] There, the being—whom Ned comes to think of as Mr. X—forces his way into one version or another of an ordinary suburban home and murders the inhabitants, one of whom—a nameless young boy—always manages to escape. These grisly visitations are, of course, scenes from Mr. X's ongoing search for the son he has been ordered to kill, and will become unwelcome elements of Ned Dunstan's birthdays from this point on.

Dreams and birthdays notwithstanding, Ned maintains a delicate balance throughout adolescence. At the age of eighteen, he goes away to college, and everything changes. At Middlemount College in Vermont, he undergoes a bizarre crisis that very nearly destroys him, and that demonstrates his susceptibility to the same forces that have laid claim to Mr. X. Like his father before him, Ned is seduced by a force that emanates from the local forest, an analogue of Johnson's Woods called Jones Woods. Like his father, he succumbs to the illusory feeling that he has finally reached the right, the perfect, place. Abandoning the responsibilities of college, he, too, finds his way to a ruined house in the heart of the forest, and experiences a vision whose significance will not become clear for many years.

> The cottage emerged from the surrounding darkness like a tall shadow in the sacred woods...When I entered, I seemed instantly to plummet through the rotten floor. I fell; I saw nothing; I did not fear. A long, shabby, once handsome room took shape before me. Out of my range of vision, a man spoke of smoke and gold and corpses on a battlefield...This was *backward,* it was *past*...I fell to my knees on the worn Oriental carpet. Before I vomited, the world melted and restored itself, and the contents of my stomach drizzled onto the ruined floor. *Home,* I thought.[18]

Unable, or unwilling, to leave his newfound home, Ned camps out in the ruined cottage and comes very close to dying of exposure. Rescued through the intervention of a mysterious stranger, he leaves school and spends years wandering from job to job and from city to city, finally settling for an orderly life as a computer programmer in New York City, a life that will be disrupted by the Dunstan-like feeling that his mother is dying, and needs him to come home.

These are some of the conditions already in place as the novel begins. There is, however, one more major element of which neither Ned nor his father is consciously aware, but which is implicit in much of what has gone before. Ned has a double, an independent shadow self whose name is Robert, and who, like Ned, has returned to Edgerton, magnetized by the imminence of Star Dunstan's death. The mere fact of Robert's existence answers a thousand questions for Ned, explains the thousand anomalous occurrences—mistaken identities, assumptions of familiarity, inexplicably hostile encounters—that have marked Ned's life. Most importantly, it provides a reason for the sense of incompleteness, of eternal *yearning,* that has followed in his wake since childhood.

> Right from the beginning, I had the sense that something crucially significant, something without which I would never be whole, was *missing.* When I was seven, my mother told me that as soon as I learned to sit up by myself, I used to do this funny thing where I turned around and tried to look behind me. Boom, down I'd go, but the second I hit the ground I'd turn my head to check the same spot.[19]

Robert, who was born just minutes after Ned and was separated from him immediately by a complex combination of circumstances involving a storm, a power failure, and a duplicitous nurse, is Ned's opposite in every significant respect. As Straub indicated in his preliminary notes for the novel,

> These two need one another to be whole. They make each other complete. Ned is Ego, Robert is Id: Ned is doubt, Robert certainty; Ned thought and Robert action. Morality/Immorality, Civilization/Savagery, Civility/Raunch.[20]

Two aspects of Robert's nature are of particular importance. First, he is hungry. The proverbial outsider, he has spent his life in the shadows, a disenfranchised witness to the daylight world that was his brother's birthright. Second, he is, to put the matter plainly, not quite human. He is, rather, another order of being, related to but different from the common run of humanity. He casts no shadow, can pass through solid walls, is able to appear and disappear at will. As Robert himself puts it, he is "pure Dunstan,"[21] a distinction that becomes increasingly meaningful as the narrative progresses.

As Ned, his father, and his unknown brother converge on Edgerton, a number of plotlines come together with typically Straubian complexity. Almost all of the stories and histories that Ned encounters from this point on intersect at some crucial point. Virtually every one of these stories hides "some other, secret story, the story you are not supposed to know."[22] As Ned rediscovers Edgerton, the narrative unfolds like a classic Ross MacDonald investigation, with Ned moving from place to place and encounter to encounter, gradually assembling a coherent portrait of the city and its scandals, past and present; and of the hidden, infinitely strange history of the Dunstans. Along the way, he catches unexpected glimpses of an older, more magical reality that hides within the interstices of the mundane world.

Ned's involvement in the interconnected dramas of Edgerton begins even before he arrives in the city. At a motel outside of Chicago, he meets (and beds) a young D. A's assistant named Ashley Ashton, who believes she is meeting Ned by prior arrangement (Robert's handiwork, of course), and who is hoping to file a criminal indictment against one of Edgerton's leading citizens, Stewart Hatch. When Ashley drops Ned off at St. Ann's Hospital, where his mother lies dying, he encounters Laurie Hatch, Stewart's beautiful, estranged wife, who is also visiting a patient in the St. Ann's Intensive Care Unit. Ned finds himself immediately attracted to Laurie, and this attraction marks the first phase of his escalating involvement in the legal and financial affairs of the Hatch family.

Ned's visit to St. Ann's also marks the first phase of his long-delayed reunion with the Dunstans. Surrounding Star's deathbed are Ned's Great-Aunt Nettie, the family's reigning matriarch; Uncle Clark, Nettie's dapper, man-about-town husband; and Great-Aunt May, a confirmed kleptomaniac whose ability to "magpie" virtually any item that catches her fancy verges on the miraculous. Other Dunstan relatives not yet present include Aunt Joy and Uncle Clarence, (who are imprisoned in their home by virtue of Clarence's highly advanced case of Alzheimer's Disease, and by the strange, pathetic creature who lives in their attic); and Toby Kraft, Edgerton's leading pawnbroker, whose eventual death will provide Ned with the first of several legacies that will come his way.

Ned's homecoming is further complicated by the fact that a group of local roughnecks believe that he has cheated them at cards, winning several hundred dollars they are determined to take back, with interest. This deliberately created misunderstanding—Robert's work, once again—puts Ned at risk and leads directly to his largely adversarial relationship with the Edgerton Police Department.

These, then, are the circumstances that attend Ned's return: his mother is dying; the father he never knew is waiting to kill him on behalf of Lovecraft's Elder Gods; his magical, long-lost shadow self is loose in the town, creating havoc in Ned's name; hoodlums armed with baseball bats are stalking him; and his dormant Dunstan nature is about to assert itself in spectacular fashion.

The key to Ned's survival—and the only thing that will enable him to navigate the maze in which he finds himself—is knowledge. He must learn who and what he is, where he came from, what he is capable of. The main narrative arc of *Mr. X* describes Ned's education in the peculiar realities of life in Edgerton, and in the even more peculiar realities of life in the Dunstan family. His education begins when his mother, shortly before the onset of a second—and fatal—stroke, tells him his father's name: Edward Rhinehart. Armed with this knowledge, Ned begins the protracted process of unearthing his father's past.

Sometimes alone, sometimes in the company of Laurie Hatch (with whom he begins an unlikely love affair), sometimes in the company of Robert (who finally shows himself at a crucial moment, and who forms a temporary—and uneasy—alliance with his brother), Ned uncovers the sordid details of his father's criminal career. A series of encounters with the friends and associates of both Edward Rhinehart and Star Dunstan, together with his researches into the public records of Edgerton, leads him, eventually, to Rhinehart's lair: a pair of cottages registered under the distinctly Lovecraftian names of Wilbur Whately and Charles Dexter Ward. Here is what Ned finds in the first of the cottages.

> Rhinehart had turned the cottage into a library...There were thousands of books in that room. I looked at the spines: H. P. Lovecraft, H. P. Lovecraft, H. P. Lovecraft. Multiple copies of every edition of each of Lovecraft's books lined the shelves, followed by their translations into what looked like every foreign language. First editions, paperbacks, trade paperbacks, collections, library editions. Some of the books looked almost new, others as though they had been picked up in paperback exchange stores. Rhinehart had spent time

> and money buying rare copies but he had also purchased almost every Lovecraft volume he had seen, whether or not he already owned it. "I think I know the name of his favorite writer," I said.[23]

Included among the bibliographical evidence of his father's dementia are multiple copies of Rhinehart's own collection of Lovecraftian stories, *From Beyond.* Although most of its contents are predictable restatements of the Providence Master's themes, one of the stories, "Blue Fire," is something different. "Blue Fire" tells the story of Godfrey Demmiman, a man manipulated into believing that he is the half-human offspring of an Elder God, and then later manipulated into destroying both himself and his ancestral home. This text within the text will continue to resonate as the narrative develops.

As he slowly makes his way toward his father, Ned makes a number of concurrent discoveries. He learns, for example, that Stewart Hatch is guilty of enough felonious financial practices to invalidate his claim to the Hatch family's considerable fortune. He learns that the Dunstans have a long history of wild talents (levitation, psychokinesis, etc.). He learns, to his astonishment, that his own legacy as a Dunstan includes the ability to "eat time"[24]: to travel backward in time and return, unharmed, to the present. On a couple of occasions, this ability saves his life. Eventually, it brings him into contact (for the first time since his mysterious visit to the past at age eighteen) with his own embittered ancestor, Howard Dunstan, the real "Elder God" whose callous manipulations have driven Edward Rhinehart mad.

Howard Dunstan is Ned's great-grandfather and the father of his great-aunts Nettie, Queenie, Joy and May. He is also a member of a "higher" order of beings that might once have been godlike, but have grown increasingly debased over the course of the centuries. "Everything," he tells Ned, "happens over and over, and each time it means less."[25]

Howard Dunstan is not the only example of the moral disintegration of the gods. Pan himself, we are told, has lived through countless incarnations (one of them as Charles Baudelaire) and has survived into the present day as a burned-out former rock star who haunts the streets of Edgerton. Another "god," who goes by the name of Walter Bernstein, appears to Ned occasionally, commenting on the proceedings and offering teasing, deliberately inconclusive hints about the nature and mysterious origins of the Dunstans. "I'm sick," he tells Ned,

> of watching the Dunstans screw up over and over. You're not the only ones who got left behind, you know. Ever listen to Wagner? Read any Norse mythology, Icelandic mythology? Celtic? The Mediterranean isn't the whole damn world...[26]

Whatever Howard Dunstan's nature or mythological origins might be, he is the man—the being—responsible for Edward Rhinehart's delusions. Out of weariness and boredom, and out of an infinite loathing for what his family has become, he has filled Rhinehart's head with Lovecraftian fantasies and turned him loose on the world, hoping to use him as an instrument in the destruction of his own family line. The Dunstans, in Howard's view, might once have been gods, but are now simply "stories" that are "ending."[27]

Ned receives this information during a hallucinatory "visit" to the world of 1935, the last year of Howard Dunstan's life. Immediately afterward, still struggling to absorb what he has learned, he returns to the world of present-day Edgerton, where the story of the Dunstans continues to unfold. Resuming his investigation into his father's life and history, he discovers two family photograph albums that were "misplaced" and have been sought by many people throughout the novel. One album belongs to the Hatch family and one to the Dunstans. Through the internal evidence of these albums, Ned learns two things: that Edward Rhinehart is really Cordwainer Hatch, the black sheep uncle of Stewart Hatch; and that Cordwainer is also a dead ringer for the profligate Howard Dunstan, who was clearly his biological father. Cordwainer/Rhinehart/Mr. X is thus both a Hatch and a Dunstan, with the latter branch, of course, accounting for his paranormal abilities. Ironically, the discovery that his own biological father was the legal heir to the Hatch family fortune places Ned in a position to inherit that same fortune.

Along the way, Ned also discovers that his father is alive and living in Edgerton under the pseudonym of Edward Sawyer, a name borrowed from a minor character in "The Dunwich Horror." On June 25th, their thirty-fifth birthday, he and Robert finally confront their father. Calling on his newly developed Dunstan abilities, Ned merges with his brother and "eats time," once again traveling to 1935, to the last day of Howard Dunstan's life. This time, he brings his father with him. Once there, Cordwainer finally encounters the author of his governing delusions, and learns that his entire life is based on a lie. Driven past endurance, he emulates the ending of his own story, "Blue Fire," and sets the Dunstan house on fire, destroying his father, himself, and his ancestral mansion in the process. Sometimes, life is like a book.

Mr. X is one of Straub's most complicated novels, and certainly one of his busiest. In the aftermath of that climactic confrontation, a number of ancillary matters proceed toward some degree of resolution. Stewart Hatch's legal problems finally overwhelm him. Ned ends his relationship with Laurie Hatch, who, in the end, is interested more in the Hatch family fortune than in Ned. Edgerton police uncover grisly evidence of Cordwainer Hatch's long and demented career. Ned receives a great deal of money from various sources and gives a great deal of it away. And, in a sort of tragic footnote to the main narrative, Ned's Great-Aunt Joy dies, and he discovers the secret she has hidden in her attic for many years: her pitifully deformed son, "Mousie" Dunstan, a hopeless, helpless creature who is not, in any recognizable way, human. In a spontaneous act of mercy that will haunt him forever, Ned smothers Mousie with a pillow and buries him in his aunt's backyard. Shortly afterward, he leaves Edgerton for good, pursued both by his memories of Mousie—the pure epitome of the debased Dunstan legacy—and by Robert, the eternally hungry, eternally dissatisfied shadow self who will follow in his footsteps forever.

Mr. X is classic Straub, a hugely assured narrative that recapitulates its author's traditional virtues and familiar concerns, while at the same time adding something new and vital to the mix. As in the best of Straub's fiction, its extravagance—and it really is an extravagant creation—is rooted at all times in the closely observed reality of the American Midwest, and in a Dickensian flair for characterization that appears to be increasing with each book.

Straub's fictional city of Edgerton is a fully imagined, deeply realized place, comparable in many ways to another fictional Straub locale, *Mystery*'s Mill Walk. Just as he did in *Mystery,* Straub takes us into all levels of Edgerton society, from the mansions of the rich and corrupt to the enclaves of the disenfranchised poor. Again as in *Mystery,* he shows us, with great particularity, the secret center of a modern American city, with its mazes and hidden corners, its secret passages barred forever to the casual, outside observer. In *Mr. X*, that hidden center lies within an area called Hatchtown, which is deliberately reminiscent of *Mystery*'s enclosed, self-contained tenement community, Elysian Fields. Both communities reflect the influence of Charles Dickens' *Bleak House*, both stand well outside the civic and social mainstream of their respective cities, and both, in Straub's words, are the indirect byproducts of "a pervading and unacknowledged corruption."[28]

The characterizations reflect a similarly wide range, and represent some of Straub's best writing to date. In addition to the superbly articulated viewpoints of his two narrators, Straub offers us a gallery of vital, vividly rendered personalities that reflect the entire spectrum of life in Edgerton. Included among them are upper-class, white-collar criminals, policemen both dedicated and corrupt, embittered ex-convicts, child musical prodigies, alcoholic crossing guards, ambitious lady lawyers, and a wide variety of beings both human and "other." The Dunstan family in particular—May, Nettie, Joy, Clark, etc.—are triumphs of characterization: funny, cantankerous, insular; generous and grasping; gregarious and secretive; indifferent to commonly accepted standards and shaped by forces outside the range of normal human experience. They are absolutely authentic creations, and further evidence of Straub's continued determination to extend his reach, and to take his fiction into new and unexpected areas.

A number of Straub's characteristic obsessions are given an airing in *Mr. X:* the importance of imaginative empathy; the need for a system of values that is unconnected to the pursuit of either money or influence; the power that parents have to shape and warp the lives of their children; the influence of the past; the fundamental importance of pursuing the truth, whatever the cost; and, of course, the complex intermingling of narrative and life, which is given a particularly bizarre spin through the story of Cordwainer Hatch and his demented belief in the reality of H. P. Lovecraft's Elder Gods.

But the distinguishing element of *Mr. X*, the element that animates it and accounts for so much of its power, is Straub's ability to articulate a universal feeling of longing, an unassuageable yearning for a lost, perhaps mythical, sense of wholeness and completion. Of course, much of this pervasive sense of yearning derives naturally from Straub's use of the doppelganger theme, with its implicit assumption that something central, something without which the world will never cohere, is missing. But the concept of the doppelganger is itself simply a metaphor for a more fundamental condition: the sense that our lives are somehow out of joint; that we are waiting, always, for that vital connection that will lead to the restoration of a lost harmony.

> Sometimes I think that everyone I've ever known has had the feeling of missing a mysterious but essential quantity, that they all wanted to find an unfindable place that would be *the right place,* and that since Adam in the Garden human life has been made of these aches and bruises.[29]

When both Cordwainer Hatch and Ned Dunstan succumb to the power of Johnson's Woods—when they are seduced by the illusory sense of having stepped from the limitations of the real world into what Donald Harington, one of Straub's favorite novelists, called "Some Other Place, The Right Place"—they are simply manifesting the basic human need to find an ideal home in the world. The home they are searching for may well be illusory, but the need to locate it is real, and universal.

Set against this pervasive sense of yearning are the eternal consolations of art, particularly, in *Mr. X*'s terms, of music. Virtually all of Straub's novels are informed, at some level, by a passion for music, but *Mr. X* takes that passion and places it at the novel's aesthetic center. Music, in *Mr. X,* is harmony, wholeness, completion, and is the closest approximation of that ideal home we are ever likely to encounter.

Music enters the main line of the narrative at a couple of points. First, Ned Dunstan's relationship with Laurie Hatch is deepened and enhanced by his affection for Laurie's son, three-year-old Cobbie Hatch, who may well be a musical prodigy. Cobbie is obsessed by music, particularly by three very different pieces: Emma Kirkby's solo performance of Monteverdi's "Confiteor Tibi," Frank Sinatra's version of "Something's Gotta Give," and pianist Zoltan Kocsis' rendition of "Jardins Sous le Pluie," the final section of Debussy's "Estampes." Straub makes something moving and genuinely dramatic out of the unlikely spectacle of two people sitting together, listening to music they love.

> Emma Kirkby's shining voice sailed out of invisible speakers, translating the flowing, regular meter into silvery grace. Cobbie sat cross-legged on the carpet, his head lifted, drinking in the music while keeping an eye on me. His whole body went still. The meter slowed down, then surged forward at "Sanctum et terrible nomen eius," and he braced himself. We reached the "Gloria patri," where Emma Kirkby soars into a series of impassioned, out-of-time inventions that always reminded me of an inspired jazz solo. Cobbie fastened his eyes on mine. When the piece came to an end, he said, "You *do* like it."
>
> "You do, too," I said.[30]

In the same fashion, Straub takes us into the interior world of Ned and Cobbie's shared responses to the Kocsis and Sinatra performances, and Cobbie continues to demonstrate an unnatural affinity for the things he is hearing. He has, in Ned's words, "the ability to hear the precise relationship between sounds."[31] Despite the fact that a portion of the novel is concerned with Cobbie's ironically competing claim to the Hatch fortune, his real legacy is his love of music, and his ability to lose himself in its various manifestations.

Like Cobbie, Ned is the recipient of a similar legacy and it, too, proves deeper and more enduring than the various financial legacies that come his way. Ned's legacy comes from his mother, and finds precise expression in her description of a jazz concert she attended one month after Ned's conception. The musicians are never named (although internal evidence suggests the Dave Brubeck Quartet with Paul Desmond on alto sax), but their effect on her is indelible and is passed along directly to her son.

> "At first, I wasn't even sure I liked that group. It was a quartet from the West Coast, and I was never all that crazy about West Coast jazz. Then this alto player who looked like a stork pushed himself off the curve of the piano and stuck his horn in his mouth and started playing 'These Fool-

> ish Things.'" The memory still had the power to make her gasp. "And, oh, Neddie, it was like going to some new place you'd never heard about, but where you felt at home right away. He just touched that melody for a second before he lifted off and began climbing and climbing, and everything he played linked up, one step after another, like a story. Neddie! It was like hearing the whole world open up in front of me. It was like going to heaven."[32]

Eventually, Ned will make use of another of his Dunstan legacies—the ability to "eat time"—and return to the scene of that concert, where he, too, hears "the tremendous story and all of its details"[33] enter the world through the portal of an alto saxophone. And just as it did for his mother, the whole world opens up.

Like so much of Straub's earlier work, *Mr. X* uses the conventions of the horror novel to celebrate the most durable legacies of human life: love, music, stories, and the unrestrained openness of the spirit. *Mr. X* also closes out the century for Straub, and rounds off nearly thirty years of single-minded concentration on the endless possibilities of narrative.

As the millennium looms, other projects are already beckoning. A novel that may or may not be called *In the Night Room* is under way, and a second collaboration with Stephen King is currently in the planning stages. Other novels, novellas and stories will undoubtedly follow, because the story tree is never empty, and the next story is always out there, waiting to be told. On that note, and with that image in mind, it seems appropriate to end this study by stepping aside and letting Straub himself have the final word. Here is the nameless narrator of "The Juniper Tree," speaking from his subterranean cell about the conditions of the life he has chosen, or been chosen, to lead.

> I live underground in a wooden room and patiently, in joyful concentration, decorate the walls. Before me, half unseen, hangs a large and appallingly complicated vision I must explore and memorize, must witness again and again in order to locate its hid-

> den center. Around me, everything is in its proper place. My typewriter sits on the sturdy table. Beside the typewriter a cigarette smolders, raising a gray stream of smoke. A record revolves on the turntable, and my small apartment is dense with music. ("Bird of Prey Blues," with Coleman Hawkins, Buck Clayton, and Hank Jones.) Beyond my walls and windows is a world toward which I reach with outstretched arms and an ambitious and divided heart. As if "Bird of Prey Blues" has evoked them, the voices of sentences to be written this afternoon, tomorrow, or next month stir and whisper, beginning to speak, and I lean over the typewriter toward them, getting as close as I can.[34]

1. Letter from Peter Straub to the author
2. *Peter and PTR* (Burton, MI, Subterranean Press, 1999), p. 6
3. Ibid., p. 6
4. Letter from Peter Straub to the author
5. Ibid.
6. *Mr. X* (New York, Random House, 1999), p. 6
7. Ibid., p. 7
8. Ibid., p. 24
9. Ibid., p. 25
10. Ibid., p. 58
11. Ibid., p. 74
12. Ibid., p. 67
13. Ibid., p. 74
14. Ibid., p. 3
15. Ibid., p. 16
16. Ibid., p. 15
17. Ibid., p. 19
18. Ibid., pp. 46-47
19. Ibid., p. 16
20. *Peter and PTR*, p. 7
21. *Mr. X*, p. 284
22. Ibid., p. 35
23. Ibid., p. 364

24. Ibid., p. 309
25. Ibid., p. 257
26. Ibid., p. 330
27. Ibid., p. 258
28. Letter from Peter Straub to the author
29. *Mr. X*, p. 49
30. Ibid., p. 211
31. Ibid., p. 212
32. Ibid., p. 11
33. Ibid., p. 482
34. *Houses Without Doors,* p. 90

Appendices

Appendix A:
Ghosts

In 1994, Straub agreed to serve as guest editor of an original theme anthology—the fourth in an ongoing, sporadically produced series—showcasing short fiction written by the members of the Horror Writers Association, Inc. The HWA, as it is generally known, is a professional organization aimed at promoting the horror genre and serving the interests of the writers who work within that genre.

The origins of the HWA go back to 1983, when a group of writers (among them Joe R. Lansdale and Robert McCammon) banded together to form a fledgling organization called HOWL: The Horror and Occult Writers League. In 1987, a radically restructured version of HOWL—now called the Horror Writers of America—was incorporated, with Dean Koontz serving as its first president. In 1993, in an effort to reflect more accurately the international character of the organization, the HWA became The Horror Writers Association. Straub himself, beginning in 1997, served a three year-term as a member of the organization's Board of Trustees.

Among the services which the HWA offers its members—services which include legal and contractual advice, hardship loans, market reports, and the sponsorship of the annual Bram Stoker Awards for Superior Achievement—are the members-only theme anthologies, all of which have been edited by prominent members of the HWA. The first of these was Robert R. McCammon's' vampire anthology, *Under the Fang* (1990). It was followed by *Freak Show,* an interconnected series of stories about a traveling carnival edited by F. Paul Wilson; and Ramsey Campbell's *Deathport,* whose stories are centered around the notion of a haunted airport built over the remains of an Indian burial ground. When Straub was offered the opportunity to edit the next volume in the series, he quickly decided to focus on one of the genre's most enduring and fundamental forms: the ghost story.

With the editorial assistance of Martin H. Greenberg and Richard Gilliam, Straub selected fourteen stories, dividing them into five distinct categories: "Dark," "The Kids," "Mom and Dad," "Cold," and "Our Work." Authors represented in *Ghosts* included veteran novelists like Chet Williamson and Thomas F. Monteleone; important, relatively recent figures such as Kathe Koja and Norman Partridge; and a number of other writers of varying degrees of prominence, one of whom, Tim Smith, made his first professional sale to this anthology with a story called "Not Far From Here." For the purposes of this study, however, the most significant contribution to *Ghosts* is Straub's own. Faced with the opportunity to provide either a story or the traditional editor's introduction, he slyly elected to do both, opening the anthology with a novella-length piece of fiction pointedly entitled "Hunger: An Introduction."

"Hunger" is narrated by Francis T. (Frank) Wardwell, a ghost. Frank begins the story by lecturing the reader on a number of common misconceptions regarding ghosts. (The primary misconception, he tells us, is the widespread but erroneous notion that ghosts don't exist.) After setting us straight on this and a number of related issues, Frank settles in to tell us the story of his life, death and afterlife. That story, despite its violent and often horrific nature, is the essentially comic account of a man shaped and driven by a variety of unassuageable hungers.

Frank Wardwell is born into the borderline poverty of a lower-middle class family, residents of a nameless American city in the early years of this century. His youthful years are marked by two major elements: his propensity for petty thefts (an early manifestation of what he calls "the hunger theme"[1]), and the day-to-day abuse of his peers (which is largely the result of his inability to refrain from proclaiming his intellectual superiority to anyone within earshot.) After two "unfortunate incidents"[2] in which he is caught stealing small sums of money, Frank is forced to leave school and go to work for Harold McNair, the domineering proprietor of a local clothing emporium. Once in McNair's employ, Frank begins to discover his true larcenous potential.

In the course of his lengthy career at McNair's, a career in which he rises from assistant stockboy to Vice-President and Chief Buyer, Frank discovers an unsuspected talent for embezzlement. By 1959, he has augmented his considerable salary by stashing away nearly $600,000 of McNair's money. Disaster strikes when, in the course of an extensive renovation, McNair discovers the secret set of books which document Frank's "peculations."[3] In the ensuing confrontation, Frank seizes a ballpeen hammer and reduces his employer to a "shapeless, bloody, brainspattered...mess."[4] Fourteen months later, following an "interesting period"[5] in the state's electric chair, Frank, newly separated from his corporeal self, is ironically subjected to the most fundamental of all hungers: the hunger that the dead feel in the presence of ordinary, unremarkable human lives. As the story ends, Frank, accompanied by a host of fellow spirits, is battening upon the most homely and ordinary of images, an image that he finds "wholly, gloriously beautiful"[6]: that of a five-year-old girl named Tiffany who is sitting in front of the television and picking her nose, watching "in wonder and awe the multiform adventures of Tom and Jerry."[7]

"Hunger" is particularly notable for the vibrantly comic voice that Straub created for his unlovable narrator. That voice is at once pompous and preening, fatuous and overbearing, endlessly self-justifying and steeped, at all times, in an unimpeachable aura of self-regard. These qualities, together with the narrator's tortured syntax, rhetorical flourishes, and uncertain grasp of the principles of grammar, combine to create a narrative tone unlike anything Straub had attempted before. Examples abound, but one will have to suffice for now. Here is Frank Wardwell, bemoaning some of the many injustices of his early life.

> And from the seventh grade on, a time when I suffered under the tyranny of a termaganty, black-haired witch thing named Missus Barksdale, who hated me because I knew more than she did, I was forced to endure the further injustice of after-school employment. Daily had I to trudge from the humiliations delivered upon my head by the witch thing, Missus Barfsbottom, humiliations earned only through an inability to conceal entirely the mirth her errors caused in me, from sadistic, unwarranted humiliations delivered

> upon the head of one of the topmost students ever seen at that crummy school, then to trudge through sordiosities to the place of my employment, Dockweder's Hardware, where I took up my broom and swept, swept, swept.[8]

The tone of comic bombast that animates this peculiar narrative voice represented a genuine departure for Straub, a new step in his ongoing evolution as stylist and storyteller. Variations on this voice would find their way into subsequent stories (such as "Mr. Clubb and Mr. Cuff" and the eponymous journal entries of *Mr. X*), adding an effective comic element to Straub's constantly expanding array of stylistic effects.

1. "Hunger: An Introduction"—*Ghosts* ed. by Peter Straub (New York, Pocket Books, 1995), p. 5
2. Ibid., p. 19
3. Ibid., p. 3
4. Ibid., p. 34
5. Ibid., p. 35
6. Ibid., p. 39
7. Ibid., p. 39
8. Ibid., p. 6

Appendix B:
The General's Wife

The General's Wife, which is probably Straub's single hardest-to-locate piece of fiction, has had an interesting and complex publishing history. Written as an affectionate homage to Carlos Fuentes' 1965 novella, *Aura,* it was originally intended to serve as a kind of autonomous internal narrative within the larger narrative of *Floating Dragon.* Straub, of course, had done this sort of thing before, both in *Ghost Story,* which successfully absorbed *The Turn of the Screw* into itself, and in *Shadowland,* which made similar use of a number of classic fairy tales. Acting on editorial advice, Straub eventually excised the narrative from *Floating Dragon,* changed the names of the main characters, and added enough explanatory material to allow the story to stand on its own. *The General's Wife* was subsequently published both in *Twilight Zone Magazine,* and as a deluxe, limited edition hardcover from specialty publisher Donald M. Grant. It has never been reprinted since that time. For various legal reasons, it is never likely to be.

The General's Wife began life in 1980, when Straub was invited to a party held at Manhattan's Books & Co. in honor of the publication of Carlos Fuentes' short story collection, *Burnt Water,* a book for which Straub had supplied an enthusiastic blurb. After meeting Fuentes, and learning that the Mexican novelist was a great admirer of *Ghost Story,* Straub chanced upon a Fuentes title he had never seen before, a slender little volume called *Aura.* Straub bought the book, read it the next day, and almost immediately began planning to incorporate the story into his novel-in-progress.

Aura is the bizarre account of a young historian hired by the widow of a Mexican general to arrange and complete her husband's military memoirs. During the course of his stay in the widow's apartment, he meets and falls in love with Aura, a beautiful young woman who appears to be a manifestation of the widow's own younger self, and who has been created and maintained through the power of witchcraft. The story had an immediate and powerful effect on Straub.

> *Aura* was a horror story, one of the best I'd ever read. It was subtle, mysterious, erotic; the details were so charged they fairly jumped off the page; it concluded with a salutary jolt, but did not actually explain itself. All this was wonderfully satisfying—it was like seeing how Robert Aickman might have written if he'd been born in Mexico City. When the story snapped itself shut, its echoes stayed, increasing in the mind. *Aura* was full of that odd poetry of the best horror (which comes from suggestive and precise detail, and from scrupulous language), and never even hinted at the flaw which ruins so many stories of its kind—the sentimental desire to wrap everything up with a fatal neatness.[1]

In Straub's version of the story, *Floating Dragon*'s dysfunctional couple, Patsy and Les McCloud, are transformed into Andrea (Andy) Rivers and her abusive husband Phil, who are living in London on a temporary job assignment. Andy, whose relationship with Phil is in a state of terminal decline, decides to assert herself and look for a part-time job. She answers an ad in a local paper and is hired by General Anthony August Leck—a World War II hero whose reputation has been clouded by allegations of cannibalism—to transcribe his memoirs. Shortly after starting work, she enters into an affair with the general's unnaturally attractive grandson, Tony.

Eventually, she learns that the general is, in fact, childless, and that Tony, like Aura in the Fuentes story, is actually an aspect of the general, given life by some inexplicable, perhaps magical, means. The story—and the affair—ends when Andy enters the General's bedroom and finds Tony's bleeding, ravaged body lying on the bed. In a sort of bizarre triple exposure, Tony's bleeding body yields to the image of his healthy, undamaged body, which yields in turn to the body of General Leck himself, who is clearly dying. In a blind panic, she runs from the room—and from an experience she will never comprehend—and returns, shaken, to her loveless and violent marriage.

When Straub began seriously contemplating this story—which proved, in the end, to be more graphic, more overtly erotic, and arguably more enigmatic than its model—he wrote to Fuentes' editor in New York, announcing his intentions. The editor never responded. When the decision to remove the story from *Floating Dragon* and reshape it into an independent novella was made, Straub again notified Fuentes' editor and again received no response. In time, *The General's Wife* made its scheduled appearance in *Twilight Zone Magazine,* and Straub dutifully sent a copy to Fuentes.

Fuentes, it turned out, had never been informed of Straub's plans, and he reacted badly. When the dust settled on the matter, the following compromise had been reached: the issue of *Twilight Zone Magazine* was permitted to go forward, as was the twelve hundred copy limited edition already in production at Donald M. Grant's publishing house. However, Straub was formally enjoined from ever reprinting the story in any future venue. Thus, *The General's Wife* never found its way into *Houses Without Doors,* and will never find its way into any subsequent collection. Anyone fortunate enough to have acquired either the magazine or the specialty press edition has sole access to a story that deserves a much wider distribution. For everyone else, *The General's Wife* is—and is likely to remain—Peter Straub's lost story.

1. The General's Wife, pp. 15-16

Appendix C:
Putney Tyson Ridge

In 1993, specialty publisher Borderlands Press issued a signed, limited edition of *The Throat* which contained, among other unique features, dust jacket material purportedly written by Putney Tyson Ridge, Ph.D. Putney, as he himself informs us, is a childhood buddy of Straub's, one always "tactfully alert to overstatement, hyperbole, pretension, sentimentality, semi-mystical incoherence, and self-justification."[1] After cheerfully eviscerating *The Throat,* which he sees as yet another example of Straub's penchant for "elevated theory and low practice," Putney ends his comments with the following recommendation.

> I prescribe frequent readings of simple, honest artisans such as Stephen King and Dean Koontz—our boy must learn to tell a story at least as well as his betters. And if he cannot learn to tell a story—from A to Z, without pointless complications—a story with clear-cut heroes and villains—I intend to suggest during one of our frequent pub crawls that he take up the saxophone instead.[2]

This is not, obviously, your typical dust jacket copy. Some years later, when Putney returned to grace the dust jacket of Gauntlet Press' fifteenth anniversary edition of *Shadowland*, he took a similar hard line with his old buddy's work.

> The reader of this laborious farrago may take comfort in my determination to return my foolish pal to first principles: begin at the beginning, end at the ending, and no nonsense in between. Unless forced to see that he began seriously to go astray with this book, he will be lost, and this companion of his late hours, this faithful representative of the sensible reader, shall not neglect his duty. One night soon, as our wayward author interrupts the guzzling of yet another libation to reach for the peanuts on the bar, I intend to speak these words: tell your story and get out.[3]

Following these two early appearances, the fictional but ever vigilant Putney Tyson Ridge began to assume a larger role as a ubiquitous, fearless critic of the evolving excesses of Peter Straub's fiction. Having created this rather endearing comic commentator—the archetypal embodiment of an aesthetic viewpoint diametrically opposed to his own, a viewpoint that lobbies for simplicity, modesty, and sensibly restrained ambition—Straub soon put him to work. Over the years, Putney has provided extensive commentaries on virtually all of Straub's books. Although he does find some kind things to say about a couple of Straub's novels, *Julia* and *If You Could See Me Now* (which he views as sensible, seemly entertainments, Novels That Know Their Place), most of his assessments are outraged, virulent, and very, very funny.

Anyone interested in further encounters with Putney should look to Straub's official web page (http://www.net-site.com/straub), which contains all of Putney's reviews, along with an illuminating biographical sketch. (Another useful source of Ridge-related information is a chapbook, published by Subterranean Press, called *Peter and PTR*, which contains a couple of excised portions of *Mr. X*, along with an amusing portrait of Putney seen from Straub's point of view.)

According to the biographical data, Putney, like Straub, was born in Milwaukee in 1943, lived next door to Straub, played in the same sandboxes and attended the same schools. After college, their paths diverged, Straub going on to an ill-advised career as an overpraised popular novelist, and Putney to a distinguished career as first and Permanent Chairman of the Department of Popular Culture at Popham College, a mythical institution that makes brief appearances in both *Mr. X* and *Mrs. God*. Putney's awards include "more than a dozen plaques and citations for his unceasing efforts on behalf of Popular Culture studies."[4] He is also a four-time recipient of the Elmer J. Atwood Award, commonly known as "the Atwood."[5] His fourth citation was personally bestowed on him by the "marmoreally pale...aristocratic hands of the Contessa Fabiana Paloma Therese de Rebas Gonzalo Loupa-Mondeale Allegro-Gonzaga y Gonzaga, patroness of the Society's mid-Iberian chapter."[6] Putney, clearly, has arrived.

From his lofty eminence as an arbiter of contemporary culture, Putney launches broadside after broadside at the works of his "misguided former playmate."[7] While his assaults against Straub cannot be effectively paraphrased, they can be excerpted. Here are a few samples of Putney Tyson Ridge pointing out the error of Peter Straub's ways.

On *Shadowland:*

> This may be the most self-indulgent work of fiction since *Tristram Shandy*, shamelessly stealing from John Fowles, pointlessly throwing off mean-spirited, vindictive caricatures of our hardworking and dedicated masters at Country Day School, rocketing backwards and forwards in time and so thoroughly muddling the distinction between what is real and what is not that lengthy passages mean nothing at all. A swamp, a noxious vapor, a will-o'-the-wisp. The cruelty, even sadism of some passages render the book unsuitable for the younger readers who might otherwise have found it palatable. It includes one passable fairy tale originally invented for the entertainment of the author's son. On the whole, the wise reader will avoid this book as if it were a contagious disease. Some of the cadences of its final pages are nicely turned.[8]

On *The Throat:*

> Disheartened, I sum up: a labored, exhausted effort at an exhaustive...No, I don't sum up, I give up, I surrender. This is a book I could not manage to read all the way through without frequent naps, vacations, and health-giving interludes spent in the company of writers I shall not name but who are clever enough to have less, in this sense meaning more, on their minds. I detect signs of extensive cutting, but the resulting moment-to-moment clarity of style only serves to heighten the reader's steadily intensifying desperation.[9]

On *Ghost Story:*

> One of my friend's most defining traits is literal-mindedness. A literal-minded person in the grip of mystic fancies can only press them to the dubious conclusion that reality itself is a variety of fiction. *Ghost Story* avoids this ripely decadent notion, but only barely—it lurks beneath the text, inhabiting scene after scene in which one character after another suffers hallucinations. That the reading public responded positively to this balderdash is...I don't know what it is, but it's extremely discouraging to a responsible educator like myself. At least the reliable Elmore "Dutch" Leonard knew what was up. His review of the book contained the clear-sighted sentence, "This isn't fiction, it is hype." The novel does contain some excellent descriptions of snow.[10]

On *The Hellfire Club:*

> Alas, almost immediately one finds oneself swimming upstream against our author's usual flood of turgid complexi-

> ties, texts within texts, ancient secrets, yawn, inside jokes, jerry-built constructions, hasty improvisations and fantastically elaborated descriptions. The pace slows to a halt, comically, whenever food is put upon the table. Not only does the lazy novelist throw in a remote country house, a confusion of birth and a resolving storm, he cynically expoits every last cliche, as these particulars indicate, of the Gothic genre the novel takes pains to ridicule. Unlike *Shadowland* or *Floating Dragon*, this book is not even good enough to be destructive. No, we must conclude, nothing can be salvaged from the wreckage.[11]

These hyperbolic jeremiads are, of course, reflections of a serious and fundamental division: the division between the reader who wants to have his or her past reading experiences endlessly replicated; and the writer who is motivated by riskier, less predictable ambitions. And though that division is unresolved, and probably unresolvable, Straub's treatment of the problem is both amusing and illuminating, and fictional critic Putney Tyson Ridge emerges as a memorable comic creation.

1. The Peter Straub website—http://www.net-site.com/straub—Putney's Observations
2. Ibid.
3. Ibid.
4. Ibid.
5. Ibid.
6. Ibid.
7. Ibid.
8. Ibid.
9. Ibid.
10. Ibid.
11. Ibid.

Appendix D:
Twenty Questions: an Interview with Peter Straub

Interviewer: Your career has undergone a number of dramatic changes over the years, and I'd like to talk about some of those changes. To begin with, you started out as a poet, but (apparently) abandoned poetry early on in favor of narrative prose. From this vantage point, how would you assess your brief career as a poet? What role, if any, does poetry continue to play in your day-to-day life?

Straub: My "brief career as a poet" was of far more value to me than to the world of poetry and its readers. For one thing, I enjoyed myself tremendously during that period. It was hugely pleasurable to work on poems and try to get them right. Also, it demanded that I pay great attention to individual words, the weight and duration of phrases, and the rhythms and cadences of the lines. All of this concentration leads to an increased awareness of verbal texture and verbal possibility, valuable to any writer.

Interviewer: Your first novel, *Marriages,* is written in a self-conscious prose that is considerably different from anything found in your subsequent work. You yourself have described it as a kind of "Ashberian anti-narrative" that is both discursive and deliberately nonlinear. I find it interesting that you turned away from this experimental style so quickly. Did you sense, way back then, that this was an artistic dead end, and that your real gifts lay in other, more traditional narrative modes?

Straub: I sort of discovered the nature of my gifts as I went along, but after *Marriages* it was clear to me that I wanted to do more with traditional narrative. It seemed to me that I was able to spread my wings a little further, and since I sensed that I could, I had to try it. I was looking for deeper satisfactions.

Interviewer: If your second novel, *Under Venus,* had met with a kinder fate—if it had been published immediately to acclaim, awards, and commercial success—do you think your career might have proceeded along different lines? Or is the Gothic impulse so much a part of you that it would inevitably have found its way into your fiction?

Straub: I don't think I'll ever know the answer to this question. If *Under Venus,* as you say, had been published to admiring reviews, then won awards and met with commercial success, my life would have an entirely different shape, that is certain. What that shape would be is a mystery. However, it is unlikely that the book would have met with anything like such critical and popular success. If it had been published immediately after I finished the writing, *Under Venus* would probably have been reviewed tepidly, won no awards, and sold fewer than 10,000 copies. In that case, I think I would have begun to explore the Gothic at about the same time I did in the life given me. Thomas Tessier and I had been talking about writers like Lovecraft, Richard Matheson, and Robert Bloch for six or eight months, and this interest would soon have found its way into my writing.

Interviewer: You once told an interviewer that, shortly after beginning *Julia,* you realized that the Gothic form represented the "emotional territory" most suited to your own gifts and temperament. What was it about the Gothic that spoke to you so immediately and forcibly? What did it offer you that the more "literary" forms did not?

Straub: While working on *Julia,* I discovered that I could create an atmosphere of unease, uncertainty, and dread, and that within that atmosphere I could build up tension and a gathering head of steam. And I liked the way an atmosphere of emotional uncertainty permitted or even encouraged ambiguity in an ongoing narrative. This framework seemed to bring everything else, characters, individual scenes, details, even plotting, into sharper focus.

Interviewer: *Ghost Story,* your third horror novel, appeared in 1979, and changed your life in a number of ways, introducing a whole new level of ambition into your work and bringing you to the attention of a huge new readership. Was the experience largely a positive one, or did celebrity bring with it a proportionate share of difficulties?

Straub: What happened upon publication of *Ghost Story* was unexpected and sometimes a little dizzying, but positive in every way. The book's reception gave me a good deal of financial and psychic security—it was a form of acceptance. The degree of celebrity that came with this popular acceptance, while guaranteeing that lots of people in any given room would know my name when I walked in, was not so great that strangers invaded my privacy. I felt sort of like the flavor of the month, a position I enjoyed but never assumed to be anything but temporary.

Interviewer: You've frequently cited the influence of Stephen King—particularly of *The Shining* —in opening up for you the larger possibilities of the horror novel. Do you think that, without King's influence, you might have continued working on the more modest scale that characterized both *Julia* and *If You Could See Me Now?* Or was the sheer, gaudy expansiveness of books like *Ghost Story, Shadowland,* and *Floating Dragon* something else you would have come to eventually, with or without King's example?

Straub: Again, this is a question that proposes an unknowable future by invoking an altered past. If Stephen King had gone into brain surgery, tree surgery, formula 1 racing, or the insurance business instead of fiction-writing, horror literature would be vastly different—we'd be in another landscape altogether. My work would be different, too, but I cannot know how. However, I probably would not have moved toward such colorful expansivesness.

Interviewer: After *Floating Dragon,* your all-out assault on the conventions of the supernatural horror novel, you deliberately changed directions, moving toward a more realistic kind of fiction whose drama is rooted in the mental and emotional states of the characters involved. Did you feel, at this time, that you had used up the possibilities of supernatural fiction, or that fiction of this type had become, or threatened to become, another artistic dead end?

Straub: The shift in direction was the result of purely personal motives. I felt as though I had exhausted the possibilities of horror for me, not that the genre itself had been played out or fully explored. In fact, I was interested to see what other writers would do with it, and since then I've been following the careers of younger writers like Poppy Z. Brite, David Schow, Richard Christian Matheson, Bentley Little, Caitlin Kiernan, Christa Faust, Jack Ketchum, Edward Lee and others with a great deal of pleasure.

Interviewer: The three novels that comprise the so-called "Blue Rose Trilogy"—*Koko, Mystery,* and *The Throat*—combine autobiography, recent American history, and "realistic" suspense elements in a way that feels more personal, more emotionally *engaged,* than your earlier novels. Were you consciously attempting to resolve, clarify or understand certain personal issues in these books? Do you feel that this big, ambitious series of novels represented either a personal or artistic breakthrough for you?

Straub: The "Blue Rose" material did feel like a kind of artistic breakthrough when in progress, and it still does. If not a "breakthrough," at least an advance. More seemed to be at stake. Yes, some of what was at stake was personal, in the sense that my involvement with the characters felt deeper and less mediated than it usually had been earlier, and I was free to deal with the central issues of grief, trauma, writing, and imagination. In general, it never occurred to me that I was trying to clarify or resolve these issues: I just wanted to represent them as fully as I could, to do them as much justice as I could.

Interviewer: The two novels that followed the Blue Rose series—*The Hellfire Club* and *Mr.X* —represent rather risky experiments in perspective. *The Hellfire Club* reflects the viewpoint of an abused and violated woman, while *Mr. X* is narrated, whether we realize it or not, by a young black man. Was this, at least in part, an attempt to distance yourself from the more personal concerns that had occupied your fiction for the past several years? Or was it simply a result of your belief that the novel is, or should be, built on a foundation of imaginative empathy, and should thus be able to go anywhere it wants or needs to go?

Straub: Both of your questions are right on target. I very much wanted to stop ploughing my own field and move into other lives, and I have always assumed that every sort of life was open to imaginative investigation. If I hadn't felt that way, I would never have dared to write about combat veterans.

Interviewer: Along with your novels, you've written a good many stories and novellas, many of which were collected in *Houses Without Doors,* many of which remain, as of this writing, uncollected. Do you have a special fondness for any particular fictional form, or are all equally valid, equally valuable?

Straub: I love novels above all, but novellas, fictions that extend themselves over something like forty to something like two hundred pages, have a special place in my affections. Novellas allow me to relax into characters and voices too intense, too singular, or too limited to support an entire novel, so in a way they encourage a kind of experimentation not advisable in the longer form.

Interviewer: Moving away from individual works for the moment, I'd like to talk for a bit about influences of various kinds. Let's start with Place. You spent more than a decade living abroad, first in Ireland, then in England. Has this multicultural background been of much value to you as a writer?

Straub: The years I spent in Dublin and London were useful in several ways. They gave me more range than I would otherwise have had, they made more fictional territory available to me. And by putting me at one remove from my own country, they let me see it in a fresh way: the American was not the only variety of authenticity. This extends into fiction, too. I'm sure I read many more novels by people like Margaret Drabble, Iris Murdoch, Julian Barnes, Kingsley and Martin Amis, William Cooper, Paul Scott and others than I would have had I never left the United States. To varying degrees, these English writers all contributed to my bag of tools.

Interviewer: When you returned to America, in the wake of *Ghost Story's* success, you lived in Connecticut for some years before settling down in Manhattan. The internal evidence of your novels indicates that the Connecticut experience was less than idyllic. Was this actually the case? And has New York City proved to be more congenial for you, more of a real home?

Straub: Fairfield County, Connecticut's Gold Coast, was very pretty to look at but otherwise a less than perfect match for the Straubs. Most of the people I met talked mainly about sports and money. They were nice people, but after a while I wanted to get into conversations about John Ashbery, Stan Getz, Saul Bellow, Philip Glass, the publishing business, paintings, small presses, politics other than right-wing, and hundreds of other things. Eventually, my wife and I realized that we belonged in New York City, and we relocated fifty miles southwest, to the Upper West Side of Manhattan, where we immediately felt more at home.

Interviewer: To come at the old, old question of literary influences from a slightly different angle, would you care to take a shot at listing, even partially, the Great Books in your life: i.e., books that, whether they consciously influenced you or not, stand out as high points in a lifetime of compulsive reading?

Straub: In roughly chronological order: A picture book about Pecos Bill, author and illustrator unknown; the Hardy Boys books, F. W. Dixon; books about dogs, I believe mostly collies, by Albert Peyson Terhune; *Frog,* by Colonel S. P. Meeker; *Smoky,* by Will James; *Emil and the Detectives,* by whoever that was, God bless him; the Sherlock Holmes stories by A. Conan Doyle; *Street Rod,* by Henry Gregor Felsen; *Slan,* by A. E. Van Vogt; thereafter, lots of early Heinlein, Asimov's Foundation novels and robot-detective books, Zenna Henderson's stories about "the People," and anthologies edited by John W. Campbell and Judith Merrill; the Modern Library Giant entitled *Great Tales of Terror and the Supernatural*; in the order read, Thomas Wolfe's *Of Time and the River, The Web and the Rock,* and *Look Homeward, Angel; Babbitt, Main Street,* and *Arrowsmith* by Sinclair Lewis; *Crime and Punishment,* by Fyodor Dostoyevski; *USA,* by John Dos Passos; *Catcher in the Rye,* by J. D. Salinger; *Swann's Way,* by Marcel Proust; *Portrait of the Artist as a Young Man,* by James Joyce; *The Great Gatsby,* by F. Scott Fitzgerald; *The Sun Also Rises* and *A Farewell to Arms,* by Ernest Hemingway; *On the Road* and the *Dharma Bums,* by Jack Kerouac; *Go,* by John Clellon Holmes; the poetry of T. S. Eliot, W. H. Auden, and W. B. Yeats; *Bleak House,* by Charles Dickens; *Vanity Fair,* by William Thackeray; *Sons and Lovers, The Rainbow,* and *Women in Love,* by D. H. Lawrence, *To The Lighthouse,* by Virginia Woolf; *Jane Eyre,* by Charlotte Bronte; *Wuthering Heights,* by Emily Bronte; *The Lord of the Rings,* by J. R. R. Tolkien; *The Portait of a Lady,* by Henry James; *77 Dream Songs* and *Homage to Mistress Bradstreet,* by John Berryman; *Lolita* and *Pale Fire,* by Vladimir Nabokov; *In Our Time,* by Ernest Hemingway; *The Tennis Court Oath, Rivers and Mountains,* and *Self-Portrait in a Convex Mirror,* by John Ashbery; *The Bell, Under the Net, A Severed Head,* and *The Nice and the Good,* by Iris Murdoch; *A Dance to the Music of Time,* by Anthony Powell; *Under the Volcano,* by Malcolm Lowry; *A Summer Bird-Cage,* by Margaret Drabble; *The Ghost of Henry James* and *Relatives,* by David Plante; *Saint Jack* and *The Family Arsenal,* by Paul Theroux; *The Big Sleep* and *The Long Good-Bye,* by Raymond Chandler; *The Ambassadors, The Wings of the Dove,* and *The Golden Bowl,* by Henry James; *Pale Grey For Guilt* and other Travis McGee novels by John D. MacDonald; *The Drowning Pool* and other Lew Archer novels by Ross Macdonald; *'Salem's Lot* and *The Shining,* by Stephen King; *Tinker, Tailor, Soldier, Spy* and *A Perfect Spy,* by John Le Carre; the Sandman graphic novels by Neil Gaiman. I could go on, but I'll stop there.

Interviewer: Other, nonliterary influences have had an obvious effect on your life and work. Your passion for music, for example, informs book after book, story after story. At the same time, there are indications in a number of your books that the visual arts—painting, sculpture —are of comparable importance. Could you comment on the role that nonverbal art forms play in your aesthetic life?

Straub: Music, especially jazz music, seemed from the first not so much nonverbal as beyond the verbal, a means of expression so pure, so open to nuance, and so responsive to immediate thought and emotion as to transcend words. It had the force of a Platonic version of speech, an angel-language, comprehensive and gestural. In the solos of Paul Desmond, Stan Getz, and Clifford Brown, along with maybe a dozen other great jazz musicians, the 14-, 15-, 16-year-old me heard ideal, heart-stopping expressiveness. Passion spoke through wit, grace, authoritative eloquence, and it always told the truth. This was a life-giving revelation. For a couple of years during my early twenties, I used to say that Paul Desmond was my "ego-ideal," meaning that he and others like him had given me a bountiful, adaptive conception of art, an aesthetic to live by.

Paintings seemed, still seem, charged with significance through the mystery of representation. The weight of a line, the gradations of color, the accumulation or rejection of detail, the composition within the pictorial space, caused subjects like cows in English ponds, empty roads in rural Holland, a bowl of apples and an empty wine bottle on a wooden table to hum and glow with meaning —the sacred meaning we would always be able to see if we had the eyes of Constable, Hobbema, or Cezanne. In fiction, representation is brought about through description, also good dialogue and accurate verbs.

Interviewer: Another major, if less visible, influence has been your decade-long experience with psychoanalysis. If I can do so without being intrusive, I'd like to ask you to comment on the effect psychoanalysis has had on your writing. Are there aspects of your later work—say, from *Koko* forward—that exist in their present form because of the insights acquired through psychoanalysis?

Straub: All I can say is that, no matter how dubious, suspect, or predictable this may seem to its numerous detractors, the experience of psychoanalysis taught me most of what I know about human motivation, the reasons why people keep acting the way they do. I learned how to listen to the unsaid and respond to it, if response seemed helpful. Certain crucial though previously unsuspected elements of my own life moved inexorably into view and proved deeply explanatory. The insights I was given, some of them of a sort I wish to call transcendant, inform my work from *Koko* on.

Interviewer: Looking back over a career that has spanned nearly thirty years, do you feel that your novels and stories have met the standards that you set for them? Is there anything in your body of work that you'd like to have another crack at, given the opportunity? Conversely, could you name the books and stories that you're happiest with, that came closest to accomplishing the goals you had in mind?

Straub: I'd say that the books that came closest to realizing the vision I had when I started are *If You Could See Me Now, Ghost Story, Koko, Mystery, The Throat, Houses Without Doors* and *Mr. X.* Yet these fell short, too. Given that one always wishes to write a perfect book, and that perfection is impossible to attain, frustration is inevitable.

Interviewer: Certain key themes seem to occur over and over again in your work: the importance of imaginative empathy, the value of meaningful work, the power of stories, the ongoing influence of past events, etc. Are you consciously revisiting these notions in book after book, or are they simply so embedded in your vision of the world that they find their way naturally—unconsciously—into the stories you've chosen to tell?

Straub: The themes you mention are present in my work over and over again, but I would not really have known that if I hadn't been reading your chapters. Their presence was not a conscious decision on my part.

Interviewer: In your thirty years as a published writer, has the business of publishing —as opposed to the business of writing —changed very much? Are any of the changes, in your opinion, for the better?

Straub: Publishing has changed tremendously since I began writing. It used to be friendly and sort of familial, and now it is unfriendly and not at all familial. It's much harder to get a first novel published, and publishing houses are much less likely to stay with a writer whose books sell in small or moderate numbers. The idea of building a writer over four or five books, which used to be standard practice, has all but disappeared. There used to be about twenty thriving publishing houses, and now there are maybe three, each with their own imprints. I don't see much to cheer about in this situation.

Interviewer: In that same period, has your relationship with your own readership undergone significant changes? Do you think that your penchant for big, complex narratives, and your consistent refusal to satisfy conventional expectations, has cost you a portion of that readership?

Straub: I've probably lost some readers along the way. I'd like to think that I'll get them back, if I keep plugging away.

Interviewer: The final question: After all these years of performing "bench presses with narrative strategies," could you envision yourself in any other occupation? Or are you fated, for better or worse, to continue telling stories for the rest of your life?

Straub: Unfortunately, I am completely unfit for any other occupation, except perhaps for that of barfly. For the sake of my liver, I'd better stick to narrative bench presses.

Peter Straub: A Primary Bibliography

Poetry

Open Air (Shannon, Ireland: Irish University Press, 1972)

Leeson Park and Belsize Square (San Francisco CA/Columbia Pa: Underwood-Miller, 1983)

Novels

Marriages (New York, Coward, McCann & Geoghegan, 1973)

Under Venus (New York, Berkley Books, 1985)

Julia (New York: Coward, McCann & Geoghegan, 1975)

If You Could See Me Now (New York, Coward, McCann & Geoghegan, 1977)

Ghost Story (New York, Coward, McCann & Geoghegan, 1979)

Shadowland (New York, Coward, McCann & Geoghegan, 1980)

Floating Dragon (New York, G.P. Putnam's Sons, 1983)

The Talisman (with Stephen King) (New York, Viking/G.P Putnam's Sons, 1984)

Koko (New York, E.P. Dutton, 1988)

Mystery (New York, E.P. Dutton, 1990)

Mrs. God (Hampton Falls, NH, Donald M. Grant, Publisher, Inc., 1990)

The Throat (New York, E.P. Dutton, 1993)

The Hellfire Club (New York, Random House, 1996)

Mr. X (New York, Random House, 1999)

Collections

Wild Animals (New York, G.P. Putnam's Sons, 1984)

Houses Without Doors (New York, E.P. Dutton, 1990)

As Editor

Ghosts: The HWA Anthology (New York, Pocket Books, 1995)

Uncollected Stories (First appearances)

"The General's Wife" (West Kingston, RI, Donald M. Grant, Publisher, Inc., 1982)

"The Kingdom of Heaven" in The New Gothic ed. by Bradford Morrow and Patrick McGrath (New York, Random House, 1991)

"The Ghost Village" in Metahorror ed. by Dennis Etchison (New York, Dell Abyss, 1992)

"Ashputtle" in Black Thorn, White Rose ed. Ellen Datlow and Terri Windling (New York, Avon Books, 1994)

"Bunny is Good Bread" (as "Fee") in Borderlands 4 ed. by Elizabeth E. and Thomas F. Monteleone (Brooklandville, MD, Borderlands Press, 1994)

"Pork Pie Hat" in Murder for Halloween ed. by Michele Slung and Roland Hartman (New York, Mysterious Press, 1994)

"In Transit" (with Benjamin Straub) in Great Writers and Kids Write Spooky Stories (New York, Random House, 1995)

"Hunger: An Introduction" in Ghosts: The HWA Anthology ed. by Peter Straub (New York, Pocket Books, 1995)

"Isn't It Romantic?" in Murder on the Run: An Adams Round Table Anthology ed. by Lawrence Block (New York, Berkley Prime Crime, 1998)

"Mr. Clubb and Mr. Cuff" in Murder for Revenge ed. by Otto Penzler (New York, Delacorte Press, 1998)

Acknowledgments

Many kind people aided and abetted me during the course of this book's creation, and I'd like to take a moment to thank them individually. If I've left anyone out—and I'm sure I have—the omission is inadvertent. So, my heartfelt gratitude goes to:

- Peter Straub—for his kindness, encouragement and patience in the face of an endless series of questions
- My brother Bob—without whom this book would probably not exist, at least in its present form
- Bill Schafer—for giving this project a home
- The rest of my extraordinary siblings—Jim, Michael, Dennis, John, Dan, Judy, Carol and Donald, for helping to see me through
- Thomas Tessier—for his conscientious readings and invaluable support
- Dave Hinchberger—for first asking me to write a review
- Hank Wagner—for companionship, and for kindly stepping aside and letting me have a shot at this book
- Paula Guran—for the use of a wonderful interview
- Chet Williamson, Roman Ranieri, and P. D. (Trish) Cacek—friends and traveling companions
- Heather—for the supplies, and for helping out so often
- Dan Simmons—for some of the most encouraging words I've ever received
- Michelle Borowitz—for caring about this project, and about me
- Doug Winter—for helping me believe I could do this
- Fiona Kelleghan—for inspiration of many kinds
- Alan Clark—for art and friendship
- Colleen McCrary—for hearts and friendship
- John and Lorie Shinn—for the cookies
- Rich Chizmar—for giving me an opportunity when I needed it
- Elena Steier—for friendship and good company

Finally, I would like to thank my parents, Bill and Anne Sheehan, for a lifetime of love and support. My mother did not live to see the publication of this book. She passed away just as the manuscript was entering its final stages, and I will miss her forever. Her love and her belief in me helped make this book possible, and influenced my life at every turn. Thank you, Mom, for everything.

Index

ABC Murders, The, 203, 209
Adams Round Table, The, 270, 271, 277
Adventures of Huckleberry Finn, The, 159, 160, 163
Adventures of Tom Sawyer, The, 161
Agent Orange, 175
Aickman, Robert, 25, 227, 228, 233, 330
Aix-en-Provence, 22, 25
Albie, 25
Althusser, Louis, 287
Ambler, Eric, 185
Ambassadors, The, 344
"America," 20-21
American Gothic, 223
American Nights, 256, 279, 280
Amis, Kingsley, 343
Amis, Martin, 343
Amsterdam, 87
Andersen, Hans Christian, 102,119
Andre Deutsch, 14, 19, 31
Anna Karenina, 29, 37, 226
Antigua, 190
Apocalypse Now, 249
Arkham House, 89
Arles, 22, 25, 56
Arrowsmith, 344
Art of Memory, The, 102
Ashbery, John, 14, 20, 24, 30, 254, 339, 343, 344
"Ashputtle" (Grimm), 119
"Ashputtle" (Straub), 264, 265-267, 277, 348
Asimov, Isaac, 343
Assignation, The, 233
At War with the Army, 216
Auden, W. H., 344
Aura, 228, 229, 329-321
Austen, Jane, 14

Babar the King, 181-182
Babbitt, 344
Bangkok, 168, 172, 174, 179, 181, 186
Bangkok Post, The, 173
Barbados, 168
Barnes, Julian, 343
"Bartleby the Scrivener," 273-274, 276
Battle Creek, 223
Baudelaire, Charles, 313
Baum, L. Frank, 159
Bed Milk Shoe, 222
Bell, The, 344
Bellow, Saul, 40, 343
Belsize Square, 31
Bendix, William, 255
Bentley, E. C., 197
Bergman, Ingmar, 43
Berkeley, 86
Berkley Books, 146

Berry, Michael, 235
Berryman, John, 344
Bierce, Ambrose, 80
Big Sleep, The, 344
"Bird of Prey Blues," 320
Bishop, Elizabeth, 14, 158
Black Thorn, White Rose, 277
Blackwood, Algernon, 46
Blatty, William Peter, 45
Bleak House, 316, 344
Bloch, Robert, 46, 80, 340
Block, Lawrence, 270, 277
"Blue Rose," 136, 169, 211-215, 237, 262, 264, 273
Bogan, Louise, 43
Bonnefoy, Yves, 14, 28
Book-of-the-Month Club, 79
Book of Revelation, The, 139
Borderlands 4, 262, 277
Borderlands Press, 333
"Box and the Key, The," 121
Boyd, William, 216
Bram Stoker Award, 273, 325
Brief Lives, 16
Brite, Poppy Z., 341
British Fantasy Award, 125
Brodsky, Joseph, 219
Brontes, The, 14
Bronte, Charlotte, 14, 344
Bronte, Emily, 344
Brown, Clifford, 344
Brown, Les, 71
Brown's Hotel, 146, 147
Browning, Todd, 82
Brubeck, Dave, 71, 318
Buffalo Hunter, The (Short), 224
"Buffalo Hunter, The," (Straub), 37, 222-227, 235
"Bunny is Good Bread," 261, 262-264, 273, 277, 348
Burnt Water, 329
Burroughs, Edgar Rice, 195
Burroughs, William, 248
Campbell, John W., 343
Campbell, Ramsey, 79, 98, 121, 123, 228, 325
Carrie, 96
Catcher in the Rye, The, 344
Central Park, 301
Cezanne, Paul, 345
Chandler, Raymond, 204, 210, 224, 226, 247-249, 257, 344
Charriere, Henri, 28
Chicago Deadline, 216, 217
Chill, The, 47
Chinatown, 180, 182
Choirboys, The, 133, 140
Christie, Agatha, 203, 209
Chronicles of Thomas Covenant, The, 159
"Cinderella," 119, 264
Clark, Dane, 216
Clark, Mary Higgins, 270, 271
Clayton, Buck, 320
Coffin for Demitrios, A, 185
Cold Hand in Mine, 45
Collins. Wilkie, 303
Columbia University, 14, 267
"Confiteor Tibi," 317
Conrad, Joseph, 173, 185, 240, 246, 249, 264
Constable, John, 345
Cooper, William, 343
Coppola, Francis Ford, 249
Country Day School, 13, 108
Couples, 29
Coward, McCann & Geoghegan, 19
Cranston, Lamont, 191, 205
Credence Clearwater Revival, 158
Crime and Punishment, 344
Crouch End, 146
Crowley, Alastair, 113
Crowley, John, 15

Dachau, 214
Dahmer, Jeffrey, 245
Dance to the Music of Time, A, 344
Danse Macabre, 59, 146
Dark Tower series, The, 148
Dark Voices, 228, 235
Datlow, Ellen, 277
Davis, Dorothy Salisbury, 271
Davis, Miles, 71
Day of the Scorpion, The, 130
"Dead Princess, The," 120
Deathport, 325
Delius, Frederick, 240, 241
Del Tredici, David, 301
De Palma, Brian, 96
Derleth, August, 89
Desmond, Paul, 318, 344, 345
Devil's Island, 28
Dharma Bums, The, 344
Dickens, Charles, 28, 316, 344
Dickinson, Emily, 211, 296-297
Disch, Thomas, M., 125
Division of the Spoils, A, 130
Dixon, F. W., 343
Donaldson, Stephen R., 159
Dos Passos, John, 344
Dostoevsky, Fyodor, 28, 303, 344
Doyle, Arthur Conan, 197, 343
Drabble, Margaret, 343, 344
Dracula, 110
Drowning Pool, The, 344
Dublin, 14, 19, 22, 23, 25, 27, 31
Dullea, Keir, 15
Du Maurier, Daphne, 189, 303
Dumbo, 151
Dunwich Horror, The, 307, 314
Dupin, Jacques, 14

Eliot, George, 28
Eliot, T. S., 229, 344
Emil and the Detectives, 343
"Estampes," 319
Etchison, Dennis, 262, 277
Eurydice, 104
"Evening Star," 43
Exorcist, The, 45
Eyes of the Dragon, The, 148

Faces of Fear, 75
Fairy Tales and After, 112
Family Arsenal, The, 344
Family Romance, 302
Farewell to Arms, A, 344
Farrow, Mia, 15
Fates, The 97
Father Knows Best, 127
Faulkner, William. 185
Faust, 274, 275
Faust, Christa, 341
Fear Itself, 98, 163
"Fee," 262, 348
Felsen, Henry Gregor, 343
Fitzgerald, F. Scott, 21, 29, 344
Flaubert, Gustave, 170
Fleming, Ian, 174
Floating Dragon, 12, 122, 125-143, 146, 147, 167, 184, 261, 329, 330, 331, 337, 347
Flow Chart, 254
Fog, The, 45
Fon du Lac, 38
Ford, Glenn, 216
Forster, E. M., 14, 28, 229, 233
Foundation novels, The, 343
Fowles, John, 101, 103-106, 112, 117, 122, 335
Fox, Joe, 280, 282, 283
Freaks, 82
Freak Show, 325
Freudian Fallacy, The, 212
Frog, 343
From the Terrace, 41
Fuentes, Carlos, 79, 228, 229, 261, 329-331

Gaiman, Neil, 16, 344
Galton Case, The, 47
Gardner, John, 154
Gass, William H., 29
Gauntlet Press, 333
"General's Wife, The," 59, 98, 261, 329-331, 348
Getz, Stan, 343, 344
Ghost of Henry James, The, 344
Ghosts, 325-328, 348
Ghost Story, 11, 37, 39, 74, 79-99, 101, 105, 117, 121, 122, 125, 126, 134, 143, 184, 232, 235, 329, 336, 340, 341, 345, 347
"Ghost Village, The," 261-262, 277, 348
Gibbsville Stories, The, 41
Gide, Andre, 28
Gilliam, Richard, 326
Giordano Bruno and the Hermetic Tradition, 102
Glass, Philip, 343
Go, 344
Goethe, Johann Wolfgang von, 34
Golden Bowl, The, 344
"Golden Key, The," 120
"Goose Girl, The," 118
Gospel of St. Thomas, The, 102, 122, 207, 253
Grant, Cary, 93
Grant, Charles L., 84
Grant, Donald, M., 59, 227, 329, 331
Great Gatsby, The, 344
"Great God Pan, The," 90-91, 98
Great Tales of Terror and the Supernatural, 344
Great Writers and Their Kids Write Spooky Stories, 348
Greenberg, Martin H., 326
Greene, Graham, 185
Grimm Brothers, The, 102, 118, 120, 219, 264
Grimm's Fairy Tales for Young And Old, 123
"Guide to a Renamed City, A," 219
Guran, Paula, 16, 30, 58, 299
Gurdjieff, G. I., 113

Hammett, Dashiell, 204
"Hansel and Gretel," 119
Hardy Boys, The, 343
Harington, Donald, 317
Hartman, Roland, 267, 277
Harvest Home, 45
Haunting of Hill House, The, 11, 228
Hawkins, Coleman, 320
Hawthorne, Nathaniel, 46, 80, 85, 86
Heart of Darkness, 185, 246, 249
Heinlein, Robert A., 295, 343
Hellfire Club, The, 148, 273, 279-300, 301, 304, 305, 336, 342, 347
Hemingway, Ernest, 233, 344
Henderson, Zenna, 344
Herbert, James, 45
Hobbema, Meindert, 345
Hobbit, The, 151
Holland Park, 47, 48, 50, 55, 56
Holmes, John Clellon, 344
Holmes, Sherlock, 191, 202, 343
Homage to Mistress Bradstreet, 344
Honduras, 182
Hong Kong, 168
Horror Magazine, 235
Horror Writers Association (HWA), 325
Household, Geoffrey, 256, 280
Houses Without Doors, 74, 211-236, 261, 321, 331, 342, 345, 347
House Un-American Activities Committee, 138
HOWL, 325
Hughes, Ted, 14

"Hunger: An Introduction," 232, 261, 326-328, 348

IBM, 36
Idiot, The, 29
If You Could See Me Now, 11, 15, 37, 38, 42, 44, 61-75, 80, 81, 300, 334, 341, 345, 347
In the Night Room, 319
In Our Time, 233, 344
"In Transit," 348
"In Terms of the Toenail," 29
International Horror Guild Award, 273
Irving, John, 238
Isaacs, Susan, 271

Jackson, Shirley, 11, 228
James, Henry, 14, 20, 21, 28, 29, 46, 80, 81, 85, 183, 229, 344
James, M. R., 80
James, Will, 343
Jane Eyre, 344
"Jardins Sous le Pluie," 319, 320
Jewel in the Crown, The, 130
Jones, Hank, 185-186, 320
Jones, Stephen, 235
Joyce, James, 344
Julia, 11, 15, 32, 45-59, 68, 75, 80, 99, 334, 340, 341, 347
Jumby Bay, 190
"Juniper Tree, The" (Straub), 170, 22, 215-219, 222, 237, 253, 254, 262, 263, 273
Juniper Tree, The (Vuillard), 251

Kalinich, Dr. Lila, 170
Kennedy, John F., 108
Kensington, 48
Kerouac, Jack, 13, 344
Ketchum, Jack, 341
Kiernan, Caitlin, 341
King, Stephen, 11, 45, 54, 69, 80-82, 83, 92, 94, 117, 125, 143, 145-164, 228, 319, 331, 341, 344, 347
King, Tabitha, 145
"Kingdom of Heaven, The," 261, 348
Kirkby, Emma, 317-318
Kocsis, Zoltan, 317, 318
Koja, Kathe, 326
"Koko" (Parker), 183
Koko (Straub), 75, 136, 142, 162, 167-188, 189, 190, 201, 204, 207, 212, 215, 237, 238, 239, 250, 262, 302, 341, 345, 347

Ladd, Alan, 216, 217
Lady in the Lake, The, 204, 224
Lake Kezar, 147
Lang, Fritz, 255
Lansdale, Joe R., 325
Lauterbach, Ann, 15
Lawrence, D. H., 14, 28, 64, 86, 344
Le Carré, John, 15, 344
Lee, Edward, 344
Leeson Park and Belsize Square, 347
Le Guin, Ursula, 15
Leiber, Fritz, 46, 80
Le Morte D'Arthur, 159
Leningrad, 219
Leonard, Elmore, 336
Lessing, Doris, 52
Lewis, C. S., 159
Lewis, Jerry, 217
Lewis, Sinclair, 344
Li Po, 240
Little, Bentley, 341
"Little Mermaid, The," 119
"Little Red Riding Hood," 118
Lolita, 82, 344
Long, Frank Belknap, 80

Long Goodbye, The, 248-249, 257, 344
Look Homeward, Angel, 344
Lord of the Rings, The, 344
Love and Friendship, 40
Lovecraft, H. P., 46, 80, 89, 303,307, 312, 316, 340
"Lover Come Back to Me," 71
Lowry, Malcolm, 29, 344
Ludlum, Robert, 171
Lurie, Alison, 40

M, 255
MacDonald, John D., 344
MacDonald, Ross, 47, 96, 204, 295, 249, 311, 344
McCammon, Robert R., 84, 325
McCarthy, Sen. Joseph, 138
McDonald's 108
McGrath, Patrick, 261
McQueen, Steve, 108
Machen, Arthur, 80, 90-91, 98
"Machine Stops, The," 233
Magus, The, 101, 103-106, 112, 117, 122
Main Street, 344
Malory, Sir Thomas, 159
Manheim, Ralph, 123
Manson, Charles, 67, 86, 295
Marlowe, Philip, 224, 248-249
Marriages, 11, 14, 19-30, 31, 32, 37, 40, 41, 42, 56, 97, 122, 339, 347
Martin, Dean, 216
Matheson, Richard, 46, 340
Matheson, Richard Christian, 341
Meeker, Col. S. P., 343
"Meeting Stevie," 98
Melville, Herman, 273
"Mermaid, The," 120
Merrill, Judith, 343
Mile End Road, 55
Miller, Chuck, 98
Milwaukee, 12, 180, 181, 183, 186, 190, 219, 238, 245, 334
Mondelieu, 238
Monteleone, Elizabeth, 262, 277
Monteleone, Thomas F., 262, 277, 326
Moore, Marianne, 14
Morgan, Frank, 159
Morrell, David, 45, 84
Morrow, Bradford, 261
"Mr. Clubb and Mr. Cuff," 273-276, 277, 301, 328, 348
Mr. Sammler's Planet, 40
Mr. X, 15, 219, 273, 301-321, 328, 342, 345, 347
"Mrs. God," 170, 219, 227-233, 236, 347
Mulligan, Gerry, 71
Murder for Halloween, 266, 277
Murder for Revenge, 273, 277
Murder, Incorporated, 213
Murder on the Run, 271, 277
Murdoch, Iris, 41, 343, 344
"My Funny Valentine," 251
"My Kinsman, Major Molineux," 85
Mystery, 12, 40, 136, 170, 187, 189-210, 237, 238, 243, 244, 250, 253, 302, 315-316, 341, 345, 347

Nabokov, Vladimir, 80, 344
Naked Lunch, 248
Narnia, 159
National Library (Dublin), 19
Nazi Germany, 38, 40
NECON, 93, 98
Nestling, The, 84
New Gothic, The, 261
Newsweek, 147, 179
New York Magazine, 174
New York Review of Books, The, 212
New York Times, The, 79, 294
Nice, 238
Nice and the Good, The, 344

Night of the Living Dead, 96

Oates, Joyce Carol, 233
Of Time and the River, 344
O'Hara, John, 41
Onions, Oliver, 46
"On Mortality and Change," 16
On the Road, 344
Open Air, 11, 347
Orpheus, 104
Other, The, 45
Ouspensky, Madame, 113

Paget, Clarence, 235
Pale Fire, 344
Pale Grey for Guilt, 344
Pamuck, Orhan, 303
Pan, 313
Papillon, 28, 29
Paris, 22, 25, 33, 34
Parker, Charlie, 183
Partridge, Norman, 326
Pautz, Peter, 99
Pecos Bill, 343
Penang, 168
Penguin/Dutton, 279
Penguin Encyclopedia of Horror, The, 125 143
Penzler, Otto, 267, 273, 277
Perfect Spy, A, 344
Perrault, Charles, 102
"Peter and PTR," 320, 334
"Peter Straub: Connoisseur of Fear," 16
Plante, David, 344
Pocket Books, 79
Poe, Edgar Allan, 46, 80, 195, 303
Pogo, 96
Poirot, Hercule, 191, 202, 203
"Pork Pie Hat," 14, 267-270, 277, 348
Portrait of a Lady, The, 344
Portrait of the Artist as a Young Man, 344
Powell, Anthony, 344
Prairie du Chien, 38
Prayer for Owen Meany, A, 238
Price, Frederick K., 141
Priest, Christopher, 303
Proust, Marcel, 28, 344
Publisher's Weekly, 147
Putnam Books, 167

"Quintessential Terrorist, The," 16

Racine, 38
Random House, 279-282
Reage, Pauline, 28
Red Harvest, 204
Relatives, 344
Rexroth, Kenneth, 240
Rhone River, 26
"Ringing the Changes," 228, 235
Rivers and Mountains, 344
Rogers, Roy, 216
Roger Williams University, 93
Rogue Male, 256, 280
Rohmer, Sax, 195
"Running Through the Jungle," 150
Ryan, Robert, 255

Saint Jack, 344
St. Petersburg, 219
'Salem's Lot, 45, 81, 82, 83, 84, 92, 93, 344
Sales, Roger, 111
Salinger, J. D., 344
Sandman, The 344
Sawyer, Edward, 314
Sayers, Dorothy, 203
Scapegoat, The, 189
Scarlet, Letter, The, 86
Scarred Girl, The, 31

Schow, David, 341
Scott, Justin, 271
Scott, Paul, 130, 343
Scott, Randolph, 153
Secret Sharer, The, 185
Self-Portrait in a Convex Mirror, 344
Severed Head, A, 344
Shadow, The, 191, 205, 242
Shadowland, 11, 13, 58, 98, 101-123, 126, 142, 184, 191, 207, 208, 210, 253, 334, 335, 337, 341
Shakespeare, William, 28, 195
Shining, The, 11, 80, 81, 92, 117, 228, 341, 344
"Short Guide to the City, A," 219-220, 234, 235
Short, Luke, 223, 224, 226
Simmons, Dan, 15
Simmons, William Mark, 16
"Simple Art of Murder, The," 210
Sinatra, Frank, 317, 318
Singapore, 168, 172, 173, 174, 175, 176, 179
Slan, 343
Slung, Michele, 267, 277
Smiles of a Summer Night, 43
Smith, Clark Aston, 80
Smith, Tim, 326
Smoky, 344
Some Other Place. The Right Place, 317
"Something About a Death, Something About a Fire," 220-222, 235
"Something's Gotta Give," 317
Sons and Lovers, 344
Stand, The, 117
"Stardust," 251
Stars and Stripes, The, 173
"Stephen King, Peter Straub, and the Quest for the Talisman," 163
Stern, Richard (1968), 41
Stevenson, Robert Louis, 303
Story of O, The, 28
Stout, Rex, 197, 203
Straits Times, The 173
Strand, Mark, 14
Stranger in a Strange Land, 295
Straub, Benjamin Bitker, 15, 102, 348
Straub, Emma (Nilsestuen), 12
Straub, Emma Sydney Valli, 15
Straub, Gordon Anthony, 12
Straub, John, 168
Straub, Susan (Bitker), 14, 15
Street Rod, 343
Strieber, Whitley, 271
Subterranean Press, 320, 334
Sullivan, Jack, 143
Summer Bird Cage, A, 344
Sun Also Rises, The, 344
Sunlight Dialogues, The, 154
Surface of the Novel, The, 14
Swann's Way, 344

Taipei, 168, 179
Talisman, The, 145-164, 170, 172, 347
Teagarden, Jack, 71
Tempest, The, 104
Ten North Frederick, 41
Tennis Court Oath, The, 14, 20, 344
Terhune, Albert Payson, 343
Tessier, Thomas, 15, 46-47, 58, 97, 125, 143, 340
Testament, 45
Tey, Josephine, 197
Thackeray, William, 344
Theroux, Paul, 344
Theseus, 104
Third Man, The, 185
Thornton, E. M., 212
Three Poems, 20
Throat, The, 12, 74, 75, 187, 188, 190, 209, 212, 219, 237-257, 261, 262, 279, 302, 331, 336, 341, 345, 347

Time Magazine, 179
Tinker, Tailor, Soldier, Spy, 344
Tolkien, J. R. R., 151, 152, 155, 159, 344
Tolstoy, Leo, 226
Totem, The, 84
To the Lighthouse, 344
Tours, 26
Tristram Shandy, 335
Trollope, Anthony, 14
Tryon, Thomas, 45
Tu Fu, 240
Turn of the Screw, The, 71, 85, 227, 233, 329
Twain, Mark, 159-161, 163
Twilight Zone Magazine, 125, 163, 329, 331

Under the Fang, 325
Under the Net, 344
Under Venus, 15, 16, 30, 31-44, 47, 54, 61, 63, 68, 69, 191, 340, 347
Under the Volcano, 344
Underwood, Tim, 98
Universal Pictures, 80
University of California, 86
University College (Dublin), 14, 19
University of Maine, Orono, 145
University School of Milwaukee, 14
University of Wisconsin, 14
Updike, John, 27, 40
USA, 344

Vanity Fair, 344
Van Vogt, A. E., 343
"Verona Beach," 145, 146
Vietnam, 13, 167, 168, 172, 173, 174, 175, 180, 181, 182, 183, 185, 211, 212, 214, 234, 237-241, 243, 246, 247, 249, 261, 263, 264, 283, 284, 286, 289, 294, 297
Vietnam War Memorial, 167, 172
Vuillard, Edmond, 251

"Walk to the Paradise Garden, A," 240, 241
Wandrei, Donald, 89
Ward, Charles, Dexter, 312
"Wasteland, The," 233
Web and the Rock, The, 344
Webster, Daniel, 160
Welles, Orson, 93
Westport, 15, 146, 167, 168, 170
Wharton, Edith, 80
Whately, Wilbur, 312
"When the Red Red Robin Comes Bob Bob Bobbin' Along," 139
Widmark, Richard, 216
Wild Animals, 32, 40, 44, 58, 63, 74, 347
Wilde, Oscar, 55
Williams, Tennessee, 212
Williamson, Chet, 326
Wilson, F. Paul, 325
Wimsey, Lord Peter, 191
Windling, Terri, 277
Wine-Dark Sea, The, 227
Wings of the Dove, The, 344
Winter, Douglas, E., 75, 159, 163
Wodehouse, P. G., 42
Wolfe, Nero, 191, 202
Wolfe, Thomas, 13, 344
Women in Love, 344
Woolf, Virginia, 28, 229, 344
World Fantasy Award, 172, 262
Wuthering Heights, 344

Yates, Dame Francis, 101, 102
Yeats, William Butler, 344
Young, Lester, 267

BOSTON PUBLIC LIBRARY
3 9999 03966 686 0